S0-BDQ-826

Ki scowled across her camp fire at the cargo she had been tricked into hauling. The head of the wizard Dresh grinned back at her disarmingly.

"Someone wants you, Dresh," Ki told him. "Someone wants you badly enough to pay gold for wind spells. And if he wants you all that badly, I don't think he will take kindly to my interference. You hired me as a teamster, not as a bodyguard."

"You fear you will earn the enmity of certain wealthy and powerful ones who wish to do me harm. You already have. The Windsingers."

The Windsingers, who control the weather, taking taxes for fair skies, and send storms to those who cross them.

"How did I ever get into this?"

"It's all in the contract, Ki."

Other fantasy titles available from
Ace Science Fiction and Fantasy:

- *Daughter of the Bright Moon*, Lynn Abbey
- *Water Witch*, Cynthia Felice and Connie Willis
- *The Broken Citadel* and *Castledown*, Joyce Ballou Gregorian
- *Idylls of the Queen*, Phyllis Ann Karr
- *Songs from the Drowned Lands*, Eileen Kernaghan
- *Harpy's Flight*, Megan Lindholm
- *Soul-Singer of Tyrnos* and *Runes of the Lyre*, Ardath Mayhar
- *The Door in the Hedge*, Robin McKinley
- *An Unkindness of Ravens* and *Death of the Raven*, Dee Morrison Meaney
- *Jirel of Joiry*, C. L. Moore
- *The "Witch World" Series*, Andre Norton
- *The Tomoe Gozen Saga*, Jessica Amanda Salmonson
- *Daughter of Witches*, Patricia C. Wrede
- *Sorcerer's Legacy*, Janny Wurts

and much more!

THE WINDSINGERS

BY MEGAN LINDHOLM

ACE FANTASY BOOKS
NEW YORK

THE WINDSINGERS

An Ace Fantasy Book/published by arrangement with the author

PRINTING HISTORY
Ace Original/January 1984

All rights reserved.
Copyright © 1984 by M. Lindholm Ogden
Cover art by Kinuko Craft
This book may not be reproduced in whole
or in part, by mimeograph or any other means,
without permission. For information address: The Berkley Publishing Group,
200 Madison Avenue, New York, N.Y. 10016

ISBN: 0-441-89248-5

Ace Fantasy Books are published by The Berkley Publishing Group,
200 Madison Avenue, New York, New York 10016.
PRINTED IN THE UNITED STATES OF AMERICA

ONE

"Excuse me, please?"

The many-fingered arms of the Kerugi reminded Ki of a fringed shawl. It turned solemn grey-white eye specks on her. The symbiotic Olo twined about the Kerugi's shoulders lifted its head and neck sinuously. Its mobile lips writhed around its little monkey mouth as it asked, "Did you require something of us?"

"Yes." Ki fumbled, trying to decide which set of eyes to look into as she spoke. "I'm looking for a Kerugi inn, built right next to a weaving hive."

The squat Kerugi stood motionless while the Olo wrinkled its tiny brow in concentration. Ki waited patiently.

"Look on any street in Dyal. We always build our inns near hives. It is good business," the Olo finally translated for her.

"So I've found. I am seeking a face-scarred Human male, with dark hair and eyes. He said he would meet me in the Kerugi inn at Dyal that is built right by a weaving hive."

Again there was a long pause as the Olo wrinkled its simian features. Its furry coils rippled as it relayed her words and got the Kerugi's reply.

"We cannot be of much help to you. There are many hives and many inns in Dyal. The Human male should have given you better directions."

"My thoughts exactly. I thank you for your time, and for having speech with me."

Ki waited politely until her reply had been relayed to the Kerugi. The Olo offered her welcome and farewell. The Kerugi with its Olo waddled off.

Ki scanned the length of the street. She had lost count of how many inns she had checked; but there was another of the tall pointed structures that housed a Kerugi weaving hive. No doubt there would be another Kerugi inn in its shadow. She trudged toward it, trying not to breathe the fine dry dust that hung in the city streets like fog. The heat of summer filled the bowl of Dyal Valley as if winter would never come, yet she knew that in another moon the streets of this city would be flowing mud and blowing wind.

A motley crowd moved through the early evening air. It was mostly Kerugi, with here and there a scuttling T'cherian or a striding Human breaking the pace of the traffic. A tall Brurjan in guard harness hulked past Ki, and she felt her belly muscles tighten as his shadow fell across her. If Dyal made a practice of hiring Brurjan guards, these streets would be safe after dark. Ki knew of no creature that would willingly cross a Brurjan. Hastily she stepped up onto a planked veranda that fronted the inn. Stooping, she swept the door slats to one side and peered within. Damn the man. He wasn't in this one, either.

She wrinkled her nose against the odors of the common room. A drunken tinker and his drinking companions were the only Human inhabitants. Kerugi huddled in clusters around the low feeding vats, Olos twined on their shoulders, twittering to one another in their own tongue. Ki watched in distaste as one of the Kerugi shuffled up to a vacant vat and, with a grunt, expelled its digestive tendrils from a slitlike aperture in its belly. A T'cherian server scuttled over to upend a jug over the vat, slopping thick brownish porridge over the Kerugi's digestive tendrils. The flatulent odor of the room increased.

Ki sighed and entered the inn, the door slats clattering behind her. She'd have food and a cold drink before checking the rest of the inns in Dyal. If she had realized how Dyal had grown since she last had delivered freight here, she would have demanded more specific directions from Vandien. "That Kerugi inn at Dyal" had seemed a sufficient description. Who could have predicted that hordes of the tiny-fingered weaver folk would have moved to Dyal?

"Carrion crows and horny old hags they are!" the tinker bellowed out suddenly. Ki eyed him warily. He was a disreputable-looking fellow. His face was sun browned, his eyes pale, his hair dusty as though he had just brought his wagonload of pots into town. A gelid pot belly cushioned him against the table, though he gestured with hands that seemed, beneath their grime, capable and strong. Once he might have been a handsome man, but age and the laxity of drink had brought a droop to his face, a sag to his lips and jowls, and leached the brightness from his eyes.

The tinker's eyes leaped and fastened on Ki's. She jerked her gaze away, shamed to be caught staring like a mannerless child. She crossed the room hastily, her dusty skirts whipping against travel-stained boots. Nervously she glanced about, seeking a table as far as possible from drunken tinkers and Kerugi with their twittering symbiots. But instead of a table, a low doorway caught her eye. She made her way to it, to stoop and peer into the dim room beyond.

The wooden floor was strewn with rushes and fragrant grasses. Low trough tables of warmed sand were scattered about the room, T'cherian diners crouched around them. Several eye stalks swiveled in her direction, then politely swerved away. Pincerlike fingers on jointed limbs resumed the conveying of food to mandibles.

Ki ducked in and stood up, savoring the muted light, the cleanliness, and the relative quiet of the place. From the common room behind her, she heard the tinker bellow out, "Bloodsucking Windsingers!" and follow it with muted curses. But here there was only the chink of pincers against the round-bottomed vessels of food snugged in the sand-troughs.

The sole Human inhabitant of the room sat with his back against the wall and his legs stretched out beneath a sand table. One booted foot rested comfortably on the ankle of the other. His head was tilted back, his eyes rolled up as, with one hand, he groped on a shelf above him. His fingertips teased a bottle to the edge, and caught it just as it began to tip into a fall. A light shower of sand came with it, dusting his hair. With a practiced twist of the wrist, he nested the round-bottomed bottle into the table before him. Two hemispherical glasses waited there, one clean and one tinged with dregs.

The man pushed the sleeves of his cream-colored tunic back to his elbows, exposing finely muscled forearms, and bent over the bottle to work off the seal. Curly dark hair fell over his forehead, partially obscuring the scar that divided his face.

Ki moved softly across the room, placing her boots with such care that she stood over him before he was aware of her. Dark eyes swept up to meet her green ones. She gave his boots a light kick. "I should have known," she grumbled. "It *would* be the Kerugi inn with a T'cherian serving room." She dropped to the floor and settled in beside him, her booted ankles crossed comfortably atop his.

"It was so obvious, I never thought to mention it," Vandien conceded. "How was your haul?"

Ki leaned back against the wall behind them and let herself relax. "Bad roads, hot weather, unfriendly towns, and ungrateful recipients on this end. They claimed the top sacks of beans were spoiled from exposure to the weather. I thought they always smelled like that. We argued a bit, and I cut my fee a little, and we parted amiably. At least, the Kerugi's Olo seemed friendly enough when I left. Who knows what a Kerugi really thinks about anything? All you hear is the carefully edited reply from its Olo. . . ."

"Um," Vandien agreed. He had resumed picking at the bottle's seal, flicking away scraps of greenish wax to expose a fibrous stopper. He reached under the table to draw a small knife from a sheath on his belt and dug it into the stopper. "I hope you're not *too* tired," he said casually. Amusement tugged at the corner of his mouth. He smoothed his small moustache to cover it, but Ki was alerted.

"Nothing a good night's sleep won't cure."

"Think we could be in False Harbor ten nights from now?"

"False Harbor?"

"About a day's ride beyond Bitters by horse; maybe two for the wagon. The road is narrow and rutted."

"But why would I want to be in False Harbor then?"

Vandien glanced up at the T'cherian server making her way to their table laden with two steaming bowls. He timed his reply perfectly, speaking as he poured a dark purple liqueur into their glasses. The T'cherian nested their bowls into the sand before them. "I've contracted us a job there."

Ki was speechless in the double amazement of Vandien actually seeking for gainful employment, and daring to commit her wagon and team without her permission. He looked up from the liqueur and laughed aloud at her wide eyes, her gaping mouth. As her eyes narrowed and she took a deep breath for speech, he raised both hands in supplication. "Before you tell me your current opinion of your dearest friend, let me tell you the details of the deal. You decide if even a stubborn Romni teamster would have walked away from it."

Ki picked up her glass and leaned back against the wall, regarding him skeptically. She took a slow sip of the liqueur. He grinned at her engagingly, already sure of himself, and shifted to feel the companionable warmth of her shoulder and hip against his.

"Three nights ago, I was sitting here, at this very table, when the strangest woman I've ever seen came in."

As Vandien began his story, a length of white string appeared from his pouch as if by magic. It settled in a loop on his fingers, and as he spoke, he twisted and wove the string into the story symbols of his people. Ki's eyes went from his fingers to his face and back again.

"She stood in the doorway and looked slowly about. She was dressed in a coarse brown smock and trousers, like a field farmer. By her body and face, she could have been grandmother to a dozen children. Our eyes met. She smiled. She'd a bottle in one hand, and yellow flowers woven into her black, black hair. All in all, a strange sight, but not an eye turned to her but mine. Straight to my table she came, and twisted her bottle into the sand. She sat down across from me as if we were the oldest of friends. And, strangely, I knew we were."

Vandien paused to take a sip from his glass and risked a look at Ki. He knew well that she could not resist a tale, especially as he told them, but he had not won her. Yet. He cleared his throat and went on.

"Well, she just sat there, smiling at me and working a cork out of her bottle. When she had it open, she took a glass from one of her sleeves, and then another, and set them in the sand between us, as if it were the most natural thing in the world. When she had filled both glasses, what should it be but Alys! Ki, I had tried earlier in the day to buy Alys in four different taverns in this town. No one in Dyal had ever heard of it, let alone stocked it. But there she was, pouring me a glass of it. And still not a word had she spoken, and me half-wondering if I'm dreaming the whole thing.

"Well, then she lifted her glass to me and said in a voice sweet as a bird's call, 'Here's to your strong right arm and the scar between your eyes!' And she drained off her glass."

"So, of course, you had to do the same," Ki murmured. She was into the spirit of the tale now, and enjoying it as much as Vandien enjoyed the telling.

He took a sip of his dark liqueur. With a fingertip, he traced the scar that began at the inside corner of one eye and ran across the bridge of his nose and down his cheek to the angle of his jaw. He gave a grave nod and resumed his story.

"When we had drunk, she told me her name, Srolan. I told her mine. She wasted no words. She said that she was seeking a strong Human with a dependable team for a very special task. She would not say who had steered her to me. I told her that while I knew of a very dependable team, they were not mine to commit. . . ."

Ki sat up slightly, her muscles tensing as she began to speak, but Vandien spoke more quickly.

"She told me what she needed done, and it seemed simple enough, even intriguing. But again I told her that I could not commit a team that was not mine. She took it to mean that I wanted a higher fee. She raised her offer. Again, I told her I must first propose it to you. Again, she raised her offer! Ki, it had reached an embarrassing level. But once more, I refused, telling her she must wait until you arrived, and ask you yourself. Then Srolan sat back, and her shoulders sagged; her eyes lost their sparkle, and her years looked out at me."

Vandien mimed her movements, becoming for an instant a downcast old woman. He held forth an appealing hand to Ki.

"She could not stay in Dyal. Her daughter in Bitters was soon to give birth, and she must go to midwife her. No one but herself would do, for the girl had had three breech births, and none of the babes survived. This time Srolan was determined to be there herself and not trust to some other midwife's fumbling. She was convinced that her touch alone could bring forth her daughter's child alive."

"How could you deny the urgency of such a mission?" Ki murmured. Vandien flashed her a self-righteous scowl at the underlying note of amusement in her voice.

"How indeed, Ki? Especially when the final offer she made was so ridiculously high for such a simple task. In money alone, she was offering, for a task that would take us at most a day, indeed, *must* be completed in a day, the extravagant sum of six tallies. Six!" he said proudly.

The number was lost on Ki. She had a grin on her face as she twisted slightly to face Vandien. "You didn't?"

He gave a quick shrug of his shoulders, taken aback by her sudden humor. "But I did. I thought that, just this once, you might not mind if I committed your team on your behalf, especially for so good a price. And besides the money, there was . . ."

"Vandien." Ki choked on a laugh, and tried to pull her face to order. "Let me guess the task, and the terms. She will pay you only after you have successfully completed it, correct? It must be done in one day, and the task is in False Harbor." At each of Vandien's cautious nods, Ki gave a bubble of laughter. "Vandien, did you agree to take a team into that sunken Windsinger temple and haul out a secret long-lost chest?"

Vandien's face fell as Ki leaned against his shoulder and shook with helpless laughter. Several of the T'cherian diners swiveled eye stalks in their direction and regarded them with disgust. Rude and raucous Humans, profaning the art of consumption with their noisy chattering, while good food grew cold in the sand before them.

"What's funny?" he demanded, his face twisting as he tried not to join in Ki's laughter. "Ki, you should have heard the tale she told me. How since the land beneath the temple sank, folk can hear the ringing of the temple's great bronze bell, under the sea, swung by the tides. During storms it swells to such a clamor that even animals stabled safe in barns are moved to panic by its tolling."

"Deep within that sunken temple," Ki took up the tale, making her husky voice deep with solemnity, "is a great metal box, containing one of the twelve secrets of the Windsingers. If it could be brought to light and put in the hands of honest folk, they could prove how the Windsingers have forsaken their sacred trust, how they have become greedy tyrants instead of the selfless servants of the world. Think of the honor that would fall to the hero who could bring such a restoration to the world. Long would the name of that teamster be remembered, heralded as the savior of . . ."

"Enough, enough," Vandien conceded, smiling ruefully. He rubbed a hand over his mouth and chin, and then smoothed his moustache. "So I was taken in by some kind of a game. But what has she to gain from it? Or is she just an old crazy who approaches strangers?"

"Oh, no." Ki sipped at her liqueur, and touched a finger to the edge of the bowl before her. She snatched it back. "Still boiling hot. It'll be a while yet before we can eat. You may as well hear the whole tale. It isn't entirely a joke. There *is* an ancient Windsinger temple, and during an earthquake that part of the coast did sink, taking the temple with it. The moon knows how long ago that was. The temple may have had a bell, and some claim to have heard it ring during a storm. There may even be a metal chest hidden in the temple. The people of False Harbor seem quite sincere in believing it is there. And every four or five years, a month comes that offers an exceptionally low tide. They can predict its coming, and they do their best to hire a teamster. Some night this month the temple will be partially exposed by the sea. At least what's left of it will be. And some fool teamster will be out there butt deep in cold water, trying to raise that metal chest."

Ki sipped from her glass. The liqueur had a sweet fruity flavor, with an aftertang that stung her nostrils, not unpleasantly. "What are we drinking, anyway?"

"Burgoon." Vandien leaned forward to refill his own glass. "That's what it sounded like when the T'cherian server told me, anyway. She wanted to heat it up to a boil for me, but I told her I'd try it cold. She's referred to me as a barbarian ever since."

"I wonder how much heat it would take to scald a T'cherian palate?"

"Why hasn't anyone ever managed to haul the chest out?" Vandien demanded suddenly.

"Damned if I know." Ki shrugged. "That part of the story I've heard a number of ways. One, that the chest isn't there at all. Two, that the chest is there, but cleverly hidden. Three, that even if you find it, it's too damn heavy to haul out. Four, and most likely to me, is that the Windsingers don't want it found or hauled out. About the time that the tide goes all the way out, a big storm hits, with a freezing wind. Makes it very unpleasant to work out there, but some fool always tries. I understand that False Harbor has made the event a sort of festival time. The teamster never gets a coin out of it, of course, but if he gives it an honest try, the village treats him well enough. A good room and decent meals, that sort of thing."

Vandien tested his food with a fingertip. "Well, at least it won't be a complete loss. We should be able to work it for a couple of days of room and board."

Ki snorted. "Vandien, I'm not going to drive my wagon clear to False Harbor for the sake of a room and a meal. And I am definitely not going to make a fool of myself by wading around hip deep in salt water on a stormy day. I still can't figure out why they would approach you with the offer. Unless . . . since you've been here, have you seen any other Romni?"

"I saw Rifa, and that dancing bear she consorts with. . . . Ki," he continued in a different voice. "It wasn't just the money she offered. There was another matter."

"Rifa. Of course. She'd find this funny. I bet they asked her to use her team, and she refused, but set them onto you, to put you in a spot. She'd guess that you wouldn't know a thing about False Harbor."

"It wasn't just the money." Vandien mumbled it this time, with a quick sideways glance at Ki. But she was not paying attention. The drunken tinker in the other room seemed to have switched tables, for his voice, raised in an obscenity, came from just outside the room. Ki glanced at the doorway in disgust. She had moved to this room to be away from the tinker and his diatribe against the Windsingers; she did not wish to hear it. His tales of woe would be usual ones: the rain taxes were too high for a small merchant like himself; the taxes burdened the farmers until they couldn't afford even his simple wares; the Windsingers were bleeding the farmers of their hard won crops. They were old tales and familiar. Ki could not think of any place her travels had ever taken her that she had not heard the same groans. But usually the complainer had the good sense to whisper them quietly to close friends, not bellow them out in public like a stricken bullock.

She glanced back to a silent Vandien. He had drawn his belt knife and was slowly stirring his food with it. T'cheria used no eating implements, and furnished none in their dining places. Ki drew her own short blade and speared a chunk of the food in her bowl. Steam wavered up from the greenish cube, and she blew on it cautiously before putting it in her mouth. She instantly wished she hadn't. Whatever it was, it

tasted like low tide smelled. She swallowed it whole to get it
out of her mouth. Not even a gulp of Burgoon could cleanse
her mouth of the taste. She turned with a tart comment for
Vandien on his food choice, only to find him still staring into
his bowl, and stirring it moodily with his blade.

"Stir with a knife, you stir up trouble."

"Romni superstition!" he snorted.

"What more *did* she offer, Vandien, beside the money?"

Slow color rose in his face and then faded. Idly he fingered
the scar down his face. "Nothing of great import, I suppose."
He stabbed a chunk of green stuff and put it in his mouth. Ki
watched him expectantly, but he chewed and swallowed with
no change of expression.

"But what was it?" Ki pressed. He wasn't finding Rafa's
stupid joke amusing. Vandien usually bore a joke well, if he
could not find a way to turn it back upon the instigator, and
Ki could not fathom his injured attitude. She continued to fix
him with a green-eyed stare as he ate three more mouthfuls.
At last he spoke.

"I did give her my word, you know. We touched hands on
it."

"And what else?" Ki demanded, sure there was more to it
than this.

"Isn't that enough, dammit? I've seen you lay your life on
the line to keep from breaking your word."

"But Rifa intended it as a joke, Vandien. I'm sure of it."

"Perhaps. But it was not a joke to the woman that made the
offer, nor to me when I gave my word. Ki, what harm could
come of us taking it on? Even if we failed like all the others,
we would have..."

"Made total fools of ourselves," Ki finished for him. "Look,
I've a team to feed and a wagon to maintain. I can't manage
that on a room and board basis." Ki paused. "There's more to
it than that. I don't take those kinds of jobs, Vandien. I haul
freight. I sometimes buy, haul, and sell likely merchandise.
But I don't do salvage, especially when the ownership of the
salvaged item is in dispute. Do you think the Windsingers
would be thrilled to have that metal chest hauled up and examined? Do you think they like the idea of anyone even attempting it? A teamster has to keep the goodwill of those in
power; or at least be unnoticed by them. I do very well at being
unnoticed, Vandien. I don't want to change that by hauling up

some Windsinger relics and turning them over to a half-crazed crone who wants to prove that Windsingers are blasphemies against nature. By the Moon, Van! Remember, I'm a Romni! That makes me target enough!"

Ki paused for breath. But Vandien was not looking at her. He had a half-scowl on his face that made crowsfeet at the corners of his dark eyes. Ki knew that when his face relaxed, those same lines would show white against his tanned skin. But there was no hope of that just now. He was listening to the drunken tinker's litany from the next room.

Ki wished they hadn't gotten into this. But she couldn't give in, couldn't let him start taking on jobs for her without even consulting her, couldn't let him drag her into things he didn't know the depth of. Damn his impulsiveness. Her careful planning of each day's travel frustrated him. He was ever willing to push on to the very edge of nightfall, hoping to find a "better place to camp." How many times had he teased her to try an unknown shortcut, only to meet with her stolid refusal. Well, let him sigh over her caution. Let him laugh and tease her about her wariness, calling it "bogey fears." He hadn't grown up Romni, moving from place to place, living only by tolerance and chance. She spoke softly.

"Vandien, my friend, the ill will of the Windsingers could follow us anywhere we might choose to go. It would not be a simple mistake, and 'excuse me, please' and backing out of their territory. There are no limits to their influence. Once they had marked us we would never know a day of fair weather again. No one would hire me, nor buy goods from me."

Vandien had finally turned to face her, his eyes meeting hers. But the damn tinker was making so much noise that Ki had to raise her voice to be heard. Around her, T'cheria were beginning to scuttle from the room. They considered it an insult to be disturbed while they were feeding. Ki didn't care what they thought. She would make Vandien understand her. It annoyed her that he was obviously half-listening to the noisy tinker. She took both his hands, raising her voice yet again. But the tinker's voice still overrode hers.

"And I say, burn them! Burn your crops in the field and scatter the sheared wool of your flocks. Let them whistle for a share! They want the best that your sweat and blood can bring them, and what do they give you? Only the rain and the gentle winds that are the right of any creature that walks the face of the world! Burn them in the fields, and let them sniff smoke and weave ash for their share! Keep only what you need for your own families. Let them suffer a winter of privation, such as the many you have known. Maybe then..."

Vandien seemed awed by the man's hysterical cant. Ki squeezed his hands and half-rose, shouting to make herself heard: "Only a fool would oppose the Windsingers! And I'm not a fool. Let someone else be a hero. I just want for us to go our quiet way, unnoticed by them. Vandien, there's you and me and the team, and not much else I care for. But, dammit, I care for that a lot, and I'll go a long way to protect it. Leave the Windsingers alone," she shouted at him, "and they'll leave us to live in peace."

To her sudden chagrin, Ki found herself bellowing into a silenced common room. The T'cherian diners were gone. Angry faces, Human, Olo and Kerugi, clustered in the low doorway, staring at her. Her raised voice had not only reclaimed Vandien's attention, but captured that of everyone else in the inn. The tinker was glaring at her, pale eyes peering around a hank of greasy hair. His wet mouth worked as he sputtered for words. Ki's stomach fell away. He, and everyone else in the room, thought that she had risen in body and voice to oppose him. An Olo draped on its Kerugi's shoulders twittered into the silence.

A T'cherian in the corner dropped her serving tray and scuttled out a low door into the kitchen. Ki glanced after her, wondering at her haste. Vandien was struggling to his feet beside her. He jostled her roughly as he stooped and seized the edge of the sand table. With a heave he upended it, spilling sand and food in a cascade across the floor. His strong fingers closed on the shoulder of her blouse, tearing it, as he jerked her to the floor behind the table. The first missile hit the table with a solid *thunk*. Bits of broken pottery and splats of stew flew over the top.

Vandien's hand went to his hip and came up empty. Even if his rapier had been there instead of on its hook in Ki's wagon, it would have been little protection against flying pottery. Their short belt knives were useful for bread and cheese but little else. As three mugs and a serving dish hit the table, she and Vandien ducked at the same moment, rapping their heads together.

"Damn," muttered Ki, rocking back on her heels as she saw

sparks of light. Several low cries of triumph came from the entryway. Whoever had thrown the mugs felt they had scored. Ki peered around the corner of the table. No one had ventured into the T'cherian room yet. They all preferred to throw from the shelter of the doorway. A metal pitcher arched toward her. Ki ducked back as it clanged against the front of the table. Her eyes flew to Vandien's. "What are we going to do?" she demanded angrily as she saw his grin. "They've gone crazy!"

It was just like him to be merry at a moment like this. "I don't know, but I promise never to stir with a knife again. What did *you* have planned, when you so aptly stirred them up?"

"I was talking to you!" In spite of herself, she felt her mouth twisting up into a wry grin to match his. "If you had been listening properly, I wouldn't have had to shout."

"The tinker caught my ear." Vandien reached quickly around the end of the table, managed to snag his food dish. He sent it spinning across the room. It shattered against the door frame, and their opponents momentarily vanished. "It seemed to me that what he was saying was just as applicable to us as farmers and weavers. But..." he cut in swiftly as Ki's face darkened and she lowered her brows. "Now is not the time to renew that discussion." Ki groped around her end of the table and came up with her glass. She took hasty aim and hurled it. From the other room came the scuffling of feet as more ammunition was gathered. Vandien went on speaking calmly. "Your words were the perfect catalyst for the situation. Not one of them wanted to agree aloud with the tinker, for in their hearts they knew the foolishness of opposing the Windsingers. But he made them feel guilty and cowardly for such thoughts. Just when they would have had to agree with him, or slink off with their tails between their legs, here comes Ki to stand up and voice their craven opinion for them. Thus making it possible for them to take out all their frustrations on us, instead of turning it on themselves or the Windsingers."

As he spoke, Vandien tried his strength against each table leg in turn. The short stout legs were firmly affixed to the sand table, possibly in foresight against situations like this one.

"I don't consider it a craven opinion," Ki hissed. "It's common sense!"

"Whatever!" Vandien shrugged and ducked at the same time. A mug clipped the upper edge of the table and bounced from

the wall to fall harmlessly beside him. He returned it quickly.
"Shall we argue about it before or after they get up enough
courage to rush us?"

"All journeys begin from where you are!" Ki grunted out
the old Romni saying as she popped up, grabbed two jugs from
the shelf behind them, and crouched down again.

"Meaning all solutions start in the now, not by looking for
someone to blame," Vandien said loftily as he snatched down
ammunition of his own. "Ki, this is decent drink, a rare thing
in Dyal. I know, for I've sampled around. You don't mean to
throw full jugs?"

"Watch me!" Ki retorted, and dared to stand to let one fly.
She had the satisfaction of seeing it shatter on the door frame,
drenching at least two of their attackers and sending flying
shards of pottery across the room. Ki laughed as they cringed.
The stinging odor of splashed Burgoon rose.

Vandien pulled her down barely in time; the basin that hit
the wall behind her spattered them both with the brown slime
of fermented Kessler beans. They gasped in the stench. Vandien's reluctance for throwing full jugs vanished. Grabbing
both of his, he rose and heaved them with a windmilling motion. Ki took advantage of his cover to seize two more jugs on
the shelf. As they ducked together behind the table, several
cries rose from the other room. "We got one!" Ki smiled savagely. As her eyes met Vandien's, a spark jumped between
them. This was dangerous, reckless, and above all a waste of
good drink, but, damn, it was fun! The tension between them
evaporated. The scar up Vandien's face rippled with his shout
of laughter as his flung jug took the tinker in the paunch and
cleared him from the doorway.

Ki heard an ululation of dismay. From the low T'cherian
door that led to the kitchen, a dark set of stalked eyes peered
at them. The shrilling rose and fell. Other eyes ventured around
the frame to peer in. The tavern keeper. Ki sent a bottle to
smash against the kitchen door, and the T'cheria darted back
to shelter. Maybe now that her stock was being destroyed,
instead of metal cups and mugs bouncing about, she would
take action.

Ki guessed correctly. Just as Vandien heaved the last jug
they could reach without leaving the shelter of the table, she
heard the warning shouts of the city guard outside the inn. The
ruckus was over as suddenly as it had begun. Ki heard the

rattle of retreating boots and shuffling Kerugi. Silence fell. She
sent a delighted grin to Vandien that changed to a dismayed
laugh as she tried to brush bean mash from her clothing. But
Vandien's face went suddenly blank, and she turned to follow
the direction of his stare. The T'cherian tavern keeper stood
in the doorway, flanked by two huge Brurjan. They wore the
neck chains and harness of city guards. Their huge faces split
in mirthless grins as the tavern keeper shrilled in lisping Common, "Those are the two! They started the riot, and must pay
the full damages!"

It was full dark when Ki and Vandien emerged into the
dusty street.

"Where'd you leave the wagon?"

"A clearing outside town. Looks like a house burned down
there, and someone abandoned the land. Good pasturage still."

They moved off down the street, taking long, swift strides.
The night was rapidly becoming as chill as the day had been
hot. Puffs of greyish road dust rose with every footfall.

"How much did they leave us?"

"Five dru." There was deep disgust in Ki's voice. "After
you settled for your room and meals . . ."

"At a reasonable price," Vandien interjected.

"After you went to get your gear, the innkeeper reckoned
up the damage—not only what we did, but also what the others
did. The innkeeper told the guard that, but for my arguing, the
tinker would have had his little drunk and done no harm. And
she insisted that the jugs of Burgoon we threw held Sheffish
brandy."

"What?" Vandien stopped and rounded on her, aghast.

"Yes." She confirmed it grimly. "That's what took most of
the money. I had no way to prove it was Burgoon. Arguing
with a Brurjan did not appeal to me."

"I doubt if there is a drop of Sheffish brandy in this whole
town, let alone jugs of it."

"Nonetheless," Ki replied, "if she was going to be paid for
liquor spilled and soaking into the floorboards, why not be paid
for fine Sheffish brandy instead of cheap Burgoon? The Brurjan
saw it her way."

"Moon's blood." Vandien spat. They resumed their striding
pace. The streets were all but deserted, and few lights showed
from slit windows. Door hides had been dropped and tied over

the slats. Beggar dogs ran free in the streets, sniffing out whatever they could. An odd sort of peace welled up in the shuttered
town.

"Well. We may as well push on towards Bitters tomorrow,
then," Vandien ventured.

Ki glanced over at him. "Why Bitters? I plan to pull my
team and wagon into the hiring mart tomorrow and take whatever is offered. Five dru will not keep the team long in grain.
I've almost run out of supplies myself. I can't go on to Bitters
on the chance of work there, and arrive completely coinless."

"But just beyond Bitters is False Harbor. There we would
have food and lodging, for a few days, and a chance to find
work afterwards."

She rolled her eyes at him. "Will you put that out of your
head? Hasn't it brought us enough trouble?"

"You perhaps. Not me. Having given my word, I intend to
see it through."

"Not with my team," she said flatly.

"Of that I'm aware, my friend. So it must be another. Which
means that I had best start for False Harbor immediately, to
allow myself time to rent or borrow a team in Bitters."

"Rent?" Ki asked incredulously.

"Payment conditional upon my getting paid." Vandien
shrugged off the difficulty.

"Well, if anyone could talk a team owner into a deal like
that, you could."

"Unless I were trying to convince my friend."

She flinched to his barb. "Are you actually angry about this,
Vandien?"

"No!" He gave a sudden snort of laughter. His sinewy arm
hooked suddenly around her waist. They strode on, hips bump-
ing. "Just shy of doing it alone. What you have said makes a
great deal of sense. Arriving with a starved team would make
our chance of doing the impossible even slimmer. No, Ki, it's
just that there are things I do best when I am in your company . . . like making a fool of myself."

"It is a talent we share," she admitted with a low laugh.
Then she sighed. "What say you to this, Vandien: I'll take
what work I can find now, but when I've coin in my pocket
again, I'll join you in False Harbor. If I'm in time for their
low tide, I'll watch you make a fool of yourself. But I'll be
damned if I'll help you. Damn Rifa's eyes!"

"She still hasn't forgiven you for taking up with such a stray dog; especially since I give you no children."

"I've had my children," Ki said shortly. Vandien veered from the topic.

"I'd best leave for Bitters right away, then."

In reply, Ki put her arm around his waist, gripping his belt just above the hip. The strength of her hug knocked him off stride. She smelled the fern sweet smell of him, like a new mown pasture in twilight when the warmth of the day rises from it. For an instant she seemed apart from all things, seeing only his dancing dark eyes, feeling the springy mass of his unruly dark curls on the back of his neck, touching the firmness of his mouth beneath the soft moustache. "Not immediately," she told him gruffly. "Tomorrow morning." The wagon loomed before them in the darkness, and Sigurd lifted his great grey head in a whinny of greeting.

Two

THE boy worked his way through the breathless market stalls, his bare feet raising puffs of hot dust. The cries of hawkers and the muted arguments of the bargainers only made the day hotter. How could folk trade on a day such as this? Yet they did, and he worked at his own small craft, the carrying of messages through the congested town. Too soon, he knew, the sudden storms of autumn would come. Then he would long for hot dry days like this as he slogged through rain and mud. He licked his dusty lips and wriggled through a knot of farmers.

He was in the hiring end of the market now. Harvest workers stood about, shovels and scythes resting beside them, hoping some late harvester would come seeking them. But it had been a dry year, as the Windsingers had threatened. Most farmers had found it short work to harvest the paltry crops the earth had let forth. The boy sought no harvest workers.

Beyond them were the teams for hire. Teamsters stood restively in this shadeless place, trying to keep the buzzing green flies from stinging their pawing, shuffling beasts. The boy skirted the tossing horns of a team of oxen, and made a quick jump away from a yellow-toothed nag that snapped at him.

The teamster laughed, baring teeth as stained as his animal's. It was not hard to spot the one he sought.

Her tall painted wagon stuck up high above the buckboards and dog carts of the others, but the hind end of her wagon was flat and bare, awaiting a cargo to haul. Her team did not stand and sweat in harness, but were tethered in what small shade the wagon offered. The teamster herself dozed on the high seat. The boy lost all respect for her. A careless fool, to doze thus in the middle of a busy market day when every second person on the street was a thief. He stood in the center of the street and looked up at her. Her voluminous blue skirts made her look even smaller than she was. Her embroidered blouse was damped with sweat. The brown hair that fell to her shoulders curled away from her forehead in damp tendrils.

His bare feet were soundless in the deep dust of the street. He reached up a hand to tug at her skirt hem. Her green eyes opened and fixed him with a stare when his hand still hovered by her skirt. "Cat eyes!" hissed the boy, and jerked his hand away without making the intended tug.

"You wanted something of me?" Ki asked, ignoring his strange greeting.

"Not I, teamster. I am but sent to say, 'If you wish to work for fair wages and a good client, bring your wagon to the black stone building, at the end of the road that runs past the smithy shops and cask makers.' Have you any questions, teamster?"

"Who lives in the black building, boy?"

The boy squirmed. "I do not know."

"What am I to haul?"

"I do not know that, either."

Ki looked down to the upturned tanned face, at the worn tunic dangerously short on the sprouting youth. "Why do you ask if I have any questions, if you have no answers?"

The boy shrugged. "It is what we say, after we have given the message. In case you did not understand what was said."

"I see." Ki fished in the flat purse at her belt and came up with one of the copper shards she had received in change from her last dru. She had spent it this morning for grain for herself and her team. She doubted the copper was enough for the customary tip, but it was all she had. She flipped it through the air and the boy caught it adroitly. He started to slip it into his pouch, but hesitated unwillingly. "The one who sent me paid all in advance, even the receiver's tip. She said she doubted you would have enough." He tossed thc small bit of metal up to Ki, but she batted it back to him with a quick flip of her hand. "Keep it, boy. I, too, am afflicted with an honest nature, and know how seldom one is rewarded for it."

The boy gave her a flash of white teeth in a surprised grin. He darted off with a flash of white buttocks before the teamster could change her mind.

Ki stretched, and wiped a layer of dust and sweat from her forehead. Clambering from the seat, she began to coax the great grey horses into their harness. She wished she knew more about her mysterious patron, including how she knew Ki was perilously low on coin. She could no longer be fussy about whom she worked for. She didn't like to think that others might know that. It attracted hard bargains and semi-legal hauls.

Sigmund stood stoically in his place but Sigurd leaned and shifted as she strove to arrange leather and fasten buckles. He had grown fractious from three boring days of standing in the hot market waiting for someone to hire them. Ki jerked the final strap flat. "By nightfall, I'll have you too tired for such tricks," she warned the great grey animal. He snorted skeptically.

She climbed up on the box and gave the reins a flip, easing the wagon forward. She edged it out into the center of the street, and then stood on the seat, shouting for the right of way. Hawkers and buyers gave way before her grudgingly. The wagon rumbled slowly through the market amid a chorus of curses at the dust it raised. Ki set her jaw and shook the reins slightly to encourage the team. Sweat began to stain their coats a darker grey.

Finding the street of smithy shops was easy. The clang of hammers falling on red metal was a sound that carried far on a hot day. Ki pitied the apprentices working bellows to blow coals red to white. Stifling waves of heat rolled out from the sheds to assault her and her team as they plodded past. She was grateful when the smithies gave way to barrel makers. But she passed the last of the cask makers shops and no black building was in sight. Instead, her wagon creaked past tottering and empty wooden buildings, where not even beggars moved. This dead section of a busy town bothered her, until she passed the dried-up public well. In a climate of seasonal extremes, she, too, would wish to live by a ready source of water.

The lumber of the old buildings had shrunk and twisted

away from the framing in silvery splinters. This had to be one
of the oldest parts of Dyal. Instead of the dangling door slats
currently popular, grey slab doors sagged or sprawled on splintery thresholds. These, and the height of the archaic rectangular
window holes, told her that this part of Dyal had been built by
a Human population. The wide, winding streets were a Human
preference. Kerugi engineered straight narrow streets and
crowded through them like seething insects in a hive.

The street gave one more twist. She spotted her building.
Black stone walls reared up above the shaky grey buildings,
as if they feared that prying eyes might breach their fastness
and steal away their secrets. The huge black stones of the walls
had been dressed by masons into precise cubes. They fitted
mortarless together, with no chink for moss or for a scrabbling
sneak thief. They glistened unweathered, but the huge dead
tree that twisted by the wall had branches bent awry by that
stony fastness. The tree had sprouted, grown and died in the
shade of the wall. Lightning had blackened it before its reaching
branches had equalled the height of the walls.

A pair of wide gates, their timbers stained as black as the
stone, gaped open. The team slowed outside them. Sigurd
snorted and chewed his bit. Ki slapped the reins firmly on the
wide grey backs, and with another snort from Sigurd the wagon
creaked forward into the courtyard.

The inner courtyard looked as abandoned as the grey wooden
buildings. Uprooted brush had rolled into all corners to settle
against the walls. Dead trees stood as markers to what had
once been careful plantings. The black stone mansion was
impervious to the dead courtyard it centered. Ki halted her
team and let her eyes drift up the high walls. Rectangular
Human style windows gaped dark, high overhead. The ground
floor level showed no openings for windows, nor for anything
else, save one stout wooden door. The stretch of wall above
the high windows was likewise smooth. Whatever chambers
were within must do without the light of the sun.

"Cheery place," Ki remarked to her horses.

"Well. Am I to stand all day holding the door open, awaiting
my lady's pleasure, while every stinging thing that flies finds
its way in?"

Ki jerked at the waspish voice. Her eyes snapped to the
black door held ajar by a black-gowned old dame. Her look

was as sour as her greeting. She reminded Ki of a gallows bird, with her wattled neck and snapping black eyes.

"Did you send for a teamster?" Ki asked, hoping this was an error.

"Yes, but I suppose you'll do. Does your rump come loose of that plank, or do your folk customarily bargain out in the sun?"

Silently Ki set her wheel brake. She gave her team a gruff command to stand and clambered down from the wagon. This was going to be bad. And without a dru in her purse, she was going to have to swallow it.

The house matron did not wait for her, but set off down the hallway as soon as Ki approached the door. Ki shut the door behind herself, with perhaps a louder thump than necessary. She had to hasten down the tall corridor to follow those swishing black skirts. Sunlight was left behind, and the few sconces were widely spaced and badly tended. Ki's shadows stretched and snapped about her, and her boots rang hollowly as she strode along. The matron turned a sudden corner. Ki broke into a half-trot lest she lose sight of her.

But as Ki turned the same corner, she found herself within an immense chamber. There were no signs of servants or other house folk. The ceiling was implausibly high; the echo of her boots bounced back at her. Grey daylight fell into the room from one of the windows she had glimpsed outside. The watery beams dimly lit a small carven table in the center of the room. It was the only furniture in the cavernous place. The house matron stood beside it and dust motes danced over it.

She halted, looking about uncertainly. How could one bargain in such a place? There were no chairs in which one could lounge disinterestedly, no wine or ale to sip to cover up a moment of thought. Ki would have been more comfortable doing this business in the sun from her wagon. Bird-eyes gave her no time to reflect.

"You are to take the freight from Dyal to Bitters. Seven crates. They must be delivered before four days have passed from tomorrow. That you must agree to, or pay the consequences. Four days will give the servants time to put the new place in order before the belongings arrive. But we shall not want to do without them for any longer than that."

"I've not said that I'll work for you," Ki pointed out quietly.

"I never said I wished you to! Nor would I, if the choice were mine. But the Master has picked you, and won't be swayed from his decision."

For the first time, Ki realized that this imperious old woman was not the owner of the mansion, but only the chief servant. The woman's attitude annoyed her, but she put it down to her age and post. Such as she must expect idleness from the lesser servants. Still, it irked Ki not a little to have the woman take that tone with her, let alone voice such an opinion.

"I repeat, I have not said that I'll accept the cargo." Ki took pleasure in being perverse now. "I conduct my business a bit differently from other teamsters you may have dealt with. I limit the weight of what my team will haul, and I take half payment in advance for any trip." She kept her words cool, but already she was thinking of the hill route that would let her make the journey to Bitters in three days or less.

"I know your terms, girl!" snapped Bird-eyes. "Do I look like some silly little maid who would hire a teamster sight unseen, with no knowledge of the rates and customs? No, Teamster Ki, you were selected, though, now that I look at you, I cannot say why! The freight will not be heavier than your usual load, and all will be packed securely for you ahead of time. The family wishes you to take the greatest care with this load, to avoid breakage. They will precede you to Bitters, so that they may receive it from you, and inspect the seals to be sure that none are broken."

Ki raised her brows appraisingly. "What do I carry to rate all this caution and mistrust? I'll warn you, my rates go higher for illegal cargo."

"I'll wager they do, and often, too. Not that it's any of your business, magpie, but the cargo is household goods; old family items of small value to any save blood relations. You need not fret about them. All will be packed securely. The city gates will not halt you. Your only task is to haul them to their destination, and there receive the rest of your pay. Now, what will you have for a trip to Bitters?"

"This time of year, thirty dru. In winter it would be a full two tallies. But the year is still mild and the roads unrutted. So thirty dru it shall be, and a bargain to you at that." Ki folded her arms sternly and braced herself for the counter offer.

"La, a bargain, she says! I warned the old Master, but no, you he would have on the word of one of his beggar friends.

What's his name to come to with the company he keeps, I
don't know. Well, he told me to pay your price. You'll get
your thirty dru advance, but mind, if even a one of those seals
be but scratched at, not a copper shard shall you get at Bitters. . . ."

"I'll be here for my load at first light tomorrow," Ki interrupted. She had expected fifteen dru advance and another fifteen at the end of the haul. But to receive thirty now, and
another thirty at Bitters . . . well, as the old matron had said,
that was small bargain to them, but one Ki would not sniff at.

"Wait," Bird-eyes said. Ki had used that tone earlier, when
she had directed her team to stand. The matron whirled with
a swishing of skirts and was out the door before Ki could utter
a word. She listened for the tapping of her feet down the
corridor, but heard nothing. The temptation to go to the door
and peer out was great, but Ki conquered it. She walked once
around the room, but found nothing that she had not seen in
her first glance. The ridiculously high windows were a puzzle
without clues.

A chink of coins spun her around. The old matron stood
beside the table. On it were two fifteen-coin stacks of dru atop
a large square of creamy parchment. Bird-eyes tapped a yellowed fingernail on the edge of the table, then gestured to the
items on it.

"Your advance. And the contract the old Master drew up
for its delivery, safe and sound, four nights hence. I will read
it to you, and you must make your mark upon it, to show you
understand and agree."

Ki advanced, boots clicking on the black flagging. She
silently placed one hand flat on the parchment. With the other
she scooped up the stacked coins and transferred them to the
worn pouch at her belt. Moving her hand so that she could
read the parchment while still pinning it to the table, Ki leaned
over it.

The grey light was uncertain. The contract had been written
by a strong hand, firm dark strokes across the smoothed surface,
in the T'cherian characters. It was brief, but tightly written.
Ki must deliver her cargo to the door of Karn Hall, in Bitters,
in four days. The cargo must be perfectly intact, no seals
broken, and all pieces accounted for. She agreed to make every
possible effort to see to its safe arrival. Should she fail to do so,
she forfeited the rest of the payment, and must return six dru

of the advance. She scowled to herself. If misfortune plagued her, she might finish the trip to Bitters with only twenty-four dru. Possible, but not likely, she told herself. And twenty-four dru was still an ample fee for such a leisurely trip as the hill route would provide. Twenty-four dru were much better than the one copper shard her purse had held this morning.

Ki drew the parchment closer to her and glanced about for a writing tool. The house matron coldly interpreted her look, and drew a small case from a voluminous pocket. Within were brushes and a vial of ink. Ki accepted them just as coldly, dipped the brush, and stroked her name in T'cherian characters. Watching the matron from the corner of her eye, she rashly added the character for a freeborn, and another for one of no political allegiance. The matron covered her amazement well. If anything, she treated Ki more haughtily than before.

"You should be on your way now."

"I intend to take on supplies first," Ki informed her.

"As you will. But, remember, you have only four days for your trip."

"Woman, look you. You have seen to your duty. Now let me tend to mine. I'll return at first light to load the cargo, but I'd like to see it now, to judge the weight. Where is it?"

"On your wagon." The matron turned on her heel. Without a backward glance, she strode from the room. As before, her footsteps made no sound. Ki snorted at the doorway. She waited for a short time by the table, and then paced the room twice. With growing anger, she realized at last that the matron did not intend to return and show her out. She had not gone to fetch the traditional ale that bargains were sealed with. Never before had Ki encountered such rudeness.

She found her own way through the bare and chill hallways, emerging to blink in the brightness of the day. Bird-eyes had spoken the truth. Seven boxes (Ki counted carefully) had been stowed on her wagon. They were of varying sizes, and made of rough yellow wood. Their seals were no more than lumps of lead crimped below the knots of the coarse rope that bound them. It was packing more fit for salt fish than family treasures. Ki sent a glare around the dusty courtyard, but there was no sign of whoever had loaded it. Only the black walls festooned with long dead vines received her scowl.

She swung up onto the wagon and climbed over the boxes,

trying to find fault with the way it had been loaded. But it was
balanced and steady. An inspection of the ropes lashing it to
the wagon revealed knots she would have sworn were her own.
It was uncanny. There was the added sting that someone had
made so free with her wagon, and she had heard not a sound
from her team. It disturbed her. She stood atop the load, frowning down on it. With a shrug, she climbed down and mounted
the seat of the wagon. She had thirty dru to spend before she
left Dyal.

By nightfall, less than two dru remained to her. The cup-
boards of her wagon cuddy were comfortably replenished. Ki
took a deep breath, savoring the smells of plenty. Strings of
dried cara root and spicy sausages swung from the central joist.
Bins held chunks of pink salt, yellow-brown flour and brown
beans. Strips of dried meat and fish rested on a shelf, wrapped
in clean sacking. The earthenware pot of honey and the rosy
Cinmeth in its flask were luxuries, but she had salved her
conscience by buying squares of leather to sew new boots for
herself. A final extravagance had been a small vial of oil of
Vanilly.

Ki wrapped the vial in a small cloth and tucked it into a
drawer. She rose from her crouch to glance about her cuddy.
It was a small and tidy space, made up of only the front half
of her wagon. No space in the tiny room was wasted. The
sleeping platform across one end of it was supported by cup-
boards. Shelves and bins, hooks and drawers lined the interior
of the cuddy, except for one small window, shuttered now
against road dust. A cover of shag deer hide had been thrown
across the wool blankets on the bed. In one corner of the cuddy,
the worn hilt of Vandien's rapier winked at Ki.

He would be in Bitters by now. Ki wondered if he had found
a team yet, and what kind of bargain he would wrangle. That
he would get a team she doubted not at all. He had a tongue
that could persuade a Dene to eat meat. If his wheedling could
not win them over, he would resort to using his personal trinkets
as collateral. If that did not work . . . Ki shut the thought out
of her mind. Vandien took care of himself. He wove his life
in and out of hers in a random pattern. He did not fear commitment; he simply saw no need for it. He was an impulsive,
reckless, and totally loyal friend, and she refused to sigh over
him. He'd be back soon enough, dragging disorder and self-

indulgence through her tidy life. It was all so much simpler when he wasn't around. The worst part of it was that he was becoming a habit with her. Damn.

She crawled out of the cuddy, sliding the door closed behind her. Settling on the wagon seat, she picked up the reins. A kick freed the wheel brake and a shake of the reins roused the team. Dusk was settling, bringing with it a small coolness. The moon had begun to claim the sky when she rolled out of the city gates, past guards singularly disinterested in her cargo. Tonight she would sleep on green grass beside her wagon, and let the team graze free. She was weary of shutting herself tight within the stuffy cuddy and listening to her beasts stomp and shuffle all night. It was good to be working again.

THREE

THE mart at Bitters was little different from that in Dyal. Except for the stink of fish. Vandien had not thought that shipments of fresh fish would stay edible over the two day haul from False Harbor, yet folk here were buying them, and smiling at the fishmonger as he wrapped his noisome wares in sacking for them. Vandien leaned forward past a customer to prod a silver fish with a firm finger. The indentation of his touch remained. Vandien gave the fishmonger a different sort of smile, and edged away from his booth, wiping his finger on his breeches.

The aroma of fresh breads wafted past him. He swallowed as he pushed his way past the booth where an expressionless Dene was listlessly hawking breads and pastries. Dark brown high-topped loaves vied with the shining flat cakes of greenish hue that the T'cheria favored. Vandien's hand went to the fat pouch at his belt. The thin leather disguised the small stones that kept company with two small coins. A carter had given him a ride from Dyal to Bitters, feeding him and giving him the coins in exchange for Vandien's assistance in unloading the bundled raw hides. The coins were not much, but were a

generous payment for the small amount of work Vandien had
actually done. He suspected she had paid him more for the
stories he had spun on the long drive than for any real labor.

He strode resolutely past the bread stall. He was hungry,
but that could wait. He had business to conduct. He hurried
past the farmers' section, past the chickens and piglets and
chattering glibs, on past T'cherian stalls festooned with strands
and streamers of slickly shining greens. A glowering Brurjan
presided over a hot meat stall, with a private chamber in back
for devouring the kill. The dying squeal of a glib, cut short,
told Vandien that a meal was in progress. To a Brurjan, "hot
meat" steamed with body heat.

He slowed as he passed the crafter's stalls. Beads and boots,
armor and amorous potions all vied for his attention. A T'cherian
merchant was politely curious about this Human browser who
looked but did not buy. Vandien smiled at him, and pointed
to a pale yellow crystal. "Two tallies," the merchant lisped in
Common. Vandien touched his purse and gave a shrug of resignation. But the smile did not leave his face as he strode away.
Now he sought the hiring end of the market. He didn't pause
to look at any other stalls.

Only three teams were awaiting hire. A scarred Brurjan
stood at the heads of two monstrous horses. Their restive hooves
were scarlet. Their harness was heavy with studs and spikes.
Manes were clipped and tails bobbed short. No farming horses
these, but coursers, trained to pull a hunter's chariot over the
brushy river plains. Those horses would follow the cries of the
questing hounds with no guidance from the driver. Vandien
veered to avoid the hooves that helped strike down prey for
their masters.

A dozing Human sat in the shade of his big plowhorse.
Vandien gave this beast only one look before discarding him.
Huge he was, but his age showed in his greying muzzle and
threadbare tail. There was no gloss to his coat, and one fetlock
was swollen.

Two mules in harness were next in the lineup. A young
Human boy stood at their heads. He had oiled their hooves and
braided their manes as if for a festival. The gawky creatures
tossed their heads, flirting their long ears at every shout in the
market. Vandien looked down into the scrubbed face looking
up into his so eagerly. "I'm sorry, lad," he said regretfully.

"They just aren't big enough for what I must do."

"They'll pull their hearts out for me," the boy countered. His eyes pleaded with Vandien.

"I'm sure they would," Vandien replied gravely. "Perhaps another time, boy. They're a fine looking team."

And that was all. He had come to the end of the teams for hire. Vandien strolled on a bit farther, considering his dilemma. He must get his team here, and drive it into False Harbor as his own, born and trained. So much depended upon first impressions. False Harbor would be expecting a teamster of skill and determination. He could not let them see him as a trickster, come to live off their hospitality and make a mockery of their customs. Ki had said that the task would border on the impossible. Let them doubt him, and he would be certain to fail. Vandien did not intend to fail.

But there was another team. The last team was stretched flat on the street, their flat feet burrowed under the sun-warmed dust. Their tails were coiled on their rumps like fat grey snakes getting ready to strike. Small eyes were closed above piggy snouts. Gouts of dust rose with their rhythmic breathing. There were four of them, their thick hairless hides mottled from grey to black. Each was as long as a horse, but there the resemblance ended. "Are you pigs, or lizards?" Vandien asked the beasts. They ignored him. Their legs were squat but thick with muscle. The four harnesses fanned out from a single large ring set over a peg hammered into the ground. Vandien glanced about for their owner, only to discover him right beside the team.

The T'cherian had decided to follow his team's example. He was mostly withdrawn into his carapace. Some passing cart had coated him thickly with the fine deep dust of the street. But for his drooping eye stalks he resembled a rock. Vandien cleared his throat and the eye stalks began to stir. Perhaps the team was not exactly what he had sought, but the owner was perfect.

The T'cherian's dark red eyes regarded Vandien solemnly for a moment. Then, in deference to Human customs, he raised his body on his jointed legs until his "face" was on a level with Vandien's. Carefully he lowered his eye stalks until his visual orbs were on nearly the same level as his mandibles. Vandien dipped his head to the T'cherian gravely, already impressed with his manners. He knew of no other race in the world who went to such lengths to put others at ease. Shrewd bargainers they were, and as callous in business as a Brurjan, but all their inflexibility was gloved with velvet courtesy.

"I wish to hire a team to pull a heavy load," were Vandien's opening words.

"My team will do so. Humans seldom use skeel. You may judge them poor beasts to look at, accustomed as you are to your long-legged horses. No doubt you find my skeel ugly beasts." The T'cherian paused in his lisping, clicking sales pitch to allow Vandien to disagree. Vandien knew that many Humans were reluctant to do business with T'cheria, claiming that their strong accents made their Common barely intelligible. But Vandien had developed an ear for the way they turned and sharpened the consonants of Common, and found dealing with them no task. Now he strove to match the creature in courtesy.

"I would not propose to judge a beast by its appearance. If you tell me they can pull, I am sure that they can, however foreign they may be to me. May I ask if they drive in the same manner as horses, or is a special skill involved?"

"A special skill to driving such as these? You honor and flatter a poor farmer like myself. No, they are the mildest of creatures, so easy to control that one of your egglings would find it as play. With a driver behind them with my turns of experience, you will find that there is little we cannot do. Even the heaviest of loads will yield to our tenacity. Would you have a field freed of rocks? Pull logs down from a hillside? They are equal to the task. And no thrifty person could hope for a better team. Having fed three days ago, they will not hunger for two more spans of days."

Vandien worked the math swiftly in his head. The beasts went for nineteen days between feedings, a particularly useful trait in his situation. Delicately, he broached the touchy part of his bargaining.

"I doubt not that your years of experience make your team the fine one that they are. But for the task I face, I would be the driver, and must be assured that they would obey a stranger. For ten days you must trust them to my care. Would you agree to such a bargain?"

The T'cherian's eye stalks moved slowly from side to side in a learned pantomime of the Human gesture for "no."

"I regret that I must refuse. My team are my children to me, and the sole means of my livelihood in these days of dry weather and Windsinger animosity. I dare not entrust them to a stranger, no matter how sincere of countenance and noble of carapace. Yet happy would I be to join you in any task you might propose. You, too, would be gladdened to see how the difficulty of any labor would be dissipated by my experienced handling of the team. Beasts always pull better for the master they know and trust. Cannot we still find a bargain here?"

Vandien heaved a tremendous sigh. He let his hands rise to shoulder height, and then fall away in a mimicry of a T'cherian's drooping eye stalks when saddened. "I must respect your reservations. My respect honors the one who feels the responsibilities ownership puts upon one. I understand the concern of the wise master for his beasts. Sure I am that no coin could dissuade you from your views. For no amount of coin would you entrust these worthy creatures to a stranger."

"No coin could buy my honor," the T'cherian repeated. He and Vandien both knew that the stage was being set for the bargain. The T'cherian waited.

"Nor would I demean your sensibilities by even offering such coins to you. What do you know of me? How can I gain the trust and thus the service I seek from you? These questions I have asked myself as we have stood here, in this unpleasantly noisy place, seeking to make a bargain like civilized folk in the midst of this most uncivilized din, in this whorl of disruptive movement and unharmonized noises. In this blatting of beasts, this heat, this caking of dust upon our countenances, in these body smells of those who pass disrespectfully close to us, how can I prove myself to you? How can I show you that I, though a Human and not endowed with those superior sensitivities that are the racial treasure of the T'cheria, am not totally without sensitivities myself?"

As Vandien slowly catalogued the discomforts that he knew annoyed the T'cherian to a far greater degree than he could imagine, he could almost see the creature shrinking back within its carapace. He shared the T'cherian preferences for coolness, dim lights, and muted sound. But in a town dominated by Human and Brurjan populations, this T'cherian must brave all discomfort to earn his algae for the day. That discomfort would turn this bargain for Vandien.

"For no coin?" the T'cherian mumbled. A T'cherian mumble consisted of aspirating the words, with almost no vocalization. But Vandien picked them out. It was the perfect opening.

A brown sash belted Vandien's short tunic and supported
his purse. Vandien's hand went to it now, but he did not touch
the purse itself. What he sought could not be bumped about
with coins. He carefully spread the rolled cloth of the sash,
until a small object wrapped in a soft grey cloth dropped into
his waiting hand. The T'cherian had followed his every move.
At first, his eye stalks had lengthened and begun to track Vandien's hand, until he recalled himself to Human courtesy and
retracted them. But Vandien was sure of his interest, and played
his moment for maximum suspense.

Carefully he readjusted the sash that had cradled the fragile
object. That done, he allowed himself a moment to straighten
his tunic, and to wipe each hand in turn down his breeches.
Only then did he begin to unfold the soft thin grey cloth. Slowly
he unwound the wrapping, using both hands to remove the
cloth as if fearful the object within would be lost. Vandien's
fingers gave the cloth a final twitch. The T'cherian gave a
sudden rattle of its mandibles. Neither spoke.

Revealed on Vandien's palm was an orange crystal, about
the same length and diameter as his ring finger. With gentle
fingers he held it to the light, as if the delicate thing would
crumble at a touch. Held to the sun, the light touched the
individual facets that made up the many crystals joined into
one structure.

Vandien made a show of lifting the crystal to his nose and
sniffing it delicately. To his nostrils, it gave off almost no odor.
The T'cherian remained desperately silent. His agitation was
betrayed by a bare tremble in the fingerlike pincers of his
primary limbs. The clatter of the market went on, but Vandien
let the T'cherian listen to the silence that had fallen between
them. When he finally spoke, he whispered.

"For no coin."

"What do you propose?" the T'cherian hissed. "It is a very
small crystal," he added hesitantly.

But Vandien was not to be fooled by the size of his ware.
"Yes. It is. And of the deepest color. A crystal such as this
would be an ornament to the richest of queens, small enough
to be carried about with one, to be enjoyed whenever the turmoil
of this workaday world threatened the inner peace so vital to
any civilized creature. I have been in the home caves of wealthy
T'cheria, who graced their walls with crystals, and hung them
in ranks from their food grids, but seldom have I seen a crystal

to match this one for color or bouquet. Long have I treasured
its comforts upon the open road. To see its blinking light, to
draw in its sweet odor of drowsy peace; these have solaced me
in many trials. By this sign, I show you that I am a civilized
creature, just as you are yourself. I am to be trusted, even when
I come to rent your team away from you, and am forced by
commercial convention to offer despised coin to you."

Vandien's brown eyes met the T'cherian's stalked ones,
radiating open sincerity. He casually began to wind the grey
wrapping around the crystal again. The tremor of one T'cherian
eye stalk betrayed him. He followed every shifting of the crystal. His mandibles rattled briefly before he recalled himself to
Common.

"Your sign impresses me, Human. Never before have I seen
one of your kind with a sopor crystal, other than as a trade
item. My name is [a hissing rattle here], called by your kind
Web Shell, for my carapace markings."

"I am Vandien." Together they bowed gravely at this formal
introduction that marked the true beginning of all T'cherian
bargaining. What had gone before was but a prelude, an ar-
ranging of forces. "Then, Web Shell, you find out today that
not all Humans are barbarians. Some of us treasure peace as
dearly as yourselves."

"What is the job you would hire my team to do?"

"A small bit of work in False Harbor."

"A rough town that is, with little to recommend it. No
T'cheria reside there; and I have heard evil things of the Humans that make it their home. What surety will I have of the
safety of my team? How can you guarantee that they will not
be stolen, or poisoned, or maimed for sport?"

Vandien slowly waved the hand holding the crystal before
his face, the Human equivalent of a T'cherian showing distress
at the mere thought of something. "May the Moon forbid such
evil deeds!" Vandien's hand went to his belt pouch. The
T'cherian still tracked every motion of the hand that held the
crystal. Vandien patted his purse so that the two small coins
chinked together. "You present me with a dilemma. You seem
to say that you would hire me your team, if you could be sure
of their safety. Have I understood you, or has the limitations
of this poor Common corrupted the thoughts you seek to con-
vey?"

"Let us take that as a premise," the T'cherian hedged. "If

I were willing to hire out to you these precious skeel, more
companions to me than work animals, what could you offer
me as a bond for their well being while in your care?"

Vandien again jingled the pouch. "What, indeed? Coin will
pay you when I return, but that is not what is needed now. A
crasser man than I might offer you coin now, not understanding
that a show of money is not always a show of good faith. But
I perceive that what is needed is not mere monetary security,
but a personal commitment. A hostage, if you will." Vandien
paused and turned his eyes up to the sky. He posed silently.
Then, with seeming reluctance, he slipped the crystal back into
his sash. The mandibles of the T'cherian rattled lightly at this,
but Vandien appeared not to notice. With tightly folded lips
and a resigned expression, he unscrewed a ring from his left
hand. It came free slowly, revealing a band of whitened skin.
With a great sigh, he held it out for the T'cherian's inspection.

The eye stalks bent to it briefly. It was an exceptionally
plain ring. The single black stone did not sparkle, though the
facets of the square cut gleamed dully. The band was of plain-
silver. Vandien hefted its heaviness.

"There is this," he said slowly. "Long has it been since it
left my hand. But if you would have a token of my good
intentions, I offer you this. From my mother's father's grandmother, it was passed to me." He paused again and took a deep
breath to clear the huskiness from his voice. "Little enough is
left to me to remind me of the heights from which my line has
fallen. But this I retain, a reminder to myself of all we once
were, and all I hope to be again. Never would I forsake it!
Never! If I were to leave this in your keeping, you could be
sure that I would return your team to you in good health, or
die trying!"

Vandien's fist closed convulsively over the ring. For an
instant every muscle and tendon in his arm and hand stood out
against his skin. He blinked his eyes rapidly. Then, gravely,
he extended his hand, palm up, to Web Shell. The hand that
held the ring trembled.

"Return your ring to your hand," the T'cherian said solemnly. "Although we put no metal ornaments upon our shells,
we understand the high regard you Humans have for them.
This one means too much for you to part with it as a token in
a marketplace."

But Vandien's hand remained outstretched. "Yet your team

I must hire. I am convinced only they could perform the task for me. Please! This discussion only prolongs my anxiety and discomfort!"

The T'cherian rattled his mandibles loudly. Vandien clenched his jaws and turned his eyes away. He had deliberately used the phrase "anxiety and discomfort," knowing well it was the standard Common translation of a T'cherian phrase that signified the mental and emotional upset that preceded severe physical damage.

"No!" the T'cherian cried out. Vandien felt it actually touch his hand with its pincers. "Take away this family token of yours, Human. Your willingness to offer it is enough! I will not require it of you! You may rent my team from me. Your display of integrity has touched me. I shall not ask advance coin of you."

Vandien stared at the T'cherian, and quickly replaced his ring on his finger. He struck a new pose. Crossing his arms over his chest approximated a humbled T'cherian. "You overwhelm me, sir! I cannot accept this generosity. I see that those who do business with you must protect you from your own courtesy. I have little to offer you, but some token of mine you must keep. I demand that you ask something of me! Anything!"

"Anything?" the T'cherian repeated, as if in wonder.

Vandien leaped gladly into the trap. "Anything! I promise to entrust you with it."

"I hesitate to ask it."

"I demand that you ask it!"

"Your crystal, Human. Entrust it to me as I entrust my team to you."

A look of dismay crept over Vandien's face. He clutched at the crystal hidden in his sash. His shoulders slumped as he let his hands fall to the sides of his body. "I told you to ask," he said, speaking so softly that the T'cherian swayed closer to hear. Vandien gave a soft laugh, and shook his head over his own simplicity. "Well is it said, 'The courtesy of a T'cherian is matched only by his shrewdness.' I demanded that you ask, and you have. Never did I consider that this would be your request. My peace, my sanctuary from the insanity of this world. And yet . . ." Vandien reached into his sash and slowly withdrew the grey-wrapped crystal. "I am a being of my word."

He extended the wrapped crystal to the T'cherian, whose

pincers instantly closed on it. Web Shell unwrapped it swiftly
while Vandien marvelled at his dexterity. Quivering mandibles
closed on the crystal. Slender cilia appeared and caressed the
crystal, ascertaining its quality. The T'cherian's eye stalks began to sag gently. Vandien smiled. It was an excellent crystal.
An itinerant trader he met near Kelso had offered it in exchange
for three measures of salt. Kelso had no T'cherian population.
As trade goods, the crystals had value only to a T'cherian.
None of the other sentient populations had any use for them.
But no T'cherian believed that.

Quickly Vandien began to ask pertinent questions about
what commands this team responded to. He made arrangements
for the time and place of their return. The T'cherian gave
dreamy replies. By the time Vandien picked up a slender prod
and moved the team off, the T'cherian was swaying softly to
the silent music of his own harmonious visions. His cilia vi-
brated around the crystal in his mandibles.

One of his small coins brought Vandien a large dark loaf
at the pastry stall. He would have preferred the greenish
T'cherian bread, but knew that he would travel farther on the
grain one. The large flat feet of his team stirred up great poufs
of dust as they moved down the street. After a few efforts at
stirring them to greater speed, Vandien became resigned to a
leisurely stroll. He slackened his pace and turned his thoughts
to False Harbor. Even at this speed it was no more than four
days away. He would be there in plenty of time to try.

And if he succeeded? Fear and hope swirled in him. He
rubbed irritably at the scar on his face. It was stiff and numb
under his fingers. Was it only vanity to wish it was gone? Was
he a fool to believe Srolan? Yes, and yes, his fear nagged him.
And that was why he had not told Ki what he'd been offered.
Because his own eagerness shamed him. He hated to imagine
how Ki would perceive it; Ki, for whose sake he had taken the
scar. He brooded on it, trudging along behind the dawdling
skeel.

And yet...his quick nature flipped his hopes uppermost...and yet imagine greeting Ki with a clear face, seeing
her amazement and pleasure. One thing he was certain of; had
he mentioned it to her, she would have come with him to False
Harbor. She would have abandoned her own tasks to help him
haul up the Windsingers' chest. And that, he decided, coming
full circle in his own personal logic, was exactly why he hadn't

told her. It would be wrong to bend her will to his by such a guile. He would not suffer her guilt or pity. Whatever flowed between them must flow freely, or not at all. But if she came, of her own will, he would welcome her. Alone, success might be as fearsome a thing to meet as failure. He would appreciate his friend's being there.

Four

THE mellow sunlight of autumn slanted yellow across the wagon trail. "Trail!" Ki snorted to herself at granting it such a title. Twin dents in the sod of the forest ran off ahead of her. Small bushes grew in between the tracks, to brush the bottom of her freight wagon as she passed over them. White birches dripping golden leaves, interspersed with cotton wood and tangles of willow, edged the side of the track. The occasional Harp tree stood foreign and speechless in the still warmth of the afternoon. She breathed the mossy forest scents and leaned back lazily on the cuddy door. She was rich, for today, in both time and wealth.

She felt only a small pang of conscience at dawdling. It was not for the sake of her customer. She could camp tonight and easily deliver her freight on time tomorrow. But there was Vandien to consider. He had not pressed her, but she knew he would welcome her in False Harbor. She would have gone, and speedily, if only it were not such a fool's errand. She bit her lip, watching the steady undulation of muscles in the grey backs before her. She added up the days; six days since Vandien had left for False Harbor. He would be there by now, unless

his luck had deserted him. As for herself, Ki could halt early
tonight, and make a leisurely day of tomorrow, to bring in her
freight on the fourth day's afternoon.

Or, she reminded herself, she could stir up her team and
push them on into Bitters before the middle of the night had
passed. Bitters was spread out, a farming place, not a fortified
town. There would be no city gates or guards to stop her. Yes,
she could do that, and then push on to False Harbor—say a
day and a half—and be there in plenty of time, but . . . damn
the man! Here she was, chewing over his little predicament as
if she were obliged to wrest him out of it. His own tongue had
gotten him into it. He had taken care of himself for many years
upon the road before taking up with her. Let him get himself
out of this one. Perhaps he would not so lightly volunteer her
team the next time. A little sweat would do him good. A wry
grin replaced the worried look on Ki's face. Let him stew it
out. She'd meet him there, on the eleventh day perhaps, when
he'd be properly thankful to see her. Let the little cockerel get
his feathers wet first.

Ki's nose twitched. She rose to stand on the wagon's plank
seat. Her slim body swayed to the steady rhythm of the wagon
as she stretched the kinks from her limbs. Her green eyes
narrowed as she tried to pierce the forest growth ahead of her.
The trail was too winding. She could not yet see the river, but
she sensed it, in the damp tang that came to her nostrils and
by the pricked ears of her team. Long habit made her glance
at the sun; she shrugged nonchalantly. She'd camp by the river
tonight. Bitters could wait. She'd make camp while the sun
was in the sky and take the time to wash and sluice the dust
from her hair. It would be good to feel clean again. She settled
on the seat.

As she approached the river, the trees thinned and receded
to a wide grassy area, fringed with brush and vines. Dead
branches and debris marked the edge of the river's spring flood
margin. The turning of the season had painted the river grasses
in warm yellows and browns. Ki turned her team into them,
pulling off the seldom used trail and paralleling the river. The
tall wheels of her wagon crunched the dry standing grasses.
The horses tossed their great heads, unhappy at encountering
the extra resistance. But she urged them on until she found
what she sought; a secluded clearing fronting on the river. Here

was grass for the team, and a shallow area of quiet water where she could bathe.

The afternoon sun was still slanting warmly down when she finished unhitching the team. The big greys moved about freely in the tall grass. Staid Sigmund munched steadily at this coarse fare, but Sigurd dropped and rolled luxuriously in the scratchy stuff. Ki smiled. They would not stray. They knew no home but the wagon they pulled.

Her camp was made swiftly. She made a routine check of her freight, tugging at ropes to be sure they had not frayed or loosened from the day's jolting. All was secure. The rest of the afternoon and the long evening were hers.

She climbed back to the wagon seat and slid open the cuddy's wooden door, blinking her eyes to adjust them to the dim interior. A little sunlight trickled in through the shuttered window. Ki turned the four catches that secured it in place, and lifted the shutter down. The afternoon breeze came in the window hole; with winter coming, she would have to buy a piece of greased skin, to cover that hole and still admit light. Glass was too expensive, and could not withstand the heave and give of the wagon. But for now she refused to worry about it.

She caught up a clean tunic from a hook, and a leather belt to buckle it about her waist. She hesitated, then dug in the drawer for the vial of oil of Vanilly. It had been an extravagance, she knew, and it would be a vanity extreme to use it out here, with no one to smell it but herself. But small vanities were due to oneself, now and then.

On the riverbank she kicked off her boots, stripped her blouse off over her head and let the skirts fall in a puddle about her feet. She stepped out of them, and set the clean tunic and the vial of perfume on top of them. She freed her hair from the two thick braids that kept it free of snarls while she traveled, shaking it loose in a thick brown mass that fell just past her shoulders. It smelled like dust and sweat.

The cool air from the river pinched her skin up in goose flesh. Ki steeled herself, shivering, and then pranced out over the rounded gravel into the river and threw herself flat in it. She came up, puffing and blowing from the shock of the cold water. Breathing in gasps, she gathered a handful of black sand from the river bottom and scoured herself with it. Soon her body gleamed pink with scrubbing and chill.

She glanced at her grazing team, and then waded out into deeper water. She ducked repeatedly until her hair hung flat and streaming. The river water finally dripped off it clean, untinged by road dust. Ki was satisfied. She moved through the water in a less businesslike manner now, kicking up splashes and sometimes ducking under just for the pleasure of feeling the water slide from her skin.

A final duck and plunge, and Ki came up headed for the bank. From the clear afternoon sky came suddenly a long note. It was a pure sound, pure as a bird's call, but long and more rounded than a beaked creature would give. It was sourceless, seeming to originate from the sky itself. Ki stood very still, senses straining as the cold river water lapped about her thighs. She made no futile effort to cover herself, but wished desperately that the rapier were on the riverbank instead of in the wagon. She preferred to be armed against the unknown.

The call died away slowly. Ki hoped it had been some long-winded river bird. She still saw no movement of living creature. Even the horses were frozen, heads up and ears pricked. Indeed, the only motion seemed to be that of the wind, come up suddenly. She shivered and hastened to the shore.

The wind grew in intensity, whipping her wet hair across her face. Ki found herself fighting for balance as she sought the riverbank. Out of the water, the chill bit her more fiercely. She began to dry herself on her dirty skirt, but the rising wind and a nervous whinny from Sigurd prompted her to pull the clean tunic hastily over her wet body.

She paused to wring her mop of hair. The wind hit her harder, pelting her with leaves ripped from the trees. She was buckling her leather belt with numbed fingers when a gust of blasting force knocked her to the ground. Ki crouched beneath its onslaught, struggling to hold her hair out of her eyes with one hand. She scrabbled across to her soiled clothes and vial of Vanilly and boots. Clutching them to her, she lurched to her feet, battling the strange air currents. She ran heavily toward her wagon. It was rocking on its tall yellow wheels. Even as Ki staggered toward it, she heard the twang of a snapping rope. One of the boxes of cargo bounced free. The rough wood slats split as it struck the earth.

A sudden stench struck Ki with the force of a physical blow. She gagged, and held her wadded clothes to her nose and mouth. Wildly she stared about, seeking a source for the odor.

There was none. The reek grew stronger, foul as old blood. But it came, like the wind, from nowhere. A strange prickling of foreboding raised the hair on Ki's chilled skin even higher. The stench was like a curtain across Ki's nose and mouth; she felt she would strangle on it. Sigmund screamed. Sigurd reared and pawed as if to strike the reek from the sky. Lather showed on his gray hide. As he came down, he wheeled and fled. She heard the thunder of his hooves through the forest as he vanished into the waving trees. The odor went with him. Ki cursed him savagely.

She tossed her bundled clothes in the hatch of the wagon, stooped to draw on her boots, then turned her attention to her freight. The crate that had fallen was a small one. She picked it up. Black enamel inlaid with small stones showed through the broken wood. Ki was gentle with it as she mounted her still rocking wagon and set it inside the cuddy. Firmly she slid the door shut.

The other ropes seemed to be holding. The rest of the crates were larger, unlikely to be tumbled about by the wind. The persistent wind stirred and eddied about her, buffeting her as she moved around her wagon. Yet the sky remained clear and blue.

No time to ponder strange weather. Ki whistled to Sigmund. Twice he pranced flirtatiously away from her before she could grasp a handful of mane and scrabble up the tall shoulder and onto his back. Vab, how she hated to ride these beasts! There was no comfortable way to straddle him. He was simply too wide. She set her heels to him and grasped a double handful of mane. Sigmund shook his head, not liking her on his back any more than she liked to be there. But he was resigned to it, and moved off with Ki clinging like a monkey. Sigurd's trail was plain. Great chunks of forest floor had been thrown up by his flying hooves, and his body had parted the brush as he passed. Following him was no problem. Catching up was the task. She urged Sigmund to go faster, and clung low to avoid the scratching limbs of the trees.

It was past full dark when a weary and bedraggled Ki, still following Sigurd's trail, rode back into her own camp. Sigurd had changed directions numerous times, and forded the river twice. She could only believe that he had been harried about by something, yet there had been no tracks in the earth but

Sigurd's own. She could not account for it. It was all a mystery.
A damnable, unpleasant, inconvenient mystery.

Right now she did not care to consider it. She was scratched
from overhanging branches, and filthy where she had been
swept from Sigmund's back into a swampy area. Sigmund was
as scratched and muddied as Ki. She returned now to a camp
unlit by fire. The day that had started off as a holiday had
become a dreary day of pointless and fruitless effort. She slid
from Sigmund's back.

Sigurd stood, head adroop, near the tongue of the wagon,
as if taking comfort from its familiar presence. His coat showed
traces of dried lather. As she approached him, he put his muzzle
down and rubbed the side of his face slowly against his foreleg.
If a horse could look abashed, he did. Ki ran a hand over his
rough damp coat. They both needed another grooming tonight.
All three of us, she amended, as she ran a hand through her
own tangled mane.

At least the wind had died. It was now a quiet autumn night,
with a sliver of moon that served more to confuse than to light.
Her camp chest was a lumpy shadow on the ground. Bone
weary, Ki stumbled toward it. First, she planned, the fire, then
wash, then groom beasts, then eat, and lastly, consider that
one of the seals on her freight was broken.

The familiar catch on the chest sprang open at her touch.
From it she took the pouch that contained her tinder materials.
A twist of dry river grass ignited readily. She heaped on the
blaze the small dry branches she had gathered earlier; the welcome light of the little fire pushed back the dark, and made it
easier to pretend that tomorrow would be better. Ki stretched
her abused body as she rose from her fire making and turned
to her wagon.

She cursed. Sigurd put his ears back at the long low stream
of invective she unleashed. When she ran out of breath, she
folded her lips tightly shut and advanced to where her entire
cargo lay tumbled and split open behind her wagon. She returned to the fire for a brand, and made her inspection. The
light did not make it any better. Of the seven crates, four
remained. All four had been split open, to reveal a strange
trove of common earth and stones. There was enough wood to
account for two more crates, but nothing to show what they
had contained. The clean slice marks on the coarse wood showed
that no wind had cracked these crates open. Ki glared at the

wreckage impotently. There was nothing she could do to salvage this haul.

Household goods! Ki snorted, and wished she could have felt surprised. Four crates of dirt and rocks. Why? And wind sorcery undertaken to divest her of her cargo. Expensive sorcery, that. Ki moved carefully away from the scattered crates, setting her feet lightly. In the morning sun, she should be able to read something from the ground. Methodically she turned to grooming her horses. Much to their disgust, she then improvised picket lines from the snapped cargo ropes, lest winds and odors return.

When she climbed the tall wheel of her wagon and slid open the door of the cuddy, a powerful blast of Vanilly hit her. The glass vial of concentrated oil; of course, it, too, would have to break when she had tossed it in with her clothes. No sense in having bad luck by halves. Holding her breath, she moved inside the cuddy to lift her last tunic off its hook.

For the second time that day, Ki bathed and washed her hair in the now dark and freezing river. She mumbled curses as she knelt shivering in the shallows to scrub out her soiled clothes. She doubted that the blue blouse and skirt would ever be free of the scent of Vanilly. As she worked, she thought of alternatives. She had none. She would go on to Bitters. She did not have enough coin to pay back the six dru of the advance. It would make a lively scene with the owners. But there was no advantage to putting it off.

Her feet were cold and stone bruised. Aches twined through every muscle of her body as she came back into the circle of her firelight. In the wagon, the Vanilly was still overwhelming. Ki took a short breath and ducked in to gather up hard traveler's bread, a sausage, a kettle, dry tea. She backed hastily out of the cuddy. On the seat of her wagon, she paused to bite off the end of the sausage. She stood chewing and considering. Then she reached into the cuddy and brought out the last box of her freight as well.

As she waited for her kettle to come to a boil, she took alternate bites of sausage and bread. She stared at the rough wooden crate at her feet. Through the crack, the stones on the enamelled box winked at her seductively. She put a measure of tea into the kettle and removed it from the fire. Her thoughts were tangled as she took an earthenware mug from her camp chest. She seated herself on the chest, poured her tea, and took a tentative sip. With a shrug, she picked up her knife. In a businesslike manner, she hunched over to pry open the rest of the rough wooden crate. The enamel box came free. She was going to have to pay full price for this misadventure. At least she would satisfy her own curiosity.

The last shard of splintery yellow wood dropped away. Ki filled her lap with the enamelled box. Turning it about, she found one plain side. She decided it was the bottom and oriented the box that way. Opening it was the problem now. There were no hinges, nor any discernable catch. Possibly it was hidden in the pattern of stones. Ki moved her hands lightly over the box, feeling for loose stones. None of those either.

She set the box down on the camp chest beside her. Sipping hot tea, she pondered. Was she being wise to even try to open it? But a stubbornness came over her. She would see what was inside it; dammit, she had paid for that much in nuisance already. She returned the box to her lap and took up her knife again.

A peculiar prickling sensation began in the fingers of her right hand. The knife fell from her lax fingers. The prickling raced up her arm. Coldness overtook Ki's heart as she watched her arm drop away from the box, to dangle from her shoulder. A poison on the stones, she realized, and was surprised at her own cool logic. She waited with dread for the numbness to spread.

But her fingers suddenly flexed and stretched of their own volition. Her hand rose to rest once more on the box. One finger settled on a red stone. Ki did not even feel the touch as it pressed gently down on it. A white stone next to the red suddenly glowed. Ki watched a finger quickly cover it. A blue stone flashed, and her thumb settled on it. The stones seemed to seize the ends of her fingers. Her arm rose, and with it, the cover of the box. Her arm set down the five-sided cover gently, and returned to unwind swiftly a linen wrapping from whatever rested on the platform that had been the base of the enamel box. Her hand tucked the linen wrapping into the empty top of the box. Her hand came back to settle gently in her lap. The tingling returned for a moment, then left it again. Ki stared at her fingers for a long breath, then gingerly flexed them. Her hand was hers again.

Ki let out a long shuddering breath. Night pressed closer,

to hover blackest over the pitiful light of her small fire. She licked her dry lips, and let her eyes be drawn back to the contents of the enamel box. It was a carved head. She set it carefully on the box beside her. Leaning back, she tilted her head to admire it.

The squat pedestal of the bust was a block of porous black stone, veined with red. Ki wondered briefly at the use of such a coarse stone as the base for such a creation. For a head as lifelike as this deserved a pedestal of crystal, a mounting of gold. In both carving and coloring, it mimicked life.

What stone was this, with a glow like warm flesh? What artist had produced the grey overcast that suggested the pallor of death? Straight black hair was combed flat to the head, to show the aristocratic shape of the skull. The eyes, pale grey, were slightly open, almost sleepily, beneath fine black brows. The nose was straight and strong above a mouth sensually full. It smiled at her, lips parted to reveal small even white teeth.

"You've made a fine botch of a simple job, Ki," it said suddenly. The head twisted about on the block as if to limber up neck muscles stiff from confinement. "I expected some problems, but I confess this is a catastrophe beyond my wildest imaginings. Where are you going?"

At the first words, Ki had frozen. As the head continued to speak, she had scrambled to her feet and begun to back out of the fire's circle of light.

"What can you do, Ki? Abandon me, your wagon and team, and flee into the woods? It wouldn't free you of those who gave you the responsibility for my journey. It certainly wouldn't do me any good. Although I retain some small powers in this diminished state, I would be vastly more comfortable with my own body beneath me, and my own hands at the ends of my arms. The body and hands, I might add, that you have so carelessly lost."

Ki remained on the edge of the firelight. Every hair on her body was acrawl with dread. Yet she knew that face and voice if only she could place them. And she had to bow to the logic of his words, even in the weird circumstances in which he uttered them. Perhaps especially in those circumstances. She stared at him, unable to flee and unwilling to return.

"Oh, come," he resumed condescendingly. "At least have some manners! I would greatly appreciate a sip of your tea.

My bodily wants in this state are few, but the mouth does become dry. Surely you won't let me, uh, sit here alone all evening."

Ki straightened her shoulders and advanced with a bravado she did not feel. She picked up her mug. With hands that trembled only slightly, she held its rim to the head's lips. He sipped. Ki set down her mug, and retreated to the other side of the fire.

"That's better," the head sighed. A little of the greyness seemed to leave his face. "But perhaps I am forgetting my manners as well. I am Dresh, lately a power of Dyal, soon to be, I hope, a power of Bitters. If, that is, you can live up to the terms of our bargain. You've made a fine mess of it so far. You realize that, don't you?"

"I realize that I was given a cargo I would not have chosen to carry, had I known its true nature!" Ki snapped. She drowned her fear in anger. "And I remember your face now. *You* were the drunken tinker that stirred up the tavern at Dyal with your wild political cant about the Windsingers. *You* urged the farmers and weavers to rebel openly, to burn their crops and wool in the field before they paid tribute to the Windsingers. And when the brawl started, you left me to pay the damage!"

As Ki spoke to him, Dresh let his face slide into the tinker's drunken scowl. His eyelids drooped, his cheeks sagged. He let his mouth dangle open. Then with a wink he straightened his features to handsomeness and grinned at her. Had the atmosphere been different, and the head atop a body, Ki might have warmed to that grin. But now it only fueled her anger.

"Someone wants you, Dresh. Someone wants you badly enough to pay gold for wind spells. Such magic is not cheap. Whoever wants you has the wealth to buy his desires. And if he wants you all that badly, I do not think he will take kindly to my interference. You hired me as a teamster, not as a bodyguard."

"'. . . to do all within my power to see that my freight reaches its destination safely.' And signed, not just with your name, but also with your status as a freeborn, and the attestation that your loyalty is only to yourself. That bit of braggadocio has bound you to me even more tightly than *I* could have engineered. And," a lifted eyebrow stemmed Ki's outburst, "you may wish to consider this. You fear you have earned the enmity of certain wealthy and perhaps powerful persons who wish to do me harm. You have. The Windsingers. Themselves. Abandoning me here will not lessen their dislike of you. As you well know, they have never been overly fond of Romni. They will see your conveying of me from Dyal to here as an act of defiance, of open rebellion. So you may as well plot further with me as to how to restore myself. At least then you will be under my not inconsiderable protection."

Kit sat glaring with narrow cat eyes, weighing the options he hadn't mentioned. She could just load his head back into her wagon and haul it to Bitters. But that might mean facing whatever allies this Dresh might have waiting for him. She could seek out the Windsingers herself, and turn the head over to them, with humble apologies. If they would believe her. If they bothered to wait to hear out her story. If she found them before they found her. And, the biggest if, if she had not already given her word to paper that she would deliver this "freight" safely. Gods, what a fix! He had her, thrice bound to him, by name, birth, and loyalty. And the Windsingers against them. Ki was in a game where the opening stakes were already too high for her purse. Dresh was the only way out.

She gave a curt nod to the head that was regarding her with a smug smile, as if he could follow the trail of her thoughts. Ki took a sip of her tea. "So. If I am to assist you in this madness, I think I must know what is going on. Let us have the whys of it."

"The whys?"

"Why are you in pieces? I dare not ask how. Why make this journey? Why pay me a premium price to haul dirt and stones? Why did you incite that riot in the tavern? Why didn't they get your head when they got the rest of you? Why do they want you at all?"

"Such a busy little mind to hide inside a Romni teamster's head! Will you not just trust me, and do as you are told? Believe me when I tell you that knowledge without understanding can cause fear that is completely disproportionate to the realities involved. As a teamster, you must know that the blinkered team may go more steadily than..."

"I am not a horse," Ki warned him.

"No. I did not mean to imply that you were one. Only that the less you knew, the safer you might feel. If..."

"You're asking me to drive a strange trail by night, Dresh, and I..."

"Ah, the quaint wordings of the Romni born. Almost like a subdialect of Common. You are stubborn, and I have no time for it. Know then, and wish you did not. It will take me less time to tell it than to talk you out of it. There is this. For some time, I have been a bother to the Windsingers. For one thing, I know too much about them. I know enough that I fear them in quite a different way from the way ordinary fools fear them. To say more would be to get into personal areas. That must content you. As to why I divided myself, let us say that I knew that the Windsingers had finally decided to free me from my mortal shell, to turn my soul adrift in the universe. The idea did not please me. The runings I had made about Dyal had grown old and were loosening. Too often had they been renewed. I need a new home, guarded by fresh runes. A suitable configuration occurred in Bitters. But there was the journey to Bitters to consider. To leave in my natural form would be useless. They would have had me before I was a step outside the gates. To leave in a disguise would make the game a little more interesting for them, but not for me. I am a wizard, Ki. That shape I project into the strata of power is distinctive. They know that shape as well as you know the scar down Vandien's face."

Dresh paused, smiling, to let Ki feel that little dart. "There are ways, but not many, to alter that configuration. I did not choose to invite a lesser spirit to join mine in my body. I did not choose to . . . well, let us not go into what else I did not choose. What I chose was to divide my body. Thus my shape on the power strata was also divided and would appear in new forms. For a while, it confused them. For a while, but not for as long as I had hoped." The head paused and sighed. Dresh licked his lips, stared at the fire thoughtfully.

Ki echoed his sigh. Without being asked, she circled the fire, poured more hot tea into her mug, and offered it to his lips. He drank sparingly, then watched her as she drank.

"The boxes of earth were to throw them off. As was the use of the black house where you signed the contract. You carried too much freight for it to be the body of Dresh. But that, too, did not deceive them for long. As for why they did not get all of me . . ." The fine white teeth nibbled thoughtfully at the full lower lip. "I think we may call it luck. They did not know how many pieces I was in. The creature they sent was of the basest level of intelligence, twice as primitive as a Romni teamster, even. It was probably told to fetch back the boxes that were enamelled. A necessary part of this magic, you will guess. My head box, within your wagon, escaped its attention. Luckily for us, they will not instantly know it is missing. Unlike some fools, they have too much respect for my boxes to try to pry one open with a knife. They will know the catch is in the jewels. Enough stones are set in each box that there are a large number of possible combinations. Yet not an infinite number, and they are determined to have them open. And they know that they have the most important ingredient of all. Time. There are definite limits to how long I can survive in this state. Time dribbles away from us already. Even now, I sense one of power busy at the box that holds my hands. A lesser one holds vigil over the box that holds my body. We must recover my parts as swiftly as possible. If they succeed in opening the boxes, they will drain me. I will die. Yet I must not act hastily and throw us into their hands. Sensing who has my parts is only half the puzzle. Now I must divine where."

The head was still for a moment. Then, with a peculiar smile, Dresh nodded at the tea mug. Ki leaned down to put it to his lips. He sipped. Then, as Ki took the mug away, he whispered, "Kiss me, Ki."

She bent forward to find his lips. They were cool beneath hers. For a long still moment his full soft lips held hers in a cold kiss. Then he broke it, and Ki jerked herself away from him.

She rocketed to her feet, the back of her hand flying to her mouth. She stared at him as if at a snake. Slowly her hand fell away. She spat on the earth before him.

"How did you do that?" she demanded in a low growl.

"You will forgive me, I trust. Much of a wizard's power is housed in his body and hands. It was just a small test to determine how much I retain. I will confess it is an experiment that has tempted me since I saw you in the tavern. You would not find it so distasteful were my body beneath my head and my hands at the ends of my arms. You have the Romni distrust for magicking. But, lacking a body, a head must do the best it can."

Dresh laughed merrily. Ki did not join in. "I am bound to you," she admitted softly. "But use me as a toy and you shall regret it. For perhaps I could buy the favor of the Windsingers with your head."

"You wouldn't," asserted the head calmly. "You are thrice bound."

"Perhaps not. But what would stop me from delivering your head to Bitters, refunding the advance, and leaving?"

"Your pride, my dear. And you lack the cash. But, I hasten to add, I shall not trifle with you so lightly again. 'Twas but a whim. I know what I wished to know. We have no more time for it now. As for when I do have a body under me again, well, you will find you feel differently. I am not a badly made man, when I am all in one piece. I have small clever hands, softer than yours, narrow hips, and shoulders wider than that vagabond Vandien's. . . ."

"What do you know of Vandien?" Ki cut in to demand.

"Ki, be assured that I know as much of you and your friend as any do. When I pick a teamster to haul my bones, I do not act without thought. As I was saying, small feet, and a flat belly. A slight scar across my left breast, but some women have assured me that it but adds to . . . where are you going now?"

"To bed. I may have to help you recover your parts, but nothing binds me to listen to an inventory of them."

"Ki, you are a basic little creature, aren't you. Lacking a course of action, and being satiated with food, you think only of sleep. But surely you do not intend to sleep within the wagon?"

"And why not?"

"It stinks awfully in there. Your Vanilly came closer to extinguishing my breath than any wind magic tonight. Bring your blankets out here, my dear. I shall watch over you."

"I bet you would."

To Ki's disgust, she found Dresh's words true. Vanilly in excess was scarcely alluring. She gathered her bedding and tucked the sheathed rapier under her arm. The one time when she might have wished for Vandien's skilled hand on the hilt of it, and he takes a seaside holiday. Her own thrusts and parries were nothing to take pride in. But it was the only weapon in the wagon. She sat on the plank seat to close the cuddy door behind her.

The strangeness of the tableau seized her. Ki crouched a moment on the wagon seat, staring. There were the small flames of her campfire, made even smaller by the immense black dome of night arching over all. The few stars did nothing to illuminate the scene. They were impartial eyes watching from an immeasurable distance. The river was a flowing sheet of darkness beyond her fire. And before her fire, silhouetted by the moving flames, was the head on its block of stone, ensconced on the camp chest.

The shiver that raced over Ki's back was not from cold. She wished fervently to be out of this whole situation. She knew of no good ever brought by magic. As for Windsinger magic: could there be a worse kind to pit her puniness against? Were not they renowned for their heartlessness and casual cruelty towards mortals, Humans in particular? Yet a large proportion of Windsingers began their lives as Human females. Ki's fear of them was tinged with disgust at the way they could turn on their own species.

She tossed her bedding down beside the fire. Not even bothering to tug off her boots, she rolled up in the bedding fully clothed. She had a feeling she might wish to move quickly. Dresh did not speak. He stared hypnotically at the flames. Ki followed his eyes. She mused sleepily on the dancing towers of flame and the crumbling ember towns. When she closed her eyes, bright afterimages of the flames danced on the inside of her eyelids.

"Ki! Awake! I have need of your hands!"

Ki was jerked from her dreams into the stranger reality. Dresh's voice was urgent; his dark brows were knotted.

"What's wrong?" Ki wriggled out of her blankets, coming to her feet alert, the sheathed rapier gripped in one hand. She peered in vain into the darkness about the fallen fire. Her team grazed peacefully. "Where is it? What?"

"Nowhere on this plane, dolt! The Windsingers have sent for one of power, great power! I heard their call. Before her, my boxes will be more useless than cobwebs. She will see right through them. But their calling has showed me where they are. I must act now, or forsake all hope. I need hands. I lack them. I shall use yours in place of my own, seeing as how you were responsible for my loss. Do all exactly as I tell you. Put your left hand on my head, extend your right arm and hand vertically...."

Ki remained motionless, frowning.

"Make haste, woman!"

"Tell me first what magic we work. Then I shall decide if I want a part in it."

"We summon a creature to make a way for us. I have located where they hold my parts. We shall go to reclaim them. Now, your left hand on my . . ."

"I wonder if I wish to go with you? Shall I leave my wagon and team here, prey to the first wandering thief?"

"I have already circled them with what power I can. Not enough to hold off a Windsinger, but more than enough to ward off the casual thief. Think you I slept as you did? Now, place your left . . ."

"What sort of creature do we summon?"

"One that moves between levels, a jointer of worlds. Must we waste time so? Can words describe colors to the born blind? Neither can they describe creatures your mind is not disciplined to see. Now please! Your left hand on my head!"

"Please," Ki whispered softly with sarcastic satisfaction. Slowly she moved to obey.

"And your right hand aloft, perpendicular to the earth. Separate your fingers as widely as you can. Blank your mind if you are capable. I do not wish your thoughts to pollute the sending. Now!"

Strange it was to let her hand rest on the soft dark hair of the wizard's head. It curled beneath her left hand, silky with warmth, a slight cushion between her hand and his smooth skull. She had a strange impulse to stroke it away from his eyes as she might pet a street child for some small favor. She resisted the impulse, but looking down into his grey eyes she felt he might have read the momentary urge. She strove to blank out her mind, only to become more and more conscious of Dresh's hair beneath her hand.

"First questions, now flattery! Was ever a power at such a disadvantage? Enough of that! Now, reach your right hand straight over your head, touching the middle finger to the palm of your hand while keeping the other fingers stretched out straight."

Ki tried to comply, but the hand position was difficult. Her smallest finger leaned far back from the rest of her hand. She felt an immediate cramp across her knuckles.

"Straighten those fingers!" Dresh barked. "So!"

One moment her hand nestled in his soft hair. The next it

was encased in a grip of ice. Cold emanated from the top of his skull, to creep up inside her arm. A sluggishly moving icy jelly was being forced up through her bones. Her fingers went numb. The feeling in her arm was lost to her. Elbow and shoulder, gone. A web of icy tendrils crept like a living mantle across her shoulders, ventured up her raised right arm. Fear hammered inside her, and she decided to pull free, to escape this loathsome inner touching. But it was as if she heard of someone else's fear and desire to flee. Her body did not move. The terror raced hopelessly around within her own mind. She was Dresh's tool, her own will impotent. Cold slugs inched into the bones of her right hand, filled her fingers. She felt the fingers straighten into the correct alignment. Surely her tendons must tear themselves loose from the bones they gripped, but now, they relaxed, and seemed to recall an earlier limberness that Ki had never possessed. The sign was made.

A needle of hot acid ripped up from Dresh's skull. It shrieked through Ki's body, traveling swiftly through her marrow. It tore across her shoulders and shot up her reaching arm in a spasm of agony beyond words or cries. She made no sound. Her mouth stretched wide and tortured, but was mute to her body's torment. The pain exploded from her reaching finger-tips, to spray out in a four fingered jet of agony across the night sky. Ki saw no sight, she heard no sound, but she sensed the signal sent through her. In some far realm there was a being that would answer such a call. Ki pictured a vulture suddenly looping and settling.

"Rest now." She knew it was Dresh, but could not tell if he spoke to her or if she simply heard him. A haze of pain and confusion scattered her thoughts. A strength not her own entered her body. She staggered forward three short steps. Then it forsook her, to let her tumble onto her bedding like a marionette whose strings are cut. Somewhere in Ki, someone was angry, was furious with Dresh. Someone would kill him, as soon as she could find her strength. But Ki was too weary to listen to her rant. She closed her eyes and sank into depths past sleep.

Five

GRIELEA paused on the threshold. Her black eyes narrowed as she measured the figure within the barren room, sensing the tension hidden beneath the graceful folds of the robe draping the womanly form. Guilt and secrets burdened her like snow on a tender sapling. A lesser creature would snap. But not Rebeke. Not she. Grielea backed up a silent step. She lowered her eyes to the floor and hissed respectfully.

Slowly Rebeke's eyes floated up from the pale blue pyramid in her lap. She sighed as she set it on a small cushion that rested on the floor beside her.

"What is it, apprentice?" Her voice was brisk, but she could not conceal all the weariness in it, nor the undercurrents of anxiety.

"Windmistress Medie has arrived. She awaits your permission to enter."

"Show her in immediately, child. She should never have been kept waiting."

Grielea bobbed a nod and vanished from the door. Rebeke arose, nervously smoothing her long robes. She gave to the soft azure drapings an icy dignity. The small feminine face that peered from the center of the high cowl was betrayed by the hooded brow that rose another two handspans above her eyes. But for the shrouded high skull, her figure was still remarkably Human. Her body, it seemed, remembered that earliest allegiance.

"Enter, Windmistress, if it please you." Grielea's voice was carefully neutral, her eyes cast down before this impressive being. Medie entered, darting her eyes in surprise around the bare room. Her cobalt robes swept the bare stone floor. Grielea remained in her servile posture in the door, but her sharp black eyes darted after the tall Windmistress and registered the hesitation in her stride.

"Welcome, Windmistress Medie." Rebeke chose the formal greeting. "A blessed wind has brought you."

"It is ever a blessed wind that brings me to your presence." Medie gave the stylized reply.

Rebeke's eyes flicked at Grielea. "Grielea, you may go. I would have you and Liset replace the watchers at the vigil; tell the two before you that they take their rest now. On your way, remind those at the watching pools to be vigilant. This is no ordinary being they watch for."

"Yes, Windmistress. So shall I do."

Grielea slipped away. Now Rebeke had no choice but to turn her eyes on her visitor. Medie was tall, much of it cowl. The darker edges of her scales mottled her thin brown features. The deeper blue of her robes announced her higher status. Rebeke's hands fluttered nervously. Taking refuge in ceremony, she advanced to give Medie the ritual kiss and words of welcoming.

"May the winds come ever willing to your call, and the airs kiss you with the same affection I do now."

Medie returned the kiss perfunctorily. Rebeke retreated a step, uncertain. Medie ignored her as she turned slowly about, studying the austere room. Her eyes played over the stark black walls, the cold stone floor, then returned to seize Rebeke in their cold grip. She stretched her lightly scaled lips into a thin line. She made no pretense at ceremony or courtesy.

"You have known for at least three days that Dresh was no longer in his residence at Dyal." Medie spoke without preamble. "Yet you forebore to act until the last possible moment. You summon me at the last, as an afterthought. If you had been successful at gathering the entire wizard, I wonder if you would have summoned me at all. You have stepped far beyond the bounds of your responsibility for watching him, Rebeke. And you have been clumsy about it. You know already what the High Council will say. That they expected such of you all along; that you have never given us your full loyalty, but continue to be swayed by unfitting emotions from an unguided childhood. Rarely do the Windsingers admit a child past her fifteenth year. Yet you we took in. Now it seems you have failed us. Is this our repayment? Why did you do this? Do you seek the attentions of the High Council?"

Rebeke turned a shade paler beneath her scales. Her blue and white eyes darted nervously about her chamber, but found nothing to rest on. She advanced a step toward Medie, then reconsidered it and stepped back.

"I do not seek the attentions of the High Council, Medie. Too long has the High Council overlooked what I have done, and spoken only of what I have yet to do." Rebeke's voice grew bolder as she spoke. "I am aware of what they say of me. I know they prefer their temple bred ones to me. They think I am weak and uncertain, not to be trusted. Why else choose me, of all Windsingers, to be put as a guard to Dresh? They hope to nod as I betray my training. Yes, I have been slow in my efforts, and that may appear as clumsiness. It is, in truth, a respect for the power that is Dresh; and a knowledge of how his mind works. I have not been totally successful, I will admit. But even had I succeeded in gathering all his parts in one swoop, I still would have summoned you to share him with me. For have I not seen you, Medie, passed over for powers and honors, seen them bestowed instead on Windsingers younger and more tractable than you? Why is this so, Medie? Unless they fear us; unless the High Council dares not pass power to us for fear we shall wield it too well?"

Rebeke paused and licked her dry lips. Her scaled lips needed no wetting; it was a Human reflex she had not yet lost. Medie had not spoken; but she had given no sign of shock at the traitorous words either. Perhaps she listened with sympathy in her heart, or perhaps she waited for Rebeke to betray herself further. No matter. This was no time for caution. If Medie would not make this move with Rebeke, then Rebeke would make it alone. Power was within her grasp. She held the hands and body of the wizard, even if the head was lacking. If only she had sent a wiser being to collect them for her; but who was there of intellect that she could trust? So she had sent the foolish winged beast to bring back the boxes, knowing he would forget the errand as soon as it was finished. So she did not have the head. She had the hands and body. Great power could be distilled from them, by one who knew the ways. And greater still was to be had if the head could be claimed as well. Medie could help her win the head. But if she would not . . . Rebeke licked her lips again.

Medie remained silent, staring down at the relaxation pyramid. Rebeke's voice was softer, almost pleading.

"Witness what I have done, Medie. Done when all the High Council could not, when they gave this task to me to watch me fail at it. Perhaps I have been careless, not to have seized the head with the other parts. But it was a difficult enough task to achieve what I have thus far, and beyond the skills of many. We both know Dresh well. He will not wait idly for us to come for the rest of him. Nor will he concede our possession of his body and hands. No, he will seek an opening, will expose himself with his own foolish riposte. Reduced as he is, he will fall into our hands like ripe fruit from a wind-stirred tree. We will have him, all of him, to drain of power. Then shall we summon the High Council? Shall we hand to them the prize we have won, and listen to them tell us that we should have delivered it sooner? Why, Medie? Why?"

Medie did not smile. But the stiffness went from her body, making her taller, more graceful; her eyes looked afar and were full of the wind. Long moments drifted by before she spoke. A light breeze sprang up from nowhere and stirred her robes lovingly.

"Once," she began softly, in a distracted voice, "once there was a young apprentice. We tested her. Set alone on the peak of a frozen mountain, she stood and sang. She sang first to lull the cold wind that lived there, to lay to rest its thousand icy tongues. She sang it to sleep, as no other had been able to do. Not content with that, she sang again, a calling song, to lure a breeze out of the far south. Long she sang, long beyond the patience or endurance of many to sing. But at last her wind came, warm still with the breath of flowers, to melt the snow from the mountaintop and send the waters down to where the peasants toiled in fields too dry to bear. I thought to myself then, her way is not the way of the High Council, and her power shall never be theirs."

Rebeke glowed. There was a tremble to her mouth and a bare sheen of wetness to her eyes. "Long have I watched you, Medie, trying to feel if you would be my ally in this undertaking. Is it possible the vigil has been two-sided?"

Medie smiled. "I felt your eyes upon me. I have not been blind to how you have been treated. In the beginning of your singership over Dowl Valley, you labored long. You set your voice to tasks others deemed required too much effort for the results shown. You showered your peasants with the most favorable of weather, bringing them rain when their lands thirsted, spreading the pollen of their crops with the gentleness of summer's breath, holding at bay the storms that would have battered ripening grain. The hail clouds you sent fleeing from their horizons. The valley blossomed under your care.

"But what was given to you as your share for this miracle? Less of a percentage than your predecessor, who, with her threats and gales, never wrung a third as much from the farmers. When you would have let your peasants keep a surplus as a reward for faithful toil, that their children might grow up to be strong tillers of the earth instead of wilting in their cradles, you were mocked. Mocked as a Tenderheart, a Peasantweeper, for your foresightedness. And Dowl Valley was taken from you and given to another."

Sparks of anger flared afresh in Rebeke's eyes. Then her shoulders slumped. Her hands trembled until she folded them together. "I scarcely know how to reply to you, Medie. I thought that my toil and my reasons had gone unseen, misunderstood by all. To hear you speak is as if the door I have strained against had suddenly swung open at a touch."

Medie crossed the room to Rebeke, taking her hands in her long cool fingers. "We shall act together, then. We shall only take what is ours by right of our toil and planning. We shall take up the reins of decision that have so often restrained us. Dresh shall be drained into us. Only then shall we let the High Council know of our success."

A brief cloud passed over Rebeke's face. Almost she looked away from Medie's piercing eyes. Then a new spirit seemed to straighten her body. She raised her chin. As she nodded, a glow of suppressed excitement lit her eyes.

Six

Ki did not see the beast come. But even in her daze, she felt its presence as a rippling in the waters of her world. There was no brushing of wind, no sound, no smell. Rather it was as if the pressures of air and earth upon her body wavered for a moment. Sigurd was scraping at the earth with one hoof. She heard the regular thuds of his hoof as he dug a trough in the sod in a peculiar stubborn frenzy. Sigmund threw high his huge head, ears pricked and nostrils flaring.

"Come Ki. To your feet now. Delay won't make things any easier. Come on, Ki."

The wizard's voice was low, comforting. She puzzled at the familiarity of the tone, then placed it. Thus must she sound to her team when she coaxed them into a particularly difficult river fording. But she found herself rising, nonetheless, to gather up the wizard's head on its mounting block of stone. She held it to her bosom as if it were a talisman against the unknown.

"Ki!" the wizard stirred her gently. "The beast is waiting, but it grows impatient. We must enter it."

"Where is it?" she murmured, confused. Her mind was

misted, as it had been since Dresh had used her as a signal beacon. Dresh's chuckle was a dash of cold water over her, rousing her to the stranger reality she now moved in. She felt her mind clear slightly even as his words aroused her fighting spirit.

"'The swallow, who was queen of the sky, is a drowning bird in the water,'" Dresh quoted maddeningly. "What a fool I can be. Of course you can't see it. And I have not time to tune your mind to accept what your eyes could show you. I must be your perception. Hold tight to me."

Ki's peripheral vision began to dim. The greyness moved in rapidly, closing out her sight until she was peering down a long tunnel at a spot of night. Then that, too, vanished. She was in a grey fog. Slowly her world began to open out again, strangely altered. The trees were taller, the grass higher. The horses loomed more massively huge than ever. With a jolt, it all snapped into perspective for her. She was viewing the world through Dresh's eyes, at her own chest level. Dresh chuckled at her dawning comprehension.

"Now that you can see your world through my eyes, let me introduce you to one of my worlds. Behold!"

Dresh blinked for Ki. The shared eyes opened to an un-night world. Yet the light of it did not illumine. The light of this world came not from moon or sun or star, but from the beings within it. Where Sigurd and Sigmund had been tethered, two great beings gave off a greenish-brown glow. Her own body, as Dresh turned their sight down on it, shimmered yellowly. "And could you but see me, I would be an opalescent glow!" There was no modesty in Dresh's voice. "And now, behold the beast!" he said invitingly, and the eyes swung to it. It was among the brownish mist of the trees. Ki walked toward it, through a dimly glowing brown sea of grasses.

The beast was not white, but gave off a translucent light. She sensed its life, but could not recognize its body. It was visible to her only as a tunnel of clear light, or perhaps she could call it a tower, for it rose hollowly into the blackness away from the solid earth. When at last Ki stood at the base of the creature, she could peer up that tunnel. The clear light shone within it as well as without. Ki's logic winced.

"Enter!" Dresh's voice goaded her impatiently.

"Enter?" Did he expect her to step within the thing's maw,

or nostril, or whatever other bodily opening it was that gaped before them?

She didn't need to move. Dresh made a sound, like a word spoken by a mouthless creature. Ki felt her hair stir, and then they were rising, or perhaps falling. . . .

They traveled streaming through the brightly glowing belly of the beast. No wind stirred her clothing, but her hair waved about her face. She did not know if they moved, or if the creature moved around them; to consider either theory of motion made her vaguely queasy. Gradually Dresh's murmured words began to reach her mind.

". . . Ki. Now, Ki. Easy. It will soon be over. I am here with you. You are safe. It will soon be over. Trust me."

"I'm not a child!" She thought she had spoken the words, but they seemed to have been ripped from her mouth and flung all about inside the creature. They made no sense as they bounced back to her. They rattled bruisingly against her flesh. The red fragments of them tumbled away.

"Ki. Ki. Ki." The wizard was reaching for her without words, trying to soothe her soundlessly. "We do not speak with our mouths. Not within this being. *You* do not speak at all, but listen to me. No, do not let your mind fly off to puzzle about what it cannot absorb; listen only to me. There will come a moment when you will hear . . . will perceive a sound. It will not be hearing, but you will know it. The pain we used to summon this creature, the agony you could not voice will come back to you. I caused you to send it forth, but as it issued from you, it is solely yours. Any more than this I cannot explain. I trust to your intuition."

Dresh paused to let the rustling of panic settle in Ki's mind. "You will know it, never fear. You will recognize it as a part of yourself, as familiar to you as your own hand. When you know it, you must seize it. Do not, however, let go of me. Cradle me in your left arm. That's right. Now keep your right hand at the ready. And once you have seized your sound, do not let it go."

Ki found that she would obey, despite a searing rage deep within her soul. Time passed, both endless and swift. They flitted on. And now they began to pass other objects in the beast; Ki saw the peal of a dirge bell, and the quivering wail of a child that had fallen down a well. She did not understand how she knew what these strange knobs of light and thorny darknesses were. But she knew them. She saw a tiny blob that was the suddenly expelled breath of a king killed by a friend's treachery. She passed through a terrible palpable orange mist of a man who had been bludgeoned to death in his sleep, but had cried aloud in his dream.

She nearly missed. She was upon hers almost before she saw it. It was white and yellow and black, angular here and swollen there. It could not be grasped with a hand. It was too large. She flailed at it wildly as it spun toward her, missed, and then, as it slipped past her, abruptly hugged it to her ribs with her whole right arm.

Ki felt she had thrust her arm into a rapidly spinning wheel. She was flung wildly and swiftly around with her right shoulder as the center of her cyclone. Vertigo overtook her. She clutched her pain and Dresh close to her, trying vainly to shut his eyes and wipe out the dizzying vision of worlds whipping past her.

She felt the pain slip back into her body, huge at first, and then ripping to the center of her being, growing smaller but more intense, until it rejoined some core within her that she had never before known. When that happened, a floor rose up to slam itself against her head and back and heels. A grey ceiling crashed into place. Dresh did not need to tell her that she had been slammed into a reality.

Ki lay motionless, the breath knocked out of her. The back of her head and the knobs of her spine had been bruised by the landing. Yet strangely she felt better, complete again. The misty indecision that had plagued her since Dresh had summoned the creature through her had gone. Whatever had rejoined her inside the beast had burned away the fog, returning to her a sense of independent judgment. Once more she was whole. And furious.

She gathered herself as her breath came back to her, staring at a ceiling patterned with grey swirls. She lifted her bruised head cautiously. It produced no change in perspective. Only when she sat up all the way, lifting Dresh's head with her, did her view change. She was still using his eyes.

The muscles of his jaw struggled under her hand. She had been gripping him by the jaw rather than by the block of stone, she realized, and had unconsciously retained her clutch. She shifted her hands quickly.

"Thank you," Dresh murmured scathingly. "For a moment

I thought myself paralyzed in your death grip."

"It would be less than what you deserve. I'll use my own eyes now."

"As you will," Dresh replied indifferently, unruffled by the icy fury in Ki's voice.

There was a swirling of mist that gradually cleared. Ki blinked her eyes in an effort to focus them. But what had been dull black walls to Dresh's eyes were to her rippling opaque curtains. She could not see what lay beyond them, but neither could she recognize their solidity.

"Enjoy your view?" Dresh asked solicitously. "Why don't you just drop me here and trot along in your own independent way?"

Ki did not respond. She tried to focus her eyes on the wall, but it defied her normal depth perception. The wall was right before her nose; it was an arm's length away; she would have to cross the room to touch it. Pride would not let her surrender, but practicality forced a concession.

"Much as I would enjoy it, Dresh, I dare not drop you here. But the reverse holds true as well."

"What you perceive as my casual abuse of you is but the haste I must make, out of necessity. Ki, if you persist in taking all this personally, we shall never get ourselves out of this."

Ki closed her eyes and felt his vision once more rise to her mind. Dresh spoke again. "We shall have to go on sharing my eyes. A handicap, and not a small one, as you seem to think. I begin to question the wisdom of this venture. I suppose we could have gone to Bitters, and perhaps I could have found a suitable body to usurp. But there is nothing like the comfort of one's own flesh. And, ah, the powers I should surrender by letting them keep my hands and body, to say nothing of my secrets the Windsingers would steal. Well, there's nothing we can do now except continue. Stand up. Let me get my bearings."

She rose in silent obedience, though her pride chafed at Dresh's assumption of control. Perhaps she would have warmed to the adventure had she been Dresh's partner; but she was not. She was no more to him than a set of legs and arms to use, like a riding beast or a docile team. The imagery jarred her a bit. What insights would she take back to teamstering? she wondered.

Dresh surveyed the chamber and Ki observed it with him.

It was a contradiction, a room of austere opulence. The dull black walls were as plain as a prison's, the air cool enough to raise the fine hair on Ki's body, but the low black bedstead in one corner was strewn with the thickest shag deer hides that she had ever beheld of the peculiar brown-violet shade that commanded the highest prices. Smoothly rolled at the foot of the bed were blankets such as the Kerugi wove from the wool of their mountain sheep, but even the tiny fingers of the Kerugi could not have fashioned such a fine weave. In another corner was a wooden table, and a single backless stool of stark design. She did not recognize the wood, but it glowed mellowly, and she coveted the tall crystal flagon filled with lavender liquid that centered the table.

"Ah," Dresh breathed out, well satisfied. "I haven't lost the touch, Ki. Not a bit. We are not only in her realm, but in her very bedchamber. This room speaks of Rebeke, if ever a room could, with her stark self-denial one moment, and her lascivious self-indulgence the next."

"Rebeke?"

"The Windsinger that stole my parts. A power hungry witch if ever there was one."

But as Dresh spoke, a double image rippled before her eyes. The room as he saw it for her remained, but she saw more— like seeing the pebbly bottom of a pool through one's own reflection. Ki saw a woman. She was tall, and her height seemed the greater for the sweeping mantle of pale green that fell from her wide shoulders to the soles of her bare feet. White anemones peeped from the grasses about her feet, and the sun glanced off the brightness of her flowing hair. "Rebeke" the wind whispered as it rustled through the grass and nodding flowers. But this was a woman, no Windsinger she, and as Human as Ki herself. Even as Ki puzzled, the image retreated and faded, until there was only the empty room before her eyes. Dresh was still speaking. Ki wondered if he had intended to share the vision with her.

". . . and therefore the most dangerous of them all. For her self-discipline is such that there is no act she could not force herself to, if she felt it behooved her. No act at all, no matter what pain or self-destruction it involved. I could wish it had been another that had stolen my boxes. But I doubt that any could have done it, except her."

"Where are your boxes?" Ki demanded. Her spine ached

with tension, and with the unaccustomed burden of carrying about a head mounted on a block of stone. She did not relish standing about in the bedchamber of Dresh's enemy. Might she not return at any moment? The sooner Ki reclaimed her cargo and Dresh got them out of here, the better. She didn't wish to indulge his chatter any longer.

"Patience!" Dresh calmly rebuked her. "Did you suppose the Windsingers would allow us to enter, reclaim my boxes, and leave? They will be guarded. Or did you suppose that I am such a trifle as to be left about in bits? Did you think to find me stashed under the bed? No, this shall be a delicate game to play. The move is now ours. In this very lack of vigilance, I smell a keener watch than I had supposed. Do we teeter on the edge of a trap? Let us consider that." But Ki's mind was elsewhere.

"The rapier!" She shifted Dresh's head into the crook of one arm, with an alarming sway in vision resulting. Futilely she felt at her belt, her stomach sinking with the knowledge that the sheath would not be there. Embarrassment and despair dropped her voice to a whisper. "I've been a great fool, Dresh. I've left the rapier behind."

"And your teapot and Vanilly as well!" Dresh added in mock alarm.

"Of what use would they be to us?" Ki growled in annoyance at his frippery. "I tell you that we are unarmed."

"And unlegged as well!" snorted Dresh. "A teapot and your Vanilly would be at least as useful as your rapier. What do you imagine, that we shall sweep into a room of Windsingers, rapier chopping, to reclaim my body over their fallen and bloody ones? What a child! Do I look like the sort of savage that would kill? The only weapon you shall find any use to you here is already on your arm. My head. So be silent, and let me think what we should do next."

"A rapier does not chop," she corrected him tersely, feeling more than ever like a fool. Dresh's bland assumption of his superiority rasped every inch of her proud spirit. Worst of all, given the circumstances, he was correct. Ki longed to thump his head down on Rebeke's table and leave him beside that lavender flask. Let his scornful words and irritating ways get him out of that! She savored the image before letting logic cool her anger. She needed Dresh to return to her own world. That she was bound to him by her written sign was another tie, and the opportunity to spite the Windsingers at their own game was an added fillip. Make free with her cargo, would they? Her grudge against the Windsingers was longer than her memory, fading back into her father's unspoken hatred of them and a dim feeling that in some way they had contributed to her unremembered mother's early death. Always before, Ki had suppressed her anger and scrupulously avoided them. Perhaps Vandien was right after all; perhaps the time had come to return their stings and insults. Fate seemed determined to lead her in that direction. So Ki expelled her breath in a harsh rush through her nostrils and awaited the wizard's desire.

SEVEN

DAINTY fingers played curiously over the glittering stones set in the black enamel box. Bare toes curled and uncurled impatiently against the thick feathers of a dikidik hide. Within the white robe of the lowest order of initiated Windsingers, a slender young body fidgeted. Grielea felt the mystery of the box hovering at the edge of her mind, an enigmatic formula based on a mathematical concept just beyond her grasp. Again her fingers played over the stones, varying their rhythm by one from the combination just tried. Grielea closed her eyes for a moment, as if by concentration she would feel the auras of the stones, hear them whisper to her the setting put upon them.

"Rebeke cautioned us not to touch the boxes?"

The lisping voice was half-questioning and half-amazed at Grielea's audacity in disobeying the Windmistress's wishes. Grielea's eyes flew open, and she glared at Liset in irritation.

Liset retracted her pale eyes from the dark sparks of Grielea's. The spidery T'cherian body hunched and quivered beneath the white robe. Grielea wrinkled her scaled nose in disdain at Liset's disapproval. Liset's mandibles twitched.

"To achieve the full rank of Windsinger, Grielea, we must

practice the strictest obedience and self-restraint. To rule others, we must first learn to rule ourselves." Even the clattery lisp of a T'cherian accent could not disguise the piety in Liset's words.

"Tend to your box. I shall tend to mine!"

Liset's mandibles clacked in astonishment. She settled her face abruptly. She wished her transformation to Windsinger would proceed more rapidly. Always the sounds and ingrained movements of her T'cherian body shamed her. If only her shell would begin to scale! No doubt that was why Grielea dared to speak to her so rudely. She had no right. Liset knew they were of the same rank of initiation. She had heard the rumors about Grielea. She had been sent to Rebeke as a last resort. Rebeke was well known to be the strictest and most demanding of the Windmistresses. And Grielea was notoriously headstrong; she had spent a full two turns in this grade already! Liset groomed her cowl smooth, and turned back to the large square box before her. So let Grielea play with her box. It would have its consequences. Liset intended to fulfill her instructions meticulously. Not for her the chilling cell and cold gruel reserved for the disobedient.

Grielea gave a thin smile of satisfaction as Liset's eye stalks swung away from her. She bent again over the box on the low table before her. Her fingers danced over the stones. Nothing. She paused, and then her hands moved again. Another pause. Another combination.

There was no betraying click of latch. The box sighed silently under Grielea's hands. She glanced over her shoulder. Liset's robed carapace was toward her. The stiffness of the crouched figure with its squat cowl showed Liset's resolution not to participate in Grielea's misbehavior. Grielea smiled mockingly at her back. She turned back to her treasure.

Silently the box slid up from its base. Grielea set the top of the box in her lap. She leaned over her prize. Her fingers nimbly unwound a long linen wrapping.

The base was a block of white stone, veined with black and red. From it, rooted at the wrists, two hands grew as gracefully as calla lilies. They clasped each other peacefully, as if awaiting a coffin flower. But a warm flush of life glowed under the olive skin of the hands. They were waiting for their master. On one of the long tapering fingers was a ring. To some it would have seemed a plain, cheap ring of black metal. But to

Grielea it fairly shouted the identity of the owner. She stiffened. Was that a light step? She bunched the wrapping back over the hands. She smiled a lynx smile as she eased the top of the box back into place. A brush of her fingers over the stones reset their lock. So he was the stakes they played for. . . . Her grey-scaled brow knotted slightly as she added that to her cache of carefully gleaned facts.

"You may leave off your vigil now. Retire to your chambers for a rest period. We shall be taking your posts for you."

Liset jumped at the sudden voice behind her. But Grielea slowly raised her chin and lowered her eyes. She smiled submissively. "Yes, Windmistress," she simpered, and "Yes, Windmistress," Liset echoed her. Liset and Grielea hastened from the room, their white robes swirling against the floor. But only one went to her chamber to rest.

Medie moved into the room slowly. There was no disguising the look of admiration she gave the two enamelled boxes. The smaller casket rested on a small table before a stool. The larger box was on the floor. The room was better furnished than Rebeke's sitting room. Here were hides of rare beasts and birds scattered about to relieve bare feet from the coldness of the highly polished floor. The walls were graced with sky windows, artfully designed living pictures of many parts of the worlds. But the only seats available were the hard wooden stools that Liset and Grielea had just vacated. Medie gave one a glance of distaste. Idly she trailed a long finger across the top of the larger enamel box.

"How best were this done?"

Rebeke paused, then settled herself upon Grielea's stool. She spoke slowly. "The boxes will take skill to open, and patience. Dresh will know that their solving is but a matter of time. He will, I think, hasten here, hoping against hope to recover his body. We could, of course, open his boxes and drain his powers now. But the doing of it might spook the quarry, in a manner of speaking."

"You believe he will come here, will try to retrieve them himself?"

"I do." Rebeke spoke with quiet assurance.

"And who would know better what he would do?" Medie dropped the words casually, but they fell into a suddenly silent room.

"Do you rebuke me with my past?" Rebeke queried softly.

"No. Not rebuke. I merely wonder at it, as many have before me. You must have known why the High Council chose you for this guardianship. A make or break test of your loyalty. Given a final choice, which will Rebeke take: the Windsingers, or Dresh?"

"And Rebeke chooses Rebeke." A tiny chill breeze rose to whisk past their ankles.

"With no regrets?" prodded Medie. There was no acid in her voice, only an elder sister's interest. In her brown and white eyes there was only concern.

"Regrets were done with long ago, Medie. Let us use a metaphor. Suppose you had a pet dog that went wild. You would let it go, in fondness, allowing it to choose the life it preferred. But suppose it became vicious, and menaced the flocks of your neighbors. Would not you feel responsible for the situation? Would you not remedy it yourself?"

"Dresh is no more to you now than a stray cur?"

"It was only a metaphor," Rebeke replied with some asperity. She rose and drifted over to a sky picture. In a wooded dell, white anemones had pushed up from the deep mosses. Tall spruce sheltered them from the wide blue skies above. Rebeke breathed deep of their fragrance, standing close to the sky window to receive it. The air of the image felt cool and fresh, recently washed by rains.

"I see, then." Medie's voice reached across the room. "We wait in the hopes of baiting him in. We do not wish to make him despair of regaining his body, for then he might choose to continue on his way and take another body elsewhere."

"Exactly." Rebeke's voice was scarcely more than a whisper as she scanned the clear skies of the window world. Her finely scaled hands rested lightly on the wooden sill. "I do not think I shall have to wait much longer."

"Did you leave word we were to be notified when his aura was felt on this plane?"

"Of course." Rebeke turned back, nodding briskly. "But I have not told my apprentices whom we await. The portion of aura he casts now is so different from the whole that I do not think they will suspect. I have described it well enough for them to know it when they see it."

"You do not trust them enough to tell them what we have here?" Medie's long fingers drummed lightly on the box before her.

Rebeke crossed the room to resume her seat. "It is not a matter of trust, Medie. They are so very young, so very full of the idealism of the Windsingers. I judged it best not to distract them with too many possibilities, or with thoughts that might divide their loyalties. Choices and loyalties are alarmingly clear at their age. Some might misinterpret what we do, might see it as treachery. I saw no need to alarm them."

"Wise. If we succeed, they will be under our protection. And if we do not . . . well, I am neither so old nor so cynical that I would enjoy seeing their innocence pay for our daring. By keeping them free of knowledge of our undertaking, you have also kept them free of what some might call our guilt. Well done, sister."

A slightly awkward silence fell. After a time, Medie began to shift on her stool. "I could wish for a more comfortable seat."

"And I. But the very discomfort of it promotes alertness. Shall we be sleeping on velvet cushions or drowsy with wine when Dresh makes his entrance? His power is not as great as he believes it, but he has a certain sly craft. I shall not make the mistake of underestimating him. Be patient, Medie. Afterwards, we shall recline, we shall eat and drink and talk together. For I think that there is much we could tell one another. What the High Council does not say to Rebeke's face, it may whisper to Medie. Am I wrong?"

Medie gave her a small and bitter smile.

Eiqht

VANDIEN'S first day of driving the team was a torture to try the patience of a Dene. He shortened his stride and slowed his pace until he felt like a shackled sacrificial beast, and still he was stepping on the heels of the team. They waddled along, blinking and squinting in the dusty street. Vandien had experimented with prodding them, only to find that whichever beast he prodded would immediately drop to its belly and sleep. The prod, he deduced, was a way of telling them to stop, without putting a limb in danger from their jaws.

He ate a portion of his loaf as he dawdled along behind them, and tucked the rest under his elbow. He didn't relish the prospect of stretching it out over the walk to False Harbor, but had no alternatives. There had been times, he remembered, when he had eaten less and walked farther.

Vandien idled along, musing on the dullness of the landscape. His trail wound through a series of hummocks and dales. Sheep droppings mucked the road before him. Wooly flocks passed him frequently. His skeel showed no interest in the sheep, but Vandien noticed that the flocks bunched and milled whenever the sheep caught the scent of his team. The cursing

Human shepherds trotted and shouted, prodding their recalcitrant charges into order. The flocks gave him a wide berth as they surged past. One flock split as it approached him, scattering to dot the hillside. Vandien was relieved that the shepherds blamed their literally mutton-headed charges and not him. Flock after flock passed him and left him behind on their way to winter pasturage. Vandien plodded discouragedly through the fresh sheep manure.

Evening found him topping a small rise. Frustration had exhausted him more than the walk. From the rise, he saw his road stretching before him like grey ribbon snipped and dropped over the land. Brushy hillocks hid it as it meandered among them. No trees nor shepherds' huts relieved the drabness. The colors of brush and grasses varied from dusty purple to dull green. Vandien sighed as his laggardly team toddled stolidly downhill, their snouty muzzles working.

Suddenly a long grey tongue whipped from one's muzzle and was sucked back. The beast gave a squeal, and Vandien felt the rope snatched from his hands. The team scuttled off, their flat feet slapping, their low grey backs undulated as they poured down the trail like water spilled from a bucket. The braided leather rope trailed in the dirt behind them.

Vandien raced after, dove on the reins, and caught them. He was dragged through manure and brush before the knotted end was ripped again from his hands. With a curse he scrabbled to his feet, wiping his welted hands down his tunic front as he ran. He slipped in sheep droppings; he sprang over spiny bushes. He paced the skeel, yelling every word for "stop" in his not inconsiderable lingual experience. They paid him no heed.

Furiously he berated himself for giving Web Shell the crystal so soon. He knew where skeel most enjoyed being scratched; he knew what algae to feed them for flux; he knew how to dose them for parasites—but not how to stop a runaway team. The dreamy-eyed T'cherian had assured him that driving the team was easier done than explained.

In the distance was a flowing stream and Vandien prayed it would block them. If there had ever been a bridge across it, it was gone now. Ruts in the trail showed that wagons and carts simply went through it, but surely his lizardly, dust-wallowing, sun-snoozing team would not. They would veer suddenly to one side or the other. With luck, he could cut them off.

Like flounders settling into sea muck, the team flowed into the stream. Vandien saw the harness strain as the beasts struggled to spread themselves flat in the flowing water. The long snaky tails uncoiled and lashed angrily, slapping the water and scoring the hides of harnessmates. Water gouted up around them. A brown wave of silt churned up by sixteen flat feet tinged the water and fled downstream. The harness jerked and tangled as his beasts wallowed, each striving to get under the others, to be flattest in the stream mud. Individual skeel were not distinguishable in the welter of tails and snapping snouts. Scaly shoulders and hips shoved and strained for position.

As abruptly as their activity had begun, it ceased. Each beast collapsed into the stream mud. All the snouts disappeared. The great staring eyes closed and the tails went lax, streaming with the current of the water. Vandien approached slowly, dread rising in his heart. They looked dead. Cautiously he picked up the braided rein and gave it a tug. There was no response.

No air bubbles rose from the sunken snouts. No muscle squirmed. Vandien gave a jerk to the reins, but all he saw was the tug of his own effort. He thought of the prod he had dropped when the team had bolted. Perhaps a few whacks with that...but he dared not leave them. He waded into the stream and planted a stout kick on the rump nearest him. No result.

Then began a miserable period of fruitless effort. Vandien soaked himself trying to pull the beasts from the stream. But no matter which tail or leg he gripped, he was powerless to move the whole. The four skeel had merged into one. All those great flat feet were anchored under mud and gravel. The low-slung bodies hugged the bed of the stream. Water flowed over all.

Vandien was wet and cold when the sun went down. He stepped back to stare down at the sculptured skeel in the stream. It was hopeless. The best he could do was to wait them out. He had driven the beasts all day over dry roads; they must have some need for air. With many a backwards glance, he trudged up the hill to retrieve his prod and loaf. The skeel had still not stirred when he returned.

Sitting down on the mossy bank, he set down his prod and drew his belt knife. Slowly he sawed off a portion of the loaf. It was dry stuff now, not chewy so much as crunchy. Then he walked well upstream, though not out of sight of his submerged team, and knelt to drink. Recognizing some flat green leaves that sprouted from the turf, he drew his knife again and grubbed up their root. He rubbed away the soil and washed the root bundle; cleaned, it was a compressed mass of white grains. He had not eaten stink-lily's roots since he was a child. Even then, he had preferred them boiled to a mush; raw, they had no flavor, just a crisp starchiness. Food was food, he reminded himself glumly. At this rate of speed, his loaf would not last him to False Harbor.

As he put the last bit of root in his mouth, he heard a sound like a pig breaking out of its wallow. It was a sloshing, sucking sound. Vandien hastily gathered his prod and loaf as the skeel began to stir.

One was stretching its neck and taking in a lungful of air with a swooshing sound. Its tail was once more curled in a neat coil on its rump. Another began squealing and bubbling until it managed to disentangle its head from its harnessmate's legs. Humping and waddling, they came out of the stream, harness tangled and wet, mud and silt dropping from their low-slung bodies. The water had washed the dust from their flat grey backs. Their fine-scaled hides shone iridescently in the dim moonlight. They were plumper and looked contented now, as they wiggled their snaky bodies and worked their jaws with wet chopping sounds. Vandien watched as they attempted to sort themselves out in their harness. They scuttled along as they did it, and he realized belatedly that they were not going to settle. They were moving away from him across the grassy sward.

With a cry he sprang after them, remembering this time that the prod was their command to halt. Poking first one and then another, he finally succeeded in getting all four skeel to drop to their bellies and lie motionless. He darted his hand in amongst them to snatch up the wet reins. One of the skeel began to stir. He gave it a firm poke. It settled again.

Vandien stood over the docile beasts with his hands doubled into fists. Then he forced himself to be calm. He kept the prod under his arm in case any of the beasts should begin to stir, and began to try and straighten the harness. T'cheria did not use buckles. The whole thing was put together with knots. Vandien found them impossible to undo in the dim light, especially since their dunking had shrunk the knots into impenetrable little balls of leather. He contented himself with tugging the harness back into place. Generous use of the prod kept the skeel still.

He had only one really bad moment. He found one skeel's tail was twined about the harness like a pea vine, instead of recoiled neatly on its rump. The full dark of night was upon them now. Vandien located the tip of the tail by feel. He pried it loose with finger pressure that brought a squeal from its owner. Vandien gave him a sharp prod and he settled again. The tail was as stiff as a woody vine as Vandien unwrapped it from the harness. No sooner had he gotten the tail free than it suddenly lashed out of his hands, its hard tip snapping across his upper arm. The tail sprang back into a neat coil on the skeel's rump.

Vandien dropped the reins and the prod to grasp at his arm, which stung as if lashed by a whip. Tears sprang to his eyes. He rolled up the loose sleeve of his tunic and fingered the welt that stood up from his skin. It wasn't bleeding. Cold stream water would take some of the sting out of it. He stooped to pick up the prod and found that the team had scuttled off, silently.

He glared about wildly, but saw nothing. He forced himself to take a deep breath, to stand still and silent. The deep mossy hillocks would not betray their passage, but . . . there! Vandien heard the rustle of one of the low bushes at the same instant that his eye caught the motion and the sudden sheen of an iridescent hide. He raced after them, but they crested a hillock before he did and he lost sight of them again. Pausing for breath on the rise, he caught the shape of their passage as they hurried over the deep moss. He screamed a curse and raced after them again.

The slope favored him and his longer legs. The wheel animals got a boot and a prod that dropped them to their bellies; two more whacks and his front pair settled. Vandien snatched up the single rein and wrapped it twice about his wrist. The knotted end he gripped in his fist. He caught his breath, prodding any skeel that thought of moving. The chill of the autumn night, merciless as the dusty heat of the day, was settling on him. He was muddy, wet, tired, and his loaf had been dropped somewhere. The trail was lost behind them in the rise and fall of the land. Vandien longed to sleep, but he feared that in the

morning he would have lost both the team and all sense of
direction. The skeel were not sleepy. They were as frisky in
the night as they had been sluggish in the day.

This time when they stirred, he let them rise. Keeping his
grip on the rein, he moved to the side of the team. They scuttled
away from him. In this way he guided them, moving from side
to side, spooking them along in the direction he wished them
to travel. He had the knack of it by the time he spied the pale
grey ribbon of the trail, silvery in the light of the moon. Vandien
let his team flow over it. They scuttled along at a pace slightly
faster than a trotting dog, while he wove along behind them,
moving first from one side and then to the other. "Like a dog
herding sheep," he commented grimly to himself. Seeing how
well they moved, he gave up all thought of a night's sleep.
Tomorrow when they wished to doze in the sun, he would join
them.

Several times that night he prodded them into docility while
he caught his breath and took a short sip from his small water
bag. He regretted his lost bread, but that could not be helped.
At least he would get to False Harbor on time. He reknotted
the water bag and rubbed slowly at the scar between his eyes.
He tried to remember what he looked like without it. He had
never been much of a man for mirrors, but he could remember
how he had felt without it.

It had used to be that folks saw his eyes first, and then his
flashing smile. He had known the power of that charming smile;
known it and used it. Now all eyes went directly to the scar,
and lingered there while he talked. His smile had become a
grimace that pulled his face awry. Some folk judged him too
hastily by his scar. Some thought him a man easily beaten.
Others judged him to have a dangerous and unforgiving tem-
perament. His scar was like a piece of cheap glass, distorting
what the world saw. Few saw his face any more; most saw
only the slash that divided it.

Ki was one of the few. She was the one who had seen him
take that slash; for her sake, he had braved the talons. She had
been aghast. She had pieced his face back together and band-
aged the flesh in place. Never again had they been strangers.
And up to now Vandien had never put barriers between them.
But he had not told her what Srolan had offered. Had he mis-
judged her, to think she might misunderstand? What did he
fear? That his desire to be rid of the scar would be confused

for a regret in taking it? He did not regret that bond with Ki, nor would he hesitate to do it again. But . . . he could wish the sign of that bond was a less visible one.

The skeel were beginning to stir again. Vandien was glad to turn his mind away from dark thoughts. The task of driving them on consumed his attention. By dawn, they were as anxious to sleep as he. He urged them away from the trail, to the shelter of some scrub willows. They settled in a tangled heap. Vandien knotted the rein about his wrist. Lying down, he stared up at the dawn sky. Sleep overtook him quickly and in his dreams diving blue Harpies were driven back by Srolan's black eyes.

Nine

Ki shifted her weight from one foot to the other. She was weary of standing still and silent, awaiting Dresh's next order. Her mind was torn between her boredom and her anxiety. Dresh's eyes, and perforce Ki's vision, were still fixed on the same spot of wall. She could find no special fascination with it. Whenever she tried to speak, he shushed her. Ki sighed loudly.

"Curse you!" Dresh barked out angrily. "How can I reach for a presence with you distracting me? You cannot be still; you let your mind run in small useless circles and then hold them up for my inspection! Cannot you keep your mind empty?"

"I had not considered that our enforced companionship might grate on you as well, Master." Ki's voice was salty.

Dresh snorted. "Well may you sneer at me as 'Master,' you who have not learned even to be master of yourself. Enough of this. I cannot use my power while interpreting the sky for a mole. Let go of me, but stand still, if you would not get yourself into mischief."

"With great relief," Ki rasped. With a solid clunk she deposited the wizard's head upon Rebeke's table and folded her arms across her chest.

She waited in darkness. Her total lack of perception puzzled her. Then a slow hot flush flooded her face as she realized her eyes were closed. So swiftly had she adapted to Dresh seeing for her! She opened her eyes to a foreign world. Ki had not stirred from her spot, and she did not now. But where Dresh's eyes had shown her a bed and hides, her own saw a palely glowing gelid mass, reminding her of a mushroom sagging into rot.

In size and structure, the table bore a faint resemblance to Dresh's interpretation. But to Ki's eyes it was made of a glassy stone rather than wood. A fibrous tube stalked up from its center. Beside the tube was a place of nothingness, a cube of darkness. From its center glowed a spark of light almost too tiny to see, but so brilliant that her eyes watered as she looked upon it. In confusion she turned away.

The opaque walls of the room rippled before her gaze, shifting pale colors like an opal in the sunlight. She moved her eyes to the floor to rest them from the sickening motion, only to discover that the floor beneath her feet heaved and wavered also. Yet she felt no sensation of movement. Her stomach protested this contradiction.

She let her eyes roam the walls again, seeking any relief from their queasy rippling. She found it. There was a window. It alone in the walls was stationary. Its homely wooden frame was as comforting and familiar as a peasant's hut. Outside was daylight. Ki felt a shiver of worry. She had never had her time sense disturbed in such a fashion. Her body told her it was late night. But the day outside was bright and clear. A few chickens scratched in the dirt of a small dooryard. An open forest of paper birch and alder was held back from the dooryard by a flower bed planted with anemones, white and purple. A light breeze stirred the nodding flowers. Ki found herself stepping forward to catch the light caress of the wind on her face, to smell with relief the smell of earth and flowers. She could see the corner of a little kitchen garden. Pea vines climbed up crooked branch supports. The tensions eased out of her shoulders. She smiled at her own fears, and tried to remember where she had imagined herself to be. Dresh had made a great show of his magic, but from the look of the countryside, they weren't far from Bitters. Small wonder he had not allowed her to see this window with her eyes. He hadn't wanted her to know how easily she could walk away from his charade.

She listened to the gentle shushing of the wind over the flowers. Her ears picked up a faint far humming like bees disturbed in a hive at night. The room behind her was silent. With a prickling sensation she realized that the only breathing in the room was her own. She swallowed her uneasiness. Weird as Dresh might be, he was her ally in this. To fear him would not help the situation. But she was glad she had found the window.

She glanced back to the table. Tiny flecks of light swirled and danced about a red spark in the cube of darkness—like flies buzzing about offal, Ki thought. Their glow was paler, softly phosphorescent like swamp-rotted stumps. She found it disgusting. She was not sure what she looked upon, but she would not argue with her instincts. She closed her eyes to the sight. She still had not mastered the queasiness the rippling walls and floors awoke in her.

There were other avenues of sense to explore. She flared her nostrils, drew in a deep breath. To her puzzlement, she no longer smelled the day outside the window. Only Vanilly. And more Vanilly. Beneath that, only a slight musky scent that she associated with Dresh's head. The strength of the Vanilly obscured whatever else her nose might have been able to tell her.

Touch: through her soft boots, Ki pressed her toes down against the floor. It felt solid. She moved her feet slightly, and was unreasonably pleased with the soft rasping noise it made against the floor. Cautiously, lest she disturb Dresh and draw another reprimand from him, she moved her hand out, to brush it against the edge of the table. She jerked her fingers back. The surface of the table was yielding and sticky, like an extremely large lump of lard on a cold day. She rubbed her fingers together, but nothing clung to them.

"Take me up again!" Dresh's command broke in upon her explorations. Cautiously she opened her eye, and fixed them on the cube of darkness. Gingerly, as if she were about to pick up a red hot coal, she reached out for the blackness that was Dresh. Before her hand could touch him, the room around her winked, and in an instant became the room as Dresh saw it. Ki shied back violently from a hand right in front of her face. It disappeared.

"It's your own hand, fool!" Dresh laughed.

She reached out again, and saw her hand appear again in front of Dresh's eyes. To guide her hands down to pick up the

head that saw for her required her full concentration. It left her
with a heaving stomach and the germ of a headache between
her brows.

"Well, if you are finished peeking about, we shall be on
our way."

"You know where your body is now?"

Dresh pursed his lips slightly and then sighed in resignation.
"Of course I know where my body is. Do you know where
yours is? How can you be so naive? Ki, Ki, if only I could
have foreseen...but enough of that. This is no time to be
lamenting what I don't have. What I do have is you. You will
have to suffice, no matter how limited I find..."

His vision streaked before her eyes, so rapidly did she thump
him back onto the table and step clear of him. She folded her
arms across her chest and stared with stony eyes at the cube
of darkness. The spark in the center waxed horribly bright,
swelling to twice its size and pulsing scarlet. Ki remained
motionless, her arms clenched tightly lest her hands betray her
by trembling. It was several long moments before Dresh spoke.

"I suppose I deserved that." The spark shrank and faded to
white. "You cannot be pleased with me as a companion, either.
Come, Ki, let us make amends with one another. Help me in
this venture in which I so greatly need your cooperation, and
I shall put a curb upon my tongue."

Ki remained motionless, but she could not keep a smile
from ghosting over her lips.

"Please." Dresh half-sighed, half-hissed the word. Ki stepped
forward and took up his head. Dresh's image of the room
snapped back around them.

He cleared his throat. When he spoke, his voice was con-
trolled. "Two Windsingers watch over my parts. Yet she whom
I feared most to encounter seems less of a danger now. There
is someone, or something, else here. I do not know what name
to put to it, and it troubles me. I fear a trap within a trap.
Though they appear unaware of us, that may be dissembling.
With so many unknowns, I hesitate to confront them. Yet to
hold off may lose us the element of surprise, which in reality
I may not possess. And the time I may survive in this state is
trickling away from me." Dresh's voice sank and he sighed.
He roused himself abruptly. "What say you, Ki?"

She shrugged. "Attack now. If we have the surprise, use

it. If we do not, what have we to lose?"

Dresh's voice was bittersweet. "Only my body and your life, my dear. But those are also the only things we stand to gain. Onward, then. Ki, as a child, did you ever play at jump-points?"

Ki frowned slightly. Like a dim echo there came to her mind the image of an old treestump in a clearing by a river. Dark-eyed Romni children danced about it. A slender young boy crouched on top of it. Suddenly he leaped into the air. "West!" cried one of the other children at the very moment that his jump peaked. With a lithe twist the flying boy jerked his body to the west, to land cleanly within a square scratched on the dirt to the west of the stump. With a grin, he leaped back onto the top of the stump, his dark hair blowing about his face. He crouched again, and again the circle of children danced around the stump. The boy leaped, and "South!" . . .

"I remember the game, wizard," Ki replied. "But it is at least a score of years since I last played it. I always lost, as I recall. The Romni used it, I believe, to train the youngsters so that they might be ready to learn the leaping and tumbling tricks that would bring them pennies at the fair. What of it?"

Dresh's eyes and Ki's vision roved about the blank black walls. "It is not only the Romni who train their children so," Dresh muttered to himself. "Indeed, one of the mysteries of the Romni is where they first learned of the exercise. What we play at here, Ki, is jumppoints on a grand scale. Where do you suppose the next chamber is connected? We shall not know until we leave this one. If your reflexes are not sharp enough to let us gain it, we will find ourselves falling through the cold dark that lies between the worlds."

"And onto the chickens," Ki replied disgustedly. She was weary of his wizardly dramatics.

"What?"

"The window," Ki spoke curtly. "If we went, for instance, out the window, we might fall through the endless void and land on the chickens."

"The window . . ." His voice trailed off in consternation. Then the Dresh vision of the room winked out. Ki found it replaced with a seeing identical to her own. Dresh's vision riveted itself to the window. "I scarcely can believe it." His voice was hushed. "Closer, Ki. Can it be the same one?"

Ki obligingly advanced to the window. Dresh's brief scanning of the room had made her aware of one fact. There was no door. The window was the only possible exit.

She felt her hand lift, to run lightly across the rough wood of the window sill. Someone used her nails to pick at the coarse grain of the wood. "Stop it!" she hissed at Dresh.

"A moment," he muttered, ignoring her anger at his casual use of her body. She watched her hand pass through the window, felt it engulfed in a cold and treacly substance. Dresh abandoned control of it, and Ki jerked it back. She felt an unreasonable urge to go and wash.

"It's the same frame," he said aloud, musingly. "And she has created the old view. I never suspected Rebeke of such rank sentimentality. Interesting. And surprisingly touching. But not a way out, Ki. We could no more leave through that 'window' than ask directions of a portrait. It's a created image, nothing more."

"Then there's no door?" She wiped her hand down the front of her tunic, then returned it to share the burden of the head. She shifted Dresh to rest on the cant of her hip, trying to ignore the stomach-wrenching sway in perspective. The damn head was getting heavier every minute. Her shoulders ached.

With a blink, Dresh returned them to his interpretation of the room. Ki saw the bed and table restored to his imaging, but no sign of the window. Dresh picked up her consternation.

"Because Rebeke does not care for the casual visitor to see it. It takes a bit of doing to make a thing visible on this plane, but invisible if viewed with the wrong attitude. More than a bit of doing. She must value it greatly to expend the time and effort. Touching." He repeated the word, and then jerked his voice away from the thought, as if fearful. "Doors. No, Ki, the problem is not that there is no door, but that there are too many exits. We may depart this chamber at any point, walls, ceiling or floor. We may assume that at some point, or points, it adjoins other chambers. At other points, it is probably close enough to permit a leap to another chamber. At all other points, there is nothing but otherness."

"How do we know where to leave?"

Ki felt the bob as Dresh's head shrugged. "Pick a wall, Ki. Your guess in this matter is as good as mine."

Ki's mouth went dry. "Some wizard," she muttered. "Even

the crossroads wizards that tell fortunes profess to see through walls." Dresh did not deign to respond. Instead, he sent their gaze roaming slowly over the walls.

"Were this your chamber, Ki, and you had set out the furniture thusly, where would the door be?"

Ki pursed her lips at the shrewdness of this method. "Not too near my bed. I should want it across the room from where I slept, that if one entered, he would have some space to cross before he could take me unawares. My way would be to enter, advance to the table there, and then across to my bed. Let us take the space in the wall across from the bed and in line with the table."

Dresh grunted. "Why not? Although all you and Rebeke have in common is your sex, in this matter you may have some insight. To the wall, then.

"To the wall, Ki!" Dresh repeated an instant later. With a start Ki realized she had been waiting to follow Dresh's lead. Shaking her head at her lapse, she moved to the spot she had chosen.

"For a few moments, I must leave you to your own eyes, Ki. This will take full thought on my part. So, if you will excuse me . . ."

The black stone walls blinked out. Again she saw the boundaries of the chamber as shifting opaque curtains. A ripple passed over them, like a wave disturbing the surface of a tide pool. Ki watched it flow past. Another took its place, rippling past. She watched it flow. For a dizzying moment, she pictured herself as inside a piece of fluted glassware that slowly rotated around her. Another ripple passed. She resisted the temptation to stretch out her hand and see if she could feel the disturbance of the wall's surface. Another ripple approached. When it was directly in front of her, Dresh's command to exit struck her. It came as no spoken word or shared thought, but as a physical compulsion to leap, mental spurs applied to her body. Ki leapt.

They passed through the wall as if through a veil of warm water. Shimmering points of light appeared like dew sparkling on the quill tips of an angry porcupine. Ki gasped in terror, but no breath entered or left her lungs. She felt she hung frozen in darkness. The wizard's head was a lifeless stone in her arms. The points of light plucked at her eyes, each one demanding to be focused on, only to retreat into distance when Ki tried to seize it with her eyes. Her hair stirred about her face in an unfelt breeze.

She fell, she flew, she sank like a stone. Then, with a silent click, she stopped. There was no thought, no breath, no tickling of consciousness nor fear. It was deeper than peace and easier than death. But Ki did not wonder at it. Ki did nothing at all, and did not even know it.

TEN

THE world was changing from deep blues and blacks to greys and muted colors. Vandien knuckled at his sandy eyes with his free hand. With the other he kept a firm grip on the braided leather that ran to the heavy metal circle joining the four skeels' harnesses. He wove along behind them, insisting that they stay on the road. The beasts made repeated efforts to scuttle off into the rocks and underbrush. They were ready for sleep. Vandien headed them off.

His mouth was dry and full of dust. He felt like his spine was gradually pounding its way up through his brain. Soon it would emerge from the top of his skull. He gritted his teeth against it.

The night winds had smelled of the sea. As Vandien crested the final hill, he saw why. The downward path was steep before him, and gullied by rains; the gentle hillocks and dales of yesterday had vanished in the night. Bony grey boulders pushed out of the earth's flesh and a few wind-twisted trees dared to poke up their gaunt branches. The trail he followed now had been laboriously cut down and across the face of a cliff. Below him, Vandien could see the flat green and small houses of the village of False Harbor. Beyond it was the sea.

No fishing vessels moored at anchor by this village. The black beaches were empty. Through the water, Vandien could see the wave-rubbled shapes of houses and sheds that had gone down into the sea in the same great quake that had split the cliff and taken down the Windsingers' temple. Their stone foundations remained, green with seaweed and dotted with barnacles. The temple itself would be farther out, closest to where the bottom suddenly dropped away and the water darkened to blue-black. Only the lowest of low tides would bar the temple, although the old village foundations might be exposed a dozen times a year. Only one tide in several years would leave the temple bared for plucking. Tomorrow would bring him that tide.

How long ago had the mountain settled into the sea? Srolan said the older folk claimed it had happened in a single day. But not one spoke of it from their own life experience. It was a tale they had heard from their grandparents; how the earth had sickened and heaved in the sullen afternoon, and mountain, village and temple had been claimed by the sea. Only the folk out fishing had survived. They returned to rebuild their village on the rise of land that had been the top of the cliff and was now just above high tide line. Gone was the harbor that had sheltered their boats, leaving a shallow bay studded with rocks and snags. They renamed their village False Harbor. They fished in the old village now, in flat-bottomed scows, catching crab and eel, squagis and octopus, where once chickens had scratched and menders had crouched by nets stretched in the sun.

One of the skeel dropped and went limp. Vandien sprang forward and pinched its tail. It roused with a squeal that made the whole team scuttle for a handful of paces. The village itself seemed quiet, though small craft worked in the shallows. As he trotted along behind his team, Vandien smoothed his dark unruly hair. With his free hand he beat the worst of the trail dust from his jerkin and trousers. He hoped he did not look as hungry as he felt.

A painted sign was swinging in the ocean breeze, and Vandien headed toward it. The sign depicted a fish leaping over a mountain. He assumed it marked the inn; it was the only two-story structure in the village. White-washed plaster had dropped away to expose patches of mortared stone. A lone horse was tethered in front of the place. Two mules were hobbled in the side alley. Taking this hint, Vandien herded his charges into the alley. Gratefully they dropped to their bellies and began their wheezing snores. He knew they would remain somnolent during daylight unless he roused them. He knotted the rein about the hitching rail anyway. With a groan, he bent over, stretching his back out. He straightened up to find a tall man assessing him.

The sea had left its marks on him. His eyes were between blue and grey. They looked through Vandien, as if the man had scanned so many horizons that he could no longer look at things close to him. Large weathered hands stuck out of the rolled back sleeves of his coarse smock. Knotted wrists joined muscular forearms. One smallest finger was missing. He stood like a man who does not trust one of his legs. Thinning hair was raked back from his face. A fisherman spat out by the sea, Vandien guessed, and turned to innkeeping when he could no longer stand his watch.

"By the scar down your face, you'd be our Temple Ebb teamster." The tall man dropped the words as if they were coins he were loath to part with.

Vandien didn't wince. He was accustomed to being identified by his scar. "I am. And you'd be the innkeeper?"

"Aye. And the festival master, this year the third time. They'll be hanging the Temple Ebb banners, as soon as they get back with the day's catch. You're to room and board at the inn. There's a nice room above, waiting for you, and a meal when you call for it."

"And a bath?" Vandien asked.

"If you want it." The man scowled as if Vandien were pressing an advantage. "Festival teamster gets most of what he asks for before Temple Ebb, and, if he puts on a good show, a nice send-off afterwards. Though," he added, looking Vandien up and down, "the fellow we had last year may have spoiled us. Dressed all in leather and chains, he did, with a team of six of the tallest mules I've ever seen. Smart, too. The mules did counting tricks before the tide time. The teamster could bend iron bars with his bare hands. Village kept him here for three days after Temple Ebb had passed. He even knew a bawdy song or two we hadn't heard before. We'd never seen anything to match those mules of his. The inn did more business

in that week than in an ordinary month." He paused, frowning
at Vandien. "You don't do sleight of hand, or somesuch, do
you?"

Ki had warned him. A dozen snide remarks rose to Vandien's lips. He swallowed them all. "No. I didn't realize it was
a requirement of the job. I thought your village wanted to hire
a team and man to remove something from a sunken temple."

The tall man ignored the edge in Vandien's voice.

"You call this a team?" The man's voice was frankly skep-
tical.

"I do." Vandien answered smoothly. He reached down to
stroke the scaly shoulder of the skeel nearest him. It responded
by surging against its harness. Wet chopping noises came from
its toothless muzzle. Vandien gave silent thanks that the creatures were nearly blind in daylight. "He's all affection, that
one," he observed fondly as he lightly rapped his prod on its
snout. The skeel withdrew its head with a sinous bending of
its spotted neck.

"We've always had them use horses, or mules, in the past.
Sort of a tradition, you know." Doubt was evident in the innmaster's voice. He scratched at silvery stubble on his chin.

"Do you want a yearly tradition kept, or do you want a
chest yanked out of an undersea hiding place?" Vandien asked
quietly. "When I touched hands on this agreement, there was
no mention of the species I must use in the team, no questions
about whether I could juggle eggs or make a scarf diappear. I
thought I was being hired to perform a task, not to reenact past
failures. Of course, it's entirely up to you."

"Now wait!" The tall man held up his large hands in appeal.
"It's not that I don't like skeel. I hear T'cheria use them reg-
ularly, plowing and hauling. But I never understood why hauling beasts would have such short legs."

Vandien looked down on his team. "Better leverage," he
extemporized tersely. His own doubts nibbled at him. The
tallest of the four came no higher than Vandien's hip, but Web
Shell had lisped earnestly of their strength and stamina. What
Vandien still could not stomach was the horrible flexings of
the skeel. They were like sharks, all muscle and bend wrapped
in thick hide. The one slash he had received from a tail made
him wonder what their internal structure was. Could anything
with bones be that flexible? But this was no time to indulge
his own squeamishness. He gave a careless shrug. "So they

are built close to the ground. That's not a fault. You can sink a wagon to its hubs in mud, and these four can still pop it out. When they get their tails braced and their feet dug in and start humping, it takes a big load to resist their pull. Look at the size of those feet! They won't get mired down in muck the way horses' hooves do. No, those big flappers just spread their weight out and give them more purchase for the pull."

"Aren't you afraid to take them out in the water?" the old man pressed. "You know, sometimes the tide doesn't leave the temple dry. You may be wading a bit."

"They're a well-trained team," Vandien responded vaguely. He would cross that bridge when he came to it.

The tall man stared at him, weighing his words. Then he hunkered down beside the team and stared at them wordlessly. Vandien felt conspicuously tall, standing over the crouched man and the flat skeel. He resisted the urge to crouch down beside them all. He leaned on the rail and waited. He hoped he would not have to wait long. His stomach was a shrunken sack tied to the end of his gullet.

"The woman I dealt with," Vandien asked suddenly. "Srolan. Is she about?"

"In the inn," the innmaster replied. He rose abruptly, and extended a large hand to Vandien.

"I am Helti."

"Vandien." They touched hands. Vandien had to look up into the taller man's face. He met his gaze solemnly. When the big man's face cracked in a grin, Vandien responded to it.

"You've a bold tongue and a strong spine, even if you're not stacked much higher than a youth. Come in and eat and rest. There'll be folk that want to meet you. I expect Srolan will want another chance for words with you. And you'll want to meet the Windsinger who will be singing against you."

Vandien closed his mouth as soon as he realized it was open. The big man laughed. "I figured she wouldn't have mentioned that to you, if she made a big sound over the chest and all. Srolan likes to pretend it's the old days, us against the Windsingers and all. She's old, and you mustn't . . . but you look empty, man, and as if you could find a use for a bed. Come on."

Vandien trailed Helti, trying to still his whirling mind. He had an uneasy feeling that too soon he would understand all, and that little of it would be pleasing.

The inn boasted a railed porch, and a wooden door after the Human style. Two large rectangular windows admitted daylight through their milky panes. The wooden floor was scarred and old, made from salvaged ship planks. Wooden trestle tables and benches stood about, with guttered candles stumped in pools of their own wax. A great fireplace at one end of the room gaped black and cold. A young boy stooped before it, shoveling the ash into a bucket. This was a clean place, by Human standards. A wide door led into the clank and steam of a kitchen. An unrailed staircase ascended to a darker upper floor.

"Sit," said the innmaster, with a friendly clap on Vandien's shoulder that dropped him onto the indicated bench. "I'll be back soon enough with food and talk."

It was good to rest on Human-sized furniture. Vandien looked around, and was struck that the whole room was scaled exclusively to Human usage. He had heard of isolated communities populated by only one sentient species, but this was the first one he had witnessed. The inn was largely deserted at this hour, except for the boy cleaning the hearth. A sulky little miss glared at Vandien as if it were his fault that she had been sent out with a bucket and a rag to oil the table planks.

And that was all. No sign of Srolan, unless . . . Vandien craned and leaned to get a glimpse of a small table set in the shadow of the staircase. Someone in robes sat there, but she was taller than he remembered Srolan. He had nearly thought of an excuse to rise and get a better look at her when Helti came back, bearing a tray.

"Cook's choice!" Helti announced as he unburdened himself with a clank.

The meal was predictable. Fish cakes seasoned with seaweed, a thick chowder (no doubt containing whatever had been netted last night) and a tankard of bitter ale. Vandien set it out before himself, as Helti produced small fresh-baked loaves wrapped in a clean cloth. The smell of the food made Vandien giddy. Helti must have read his face, for he gave a ringing laugh.

"You eat, I'll talk," he offered, and Vandien needed no further invitation. Steam from the hot fish cakes scalded his uncaring fingers. The crusty brown crust broke open to flaky white fish inside. Vandien took a bite to keep his jaws busy while he stirred up the dregs of the chowder to let it cool.

Cubes of cara root swirled past keeping company with shucked limpets, mussels, and less identifiable shapes. His spoon clacked against shells in the bottom of the bowl.

"Srolan." Helti shook his head. "She's probably gone upstairs. Won't stay in the same room with the likes of *her*," and he tossed his head at the robed figure at the shadowed table. "I shouldn't have let Srolan go out this year. It's a youngster's job, the walking of roads until a fit teamster's found. But she insisted, and I was not the man to say 'no' to her. . . . She's a granny to half the village, and aunty to the rest. Who's to tell her she mayn't go? So off she went, and though I knew she saw Temple Ebb differently from the rest of us, I didn't think she'd mislead you. She's old. Even older than you might guess. I hope you won't be holding a grief against her?"

Vandien swallowed. He took a breath, feeling the food in his belly beginning to warm him. Slowly he broke one of the warm loaves, smelling the homey smell as it rose from the bread. "Tell me why I should be grieved, and then I'll be able to decide."

Helti looked uncomfortable. His eyes reminded Vandien of fish darting about in a tide pool, seeking escape. "Temple Ebb, you see, has been . . . since I was a boy, it's been a time of merriment, a time for sweet cakes and the best of fall's harvest from Bitter's farmers. The fisherfolk forget for a time how bitter cold it's going to be, fishing all winter. It's a time for forgetting the realities of work, to lose yourself in a spectacle, whether it's a counting mule or doves from a cup. The big finish is to watch someone else get as wet and work as hard as we expect to do all winter." Helti paused and Vandien nodded, chewing. He watched the big man shift awkwardly on the bench. But he left the speaking to Helti as he took a welcome draft of the cold ale.

"Let me tell you how we see it. Sure, there's a legend of the Windsingers' chest, buried in the muck of the temple. But the idea of someone hauling it up is just spiced sugar on the top of the cake. It's the pageantry of it, the drama of a teamster up to his armpits in icy water and waves, trying for that chest while the Windsinger stands on the hill above, her blue robes blowing in her own gale, and does her best to keep him from it. One old rhymester that came among us called it 'the ancient battle of man against the elements of wind and water': wrote a whole school of verses about it. He's the one that told us it's really the pageantry of it that we love. Likely you'll hear his song in this very room this evening, if Collie's fixed his harp yet."

Vandien found himself nodding. He was just as glad that Ki was not here to grin at him across the table and be so damn right. He continued to eat, but the food no longer had flavor. So it was all to be a farce, and he was the hired clown. Yet, "Srolan offered me a very large fee, in more than coin," he said softly.

"Oh, yes!" Helti chimed in anxiously. "And it's sincere! If, that is, you bring up the chest itself. Srolan would never offer more than she was in power to bestow. The village council is always generous with the pot it sets aside for the festival teamster. Probably because it's never had to pay any of it out." Helti hesitated a moment. "They usually reimburse me for the teamster's keep. The rest they use up on the Midwinter Fest. They don't mind contributing to their own fun," he confided.

"I see." Vandien stirred his chowder aimlessly. His belly still hungered, but suddenly eating seemed too much of an effort. There was no real chance of lifting his scar, nor even of turning a profit. A man who put less value on the touch of his hand would leave now, not even make the attempt. But he *had* touched hands on this. While the opinion of others mattered very little to Vandien, he would not tarnish his own opinion of himself. So he had given his word that he would make a public fool of himself. That was how it was, then. If it must be done, he might as well do it with good grace.

Helti was amazed and a little alarmed as he watched the teamster's melancholy face light with a sardonic grin. Trust Srolan to find one like him. Vandien raised his mug and drained it, returning it to the table with a thump. Helti in turn lifted it and waved it at the boy, who stopped scraping ashes and clinkers to take it for refilling.

"Any other little revelations about this task you would care to enlighten me with?" Vandien inquired genially.

"No. No. Unless, well, perhaps you would like to meet the Windsinger you'll be opposing. I mean, no sense in going into this thing with hard feelings. You two are the village's guests during Temple Ebb. It's not like she picked you to defeat; you just happened to be the one this year."

"Precisely. No hard feelings, good fellowship all round, and here's to you, my competitor!" The boy had returned with the mug and Vandien raised it again.

"Exactly." Helti was not totally reassured. Vandien's words were sporting enough. But the merry lilt had sharp edges. Still and all, it was too late to find another teamster. Helti made a silent resolution that next time he would send someone else to find a teamster. This fellow promised no sport or show at all. Worse, his capacity for food and drink seemed limitless. A poor bargain, but too late to change now. He tried to mellow the teamster's mood. "They've sent us a fine Windsinger this year. Not like in early years, when I've heard that the Windsingers took the whole festival poorly, and turned gales and storms on the village for weeks afterward. No, they've come to see it for what it is, a bit of pageantry, a break from this workaday world. Quite a merry little one they've sent us this year! She plans to stay right here in the inn with us, just as if she were folks. Not much past being an apprentice, by the color of her robes, and so fine-scaled that you'd swear she still wore her own skin. She can blow up a fine wind though. A sweeter tempered Windsinger you've never had to do with. Last eve she was making breezes for the children's kites, so that even the youngest ones could get one flying. Now that's a new one to us; most have been courteous enough, but acted more like they were tolerating the festival. This one seems bound to enjoy it as much as us. Picture this; here we were, last night, all gathered about the fire of an evening, beginning to do a bit of singing. Festival has a lot of songs, it being an old holiday, and we were tuning up a bit on them. We had got into it pretty fair, more loud than tuneful, you understand, for singing is not a thing we do that often. We had just got to the middle of the chorus, mugs beating out the time, when we hear a voice join in that we know isn't one of the village folk. High and clear like a bird taken to Human tongue. Everyone stops their singing, and looks about, and there she is, on the stairway. It gets all silent, you can imagine how we are, thinking, how long has she been there, how much has she heard—for some of the old songs aren't too kindly spoken of the Windsingers. But what does she do? She finished out the chorus alone, and gives us a smile and comes on down. 'Bring me a mug of your best!' she calls out, just like she was folks, 'and I'll sing you one you've not heard before, even though it's about your own village. We call it The Village That Plows The Sea.' And in she starts, singing to an old tune, but set so high that no one in the village could have matched one note of it. And it *is* about False Harbor, and how we harvest fish from the sea, and it makes a joke of it, saying we plow the waves at Temple Ebb, seeking for what is not there."

"I don't get it," Vandien put in slowly, his low voice a marked contrast to the innkeeper's amazed and jocular one.

"Why, you know! We send out a man with a team, and he slashes and turns through the waves, like a farmer turning up furrows to plant a crop, and we harvest a crop of fish from the sea . . . but I'm just telling you in words, you have to hear it all done in rhyme, with the words turned to mean two things at once and . . ."

"No." Vandien's voice was as soft as ever, but cut right through Helti's flow of words. "That much is obvious, even to me. What means the part about plowing for what is not there?"

"Srolan!" Helti hissed the name out in frustrated rebuke. "You make me feel bad, young man. Has she not told you that the Windsingers have always denied there is anything to be found in the temple? They send the storms, they tell us, only because such as we should not be desecrating their fallen temples with our curiosity."

"Is there, or is there not a chest I am to bring up?" Vandien demanded in a flinty voice.

"There is not."

The voice from behind his shoulder was silky soft, pure and strong with years of training. Vandien turned to it slowly, refusing to be startled. Few could approach him without his hearing, but she had.

"Windsinger Killian," Helti breathed deferentially. "I hope our frank speech has not irritated you. The man was hired, knowing little of our customs and what we truly expected of him. I was only . . ."

"Peace, innmaster. Why should I take offense at the truth? Your name, teamster?"

Vandien looked up at her and held his name in his mouth. Her height was not impressive. She had more than half a head over Vandien, but most of it was cowl. What had been her forehead when she was Human would have been on a height with his own. She was slender in pale blue robes that fell to

cover even the tips of her toes. But it bared her face and hands
and wrists to Vandien's quick eyes. Finely scaled she was, the
scales only beginning to be edged with a bluish tinge. It could
have been a flawlessly applied cosmetic, but it was not. Her
fingernails were already turning to a heavier layer of horny
scale, the eyelashes and eyebrows long fled from her face, even
her lips were masked in scales of a slightly rosier hue. She
was a Windsinger, and Vandien had been warned all of his life
not to gift one of such power with his own name. He was mute.

"He is Vandien," Helti broke in as the silence became awkward. "Pray, seat yourself, Windsinger Killian. Shall I send
for something from the kitchen for you?"

Vandien had lowered his dark eyes. Now he picked up his
mug and looked boldly at the Windsinger over its rim. He took
down half of it. Helti was becoming more and more agitated
every moment, but Vandien cared little; Helti had made free
with his name, now let him swallow discomfort and choke on
it.

But Killian appeared not to notice any awkwardness as she
seated herself beside Helti. Her tall cowl bobbed gracefully to
her movements, like the soft crest of a wading bird. But for
that cowl she could have been a prudishly swathed young woman.
Her grey eyes, so Human, looked into Vandien's with the
charming frankness of an innocent girl. And yet, he reminded
himself, she was neither innocent nor Human. Not anymore.

"And does your teamster speak?" Killian teased.

"When he has words to say," Vandien countered.

"And have you nothing to say to me, who will oppose you
tomorrow?" Her eyes smiled at Helti's, past Vandien, as if he
were a difficult child and Helti the doting parent.

"I think not," Vandien rasped.

"A pity. I had so looked forward to meeting my competitor,
and seeing if he was worthy of opposing my skills. So silent
you are, I think you cowed already. Will you slip away in the
night, Vandien, before we have a chance to try one another?"

"Will you?"

"Um. You think that would make your task easier? That if
there were no wind whistling about you, you could splash about
to your heart's content and find something in the old temple?
Were it not that our temples, old or new, are consecrated only
for us, I would be tempted to let you try."

"Now, now!" Helti intervened anxiously. He rose and pressed

a heavy hand on Vandien's shoulder. "You've no call to be so bitter of tongue, young man. It's true, you were misled about your task. I'm sorry that was so. But take it with a good spirit, as befits a man of honor. Buck up, and make the best of it! Is it so hard a thing, to face two days of free food and drink, a clean warm room with soft blankets, and whatever else you can think to ask for? It's true you don't stand to gain much in coin, but surely Srolan told you how we treat our teamster guest. Would you have a new cloak? A pair of boots? Ask for it, and it's yours. You'll see we're not a niggardly folk when it comes to our guests. Perhaps you've been tricked into this part, but it need not be a bad thing for you. Think what you're to ask of us, and warm your heart a little. And, Windsinger Killian, begging your pardon, but I hope you won't be taking our teamster's sour words too hard. A long and weary way he has come, dry of throat and hungry, thinking of gold for his purse, only to have his dreams turned to fish chowder and boots. It's enough to sour any man. Likely he's just a bit tired. A hot bath and a bed is what you need, man. Now isn't that so?" The big hand on Vandien's shoulder tightened suggestively. It did not leave his shoulder as he rose, but subtly helped him to his feet and steered him to the stairs. "You'll see. It will set all to rights with you. You'll face tomorrow with a grin on your face and a new spirit."

"No doubt." Vandien's words were for Helti, but his eyes locked with the Windsinger's. What parents had given their daughter such eyes? How had they felt when they lost her to the Windsingers? Or had she, like so many other little girls, gone out to play one day and simply never returned? Did she even remember them? And then the large grey eyes dropped him a wink, so girlishly flirtatious that his blood ran cold.

He climbed the stairs slowly. Down below, he heard Helti bellowing for someone named Janie to fetch him a bath. The stairs led up to a hallway, dimly lit by windows at either end. The stairwell was not railed. Vandien resolved not to drink too much this night. Of the six doors facing onto the hall, two were closed. He made a hasty inspection of the other four and chose the largest and airiest bedroom. The window shutters had been latched open and a fresh breeze off the sea flavored the chilled room.

It was a well-furnished room by any inn's standards. The stout wooden tub, long and deep, had been designed for someone larger than Vandien. A wooden stand, plain but graceful, supported a basin and ewer. The wooden bedstead boasted a straw stuffed mattress with two thick coverlets and a folded woolen blanket at the foot of it. There was even a trunk, if he had needed a place for his possessions. Two worn hides graced the floor, one by the bed and another by the tub. A wooden stool completed the room's furnishings.

Vandien sank gratefully onto the bed. For a moment he let his shoulders slump in defeat, then he straightened, knuckled his eyes, and pushed his hair back from his face. There was a knock at his door. Before he could answer, it was shouldered open. Janie was obviously the older sister of the child cleaning tables; the resemblance was unmistakable. She carried two heavy buckets of steaming water. The serving boy behind her was similarly laden, and two rough towels were slung over his shoulder.

"Your bath, teamster," the boy announced, dumping his water into the tub.

"I doubt he thought it was soup," giggled Janie. She rolled her eyes at Vandien, and shrugged at the boy's stupidity. Her young breasts heaved alarmingly. Vandien couldn't decide if she were flirting with him or the serving boy.

The boy ignored her, setting the towels on the stool and clumping out of the room. Janie glanced about casually, pulled a handful of herbs from her apron pocket, and tossed them into the water. As she bent over the tub to stir them in, she watched Vandien from the corner of her eye. He sat silent, waiting. Then she straightened, slowly drying her hand and arm on her apron.

"Is there anything else, teamster?"

"Nothing. This is much finer than I expected. Thank you."

"You know, you've but to ask for whatever comes into your head. Nothing is refused to the Temple Ebb teamster. So don't be shy."

"I won't," Vandien responded gravely.

"Well then." Janie gave a short sigh as she inspected the room again. "I'll go then. Enjoy your bath."

"I will. Thank you."

She sauntered to the door and gave Vandien a bright smile before she shut it behind her.

Vandien sighed and bent down to pull off his boots. Maybe he should ask for a new pair; these had certainly seen better days. He stripped his tunic off over his head and let it fall to the floor. His romp in the creek and days of dusty travel were recorded on it. He kicked his road weary trousers onto the same heap.

The water was too hot, but as he eased into it he felt the weariness lifting away from him with the dirt. He raised a dipperful of water and let it stream over his head. Leaning back, he sank into the tub until the water lapped against his unshaven chin. He lolled his head back on the tub's rim and closed his eyes.

"I've forgotten my buckets!"

Vandien wondered why he wasn't surprised. When he opened his eyes, Janie stood in the door.

"I only came to get my buckets," she repeated, and defiance mingled with a taunt in her voice.

"I'm glad you came back, actually," Vandien conceded. "There *is* something you could do for me."

"Is there?" Janie's eyes were wide.

"When you take your buckets, would you take my tunic and trousers as well? They need washing. In fact..." Vandien hesitated. "If you could also find some new things of the same size, I'd be very grateful."

"Yes, teamster." Janie's voice was suddenly subdued. She scooped up her buckets and slung his dirty clothes over one arm. Vandien winced at the slamming of his door. Well, it couldn't be helped. He wondered if he had ever been as young as Janie. Slowly he let his body slide deeper into the hot water. He had not realized how cold he was until the heat of the water began to chase away the deepest chills. He lolled his head back and relaxed.

The door was eased open. Vandien did not turn. This was beginning to be wearing.

"Wouldn't the teamster like his back washed, perhaps?"

"Janie, my back has been in the same place for as long as I can remember. I think I can find it to wash it. Do this for me instead: go walk on the beach, pick up all the pretty shells you can find and put them in a box. Someday, when you are as old as I am now, and feel twice that age, look in the box and remember when you were a little girl who couldn't wait to grow up. Now scoot!" Vandien turned with a slosh of water to point at the door.

But it was Srolan who stood with her back pressed against

it, a grin of mischief on her face. Her black eyes sparkled. "You've more about you than shows, teamster Vandien. Even at this moment."

Vandien sank back into the tub, embarrassed and feeling more flustered by Srolan's presence than by young Janie's.

"I must sound a pompous fool to you. I won't try to explain."

"You needn't. I saw her face as she left. . . . There is a certain kind of woman—she may be any age—who isn't certain of herself, who won't risk being rejected by a handsome man. But when she sees a man with a disfigured face or a withered arm, she says to herself, 'Surely no one besides myself can see past that scar to the worth behind it. Surely he will be flattered by my attention, and I will be giving him a gift he seldom receives.' So, she offers, and expects you to be amazed and grateful that any would find you attractive. Am I wrong?"

She wasn't, and that hurt. But Vandien only said, "Srolan, I am in no mood to speak of scars just now. If I had realized the teamster's ablutions were a public ceremony, I would have had the tub brought down to the common room. Would you mind?" He jerked his head toward the door.

"Yes, I would. And so should you. This will be the only private chance I'll have to talk to you; the common room is ever full of ears. My own home is never free of neighbors seeking a cure for a toothache, a plaster for a sore belly, an oil for a pulled shoulder. So we must set aside privacy and meet here."

"Why? How will you explain when Janie finds another excuse to pop in here? She'll be back soon, with clean clothes for me."

"Knowing Janie, she could find an excuse faster than that. She's a resourceful little snip. This inn will be a more restful place when she finally finds someone to oblige her. But, to answer your question, she won't pop in because she saw me come in as she was going down the stairs. She'll be afraid to open the door now for fear of what Granny might be doing with the stranger. But enough of this. Stop worrying about your flesh, and listen to what I have to say."

Vandien waited for her to continue. He watched as she roamed the room smoothing the coverlet on the bed, shaking and refolding the towels, and finally perching on the foot of the bed. She pushed back her black hair and gave her head a shake to set it free down her back. Her gesture was as young

as Janie's, and not so contrived. When she turned to face
Vandien, her years had hidden themselves. The lines in her
face and her bony knuckles lied, her eyes asserted. Vandien's
attention was riveted to her.

"You think me a foul old woman, perhaps, to deceive you
so about your task?"

He had, but no longer did. "Well..."

"But I did not deceive you. Every word I told you is true.
There is a Windsinger secret in that temple, and if you bring
it up, you shall have six tallies, and the scar lifted from your
face."

"One's as likely as the other," Vandien muttered. Helti had
made him feel ashamed for being so gullible. Now, with a
word and a smile, Srolan made his doubts seem a weakness.

"Damn Helti!" Srolan blazed. "Damn the fool, and that pet
Windsinger they have sent us. His words take the heart out of
our teamster. What man can win when he expects defeat? It is
the same every year. After Helti has been at the teamsters, they
do not even look for the chest. They splash about with their
beasts for a few hours in a storm, and then back to the inn
they come, for a drink and a hot meal and a willing bed partner.
They've changed a worthy quest into a fool's show. Cannot
you see the slyness of the Windsingers in this? Vandien, do
you think it was always this way? It was not.

"When I was a babe, Temple Ebb united our village. There
was no need to hire a teamster. Every able-bodied adult in the
village was out in the shallow waters of low tide, trying to
bring up that chest. Back then, the storms of the Windsingers
lashed us all, but could not dissuade us. Now they call the
chest a myth, because for a fool's life no one has seen it. They
disbelieve the stories of their fathers. Yet there are folk in this
town descended from those who have touched the chest. The
same ones that told us it's too heavy for a man's hands. Only
a team could haul it up, they said, for there're stones that must
be moved, as well as a heavy chest to haul.

"And so we began the hiring of teamsters every year. But
love for wealth is not spur enough for a man when the Windsinger's storm is upon him. No hired teamster will bring up
that chest for coin alone. The teamster would need a reason
more compelling than that. For years, I tried to tell them that,
but they wouldn't listen. They don't know how a sung storm

chills the heart and leaches away resolve. They've never battled the Windsinger's storm. So this year I did it myself. I found a teamster and gave him a reason to keep his heart hot. I found you."

Srolan's eyes were piercing. Vandien, who had so often unleashed the compelling charm of his own dark eyes, fell victim. Srolan's cause became his; her resolve fired him.

"Why have they lost the spirit that moves you?" Vandien wondered.

"They do not remember; some do not even know!" Srolan cried. "What do you suppose made the earth shake and fall? It was the blasphemy of the Windsingers that sent our village beneath the waves! So I heard from my own grandmother!" She fell silent, too outraged to go on. The heaving of her breast testified to her emotion. Vandien stared at her.

So old she was, and so young. Her words had added sparks to her eyes, brought the color to her cheeks until the withered skin flushed with youth. Damn, he liked her! It was as instinctive as breathing. He *knew* her. She was sound, a friend to be trusted as if he had known her for years.

But.

His common sense nagged him in Ki's voice. The woman was either senile or crazy. Her story was full of holes. Revenge for her long drowned ancestors? He should listen to Helti, and get through this with as little scraping as possible. Did Srolan think him a gullible simpleton? Or did she believe he was as crazy as herself?

"Your bath water must be getting cold."

Vandien started, suddenly realizing how long the silence had lasted. He shifted in the water. If Ki were here, she would call him a fool. She would tell him not to get involved in other folk's quarrels. She would tell him not to be impulsive. But Ki wasn't here.

"Is there a chest?" he suddenly demanded.

"Yes." Her answer was simple, ringing with truth.

"And can it be retrieved from there?"

"Where Human hands place a thing, other Human hands can remove it."

Only one question was left. It nearly choked him. "And can you pay me six tallies, and truly lift the scar from my face?"

Srolan rose. She gave him a smile that she had saved since

she was born, just for him. It held the promise of all promises. "If you do your part, man, do you think I will do less than mine?"

"But how?"

She knew he wasn't asking about the money. She smiled at him silently. Rising, she took a towel from the stool and tossed it to him. He watched the door close softly behind her.

Vandien rose from the lukewarm water, stretched, and swathed himself in the towel. His fingers were wrinkled into ridges. All his lax body could dream of was sleep.

The door opened.

"These were outside your door." Srolan stepped in. On the foot of his bed she placed a clean brown fisherman's smock and trousers. She stepped out again. Vandien was not given time to speak.

He fell into the bed, not even bothering to dry himself or call thanks after her. The coverlet was stuffed with down, warm airy stuff, light as sunshine on his body. The door opened.

"And, Vandien?"

"Does no one knock?" he muttered wearily.

"No one. It would do her no harm if you let Janie know you thought her pretty and sweet. A kind word or two from you might make her feel her own self-worth, and keep her from throwing herself at the next stray traveler that happens along. And there are things she could tell you, if she had a mind to."

Srolan began to withdraw. Vandien sat up.

"Wait!" When she paused, her head thrust into the room, he asked, "Is there anything else? Is there any other reason why any one else is going to barge in here?"

Srolan smiled at him. "There's only one last thing I'll say. Close the window shutter before you take a cough. No, stay where you are. I'll do it for you."

With quick steps she crossed the room to lower the shutter with a thud and latch it against the gusting wind. Vandien was plunged into restful darkness.

"Thanks," he murmured, shouldering himself deeper into the bed.

"My hopes are riding on you, teamster," she spoke into the darkness.

He had not heard her come near, but he felt the sudden press of lips upon his forehead, warm as a lover's and as impersonal as a goddess's. It was a strange caress, outside all forms of courtesy Vandien knew. Yet it did not startle him. All the things tight inside him, all worries, all doubts, all the tiny muscles of his face and scalp, loosened. Sleep was softer and warmer than the down coverlet, and bottomless. He never heard Srolan leave.

Eleven

LIKE an opalescent grindstone, there winked into view a place. It wheeled impossibly huge before Ki. It eased toward her ponderously. In some long forgotten reach of her brain, an instinct stirred. Ki's left arm and hand freed themselves of Dresh's head. She watched idly as her hand crabbed out toward the distant glittering wheel.

She did not swim, nor crawl, nor perform any act of locomotion. The wheel was two body lengths away from the tips of her fingers. It was a lifetime away. It was on the far side of the glittering points of light. It was not a place at all, only a bright mural on the far wall of the sky. A placid sleepiness wrapped her. Always she had been here. She recalled an ancient dream of reaching; she did not remember what she reached for, nor why. There remained in her only a remote spark of purpose that bade her left hand continue its scrabbling, finger-waggling crawl. It was fitting that she do so. That movement was a part of this light-sprinkled darkness, was one with her eternal arching flight. Ki dreamed a dozen lives away.

Contact! Her fingers brushed the shining opal wall. The tips of her fingers wiggled into a warm, yielding surface. Her hand

sank into it. A sudden tingling seized it, an awakening from
numbness. Like a drowning swimmer whose face breaks the
surface of the water, Ki fought. The glittering wall yielded to
her fingers, but provided no handhold for her to pull her body
along. Rather she was drawn in, sucked up. Her face touched
the warm surface and broke through. Life scintillated in her
veins. Her skin sang with it. The sudden wash of sensation
engulfed her and drained her. She sank in a heap.

"Up!"

Ki was given no time for thought or recovery as Dresh drove
her body to its feet. She hurried along a shimmering corridor
lined with identical closed doors. The head's eyes flickered
back and forth, scanning each door as they passed; grey wall,
grey door, grey wall, grey door. Her vision was tied to Dresh's
once more. His darting glimpses were making her sick. She
was giddy with the flashing images, too young to her reborn
life. She staggered along, confused and disoriented.

He jerked her to a halt before a door, no different from any
of the others. "In here!" he barked, activating her body before
she could comply voluntarily. The door swung open to her
touch and closed silently behind her.

Ki found herself in a small austere room. As her breathing
steadied, so did her vision. The room was almost a cell, devoid
of furniture but for a low bedstead with blankets folded across
the foot of it. She sank wearily onto it, placing the head gently
at her side. She rubbed her aching shoulders, trying to comprehend such things as time and physical spaces. Blindly, she
fingered a smarting semi-circle of indentations in the flesh of
her arm. Teethmarks. Dresh picked up her thought.

"I was forced to hold on anyway I could. You very nearly
dropped me, you know. But," grudging admiration came into
his voice, "for one who claimed no skill at leaping, it was a
prodigious feat. It is typical of Rebeke to gamble her life on
her superior skill. And yet we matched her."

"I cannot do it again. You must not ask it of me."

"So say all women after they have birthed their first child.
Yet when the need comes upon them again, they find the
strength. So shall you, Ki, for you must. But do not think about
that right now. Worrying will only weaken you."

She snorted derisively. "Do you think I'm not worrying
now? We seem to have leaped right to the center of their hive."

"Quarters for the novices, if I am not mistaken. With safe

corridors for those not yet adept enough to trust their daily
lives to leaping. It is not quite where I had hoped to find us,
yet it is closer to where we must be. My body is not far from
us now. The closer we get to it, the more I may draw upon
the powers of it."

"Let's get this over with." Ki picked up the head and settled
it firmly into the crook of her left arm. A strand of dark hair
fell across her eyes. She brushed at her forehead but it didn't
move. She sighed, and brushed Dresh's black hair back from
their shared eyes. The wizard let go a short chuckle.

"So swiftly do we adapt to one another, Ki. Perhaps we
were wiser to forget about regaining my body. Let them keep
it. I shall tap your body for my needs, and you shall remain
my faithful steed and companion."

"Not likely. Sooner would I be a house slave to a Brurjan.
Dresh, no more bandying of words. Many doors must mean
many novices. Might not one enter at any moment?"

"Do you have so little respect for my powers, Ki? This room
has been empty long. It has almost lost the imprint of the one
that last used it. That does not mean it is absolutely safe, but
it is the safest haven we shall find in a Windsingers' nest."

"Hush!" Ki's quick ears had picked up a muted murmur of
voices passing by the door. Fear swept over her. She listened
long to the footsteps retreating down the hall. When silence
fell again at last, she expelled her held breath in a ragged sigh.
"Can we go and get your body now?" she pleaded.

"Certainly. Just step out in the hall and ask directions of
the first novice you meet. Trot on in, and ask Rebeke sweetly
for any boxes of wizard meat she happens to have around."

"So how do we do it?" Ki asked grudgingly after her surly
silence had been ignored.

"I don't know. Dammit, do you think I am in the habit of
losing bits of myself to the Windsingers? It all depends on what
they do. I haven't the power to meet Rebeke and the other full
Windsinger I sense hovering over my body. We must wait until
they leave off their watching, or until we have found a weapon."

"And if they open the boxes?"

"If I sense that happening, then we must risk all and try to
reclaim my parts."

"You would know if they had broached your boxes?"

Dresh expelled a long breath in a hiss. "I believe I would.
I hope I would."

"But you are not sure?" Ki pressed him in dismay.

"Ki, do you know what my powers are? No. You know only enough of the stuff of wizardry to fear me, and to make you angry. You take a foolish pride in being 'only Human' as if my wizardry were some freak of my birth, and not a prize hard won, at much sacrifice; as if my skills were a monstrous unfairness to those who do not have them. So you credit to me powers beyond the skills of any to attain. I, who possess wizardry, know the limits of my arts. But of the Windsingers? Who can say, except one that is a Windsinger? I am a wizard, and the ways of magic are not unknown to me. But the fear and loathing you feel for a Windsinger, who has forsaken the shape of her birth species and taken on the attributes of a race that no longer exists... those feelings I share. I can guess at their limits. But as I am not a Windsinger, I cannot plumb the depths of their arts. What skills do they truly possess, and what ones do they pretend to, that they may better control the masses?"

"You aren't sure," Ki confirmed it for herself. "For all you know, they could have both boxes open by now." Slowly she set the head back on the bed beside her.

"I would sense that!" Dresh asserted. "If they drained my body and hands, do you think I could survive in this state? If I had taken another body when they drained me, I'd survive. But that is all it would be; survival. Wizardry is an art of the body as much as the mind. I'd have all my long training to begin again...." Dresh's voice trailed off desolately.

But Ki's mind had followed a different path. "And what of me?" she demanded angrily.

"Eh?" Dresh asked, distracted.

"What about me? If the Windsingers drain you while we're here, I'm left holding a dead wizard's head. Then what?"

"The Windsingers would stop you," Dresh explained calmly. "Surely you've realized that."

"Kill me?" Ki pressed.

"No!" Dresh snorted. "We aren't all savages. No, not kill you. Stop you. Put you in a void room." Ki's face was pained as she tried to grasp his meaning. "Sort of like putting a turnip in a root cellar," Dresh elaborated.

"Like when we jumped?" A tingling dread ran over Ki's body; a mindless forever of frozen dreams.

"Exactly," Dresh agreed, pleased she had grasped it.

Ki put her own head into her hands. Her eyes were closed against her palms, but her mind shared Dresh's view of the wall.

"Why me?" Ki asked rhetorically.

"Because you said you would do all in your power, and signed your name to it. It's all in the contract, Ki."

"It always is," she mumbled.

·Twelve

VANDIEN awoke to warmth and darkness. For long moments he lay still, savoring that time of peace that hovers between waking and sleeping. He tried to drift back into sleep, but found he could not. His body felt rested and healed, his mind cleared to alertness. He found he had ideas he had not had when he dropped in sleep, and a drive to begin his task. The will to work possessed him.

Rolling from bed, he lifted the window shutter for a look. Late afternoon greeted him. He looked down on his team, still huddled peacefully. He resolved to check their lines before nightfall, to be sure they would withstand any nocturnal tugging. Letting his eyes wander farther, he looked over the low dwellings of False Harbor. Holiday banners fluttered from cottage windows. A puppeteer had set up a booth in the street. Children too young to fish were standing about it. Shouts of laughter rose at regular intervals. Vandien smiled at the sound.

The tide was going out. He stood holding the shutter open, watching the slow retreat of the waves. It was so deceptive, their rise and fall. Each nibbling wave seemed to fall on the shore and lap up to the same height as the preceding one, but already the high tide line was clearly visible, a tracery of small flotsam, shells and seaweed stranded across the sands in a wavery line. Later tonight, he knew, most of the old village would stand exposed. The broken house walls would rise from the sea like the decayed teeth of some monstrous beast. The tide's full retreat would be under moonlight, and would expose almost all of the old settlement. But not the temple. The temple had been closest to the sea, standing between the ocean and the village. When the land sank, the temple had gone deepest and taken all its secrets with it. Had any Windsingers drowned along with that mysterious chest? No one had ever mentioned that to Vandien.

There were boats in sight, some beaching, some heading out to sea. There were flat-bottomed scows prowling in the shallows, and double-ended dories that would venture into deeper water and fish the true sea. Close in, Vandien saw youngsters in makeshift vessels or on rafts. Armed with sharpened sticks of driftwood, they lazed silently along, waiting for some sea creature on the bottom to betray itself with a ripple of fin or a twitch of claws. Then the sharp spear would plunge down, and sometimes return with skewered bounty. The wind was chill on Vandien's face, and he could imagine the iciness of the water. Yet the youngsters were barefoot and shirtless, or nearly so. "Oh, for the youthful ability to ignore the weather," Vandien sighed to himself.

He used a towel to wedge the shutter ajar. It gave a dim light to the room as he fumbled his way into the unfamiliar garments. He must remember to ask for candles. The brown smock was loose on him, sewn for a man wider of shoulder and taller than he. He belted it at the waist with his own belt. The extra bulk of unneeded cloth was annoying, but the clean soft smock felt good against his skin. The trousers tied at the waist with a drawstring. They were also too long, but Vandien found their unaccustomed looseness pleasant. He had no doubt that he struck a comic figure. Well, let them laugh. The rest of the village might as well get their money's worth, if not Srolan. He looked about for his boots, but they were not where he had dropped them. He found them by the door, their mud scraped away and the wrinkled leather freshly oiled. Srolan or Janie? he wondered, and shook his head over his own unwariness. What other visits had he slept through? Luckily he had nothing worth stealing. He pushed his feet into his boots, tucking excess trousers into them.

The common room below was a noisier, busier place than it had been in the morning. Vandien paused a moment on the stairs. The fisherfolk below were taking their ease in most energetic ways. The sound boomed like surf, the voices rising and falling in waves crested with laughter. Most of them were garbed to match Vandien, but in brighter colors. One woman big with child was robed for comfort, but the rest dressed like their men, in smocks and trousers. Their hand motions were extravagant as they talked, big hands thrown back, mouths wide with laughter. They were large folk for the most part, making Vandien feel like a youth. Smells of drink and hot chowder rose to him. The big fireplace roared now. Benches had been pulled up before it, and folk sprawled on them, their boots smoking in front of the blazing logs.

Vandien's quick spirit soared with their good humor and easy laughter. The fellowship below was as appetizing as the food, and more heartening. His earlier melancholy evaporated before the warmth of it.

"Vandien!" Helti roared it out, and the din stilled for an instant. "Here's our teamster, and looking more the part now. Come on down, man! Make him a place at the fire, there! Janie! Fetch a bowl of the kettle's best, and a mug of the coldest!"

Vandien's boots rang on the stairs as he descended. The talk picked up, not quite as loud as before, but it was a comfortable sound. Fisherfolk moved aside to let him through, with affable nods. For every eye that clung to his scar, Vandien saw a hand or a leg or a face as marred as his own. His scar might be a little more prominent than most, but a missing finger or a hook-torn arm was little to these people. He felt acceptance, and, if anything marked him as an outsider in this crowd, it was his slighter stature and girth. He eased down on the bench like a boat moving into its berth. Janie put the hot bowl into his hands almost before he was settled, and set the mug on the bench beside him. He took the chance to send a smile and a look into her eyes. To his surprise, a blush rosed her cheeks and she scowled at him. She fled back to the kitchen.

He nodded to introductions too multitudinous to note. Vandien was at his best in dealing with folk; he was as skilled as a stray cat in moving into a warm place by the fire and making himself agreeable. He could remember too many times when his hopes of a meal and a bed had hinged upon how affable folk found him. He felt no cynicism about this; among his folk it was the oldest and most basic idea of hospitality. In his own land, the man with a tale to tell, a smiling face, and a listening ear was never turned away empty.

And that was the trick of it, as Vandien had long known. A tale or two of a stranger's travels were welcome new meat in a village where the doings of one's neighbors were not all that different from one's own. But even more welcomed by folk in isolated villages was the chance to tell their own tales to new ears. Vandien listened, his eyes bright, his lips curving in appreciation of the story. Before the chowder was gone, he had heard of their catch for the day, and the week before. He had commiserated with Red, who had inadvertently netted a creature too large for his boat, and lost not only nets but part of his rigging. He knew that Sara's baby was expected before the next moon, and that the child's future luck as a fisherman would be foretold by what catch the afterbirth lured into the nets. Berni was crouched on the floor before him, sketching on the boards with a bit of charcoal taken from the fire as she argued with Helti about exactly where Dea and her crew had gone down in the big storm just before festival, five years ago.

A young man with a cloth-wrapped harp came pushing up to the fire. Collie, Vandien guessed. His face and hands were still red with chill from his fishing. He had a large square face, and square hands to match it, with thick stumpy fingers that gave no hint of the music in them. But when he took the cover from the harp and began to test the strings, Berni and Helti stopped their arguing and all the common room drew closer to the hearth.

Collie wet his chapped lips and looked around with a smile at the silence he had caused. He looked to Vandien, and Vandien conceded all attention to him. Smiling, he plucked a few notes on the harp and looked about him questioningly.

"Not that one!" Helti decided. "Too sad for the night before Temple Ebb. Give us something with a merrier tune."

Collie's sandy brows danced with mischief as he plucked out another set of notes. "Collie! There's children still up and about!" Red was scandalized. "Save a tune like that for later in the night, when the small ones are off to sleep!"

"He speaks with his harp," said a soft voice by Vandien's ear. He looked round to find Janie had wrangled a place at his shoulder. "All the village laughed when his father traded half a season's catch for that harp, and gave it to a simpleton. But once the boy mastered it, no man in the village had a sweeter voice."

Vandien nodded silently, hearing both stories in the tone of her voice. Janie was not only telling him how Collie had gained a voice, but in all innocence had told also where her heart longed to be welcomed.

Collie looked askance at the room. With a shrug of his shoulder and an upturned hand he asked what they would hear.

"Give us the net menders' song!" called a voice Vandien knew. He glanced up to where Srolan sat on the stairs. She was above the level of the flickering candles. Her face and form were a maid's in the semi-darkness. Vandien wondered how long she had sat there, looking down on them, watching the interplay of the village without being seen. Collie's fingers were already drawing out the notes of the melody. The surging voices of the fisherfolk followed his fingers. The chorus was a simple one. Before the song was done, Vandien was shouting it out with the rest. Stamping boots kept the time.

"That's one we haven't sung in a good long while," Helti observed into the silence after the song.

"And it puts me in mind of another one!" called a grizzled old man in the corner. "Can't remember its proper name, but Collie should know the tune. It's the one that begins, 'Moon follows my wake and silvers my nets . . .'"

"The Candlefish Moon!" Srolan's voice came dropping from the upper dimness.

"That's it!" the old man exclaimed, and Collie put his fingers to his harp strings. This song most of the younger folk listened to, joining in as soon as they knew the refrain. The words were in Common, but in archaic forms to fit the rhyme. An old song, Vandien guessed, and so seldom sung that the younger folk did not know the words. It was a courting song, too, that had many of the oldsters looking at one another with youthful eyes, while Janie's voice came from behind Vandien to sing the refrain with heartfelt sweetness. He stole a look in her direction, but she never noticed. Her eyes were on young Collie.

Collie did not let that song die completely, but used its ending notes to lead into another. The old man in the corner

grinned delightedly as he recognized it, and he led the others
into the words. Again the turnings of the words betrayed the
age of the song. It was a stirring ballad of an earlier time, when
the Humans of this village had disputed their fishing grounds
with T'cherians from across the bay, and won. Vandien sensed
about him a quickening of spirit. The old folk were caught up
in singing of this past glory. The younger folk listened or
hummed along in wonder. Vandien glanced up the staircase.
Srolan was all but invisible. After the battle song, there was
another, this one sad, a lament of the folk who returned from
fishing to find their village sunken, their kin gone. A bonding
was taking place here; Vandien felt it on an instinctive level.
Was the old man in league with Srolan? Were they working
together to turn the villagers' minds back to the past? Some
eyes were moist at the end of that song, and Collie let the last
notes die to silence.

Helti himself was quiet as he moved through the throng with
a tray of cold mugs for the newcomers, while Janie dispensed
cold bitter ale from an immense pitcher. There was little talk,
most of it muted. Kinship. That was what thrummed throughout
the room. It was more than friends and a warm fire on a cold
night. Vandien could almost touch the unity of the village.
Berni suddenly looked up from her idle sketchings on the floor
to say, "Collie. Play the Temple Bell Song."

A hushed expectancy settled in the room. Collie sat still for
a moment, his lax fingers numbing his harp strings. Vandien
did not look up at the darkened staircase. He did not need to
see Srolan to know her triumph. She had primed them, and
perhaps the old man had helped. But now village feeling was
running high and free, on its own, as unstoppable as a river in
flood.

Collie's fingers swept into the music. No one sang. Vandien
heard the deep plucked notes like temple bells ringing slow
and mournful behind an intricate weaving of somber melody
that grieved too deep for words to flow. The candles seemed
to burn more slowly as he played, and the mourning seemed
to ebb and flow as endlessly as the tides. Then first one voice
and then another began to rise. And Vandien could not understand the words at all, but both old and young sang them
well and with feeling. He knew he was listening to a tongue
so old it was no longer spoken, the vestige of whatever language
had been spoken here when the village sank. Common was a

good enough tongue for everyday dealings, but like many another folk, they had turned back to their native tongue to sing
of a sorrow too deep for words, too personal for outsiders to
share.

It was a long piece of music, not the usual tavern ballad of
eight or ten verses, nor a courting song with three or four verses
and a sweet refrain. This song was a tapestry, composed of
sections where the harp grieved alone, and then was joined by
Human voices, that tapered away and left the harp sobbing
alone again. The singers were intent as they sang, rapt when
they listened. Vandien marked that no mug was raised to slake
a dry throat, no one tossed more wood into the blaze, even
though it had begun to wane. He found himself drawn into it
almost as strongly as the villagers. He did not feel restive as
he listened, despite his ignorance of the words. There was a
power to this song, an emotion that was almost racial. The
song tapped their ancestry, swirled them all back to a time
when grief was fresh as a bleeding slash. It was all so hopeless,
so very hopeless.

The light in the common room dimmed with the falling fire;
the candles were burning to stumps. Shadows were longer
where they fell on the rough walls. The voices were stilled,
and the harp's sound died away to almost nothing, whispering
to itself. Vandien could hear the shushing of the waves outside.
The harp fell silent. Then, with a crash of chords, it came back.
The voices suddenly rose to roar out a defiant chorus. Three
times that chorus was shouted out, each time angrier and more
implacable. Then, with a final shout, voices and harp were
still.

Vandien found himself trembling in the dark. No one moved;
even Collie's hands, dimly limned by the red firelight, rested
still on the strings. The silence was not peace; rather it was a
tingling awareness, a remembering of a promise made, of a
duty to be kept.

"The Windsingers!" The old grizzled man in the corner
spoke with soft contempt. Someone spat loudly.

Vandien heard a step, and sudden light came back as Helti
kindled a fresh candle from a guttering stump. Janie was passing
another. Berni turned and began to reload the hearth. There
was little talk as light and warmth came back to the room. The
returning light showed Collie's head bowed over his harp. His
fair hair was plastered to his forehead and neck with sweat.

"Best bring the harper a mug, Janie," Vandien suggested softly.

"Whatever the teamster pleases," Janie replied meekly, and went swiftly to this chore.

Talk was resuming, eddying in small pools throughout the room. There were no rowdy stories as Vandien had overheard earlier. The voices were serious. Vandien noted that the speakers were the older folk in the group, with the younger generations listening most respectfully.

Collie wiped his damp hands down his trousers and took the cold mug Janie offered. The muted conversation began to fill the gap left by the silenced harp. Janie stood at Collie's shoulder, waiting to take his empty mug from him. Berni continued to sketch aimlessly on the floor at Vandien's feet. He thought how Berni had looked in the firelight as she sang. Her wavy brown locks cascaded down her back. Her alto had sung each word clearly, enunciating them so that Vandien had found himself trying to bring meaning from those crystal syllables. The song had moved her. Even now, the flush of it showed in her brown cheeks.

"What did they mean?" he asked quietly.

Berni started as if roused from a dream. Her eyes were a soft brown, lighter than his own. They gentled her competent face. Now they were puzzled. "What did who mean?"

"The words of the song. The Temple Bell Song. What did they mean?"

Berni was at a loss to explain. "It was the story, you know. We have it every year, but it doesn't always sound like that. I've never heard it sound like that before. It tells how it started, and all."

"I don't understand. How all what started?" Vandien slouched on the bench, resting an elbow on his knee. He smiled and said no more, knowing that silence would best prompt Berni.

"It tells how Temple Ebb Festival started. It's the song of how the village sank, and all." Berni hesitated. "I don't know if I can put it all into Common. I could give you the gist of the tale, I suppose." She took a deep breath, glancing about as if seeking a starting place. "Long ago, our village was a peaceful place, with a good deep harbor and a sturdy fleet. The Windsinger temple stood on a spit that ran out into the sea. And if they were not our favorite neighbors, neither did

we seek their wrath. Mostly we ignored one another, the village
and the temple. Their temple bell rang at the high and low tides
of the day. We lived in peace, if not friendship. Until the
Windsingers made the earth shake, and let the village slide
beneath the sea."

"How?" Vandien interjected softly.

Berni frowned. "The song doesn't say, not clearly. I can't . . . I
have no words to translate exactly what the song says. But the
Windsingers sang our village into the sea. It was their fault.
Their fault!" Berni's breath quickened. Vandien nodded, not
wishing to delay the rest of her story. But why? The question
tickled at the back of his mind. Why would the Windsingers
sing, not only the village, but their own temple into the sea?
And how? Their power was over the winds of the air, not the
bones of the earth.

"Most of the village folk were out fishing when it happened.
In the village were our old people, our babes, and those of us
sick or injured that day. Alone and defenseless they were, when
the earth trembled and the sea went dry. The folk out fishing
rode out the great series of waves that came crashing from
nowhere. We heard the wild tolling of the temple bell. We did
not know, until we came back, that our beautiful harbor and
our village were gone." Berni was as caught in the telling as
she had been in the singing. She was one with the "we" in the
tale, telling it as she saw it herself.

"The village was gone. The green hill above the village was
gone, riven and sunk. The floor of our harbor had heaved and
buckled, so that our large boats could not even come into
anchorage anymore. And everywhere, floating on the sea, were
bits of our lives. Limbs of trees and house timbers, with here
and there a body.

"One little girl they found clinging to a beam. A fishing
boat picked her out of the water. She was half-drowned, her
robes draggled about her. At first we thought she was one of
our own. She was only a little girl, probably stolen by the
Windsingers, stolen away from her own folk who loved her.
She wept, when she wasn't gagging up salt water. But finally
she told it, as a child would tell such a story. She and a group
of little ones like her had been down below when it happened.
Down in a great chamber under the temple, that we village
folk had never known was there. It was a schooling place, or

a worshipping place; something like that. When the little ones
felt the earth shake, and saw the water begin to squirt through
the walls, they tried to save the precious Windsinger things.
The little girl told how they had tried to carry up the heavy
chests, five and six little ones to a box, trying to lug them up
the stairs. She tried to help. But the whole temple was coming
down on them. A falling stone broke her arm. She could hear
the screams of those that were trapped and dying. The salt
water was rising around her, and she was scared. So she did
what any scared child would do. She tried to get away. She
couldn't say how, but she got out, and somehow when the
water swept her up, she managed to catch hold of a floating
beam with her good arm. There she was, and fisherfolk picked
her up, her little white gown all soaked and her arm bone
gleaming white where it poked out of her flesh. She looked so
like a Human child, with just a bit of scaling on her chin, and
most of her ears still there and showing through her cowl. But
her heart was already Windsingered. Though we dried her and
wrapped her warm, we could not stop her weeping. All she
could do was cry for the chest she had not saved. She sobbed
that she was no longer worthy of her cowl, a disgrace to all
Windsingers, and especially to her sisters who had died trying
to save the thing she had abandoned. We thought she had cried
herself to sleep. But when we touched her, she had wept herself
to death. At that very moment, the temple bell rang, speaking
in a drowned voice from beneath the sea."

Berni paused. Then her brown eyes came up to Vandien's.
The softness had burned out of them. "And that is how we
know that the Windsingers left things in the temple! Things
they thought worth dying for! We were told by the dying voice
of a little child once Human. We do not know what they left.
But we shall find it. And when we do, we shall use it. They
shall be made to grieve, those who brought our village down,
those who stole the lives of Human children with their own!"

Her eyes locked with Vandien's. Sympathy stirred within
him. He felt the fire of her vengeance kindle in his soul. But
Berni broke that newly forged bond. She reached behind her
to the hearth, to take up her mug and drink deep of it. When
she set the mug down, she smiled up at him sheepishly. "So
goes the song. It's a moving tale, one that always catches me
up in it. It was made by a minstrel who knew how to play folk

as well as his harp. How I love the old tales! I wish I knew more of them. But if you would like to hear more of them, you must ask someone older than I. Srolan, perhaps, or Correy."

"You tell a tale well," Vandien complimented her. Looking about the tavern was like waking from a dream. The almost religious intensity of the Temple Bell Song was only a fading influence. Now folk were in little knots at tables, lifting mugs and warming themselves for tomorrow's festival. No boat would leave shore tomorrow. There would be baking of holiday treats, and the holiday banners would flutter. Folk would dress in their newest winter finery, and while away the day in the village streets. The puppeteer had said that some jugglers planned to come from Bitters, and perhaps a fortune teller as well.

There was talk, too, of past teamsters. Some they recalled with laughter, for their pitiful efforts, or in delighted remembrance of their showmanship. Srolan, who had come down the stairs to move among them, deftly turned the talk back to earlier days and earlier teamsters. Vandien found himself listening intently. He heard of mired teams that drowned when the tide came in, and of a teamster whose ribs were caved in by the fury of the Windsinger's gale that flung him against the temple walls. There were many stories like that, but none gave him the specifics he sought.

In a quiet moment, he asked, "What exactly does the chest look like?"

"What chest?" a dark young man asked snidely, and several others snickered. But the stabbing looks of their fellow villagers silenced their skepticism, if it did not dispel it.

"No one knows," Berni dreamed aloud.

"No one's ever seen it," Helti filled in.

"That's not true." Janie's young voice was shyly defiant. "My mother's father held it in his hands."

"Then why didn't he bring it back to shore?" scoffed the same dark young man.

"Because he couldn't. Because it was too heavy, and Paul . . ." Janie's voice was losing its courage. Vandien could tell that she had been badgered about this story before.

"What about Paul?" the young man demanded.

"I won't say. You only make mock of me, and him."

"He lived as drunk as he died. There were lots of things he

couldn't explain," chimed in another voice derisively.

"Shut up!" rasped Berni, but Janie was on her feet, ready to square off with them.

"Did you know him then, Dirk?" she asked sweetly, eyes flashing. "How young you look, for a man of your years!"

"No more than did you, Janie!" Dirk snapped.

"No, but I knew my mother, and she told me as he told it to her."

"Yes, a lot of folks knew your mother."

Dirk's taunt seemed to have a private sting that was publicly known, for Janie whitened and then flushed to her hair line.

"Shut up!" Berni roared again, but the damage had been done. Janie left the room, not fleeing, but defeated all the same. Collie rose, to drape his harp silently. His motions said what his bound tongue could not; that he would not play music only to have it defiled afterward by this kind of talk. His leaving seemed to break the gathering. Others shifted, rising and dragging outer smocks down over their heads, bidding good night to friends.

"Damn Dirk and his flapping mouth!" Srolan spat, sitting down beside Vandien. "Everytime Janie is moved to speech, he finds a way to silence her. And for no reason I can discover, except his own ill nature."

"What was the rest of the story?" Vandien asked softly. Although the tavern was emptying out, it was still a less than private place to talk.

"No one knows. That's the bite of it. Janie had the story from her mother, who told it to no one else. Who's to say if there is any truth to it? Many's the time I've had Janie alone, and tried to get her to talk. But she's a tight-mouthed girl when the talk gets too close to her own. Janie will give you anything you want, except a glimpse of herself. When the talk gets too close to her family, she either clams her mouth, or says what the rest of the town says, and just as heartlessly: that her mother was a drunk, as her mother, and father, and grandfather were before her. And a drunk will tell any story to get another drink."

"But Janie's mother did not tell that story to anyone but Janie?"

"Exactly. And that's why I think there may be a bit of truth to it. What did that poor woman have to give her child, other than borrowed fame? 'Your grandfather was the last man known to have held the Windsinger's chest.' She gave her girl a tiny bit of family pride to cling to, and was at least woman enough to keep the story a private one, not one bandied about and laughed over. The story is as her grandfather first told it, pure and unaltered. Any fool in the village can tell you what his grammy said that Janie's grandfather said. But it's all fifth hand and two generations old. Any useful bit of information is twisted to rumor. Only Janie knows the story as her grandfather told it."

"Would she tell it to me, do you think, Srolan? She seemed anxious to please me earlier. . . ."

Srolan was shaking her head. "Try to speak to her now, and you'd find all her walls up. She was willing to bed you earlier; bedding takes no talk. She'd gladly give you what the village boys dare not ask for. They won't court her, for she seems ever angry to them, always sharp of tongue and derisive. And so she is, for she believes they won't court her because they despise her. She'd bed you, to show them that others want what the village boys turn their noses up at. Also that she'd rather bed a strange teamster than sleep with the likes of them."

"I don't understand." Vandien was confused.

"Neither does she, poor pet. So she goes about paying for her mother's reputation, and makes herself lonely in the process. But you won't get a word out of her tonight. You've refused her once. She won't offer again, and take the chance of your disdain. Nor will she ever admit, by word or sign, that she made you such an offer. She's so careful, she even fools herself."

"What am I to do?"

"What the teamster does every year. Go out, and waste more than half the tide looking for the chest in every wrong place. Go out there, with no idea what it looks like, or how large it is, or where it is. Splash around a lot." A gusty sigh drained her smaller on the bench beside him. "I'm an old woman, Vandien. Each Temple Ebb year I hope it will be the last, that this year the chest will be found. But it isn't. Likely it won't be this year, for all that you'll do your best. Go up to bed, man. Get some sleep, and be ready for tomorrow. The low tide will not be until tomorrow evening, so sleep in a bit. Good night."

She rose, and went away, walking old. Vandien looked

around to find the common room empty of customers. He was alone by the failing fire. Janie sullenly gathered mugs onto a tray at the other end of the room. Vandien rose and stretched and sent her a smile. She stared through him. He went to check his team, and then to bed.

Thirteen

REBEKE swivelled her head. Had she imagined a low hiss at the door? She let her eyes meet Medie's for an instant. They both waited. The hiss was repeated.

"Enter."

The pale azure robes swirled about her bare feet as the apprentice edged nervously into the room. She wet her pink lips, unmarked as yet by scales. Her eyes jumped from Medie to Rebeke nervously, as if uncertain who to address.

"Speak, child," Rebeke commanded testily. "What is the matter? Did I not set you to watching at the pools? What do you here? Has one relieved you at your post? I have given no such order."

"If it please your Windmistresses," lisped the girl. Beneath her cowl, her face was that of a young Human girl of perhaps thirteen years. Her voice quaked. "I and Lizanta, and Kirolee were watching at the pools. We held in our minds the shape of the aura you told us to watch for. We resolved to be alert, and to watch for it and no other. We knew we were to call at the first sign of it." The child paused, her trained voice thickening with panic.

"Speak on, little one," Medie's voice was kindly. "No ill will come to you, if you have done your duty as you knew it."

"I fear . . . I fear we have not done well, Windmistress. A glowing came to Kirolee's pool. She called that she had the expected intruder. But, before I could even speak, the glowing changed. Well do I know that such a thing cannot happen," she hastily went on, even as Rebeke angrily opened her lips, "but such it did, I swear. An aura changed. It was no longer what you had commanded us to watch for. And so I thought that Kirolee and I were mistaken, that perhaps some stray breath of ours had furled the pool and made the seeming change. So, as the singer of rank, I commanded that the watch go on, for this aura was not what we were seeking."

"That does nothing to explain why you are here, when you should still be watching the pools." Rebeke's cheeks glowed with embarrassment. That one of her apprentices should show herself so uncertain and unreliable in front of Medie! But Medie leaned forward as if the information the child was spilling forth were of the greatest import.

"What happened then?" she coaxed, ignoring Rebeke's rebuke.

"We went on monitoring the pools. I bade Kirolee to observe the strange aura, but not let it distract her from her duty. A time passed. Then Kirolee called out that the strange aura had changed, that it was once again that which we were watching for. This time both Lizanta and I were able to see in Kirolee's pool. She was right. But even as all three of us watched the aura changed again."

"An aura cannot change." Rebeke stated the fact coldly. "It may be altered, but it cannot flicker back and forth between forms as you describe." Even as she spoke, the little apprentice sank down onto her knees, her blue robes puddling out around her. Her eyes grew brighter with unspilled tears.

"I know that, Mistress." She choked the words out. "I know. But if only you could come look upon this strange aura and tell us what it means. I know I have failed in my watching. I am ashamed . . . and fearful." The last words went husky and faded.

"She is only a child, Rebeke," Medie whispered gently. "She seems possessed of wit and courage to report to you as she has done. The blame she takes upon herself. This is a Singer of promise. Let us not be too harsh with her."

Rebeke folded her lips tightly. The outlines of her scales shone out against her face. These apprentices were her responsibility, not Medie's. That Medie should dare to assume authority here, to tell her how to handle such a situation. . . . But Medie was smiling gently at Rebeke. She felt her anger ebbing away. They would work well together; they tempered one another. Rebeke returned Medie's smile, and rose from her stool.

"Wipe your tears, child, and return to your post. I shall join you shortly, to inspect this changing aura. Swiftly now!"

The apprentice vanished from the room in a swirl of robes. Rebeke clicked her tongue and turned grave eyes on Medie.

"They are taking them too young these days, and putting them into blue before they are even women grown. Do they think we shall become an army, to subdue the world by numbers alone? Greed. It is greed, Medie, that will be our downfall. It will bring the final uprising, unless such as we can check it. Well, I shall go and see to the child's pool. I shall make her punishment a mild one, as you suggest. But we must remember that a strong will is born only of strong restraints. Spirit as fine as hers can be spoiled by too light a hand as well as too firm. Keep watch for me; I shall return shortly, after I have laid their fears to rest. A changing aura. Too young, too young . . ."

Still shaking her high cowled head, Rebeke left the room. Medie remained perched on her stool, seeming to listen to some inaudible sound. Then, eyes full of wariness, she slipped from the stool and hurried over to the small enamelled casket on its black table. Her eyes devoured it as she weighed her decision. One more glance at the door. Her long dark fingers flickered over the colored stones in their settings. She was deft and sure in her touches.

But the casket remained closed. Medie stood for an instant, letting one finger tap thoughtfully upon the box. Then a thin smile stretched her scaled lips. More slowly, with deliberate pressure, her fingers probed the casket. She sighed. The lustrous black lid loosened and rose in her hands. She set it carefully aside. Wariness froze her.

She stared at the linen wrapping carelessly bunched over the casket's contents. It was not right. Someone had been here before her. Her eyes narrowed speculatively. Rebeke had not wanted her to open this casket. Was it because she had already opened it herself? How many veils, Medie wondered, must she lift before she beheld the true Rebeke? Beneath the many shells of deception and wariness, was there a Windsinger at all? Her guilt at opening the box vanished in the light of Rebeke's deception of her. Unhesitatingly, she twitched aside the linen wrapping. She stared down upon the wizard's folded hands joined to their block of white stone veined with red and black.

In cool curiosity, Medie touched them. They were cold, the long tapered fingers stiffly unyielding to her gentle pressure, but not with the stiffness of death. She tapped an envious finger on the black stone set in the simple ring. She longed for it, but longed with the knowledge that such things must be taken correctly, if they are to be taken at all.

"So she has you at last, Dresh. But not as she once would have wished it. I wonder if you ever supposed it would come to this. None of us did. I wonder if she will have the spirit to carry this thing through. She thinks she has the will. But there's a deal of space between the dream and the deed."

FOURTEEN

"I'VE never seen anyone row that way before," Vandien ventured.

Janie pulled her eyes back from the horizon and gave him a disdainful look. She made no reply. Vandien abandoned his attempt at conversation and contented himself with observing.

He sat on the fishy floorboards in the bottom of a double-ended dory. The brisk wind licked his face, making the scar tighten with the cold. It did not hurt—yet. He appreciated the heavy cloth of the smock and trousers and the extra material that held the warmth against his body. Janie had furnished the knit wool cap that snugged his curls to his head and covered his ears. Janie's blue-grey smock and trousers made her eyes show their true color. A cap of grey wool proved oddly flattering to her. Her high cheekbones were touched red by the wind. Her blond hair escaped from the cap to wave loose against her shoulders. She wore loose soft boots, shorter than his. Vandien remembered what Berni had said about boots last night. "No one hereabouts wears boots like yours. What if you fell into deep water in those? They'd fill with water and drag you down before you kicked them free. Loose enough to slip out of, and soled to grip the deck without scarring it; that's what you need hereabouts. Helti! Better look to boots for our teamster before tomorrow's tide!"

The dory rode like a seagull. It was clean, with not a string of dried gut or a scale to show its use. *Rainlady* was burned into her nameplank. Janie stood in the center of her, looking toward her goal. The long oars dipped and rose steadily. She pushed on the oars, lifted them clear of the water, drew them back to her chest, sank the oars into the water and pushed again. Vandien marvelled at it. He did not volunteer to take a turn at it. He was sure he could find other ways to make a fool of himself soon enough. And yet she made it look easy; the motion was all in one piece, without jerks or hesitations. He should have suspected those muscles in her shoulders, he realized, remembering the easy way she had handled the large buckets of water. Her mouth was set in a grave line. She would speak when she was ready.

Janie had awakened him in the dark, shaking him roughly by the shoulder so that there could be no mistaking her intention in coming to his room at such a time. He had stumbled about in the dark, for she had brought no candle and would not let him light one. "Meet me by the back door!" she had commanded him as soon as she was sure he was fully awake. She had left him to dress and puzzle in the dark.

The inn was silent as he came down the stairs. The only light in the common room came from the dying embers in the fireplace. He found the great door unlatched; it opened to his cautious push.

Janie waited by the back door. She shushed his questions, pushing the wool cap into his hands. Then she had led him away into the darkness, although the smell of dawn was on the air. "I wanted to catch this tide," was all she would say. "And I like to be up and about when the rest of the village sleeps still." He had followed her to where her dory was tied to a sagging little dock. "Sit flat on the deck!" she had commanded him in a hiss. "*Rainlady* rides high and light with such a small load. She'll be lively enough for me to handle without your leaning over the side." Vandien had sat, and been as silent as his companion.

Morning showed in the face of the water before it touched the sky. The oily darkness of the waves gave way to a silvery greyness, and then the sun was edging up over a watery horizon.

"Holiday. Whole village will be sleeping in after last night. We've the sea to ourselves, for a while." Janie told him that, and seemed to think it was all he needed to know.

Vandien was content to watch her manage the boat. He glanced back once to see how far they had come. Not as far as he had thought, and yet the distance seemed much greater than if he had been looking back over a road on solid land. The insubstantial terrain of the sea lent its strength to the distance. Vandien suddenly felt that shore was a tremendous distance away. The dancing dory seemed a temperamental thing to trust his life to; it was no more than a few lapped planks, bowed and fastened together. It rode the waves joyfully, rising to show them the world, and then sliding down to diminish their horizons. Vandien would have preferred a more sedate vessel. "Like riding on a gull," he told himself, and found the image of webbed feet propelling the boat more likely than the rigid oars rising and falling in unison.

The rhythm was broken. Janie stood still, letting the oars trail in the water. "This is where it starts to drop off. We're over the old village. It was built on the gentle slope at the foot of the hill. The temple was built out on the spit. Some say that at high tide, the sea surrounded the temple, and that at low you could walk to it across the sand spit. But that was all a long time ago. No one can say how it truly was. All that is certain is that when the village sank, the temple sank even deeper. At least one tide a month will bare part of the village, but only the lowest tide of the year reveals the top of the temple. Only one year in three has a tide low enough to make salvage possible."

Vandien was silent. Janie seemed to be waiting for him to say something. He didn't. If she was going to talk, he would let her. He sensed that she would welcome an excuse not to talk. No matter what he said, that angry face would darken and put all his words in the worst possible light. He would not ask her why she had brought him out here. He just met her grey eyes solemnly and waited.

But not even silence could placate her. Having decided to speak, the words boiled out of her, merciless and scalding. "You asked a question last night, teamster. It was never answered. Instead, you listened to the village scoff at me. When they were through, you didn't bother to seek for any other answers. What did they tell you after I left? That my mother was a drunk, like her parents before her? That she would say anything, *do* anything for a drink? Well, teamster, that's true. But two things she left to me: *Rainlady,* who belonged to my father before the sea took him, and a story. The story she never told for a drink. The only story she saved for me."

She paused. Her color was high, her cheeks bright with more than wind's kiss. To agree with her would be just as bad as to contradict her. So Vandien waited.

"My grandfather told it to her," she went on a bit more calmly. "He was a very old man, and some said he was wandering in his mind when he told it. Others said he would never be sober again. So they didn't bother to listen, except for my mother. That's why they all know of the tale, without knowing the details. I have never told it to anyone. Let them live in ignorance. I won't stand up and let them call me a fool over what I cannot prove. That was what I always said to myself. That is how I'd keep it until I die, except for . . ." Janie sighed. She suddenly broke the thread of her talk.

"There is one person in the village you can believe. Srolan. She's old and crazy, but not so crazy that she doesn't know the truth. I've never known her to break faith with anyone. She . . ." Janie suddenly looked at Vandien, really looked at him. In her eyes he saw sympathy and understanding beyond her years, the kind that is only taught by cruelty endured. "She told me why you came to do this thing. No one else knows, but Srolan and I. The village council knows of the money she offered. It doesn't worry them, for they don't expect to pay it. But Srolan told me why you truly came; to have the scar lifted from your face. She said that, if you are a man that can see she is sincere when she offers to do what most would deem impossible, if you can look at her and are wise enough to see that she would not offer what she cannot deliver, then you are a man that will hear my tale and know the truth of it. She did not ask me to tell it to her. She knew I would have been able to say no to that. All she said was, 'Try him yourself,' and left me to sleep on that."

Vandien looked at her quietly. The chill wind outlined the scar across his face; it was a stiffness he was always aware of in cold weather. The colder the wind, the more insistent the old wound became, beginning merely as a dull ache. In the coldest weather, in times of blowing snow, the scar pressed between his eyes and down the side of his nose with a pain that was nearly as sharp as a burn, but constant. If he spent any time in the cold, it pulled at his whole face. Ki knew of the pain, but did not suspect the extent of it. He no longer complained about it. He had not mentioned it since the evening he had lain in the wagon, giddy with agony, while she prepared a steaming compress for it. She had been careless as she leaned over him to arrange it on his face. He had looked up into green eyes full of guilt, mirroring his pain. He had been shamed, for he was not a man to manipulate others with emotions. The next day he had ridden through the snow all day, and never mentioned that his eyes were separated by a line of fire. Ki never heard or saw his pain again.

Even on fine days, he could not lose the shadow it cast over his face. Vandien was a man behind a scar, ever concealed, always distorted by his own face. Now this fair-faced child was looking at him as if she understood.

"Why do you stay in False Harbor?" he asked her suddenly.

She was startled, caught without words. Vandien wondered why he had given her the question. "Never mind," he said hastily. "Just tell me your story, if you will. I think we can understand one another well enough."

Apprehension showed on Janie's face as she pondered him. It made her grey eyes stern as her mouth went sullen. He thought she would row him back to shore. But her need to tell someone won out.

"Look over the bow," she commanded him. "Keep your body low in the boat; just lean your head over so you can look down. That's right. You may have to shade your eyes from the glare of the sun. Keep watching."

Vandien saw nothing but water. He shaded his eyes and peered, but the surface of the water baffled his eyes. He saw bits of seaweed floating by. Rising bubbles like seed pearls. Then his eyes caught the trick of it. Tiny black fish wriggled beneath the surface of the water. He leaned over more, both hands cupping the sides of his face and looked down. He could see bottom. Seaweed-covered foundations stared blankly up at him. Off to one side, a chimney still stood as tall as a man. The rest was tumbled into a rubble, the lines softened by the sea life clinging to it.

"See the houses? Hard to imagine folk living there, eating their supper around the tables, mending their nets by the door. Keep watching."

Janie took up her oars again. The boat glided up and down on the waves as Janie pushed it forward, and through all that motion his eyes tried to focus on the uneven bottom. He felt a moment of queasiness. He saw patches of sand rippled into ridges by the sea, and fine seaweed that trailed airily from sunken housewalls. Flounder stretched flat on seaweed-mossed hearths. Clouds of fingerlings hung suspended. Crabs imitated barnacle-crusted rocks that might have been other crabs. The sea floor began to drop away.

"We'll be over the temple soon. It's harder to see, because it's deeper. But I don't like to go above it on a low tide. Things happen to boats that do that. Fishing's no good there, anyway. The fish don't collect around the temple like they do the old houses. Can you see it yet?"

Vandien glanced back at her quickly. She nodded at the water impatiently. Her hands were busy on the oars, making the small paddling motions that kept them in position. Vandien looked down again. He strained his eyes. Just before the depth of the water made all blackness, he thought he saw the outline of a wall. That was all.

"Now this is what my mother said her father said. The tale is older than you might expect. She was born very late in his life, and he told it to her when he was a very old man. Because of who her father was, my mother did not take a mate until late in her years; I was born to them long after they believed her barren. They say my sister, who came after me, was the death of her. Women that old should not bear, for though they may survive it, their health is never the same. But, old as it is, here is my grandfather's tale." Janie cleared her throat. Her voice changed; now she recited. She began, "This happened a long time ago, Carly. I was a fine youth, then, a fine strapping youth, and the best fisher in the fleet. Back then, we cared about our village, and we still remembered how the Windsingers had sunk it. We wanted to right that wrong, and we wanted to do it on our own. None of this hiring foreign teamsters to come in and do our dirty work. None of this looking for a stranger folk to make our revenge on those who'd done us evil. None of this dragging outsiders into our quarrels. We were a proud folk, then. Proud. And I was a fine youth then, a fine strapping youth, and the best fisher in the fleet. Maybe I was the proudest of a proud lot. But back then, we didn't count that a bad thing. When Temple Ebb would come, all the younger folk would drop their fishing for a day. No matter how good the catches had been, no matter if crab were swarming up the beaches, we dropped it all and did our duty. We'd follow the tide out as it went, so as not to lose a minute of it. As soon as the water was less then neck deep in the temple, in we'd wade. And we'd begin to search. We weren't certain just what the Windsingers had lost there. But we were determined to have it.

"I'd been out to the temple at every Temple Ebb, since I was tall enough not to drown there. Others turned back, for the Windsingers did their best to stir up a drowning storm, even in that level of water. But not I. I was out in the temple, wading in that tumbled mess, searching for whatever that little Windsinger child had lost there. Others were content to wade about a bit, poke where they'd poked every year, and go back to shore. But not me. I lifted stones, I shifted water-logged timbers. Waves and tides move things about with a strength beyond men, and the quake that dropped the roof in and most of the walls could have buried anything. Only a fool would expect to find the Windsingers' chest sitting on the top of the rubble. And I was no fool.

"Most of the others had given it up that year, and gone back to shore. But I stayed, and I wasn't alone, for Paul stayed with me. The village no longer speaks of Paul, does it? Paul, who was their darling, as I am their dastard. He was my friend, when all the others used my name as a curse. No matter how often I was drunk, Paul was there, sober, to see me safely home. If my catch was poor, he shared his with me. Let any man speak ill of me, and Paul would speak out on my behalf. He was all a man should ever be, and my one true friend. None could help but love him, man and maid alike. No one doubted that he would do great things. No one was surprised that he stayed in the temple on the black night of that Temple Ebb.

"Water was up around our hips, but we didn't care. We went to work on some of the bigger blocks, ones a single man couldn't lift. Together we'd toppled them over and looked underneath. We were in the southwest corner of the temple. We had moved a number of stones, not being too careful where we put them. Just getting them out of our way, to see what was under them, and not finding much more than crabs and sand. In the very corner was one big brute of a stone. Even together, we couldn't budge it. But we were stubborn. Paul

waded back to shore, through that howling tempest the Windsinger was brewing. He went to the tavern and asked for help.
But no one would come. 'It's cold,' they whined. 'It's wet and
the tide will soon turn. Stay with us, Paul, and drink. Duce
will come in soon enough.' But Paul had honor. He wouldn't
stay to drink or warm himself. Back he came to me, with an
old broken oar. We stuck it under the stone, and he lifted, and
we heaved, and up she rose. Neither of us could take our hands
away from the oar, for the stone would've dropped again. So
I just sneaked a foot under there, and scooped out whatever I
could reach. Mostly sand, and then my foot caught on a thing
that dragged. Slowly it came out, and all the time we pressed
down on that oar. Little by little, I scraped it alone. Out it
came. We both stared. We knew that we had it.

"We'd found the Windsingers' chest. Ever so careful, we
eased that rock down. Paul just stood holding the oar, staring
down at it through the water. But I knew the tide was turning,
and we had no time to waste. I took my breath and stooped
down and got my hands on it. Cold! So cold it burned my
hands, but I was a fine youth, a fine strapping youth, and I
didn't let it go. Paul crouched beside me, and took his end.
Together we strained. I felt my knuckles cracking, and heard
the creaking of his shoulders. We brought it up, our lungs
nearly bursting with the effort. How little Windsinger children
had ever lifted it, I'll never know. It took all the strength in
both our bodies to raise it. Maybe its time under the sea had
soaked it full and swelled it heavy. But we had it. *We had it!*
I looked to Paul, and he was grinning like a skull. 'Let's get
it to shore,' he said, and I nodded. Then it happened. We heard
the bell toll. Know where that bell is, Carly? Know why no
one's ever seen it, but the whole village has heard tell of it?
Because it's down there in the Windsingers' cellar, that's why!
That cellar never caved in, it just filled up with water. That's
where the bell hangs, and the right tide can ring it. We heard
it bong, to shake the very earth under our feet. We knew the
tide was turning. Time to go, and fast. Paul took a step, and
I started to follow. Then he gave a yell and stopped still. He
jerks about, looking scared, and right away I can tell it's his
foot. We ease the chest down beside him. His foot was jammed
deep between some of the stones we had shifted. He couldn't
get out. Well, I can't hold that chest and pry him loose. I can't

carry the chest alone. And even if I could, it's too late. The tide had turned. Before I could be back for him, he'd be under. I was a proud man, Carly, and not one to let a friend down. I put the chest from my mind.

"I took the oar up and went to work. But most of those stones we'd moved, we'd moved together. I could see there were three I'd have to shift if we were to get him out. Paul could help me with it. 'Take the chest, Duce,' he told me. 'I can't carry it alone,' I told him. 'Besides, you're just trying to get out of your share of the work.' We both laughed, and he knew I wouldn't leave him to die. I moved one stone, though I left skin on that oar to do it. I started on the second one. I pushed on that oar, feeling the pains of trying too hard, things popping loose in my shoulders and back. But there's Paul and the chest at stake. It has to be! So, I close my eyes, see, and push with my death strength. And the second stone moved. Paul could see what it done to me. 'Don't Duce!' he tells me. 'Back to shore with you! Come back for the chest at the next low tide. You can get it then, now that you know where it is.' 'Not with your corpse in the way,' I told him. He knew I wouldn't leave him. We had a bit of pride, back then. I got the oar under the stone, though I can see that the pain of me shoving on that stone is nigh to killing Paul. He doesn't say, but I guess that his foot is being crushed. 'Don't faint!' I told him, and that makes him laugh the laugh that men use when they fear to cry. The tide is still coming in, getting deeper every minute, and the damned Windsinger still howling up the wind. The water was lapping around our chests, sucking the heat from our bodies and the strength from our legs. Only a little bit of the chest is still above water, but I knew where it was. I planned to get it later. I put my weight on the oar, and Paul screamed. A terrible scream. All the others have long gone back to the village. It was getting darker, the water is getting deeper, but they're all in the tavern, drinking deep, waiting to make jokes of us when we come in, the last fools, cold and wet. But I remember thinking, 'Can't they hear his scream? Can a man make a sound like that, and not be heard?' But no one heard but me. It took the heart out of me. Every time I put my weight to that oar, Paul screamed. Yet I knew I had to lift it that way, it's the only way there was. He'd turned grey, only fear of drowning kept him from fainting with

the pain. I promised him, 'Paul, this will be the last heave.
I'll either free you, or give you my knife.' He nodded and tried
to smile. The waves are rising.

"I took the oar in both my hands, and my soul cried out to
the villagers taken by the sea. 'Help me!' I beg of them, and
I pushed. The stone moved. Paul dropped down in the water,
but I caught him up. The tide was coming in faster, and all
this time the Windsinger on the hill is stirring the waves with
wind. I know I'll have to fight the wind, too, once I'm outside
the walls of the temple. Paul was heavy in my arms, and hardly
awake. 'The chest!' he said, and 'Friends first!' I told him. I
knew it was too late for the chest. I couldn't even see it anymore. The sea had taken it back.

"I got Paul back to shore, though we were both more drowned
than dry. Not a one of the damn villagers ever came to look
for us. We lay on the beach, too tired and hurt to drag ourselves
up to the houses. By morning, when they found us, Paul's leg
was swollen to the knee, and he was gone in a fever. He never
woke up to say my story was true. The others were too ashamed
to believe me. Easier on them to tell one another that my
drinking and carelessness had put an end to my best friend and
the likeliest man in the village. So they didn't have to admit
what cowardly weaklings they all were. If only one of them
had stayed, we would have had the chest that night, and Paul
too. But no one did, and Paul died and the sea took the chest.
I rowed out at low tide days later and looked down through
the water, but it was gone. The sea had hidden it again. Though
I searched the temple at every Temple Ebb until my youth gave
out, I never laid hands nor eyes on it again. But it's there,
Carly, and some day someone will bring it up. Some day it
will be proved that this old man wasn't a liar. Shame as it is
to bring in a teamster every year to do our duty for us, well,
perhaps it's better that an outsider do it rather than one of
these damn weakling cowards that lost us the chest and left
Paul to die.

"That's how he told it to my mother, and that's how she
told it to me."

The contrast in Janie's voice jerked Vandien back to the
present. During the telling, she seemed to speak with an old
man's quavering voice. He knew as well as he had ever known
anything that Janie had not made up this story. Neither had her

mother, he guessed, for the cadence of the words, the turning of the accent put him in mind of the old songs they had sung last night. Whoever had first spoken those words had said them just as naturally as he would sing one of those archaically phrased songs. The only question left was, had the old man lied? Vandien didn't think so.

"And that's why you stay in False Harbor." Vandien said it quietly, but Janie flushed. Her eyes raged as if he had accused her of child-stealing.

"I stay in False Harbor because it is my home. I stay here because I choose to. It's a life I know."

"And that's why you stay, no matter how badly they treat you. It has nothing to do with waiting for your grandfather's story to be proved true? There is not some part of you that cherishes his ancient anger, that wants the others to be proved faithless? You have no dreams of being vindicated, of having them come to you to apologize for their blindness and ill treatment of you? You have no visions of a moment of glory when you stand before them with the chest and cast off the stigma they have put upon you?"

Vandien had watched her face as he spoke. There was a poignancy in the way it shifted from sulky child to angered woman, and back again. She calmed her features and her voice was impassive as she observed, "There is more than one kind of scar, teamster. Shall you shame me because I would like mine lifted from my life?"

Vandien nibbled at the lower edges of his mustache. He wanted to choose words that she would hear, not ones that would drive her further into anger and stubbornness. "My scar is on my face, Janie. On my skin, and between me and the world as I meet it. But the scar you speak of is felt upon your life because it is in the hearts of the others. Do you think they will be glad to cast off their contempt for you, the granddaughter of a drunken liar, and take up instead contempt for themselves, the descendents of cowards and weaklings? Janie, I don't know fishing or boats. But I know Humans. If you think my finding that chest will justify your life and change how the village regards you, you're wrong."

Janie stood at her oars, staring past him at the horizon. Her mouth was set. Suddenly, one of her arms tightened, and pushed hard on the oar. With great driving sweeps she turned the dory back toward shore. Vandien slid back onto the deck in the bow of the dory. He looked up at her, studying her face unabashedly as she ignored him.

"I have my scar," Vandien mused aloud. "And you have yours. But what is Srolan's stake in this?"

A bitter smile twisted Janie's lips. "She says it's because she remembers the old ways. She should. She's been around long enough. Gossip is that if she can ever lay hands on that chest, there's a way she can become young again. Really young, not just her tricks and fancies."

"Cattiness ill becomes you, Janie."

"Her reasons ill become her. They are not worthy of her, for she is a better woman than that. Only in this is she a fool, to be tempted by the impossible."

"Aren't we all?"

She shot him a wicked glare. "You mind to your duties, teamster. I'll mind to mine."

Then, startlingly, the keel of the dory scraped sand under Vandien. Janie shipped her oars. She grudgingly let him help her drag the dory up onto the beach. "Best get a good meal," she advised him stonily before she left. "And a bit of rest. I'd follow the tide out, if I were you."

"How old is Srolan, Janie?"

With a snort of disgust, Janie turned and strode off.

Fifteen

"Ki!" Dresh hissed.

"What is it?" she mumbled. How long had it been since she last slept? She hovered on the edge of sleep, seeing only because Dresh kept his eyes open and fed her the images; her own eyes had sagged shut long ago.

"Wake up, fool!"

"What is it?" she repeated. She picked up the head and put it on her lap again. Tension emanated from him, Ki felt a trembling in her fingertips that was not her own nervousness.

"My hands. I feel a coolness on them, a touch of power. Someone has opened my box."

She shifted Dresh's head against her arm. The weight of it pulled at her weary shoulder muscles. Their eyes were fixed on the wall, but Dresh saw more than Ki did.

"It's the end of the game, isn't it?" Ki whispered.

"Not quite. We're too close to give up now. Only one of them watches over me; of that I am sure. We must act now."

"What are we going to do?" Ki got to her feet, Dresh riding heavily on her arm.

"I don't know. We shall have to act as our impulses dictate. Out the door and into the hall, Ki."

She eased open the door of the Windsinger's cell and poked her head cautiously out. Then she drew it in with a sigh, and projected Dresh's head into the hall instead. She took in an empty vista. Awkwardly she rotated the head on its block to scan the other direction. Safe as well. She clutched the head to her body again and hurried out and down the hall.

They had gone no more than a hand of paces when Ki heard the rustle of robes and the patter and slap of bare feet.

"Someone approaches!" Dresh hissed.

Her shoulder jarred against a door that shockingly offered no resistance, and she found herself clutching the wizard's head as she skidded and fought for balance. The closing door clipped her hip as it swung shut silently behind her. Her thrust had carried her into the center of a room. The sole occupant, her dark eyes wide in shock, shot to her feet, a small ovoid of blue stone clutched between her pale hands.

As Ki regained her footing, the Windsinger crouched to set the ovoid carefully on the floor behind her. Then she rose to full height, her cowled and knobby skull towering over Ki. Ki did not wait for Dresh to react. She dropped his head and flung herself at the white-robed figure.

Ki's tanned hands closed on the scaled wrists, but to Ki's eyes, deprived now of Dresh's sight, she wrestled with a pale tower. From the tower's peak shot a fall of blazing fire. The shimmering walls of the room spun around her, but she did not loosen her grip. A Windsinger seized was as a snake pinned: more deadly to free than to hold. They struggled in silence. Red sparks darted from two dark holes in the tower, stinging against Ki's face.

Hands that can hold a plunging team in check; shoulders that have spent a lifetime loading freight and bundles; these do not tire easily, especially while enmeshed in the web of fear. Ignoring the sparks tingling against her cheeks, Ki jerked forward and sharply down. The tower collapsed, to less than Ki's height, and Ki flung herself upon it. They crashed together to the heaving floor. The struggle was suddenly over.

Ki froze. The pale tower was a warm and lumpy mass beneath her elbows and knees. She did not release her grip on the wrists. Even the lack of sparks from the now pinkish eye places did not reassure her.

"Dresh!" Ki called hoarsely. Only now did she think of the abrupt way she had dropped him. She cast anxious eyes about the chamber. The wavering translucent walls mocked her. Would the block of stone that the head was rooted to shatter under such an impact? If the back of his head struck first, would he be unconscious, perhaps worse? She could find no trace of him.

Systematically, she began at what she guessed had been the door; a more pronounced ripple in the surface of the quavering walls. She lowered her eyes and fought the vertigo that assailed her, sweeping her eyes in slow passes over the palpitating floor. Even when she finally spotted the cube of darkness and its ever lingering spark, she found it strangely difficult to keep his location fixed in her mind.

He was, she guessed, a hand of paces away. It was so difficult to tell. She gazed at him hopelessly and fought down a wave of panic. She could not reach Dresh unless she released her prisoner. But she would not know until she reached Dresh if it were safe to release the Windsinger. The body beneath her was still and limp and as terrifying as ever.

"Dresh!" Ki ventured again. Was that a muttered reply? Gradually she eased her weight off the body beneath hers. One of her hands strained to encompass two of what Ki fervently hoped were wrists. Feeling both foolish and frightened, she began to extend her body in the direction of Dresh's cube. She tried not to imagine what her disadvantage would be if her captive began to stir while she herself was stretched full length upon the nauseatingly shimmering floor.

But even the full length of her body did not reach Dresh. She could not decide how far away he really was. She gave a tug at the Windsinger, sliding her across the floor. She reached again, but found no Dresh. Four times she tugged her unconscious captive along, before a questing fingertip brushed against Dresh's head. His world snapped into place around her.

"You look ridiculous," Dresh pointed out. Ki stared at herself ruefully. A tiny trickle of blood was making its way down from the left corner of her mouth. From this disconcerting angle of perception, she deduced that Dresh's head was resting on its side.

"I trust you are not harmed?" she inquired apologetically.

"Less than one might expect, given the circumstances. Ki, let go of her. Can't you see she's unconscious?"

"No, I can't. One can never trust a Windsinger," she replied, her voice going hard. But she released her grip. To her chagrin, she saw that her victim would scarce have reached her shoulder, were it not for the loathsome cowl. Dresh read her thoughts.

"What you saw with your own eyes was, in this case, more accurate. She glows with a more powerful aura than I would expect of one of her rank. Even more strange is the restraint I read upon her. As if she were at all times pretending to be less than she is. It is a phenomenon I have never before encountered in a Windsinger. Yes, as you say, one can never trust them. Do they send you the rains out of love and mercy, or only so they may tax you the more?"

"Save your mind-wrestling for the tavern crowd, Dresh. Let us be more practical now. What are we to do with her? When she awakes, she will surely rouse the whole hive of Windsingers."

Dresh clicked his tongue. "The answer is clear, Ki. She shall not awake. We shall slip her out through the walls."

Ki had crawled the rest of the way to Dresh. She watched herself loom larger as she came nearer to the wizard. Now, in her odd half-blinded way, she watched her hands grope for his head. It was the one thing his eyes could not focus on for her. Gently she felt out the shape of his head. She used both hands to put the head and block of stone upright. Transferring him to her lap, she brushed the hair from his forehead. She ran light fingers over his face, trying to tell by touch if he had been injured in the fall. She fingered the beginnings of a lump just back of his hairline.

"Stop that! I was stunned, but only for a moment. If I needed your ministrations, I would tell you so. We may not dally now. We must dispose of this Windsinger before she awakes."

"You must, perhaps. Not I. I cannot do such a thing; not in so cold-blooded a fashion, anyway. Were we still struggling in the heat of terror, I could kill her. But to push her out into that emptiness we jumped . . ." Ki shrugged, then shook her head. "I cannot."

"This is foolishness! We would not kill her. We would only . . . 'pause' her life. Eventually she might be found to resume it. Consider her as a viper found nesting among the blankets on your bed."

"Then I should lift it up, blankets and all, to shake it out in the woods."

"Fool that you are, I believe you would. And it would bite you another day for your mercy. Come, then, let us bind her, if that is the best you can do."

But as Ki lifted Dresh and rose, the Windsinger on the floor stirred. Ki's vision of her narrowed as Dresh squinted at the revealed face in surprise.

"I have seen this Windsinger before," he mumbled, half to himself. "But she was not robed as an apprentice then. Ki! Help me find the blue egg she was holding when we came in."

Nervously Ki rotated her body so that Dresh could scan the floor of the chamber. Could not he see that the Windsinger was struggling to rise? Her own impulse was to fell her again, or at least to flee.

Ki pounced, but not on the Windsinger. Once more Dresh had pre-empted her physical command of her body. She had caught up the blue thing in her hand before she was aware of seeing it. From Dresh's mouth came a hoarse caw of triumph.

"No meditation orb this! I thought the blue too deep a shade! Now, little bird, what does a white-robed apprentice have to do with a speaking egg? What information could you possess so vital that a Windmistress would trust you with one of these pretties?"

Ki held the egg up for the captive's inspection. It was about the size of an apple, but smoothly egg-shaped. It shone transparent blue, but for a single white spark frozen in its center. It reminded her of nothing so much as Dresh's head as she saw it on this plane. The texture of it made her uneasy. It was heavy for its size. Despite its crystal shine, it felt leathery in her hand, rough and raspy against her skin.

Dresh's eyes snapped away from the egg, to clash with the dark ones of the Windsinger on the floor. She was sitting up now, one hand gingerly smoothing the white cowl over her high brow. She lowered her hand shakily, opened her lips as if to speak, and then firmly shut her mouth. Anger flashed in her eyes.

"Come. I've seen you before. You were in the company of Shiela, of the High Council, and your robes were as blue as morning sea. What is your name, little breezemaker?"

The woman on the floor glared at Dresh. Then, like the moon breaking free of cloud cover, she dropped the anger from her face. When she spoke, her voice was a low musical alto. It held no emotion.

"Do you think, Dresh, that I would be so foolish as to gift you with the power of my name?"

"Um. She wants to spar, doesn't she, Ki? I do not think we shall learn anything from her that we have not already guessed. Such as, that Rebeke has no idea of your true rank among Windsingers. That explains the cloak of restraint you hide behind. And consider her silence, Ki. Not a sound from her when we burst in, nor during your amusing little wrestling match. I think she would rather face strangers alone than have anyone come upon her with the egg in her hands. What we have here, Ki, is a scorpion in the adder's nest; a spy among her own kind."

The Windsinger's expression did not change. She resmoothed her cowl again and tugged the sleeves of her robe to even them. She did not smile as her eyes came up to meet theirs.

Dresh's eyes clinched with hers. "You might get away with killing Ki. But it would take some explaining, to both your mistresses, if my aura abruptly winked out. Nor do I think Rebeke would be the one you would fear most. Whoever awaits your word through the egg would be the more awesome in her wrath. So put aside the poisoned needle you just drew from your sleeve. It cannot help you."

The Windsinger's dark eyes were catlike in their unwinking stare. The needle made a sweet ringing against the floor. Slowly the Windsinger rose.

Ki felt her courage ebbing out through the pit of her stomach. Her mind tried to add up the levels of danger facing her. First the Windsingers, whose realm they were in; secondly from this spy among the Windsingers; thirdly from whomever this creature spied for. And even if she could safely avoid them all and reclaim Dresh's part, even if she could safely regain her own world and pick up her life strings, was not Dresh himself a danger to reckon with?

"Steady, Ki," muttered Dresh, as if sensing her forebodings. "We have been gifted with a weapon deadlier than any rapier hand has ever held. For the time being, at least, I think that our interests are in line with this traitor's."

"You are proposing an alliance?" The Windsinger stated it coldly. Her fine dark brows arched up to her cowl.

"I am. You aid me in locating and regaining my boxes. In return, I shall not betray you to Rebeke."

"My gain is too small."

"As you please. We know that I cannot remain undetected on this plane for long. Surely Rebeke has posted watchers for my aura. They will pick me out, they will come searching. They will find me here, with you, in your room. They will find the egg of speaking. It will be my end, and Ki's. But our final request shall be to hear you explain your way out of it. You are a spy to Rebeke, and an embarrassment to . . . the High Council, perhaps?"

"My patron is a powerful one. Rebeke will not dare to harm me, no matter what my transgressions."

Ki felt Dresh shake his head, and heard the clicking of his tongue. "You have not been here long, if you know no more of Rebeke's temper than that. She will rend you first, and then wonder if it was politic. Even when Rebeke was a Human, her temper was savage. Windsinging, I imagine, will have refined its edge."

Was it uneasiness or mere restlessness that caused the woman to shift her feet? Ki wondered. Dresh was quiet, letting the silence grow huge in the room. Ki resisted the impulse to fidget. A memory floated to the surface of her mind. Ki snared it. Thus had she used to stand, in bored and useless anxiety, while her father haggled over horses. Her interest in the matter was vital, her power in the exchange null.

"When you interrupted me at the speaking egg, I . . ."

"Come, come, let us stop the falsehoods before they begin. Had you even begun to speak through that egg, it would have been hot enough to blister Ki's untrained hands. You have spoken to no one as yet."

The Windsinger bit her lower lip. The hidden anger flashed out once from the dark eyes, and was gone again. "You offer me nothing, wizard. If Rebeke knew I spied on her, she might kill me. But if I help you to regain your body and escape, will not both Rebeke and my patron take a vengeance on me?"

Ki knit her brows over her closed eyes, but Dresh's voice was smooth as honey. "Of course they would, if they knew it was your doing. But it seems to me that if you have played a two-faced game this far, it would not overly tax you to make it three-faced. Put your mind to it, breezemaker. I shall make it simple for you. All I ask is that you escort me safely to the place where my body is held, and draw off any guards. I shall handle my own escape from there."

"Certainly," the Windsinger replied sarcastically. "And shall I pack a moon for you to take along?"

Dresh smiled hard. "Don't bother." He lifted Ki's hand with the speaking egg in it. "I shall be content with this."

The woman stood still, listening perhaps. Her dark eyes were veiled with her own darker thoughts. Ki shifted her weight, juggling the head and egg into a more comfortable counterbalance.

"My time is short," Dresh warned her. "Debate on this too long, and others will decide for you. You must agree, or be discovered."

"Do you think I don't realize that, head?" the Windsinger asked coldly. A slender hand strayed up to touch her mouth. "Wait here for me, then." And she was gone, moving swiftly and silently.

"She will bring them all down on us," Ki muttered.

"Not while we hold the egg. She will do anything in the hopes of regaining it unharmed. But it all rides on our little traitor now. If she is creative enough in her deceits, we may yet win back my body."

"And if she is not?" Ki's voice was flat.

"Then hold that egg ready for throwing, my dear. We shall open a doorway that lets in the otherness as we wink out. We shall not die cheaply."

"A grand comfort, that," Ki replied sourly. She shifted egg and head again. The egg weighed heavily at the end of her arm. Her shoulders and back ached. The strain of seeing through Dresh's eyes fuzzed her mind. Her reasons for accompanying him on this ridiculous quest had paled to idealistic idiocy in her own mind. Pride and honor seemed but foolish trinkets compared to the living of life to its end. She found herself wondering if Dresh had not somehow bent her mind into going along with it. That kiss . . . if that was not proof of how he could twist her will, what was? And to so demean her independent will must be an indication of his small regard for her. She was a tool for him, a mindless gadget to be used at his whim. And what real grudges did she have against Windsingers? A few unvoiced forebodings in the back of her mind, her father's vague accusatory hints, Vandien's foolishness, Dresh's own long-winded harangues. In fact . . .

"Ki, if you let the egg seduce you now, we are both lost."

Ki jarred back to wakefulness. Dream cobwebs snapped in her mind. Pyramids of reasoning collapsed under the weight of their own conclusions. She brought the egg up to Dresh's eye level, but he flicked their gaze away from it.

"It is dangerous enough that you hold it in your bare hand, with its hide against your skin. It would be folly to gaze untrained into its depth. Its loyalty is to the Windsingers that feed it. Listen to it, and it will bid you to dash out your brains against the walls, to cut your own throat, and you will obey. Concentrate on our task."

She shook her head. She felt spidery hands tugging at her mind's skirts for attention, but she joined her thoughts to Dresh's vision and stared at the chamber door.

"She comes," whispered Dresh.

Ki held her breath, listening. She heard nothing. But the door swung open, and their Windsinger peered in.

"Come swiftly now. I have lured them all from their watching, sent the last watcher to follow Rebeke, telling her that she was summoned. The body is yours for the taking. But you must come swiftly, for this ruse will not keep them away long. Come!"

Ki shrugged her load up and followed. She moved out into the passageway behind the Windsinger. Cautiously she pointed Dresh's head first in one direction and then the other, to be sure all was clear. Then she followed. Her lips tightened in a smile as she realized she was using Dresh's head as a torch. It was his turn to be the tool.

It swiftly became apparent that what she had regarded as a corridor was part of a labyrinth. When the Windsinger turned left through a door, Ki shadowed her, but instead of the expected chamber, she found herself in another passageway identical to the first one. They wound their way through a universe of stark walls and plain doors. Ki tangled her mind trying to remember how many doors they had passed each time before turning, and the directions of each turn. After a hand of turns, she gave up the notion. She snorted softly as she decided that even if she had been able to retrace their route, it could only lead them back to the dubious sanctuary of the Windsinger's chamber.

So it was that Ki was totally unprepared when her guide stepped through one more door, and stopped. Ki trod upon the hem of the Windsinger's gown before she realized they had arrived. Swiftly mumbling an apology, she stepped back and swept Dresh's gaze over the room.

There was little to see. Ki ignored the sky windows. There were the two empty stools for the watchers. There was the small black table with Dresh's bared hands resting upon it. Ki's heart squeezed at this eerie sight; it was as chilling as her first glimpse of the bodiless head that she now carried so casually. Yet this time it was not just the magic that appalled her, it was the evidence of the superior skills of the Windsingers to undo it. The lid of the hand casket had been left on the floor. Beside the other stool was the square enamel box that contained Dresh's body. Another sweep of Dresh's eyes flashed over the sky windows, and the lush hides scattered on the floor. The high ceiling receded into shadows. A sourceless light gave an appearance of afternoon to the chamber. It did not come from the sky windows; some of them were in full night now, while in others the rising sun stained the skies. Ki wasted no time on what she now knew were illusions. She swung Dresh in a swift scan of the room, seeking other exits.

"Confound it, girl!" the wizard growled. "Whirl me about once more, and I shall be as sick to my stomach as a head without one can be. My eyes *do* move independently of my skull. Besides, we have no time for gawking. This procedure takes some little time, even under the best circumstances. We cannot make even one mistake now, for I doubt if even our little friend's fertile imagination can invent lies enough to keep Rebeke away for long."

"At least your hands are already opened for you," Ki pointed out.

"I shall have to remember to thank the Windsingers for that small saving of time. Take me over by the casket. I shall require your hands again."

"What about her?" Ki asked, jogging Dresh's head in the Windsinger's direction.

"What of her? Do you propose to stand a watch over her to prevent her escape while I work this magic? Be logical, Ki. Should she begin to scream and run, what could we do? Shall you chase her down the hall, my head ajounce upon your arm, to fling me rudely to the floor when you catch her? No, all we have to bind her with is her own deceitfulness. And a small blue egg. Come. To work now."

But when she stood beside the coffin, a second problem arose. With Dresh on her left arm and the egg in her right hand, she had no hands left for stone pressing. After a moment's juggling, she settled Dresh's head with the egg tucked under his chin in the crook of her elbow. She took a deep breath. With a shiver of trepidation, she set her free hand on top of the casket.

Just as it had by her campfire, her arm took on a life of its own. Through Dresh's eyes, Ki watched her hand dance over the colored stones on the lid. A center crack appeared. Gently her hand eased back the two sides of the lid to reveal Dresh's body. He was huddled within the box, neatly tucked into the cube. Neck and wrists were neatly stoppered with black cubes of red-veined stone. Ki returned the egg to her right hand and hiked Dresh's head higher for a better look.

"Now what?" she whispered to Dresh.

"Now the work begins," Dresh growled in reply. "Step back, Ki, and give me some room."

She stood back from the coffin. An eerie foreknowledge afflicted her. She was not surprised, but strangely revolted when a forearm that ended in a block of stone groped its way over the side of the box. Next, a brown-clad shoulder pushed itself into view. With a sudden heave, the chest and block head swayed upright.

"Deucedly hard to balance a body with no head on it," Dresh grumbled to himself.

The body braced a block hand on the edge of its crate and awkwardly clambered to its feet. An unnaturally high step, like a marionette in an amateur's hands, and the body placed one of its feet on the floor. The other foot followed, and the headless, handless body swayed on its feet. Ki and the head looked it over. Dresh's claims were true, Ki found herself admitting; he was not a badly made man. An acorn-brown tunic covered his torso to his hips; the bare arms that moved and flexed now were evenly muscled. Hose of a darker brown sheathed his muscular legs. His feet were shod in light buskins. Not ill made at all. But at each wrist and on the stump of the neck was a block of the familiar red-veined stone. With a queasy feeling, she noted that the chest rose and fell very slightly; she had no doubt that within that chest a heart lightly fluttered. Slowly the body extended a stone-ended right arm in Ki's direction.

"Body, Ki. Ki, I'd like you to meet my body. Touch hands,

or whatever!" Dresh barked out a macabre laugh. Ki shuddered and took an involuntary backward step.

"Enough levity!" Dresh thundered suddenly, as if she had been the one to begin it. "We have no time for it. We have the pieces, Ki. Now we have to put the puzzle back together, and then return to your world. We shall need a piece of brown chalk. I think you will find some in my purse, at my waist. Place my hands at my feet. Then draw a circle around my body equal to my normal height. And, Lord of Fishes, hurry!"

She suppressed a shudder as she gently frisked Dresh's body for the chalk. Once more she had to jumble egg and head together as she moved the hands over to Dresh's feet. When one of the hands on the block stirred and gave her a pat on the wrist, she did not find it reassuring.

"Put the egg in my hand. I suppose I can trust myself with it," Dresh remarked gaily.

Ki was beginning to wonder if he was mad. But his fey mood was infectious. Head tucked securely against her, she crawled in a backwards circle around the body, sketching in the circle with the soft chalk on the polished floor.

"And now?" she asked as the two ends of the circle nearly met.

"And now set the head upon the floor and back away from it, mortal!"

Dresh's eyes flickered to the doorway. A tall Windsinger robed in deepest blue was poised there. Her brown eyes had the wide white rims of the full Singer. Their mocking stare froze Ki's blood. She remained crouched on the floor, chalk poised in her hand to finish the circle. Dresh's head was clutched to her breast.

"Do as I say, mortal!"

The Windsinger's voice brooked no denial. Ki moved to place Dresh's head upon the floor. But she did not move. The hands she willed to lower the head remained clutching it. The legs she willed to back away from Dresh remained crouched. In her hands she felt the muscles of Dresh's head harden in a grin.

"Medie! I had scarcely expected to encounter you here! Something more than my sundered body has drawn you here, I'll wager. Now, now, cast not your eyes so menacingly upon Ki. Would you slay the cow because the farmer displeased you?"

"Not a farmer's cow, Dresh. But I would slay the battle horse that carries the warrior. So!"

Medie raised her hand. Something flashed in her fingertips. Ki squinted her eyes more tightly shut, but Dresh's went on seeing for her. She flinched in anticipation.

It seemed to Ki that Medie grew taller as she stood, her threatening hand raised for an eternity. Her brown and white eyes were wide and staring. Her scaly lips moved silently. The raised hand wavered. Like a great tree falling, Medie swayed forward. She struck the floor face first, making no effort to catch herself. Whatever had flashed at her fingertips ran sparkling about the floor for an instant, and then dispersed. Medie lay still, soundless.

Ki breathed again. "What did you do to her?" she whispered in awe.

"I? I did nothing," Dresh said softly. "Medie lies dead, Ki, not merely struck senseless. That is not my way."

"No. It is my way." Stepping through the doorway, their traitor-ally stooped over Medie's body. Ki felt her gorge rise as the younger Windsinger drew from the concealing folds of Medie's robe a long narrow blade. With a dainty wiping motion, she fastidiously cleaned the blood from the blade with her fingertips, and dried them upon Medie's robe. She smiled as she looked up and her eyes met the wizard's.

"Now you may set the head down with the other parts and back away," she coolly informed Ki.

"Think well on what you do, breezemaker. Medie may be dead, but that will not free you from Rebeke's vengeance. In fact, it will cause her hands to fall on you more swiftly. It was the act of a fool!"

The Windsinger raised her thin eyebrows in mock innocence. "On the contrary, wizard, Rebeke will be indebted to me. Have I not slain the traitorous Medie, an obvious informant to the High Council, here only to trap Rebeke with her own words? In your own hands you grasp the egg that is the proof of my words. Did not Medie gather here the parts of the wizard, Dresh, that she might claim his power for herself and the Council? No, wizard, I think my act has earned me the gratitude of Rebeke, not her vengeance. Put the head at the feet of the body, girl!"

There was whiplash in the sudden command. The wizard's mind held Ki's body motionless. Ki remained crouching at the gap in the chalk circle, the head grasped close to her.

"Think you truly that Rebeke is to be fooled so easily, breezebringer? Then you do not know her. As a mortal woman, she was clear of sight, more clever than any vixen that ever led dogs away from her kits. She could tell a man's mind before he spoke it, know what a child would do before the child did it. Your own training should tell you that her Windsinging days will only have enhanced those abilities. Will you pit your petty guiles against such a one?"

"Silence, head!" snarled the Windsinger. "Let the teamster obey me, or let her die as she grasps your empty skull. I care not. You both shall go soon, anyway."

Dresh's eyes gripped the traitor's. But Ki was aware of her hand, unwatched by herself or Dresh and unnoticed by the Windsinger, as it moved the chalk swiftly and secretly. Even as the Windsinger finished speaking, Dresh's will jerked Ki within the completed circle. A darting glance of Dresh's eyes showed Ki a tiny rune chalked upon the floor at her feet. The silence settled slowly in the chamber like dust settling after a heavy cart on a summer trail.

"Do you expect me to be impressed with this? Why not juggle three eggs, or make a handful of colored glass beads appear? I should be just as awed, little wizard. How long do you think an earthrune will hold, chalked on the floor of a Windsinger's chamber?"

"Long enough." Dresh was grim. Ki held herself still and small. She was, she reflected, a puppet, a body to jerk about when the right strings were pulled. These two would not even hear her words, should she speak. They played for stakes she could not afford; her life was less than a copper shard on their gaming table. Ki ground her teeth silently, cursing all magic, whether of earth, sky, or water. She longed with sudden pain for the feel of Sigurd's coarse mane, for the homey smells of her cuddy and camp, even for Vandien's acid wit. Dispassionately she thought of the rapier, sheathed and useless in another world. As useless as it would be here. I can but die, she thought to herself, and took an odd comfort from the thought.

The young Windsinger drew from her robes a small cube of blue chalk. Outside the circle, opposite Dresh's rune, she crouched, swirling markings upon the floor. But Dresh's eyes did not linger upon her. He drew Ki's body across to his own, took into her hand once more the blue egg.

"Shall we try to reassemble you now?" Ki ventured. Dresh seemed to have forgotten about her mind, using her body as freely as his own.

"Hopeless." Dresh stated it factually. "Under these stresses, the correct convergences could never be formed. I would be certain to die under the operation. Almost as certainly we shall both die now. Unless. Unless." He turned his vision back to the doorway. Medie lay as she had fallen. A small area on the back of her blue robes was stained a darker color. The hidden contents of the tall cowl were limp on the floor. Ki shuddered. Death would never fail to awe her, no matter how often she saw it. A coldness swept up from Ki's stomach.

Dresh's eyes flicked back to their enemy. She made a final flourish and looked up at him, triumph leering from her dark eyes. A cold voice cut the air of the chamber.

"Guests, Grielea? Have you chosen to entertain them without consulting me?"

Like a curtain falling, a veil of innocence cloaked the triumph in Grielea's eyes. All eyes in the room, even Ki's closed ones, turned in the direction of the voice. Rebeke had entered silently. She rose now from where she had bent over Medie's body. For a moment she contemplated the scarlet stains on the tips of her long fingers. She rubbed the tips of her fingers together, and then extended them in Grielea's direction. The gesture had the eloquence of a thousand questions. Grielea broke before that moment. She strove to answer them all at once.

"She was a traitor to thee, Windmistress. See, I did find her with the wizard's parts, and the speaking egg. I heard her as she began the summoning words that would call the Council. I . . . I guessed at her betrayal. In my anger that she could do so to one I loved, I slew her. I beg your forgiveness."

Tears dribbled from Grielea's black eyes. Slowly she dropped her head, and her tall cowl bobbed to obscure her eyes. Rebeke stood silent. But Ki was shocked beyond measure at the look in her eyes. Dresh met her gaze unwaveringly. Ki eavesdropped at the language of their silence, but could not believe the message that passed between them. Never before had Ki seen sorrow in a Windsinger's eyes. Dresh began to speak, his voice low, conversational.

"One might ask her, Rebeke, why she wears the white robes of the apprentice if she knows the words that activate a speaking egg. One might even wonder where a mere child such as she got the knowledge to form such a sky rune as is drawn at her feet. Or even why she carries the blue chalk cube of the Wind Runester. One might ask those things, Rebeke."

Rebeke sighed gently. "Why would I waste time with questions when the answers are before me? Would *you* pretend, Dresh, that betrayal is a new experience for me?

"Rise, false one. Look on the Windmistress you have slain, and reflect what thy portion shall be."

Grielea rose nonchalantly. Her narrow hands rose to smooth the forehead band of her cowl. Her small mouth smiled coldly at Rebeke. "You dare not slay me, Rebeke. I am high in the favor of the Council."

Rebeke laughed. It was a short laugh and she choked on it. Her eyes fell to Medie. They shone brightly when once more they rose to meet Grielea's. "The Council's favor? Tell me instead of the sun's coolness. A favor indeed they have granted you, to send you here on a fool's errand. A knife such as you cuts two ways, Grielea. It has no handle. It is never safe, especially to the hand that holds it. Did you think they would allow you to live, after they had taught you and used you? They do not expect to have to dispose of you. They know I will do that, and, in that act, seal my own fate. But I shall not play into their hands that way. I have my own methods for dealing with such as you."

Ki saw Grielea's eyes go wide. Her glance ricocheted from Rebeke to Dresh, and back again.

Rebeke sighed. "Grielea. Look here."

Rebeke's narrow fingers cut a sign in the air. For a minute the flowing blue rune seemed to hang there, visible to Ki through Dresh's eyes. Grielea stared at it. And continued to stare, even after it had faded from Ki's sight.

"That will keep her occupied while I look to you. It was clever of you, merging your aura with the teamster's. Who would ever have suspected her of having one? The puzzle of it kept me long at the pool. Long enough for Medie to die, Dresh." A sudden huskiness muted her trained voice. "Dresh, Dresh." She coughed. Her proud shoulders drooped. "Why have you put this upon me?"

"I put this upon you? You made the choice for both of us, Rebeke! Did I drape you in robes of blue, cowl you with the high cowl of the Windsingers, poison your body with their essence to scale your face? Did I make you both more and less than Human woman?"

"No!" flashed Rebeke. "I did those things for myself! You would have made me a wizard's wench. I could have watched from a darkened corner as you conjured the powers of the earth, and applauded your successes. You would have given me balms to keep the youth upon my face. I would still be a pretty toy for you to while away your spare moments."

"And that would be so much worse than to wear the scales of a Singer, and be the toy of the High Council, Rebeke?"

Ki let out a silent, shuddering breath. This strange give and take between Rebeke and Dresh was fearsome enough in a blasphemous way. But there was more to fear in this room than they. With an effort of will, Ki forced her own eyes to open. She panned them over the alien scene, trying to reconcile it with what Dresh's eyes had shown her.

"The High Council is not the ideal, Dresh. That I will admit. I will even whisper to you that they have corrupted the destiny of the Windsingers. But it shall be put back onto its course, by ones such as I. And I believe that is a worthier goal than for me to primp and paint myself so as to retain your favors."

Ki glanced down at her hands. But all she saw was the infinite void of the cube that was Dresh, supported by pale white strings. Her own hands in this dimension, Ki suspected. From the cube emanated a voice, or perhaps only a stream of thoughts.

"You give me so little credit, Rebeke. You speak as if it were only your body I loved. Your flesh could fade, could take on the forms of age, as is only seemly. And still, I would have loved . . . as still, perhaps, I do."

Silence drenched them all. Ki's eyes wandered. She fixed on a pale tower, oddly familiar. Grielea, she surmised. Yes, there were the twin red sparks of her eyes. And did those sparks shift, did they dance toward Ki's own gaze? It was impossible. Rebeke had frozen her with a windrune. But it seemed to Ki that the tower did move, that it ventured toward the circle that Dresh had drawn, taking impossibly small steps, but advancing, none the less.

"Perhaps?" The sharp note in Rebeke's voice shattered the stillness, jarred Ki so that Dresh's vision once more snapped into her mind. "Perhaps! Do you throw that word to me as you throw a bone to a hungry dog, Dresh? Or do you just try to make my task more difficult for me? Medie is lost to me, Dresh. I shall miss her strength sorely. Deprived of it, I have all the more need of the powers you have gathered. I have a goal. Left to myself, I would never harm you. I shall not bandy words with you, nor leave you to guess. I still have feelings for you. But should I let them interfere with my chance to realign the Windsingers with their proper goal? Shall I let such a chance slip away by letting you seduce me with conversation? No! If I must do it, I shall do it as hastily as possible. Why draw out our mutual torment..."

With a physical wrench, Ki turned Dresh's eyes in the direction of Grielea. She had moved! She stood within the circle, a smile of triumph on her face. Her hand was raised and death sparkled on her fingertips; her target was Rebeke!

The next move was Ki's, done with a swiftness that surpassed Dresh's skill to command her. With the strength that is born of terror, she hurled the blue egg at Grielea's head.

Dresh's cry of warning to Rebeke changed to one of horror as the egg met Grielea's cowled head. It passed through her face and skull like an arrow piercing overripe fruit. Bits of flesh and splinters of bone seemed to hang in the air before Ki's astounded eyes. Then the egg met the wall behind Grielea's slumping body. The wall vanished in an echoing roar of blue flame.

Grielea's lifeless body tumbled out of the hole in the wall, falling away from them into the void outside the punctured room. Even as Ki watched Grielea flopping away like a spoiled doll hurled down a well, she felt herself whirled toward the void. An unmerciful wind swept her up, and Dresh's torso came flailing along with her. She felt nausea sweep over her as the body seized her in a clumsy embrace. The hands were clinging to one of the body's legs. Dresh's head remained in her arms as they were swept out into darkness.

Ki retained one last image of Rebeke staring after them in wonder mixed with agony. Then the walls of the punctured room healed up behind them. Rebeke was lost to her sight. Together Ki and Dresh tumbled through the emptiness about them. She realized that she was no longer breathing, but it was only a passing disturbance in the drowsiness of her thoughts. She had had this dream before. There were the points of light again. Once more her hair stirred faintly against her face though she felt no breeze on her skin. She felt no panic, not even an interest in her situation. She drifted through an infinite void, a wizard's head clutched in her arms, a wizard's body embracing hers. The future did not worry her. She had no past to give it perspective, no present to consider it from. She was content to drift effortlessly, unbreathing, unthinking, unbeing. The head in her arms struggled with her mind, trying to impose its worries on her clean soul. Ki would have none of that. She let all her thoughts unravel as quickly as he knit them. She turned her mind to silence.

Sixteen

Vandien's team was as he had left it. He looked down at them
snoozing in the dust like a litter of puppies. Damnedest things
he had ever dealt with. He hoped he would be able to get them
to stir when the time came. With a shrug and a sigh, he turned
to the tavern. Breakfast would be welcome. He was not used to
such early hours, especially on an empty stomach.

The Windsinger stood solidly in the center of the alley; a
light wind stirred her pale blue robes. Her eyes were fixed on
Vandien. The tight blue cowl framed her face in an oval,
making her eyes seem even larger than they were. The dim
morning light made her look more girlish than ever. At this
distance, the light scaling of her face was invisible. Her hands
were small within the voluminous sleeves. Like a child dressed
up in her mother's clothes, Vandien thought to himself, smiling.

Her face was unsmiling as she stared at him. She made an
annoyed flick of her hand and the wind dropped. With that one
gesture, she was no girl, but a Windsinger. Vandien felt his
stomach do a slow turn. Had he been comparing her to a child
but a moment before? Fool, to be put off guard by a sweet
face.

"It's a lovely morning, teamster. The skies are clear and one can see for miles from the hilltops."

Her musical voice was charming, but her face did not mirror her gentle greeting.

"It is," Vandien agreed shortly. He began to walk toward her, intending to stride past her. The less he saw of this Windsinger, the safer he felt. But just as he would have passed her, she sidestepped quickly to put herself in front of him. He had to halt or knock her down. Vandien stood still, closer to her than he felt comfortable, but unwilling to retreat.

"What do you want?" He asked the question in a soft flat voice that made no pretense of courtesy. This was a Windsinger. He had no desire to stir her anger, but neither would he crawl before her.

"I have been walking on the hilltops this morning, teamster. Did I mention that one can see for miles in this light?" The voice lilted along. "And what do you suppose I saw in this fine clear light? A little boat upon the water. A little boat, floating above the ruins of a temple consecrated for Windsingers alone. For a moment, teamster, I considered bringing up a gale. I could have whisked that little boat miles from the shore, far beyond your power or hers to row it back again. Imagine, teamster. Imagine. But I was generous. I didn't. I will wait for this evening, when the tide goes out, and then we shall be matched. I look forward to it."

"Is that all you came to speak to me about, Windsinger?"

Mild distaste showed in those wide grey eyes, pursed her sculptured mouth. "Festival here is an old tradition, teamster. I would advise you not to strain yourself turning over heavy stones in a seething sea. Put on a good show, by all means. We Windsingers understand the need of the populace for ritual. Let them have this outlet for the little hostilities, and we will have a happier flock the rest of the year. We do not begrudge it to them. We even send a representative every Ebb year to make a token resistance to their feeble efforts. An outlet like this is a healthy thing for them, teamster. But, just as a nervous cow does not give the sweetest milk, so a people, over stirred, do not harvest as well as they might. They become restless, and give trouble at unexpected times. This is not good for them, or for us. And especially bad for you, teamster. The songs that were sung last night, teamster—we were not pleased to hear them sung that way."

"Are you finished?" Vandien broke in, knowing full well she was not. The trepidation he felt at being unsubtly threatened by a being of unknown powers was manifesting itself as anger. The blood pounded in his face, pulsing past his scar. He refused to be frightened. His jaws hurt at the corners where he clenched them too tightly. He wished there were more people about on the streets, to see their sweet Windsinger now. But they were all sleeping this holiday morn. He was alone.

She laughed at him. "Finished? Why, you would silence me before I tell you the most entertaining thing of all. But since you are so impatient, I will be quick about it, and let you be off to your important business." The smile fell away. "We know who you are, teamster. We see the company you keep. We are not to be trifled with. We think you should decide now that you have ventured beyond your depth. You need say no words to anyone. Put on a good show tonight. Be jovial about it. Tomorrow, go on your way with a whistle on your lips and a fair wind at your back. No one need think the less of you. Some might even think better of you. Show wisdom belatedly, rather than not at all, and you may keep the storms clear of your friends."

The Windsinger turned slowly. She had taken two steps before Vandien found his voice.

"Windsinger Killian!"

She turned to look at him coolly. "More words, teamster? I thought you were anxious for me to be finished."

"Be plain with me. Whom do you threaten?" Vandien's eyes were flinty. "My companion this morning was but a child, embittered by a lifetime of ill regard from her own folk. There are no devious plots in her. Her anger is not even focused at the Windsingers, but on her own people. She does not seek your secrets to harm you, but only to redeem herself in the eyes of the fisherfolk. Do you say that if I search for that chest tomorrow, your anger will fall on Janie? That's a fool's threat. Janie will continue to search and crave for your secret, even if I left this village tonight and never ventured into your temple. She has searched for it in every past Temple Ebb of her short life. Will you pretend that this year your wrath will suddenly fall upon her if I search also? You flatter me, but you do not convince me."

Killian smiled down upon him. Vandien did not know how she did it, when they were of a height, but she managed.

"Janie!" she snorted out the name. "Throw dust into the wind, teamster, and it only blows into your own eyes. Of Janie, we know all. She is no more to you than a girl met yesterday. You can throw her to our wrath, but that will not appease us or deceive us. No, teamster, I speak of Srolan, who brought you here. And I speak of the Romni who meddles in things beyond her. Do not make wondering eyes at me, and pretend to innocence! I will tell you plainly that Ki has been only an inconvenience to us. No more than that, and we have let her pass unharmed. But if you continue to pry and meddle, little man . . ."

"Bluff and bluster, like the wind you croon to, Killian. Srolan's determination is independent of my own. Even if I fled, she would continue to 'pry and meddle' on her own. You cannot put your persecution of her on my back. And Ki? A free spirit as well. If you had her in your power, you would not threaten—you would dangle her before me. No, all you have of Ki is her name. So whom do you threaten?" Anger made him bold. He would not let her see that her possession of Ki's name was enough to chill his blood.

"Subtlety is wasted here, I see. Sample this, Vandien, and decide whom I threaten." Her little hand rose swiftly, to flicker in the air before his face. Vandien jerked back from the expected slap. But her fingers did not touch him. Instead, a scream of wind whipped down the alley, throwing dust from the street into his face and eyes. Killian was gone. He squinted his eyes against the blast of air. A sudden buffet of cold drove him back down the alley, arms shielding his face. He crashed against the railing, falling over his huddled team.

He coughed dirt, tried to draw a breath through his sleeve. The piercing cold burned his scar like a brand and drove feeling from his fingertips. He staggered against the wind and slammed into the side of the inn. He forced his eyes open to slits; tears streamed from their corners. The wind drove him to his knees. He grovelled before it as he had not before Killian.

The roaring in his ears deafened him. It took a handful of breaths before he realized it was no longer the wind he heard, but only the rush of his own blood. The wind had stopped. The wan autumn sunlight was trickling down upon him, apologetically trying to warm him. Battered and numb, he slowly pulled himself up by the coarse stones of the building. Leaning against it, he blinked his begrimed eyelashes to clear his vision. The sight that met him was chilling.

The street was undisturbed. No loose boards were flung about, no shingles had been ripped loose. Temple Ebb banners hung limp. It was a quiet, sleepy street, a holiday morning street. The alley wind had been a special wind, a wind for Vandien alone. Killian had given him a sample of her skill. No reason for her to disturb the fisherfolk. Discipline only the teamster, who threatened to stampede the docile herd. It was as she had suggested to him. All he had to do was change his own mind. No one else would know, or think the less of him for it.

Ki? The Windsinger had said she was meddling in their affairs. In his dazed state, Killian's words still made no sense. Ki had always steered well clear of the Windsingers. He flexed his hands. Blood and warmth were returning to his fingers. Ki. Trust her to get herself into trouble when he was immersed in his own problems. He rubbed loose dust from his face. What should he do? Abandon his task here, go seeking for Ki? But the Windsinger had said that no harm had come to her. He winced, imagining how Ki would react if he came charging to her "rescue." No, Ki had said she would meet him here. She would expect him to be here, would come to False Harbor if she was in any real trouble. He had best stay where she could find him.

He stumbled into the common room and glanced around at the empty benches. The same boy was clearing the hearth, the same girl was oiling the tables. He wondered where Janie was. No one spoke to him as he made his slow way up the stairs and went into his room. The water in the ewer was lukewarm from standing, but it lifted the dust from his face. He dropped onto his rumpled bed. Lying flat on his back, he gently massaged the edges of the scar on his face. The concentrated ache began to ease. He already dreaded tonight, with the cold and the damp of the sea that would pucker the scar to new pain. If Killian were on the heights blasting him with wind, how could he hope to stand in that water, let along dig for some chest?

Misery and discouragement engulfed him. There was no sense in even trying. He'd only be making a fool of himself. But if he did not try, the Windsinger would think him cowed;

and he would lose whatever chance he had of lifting the scar from his face. His cautious fingers went on kneading, coaxing the stiffness from his face. Sometimes Vandien fancied that the scar was a living thing that had eaten into his face and would chew through his skull bones eventually and gnaw his life away. He let his hands fall back and was still. Loosen, loosen, he mentally pleaded, and slowly the muscles of his face went lax. The throbbing eased.

Warmth was seeping back into the rest of his body. The cold that had been knotted around his spine was loosening. He had been chilled by this morning's boat jaunt before the winds hit him and blew away his last reserves of body heat. He felt about and pulled a corner of the blanket over himself. His mind began to empty, his body to quest after sleep.

"Vandien! Wake up!"

His mind balanced on the razor edge between sleep and wakefulness, he slid his eyelids open, to gaze dreamily at Srolan hovering over him.

"No." He started to close his eyes.

"Yes!" she insisted, shaking him.

He heaved a sigh and sat up on the bed. She immediately perched on the foot of it. He had to marvel at her. A huge cloak hung from her shoulders, the blue hood of it pushed carelessly back. The bright kiss of wind on her cheeks showed that she had but recently come indoors. She pushed her tousled black hair back from her face, and settled her hands in her lap, hugging them between her thighs to warm them. Her eyes were bright as gems, her mouth both bitter and excited as she told him, "It's a wasp's nest you've stirred up!"

"Me?" Vandien was incredulous. "I came to this village, an honest teamster in search of a quick job for easy money. Instead, I find myself flung into intrigue centuries old, and involved in a three-way tussle between an innkeeper who wants the folks entertained, a young lady who'd like to see this town humbled as she's been humbled, and a crazy old woman who . . ."

"Wants to see justice finally done!" Srolan cut in. She laughed merrily, a young woman's flirtatious laugh. Vandien found himself looking closely at her. There was a magnetism about her, a vitality that called to every instinct within him. He was not unaccustomed to the urges that a healthy lively woman could stir in him. In his younger days he would have been preening, shaking his dark curls, pulling himself up straight, swelling his chest with a breath. But he was a man grown now, and scarred across the face, no longer prone to strut for show.

And this woman? She was old enough to be his grandmother, his great-grandmother perhaps, though she made his skin tingle and his ears ring. She filled him with desires, but none of them were physical. He wanted . . . Vandien fumbled within his own mind. He wanted to stand proven in her eyes, to have her respect. He wanted those black eyes of hers to shine upon him. He wanted her to single him out in a crowded room as the only man worthy to hold conversation with her. He hungered, deeply and suddenly, for her friendship, and her trust.

She read him. "I chose you well!" Her voice was warm. "There are those who think deeper, men of greater stature and strength than you. There are better teamsters, and more cautious ones. But, Vandien, you feel. And by your feeling, you do things. You are as generous with your loves as with your hates. Out of a thousand, you are the one."

His blood seethed with pride. Vandien found himself smiling without making sense of her words. The nibbling doubts he had felt about Srolan's motivations since his words with Janie were stilled. She came closer and took his hands in hers.

"What did she tell you? Janie?"

"Her grandfather's story. She spoke it like a litany, in his words, and, I swear, in his voice. What a burden to put upon a child."

"The old are more often righteous than kind. And was it any use to you?"

Vandien shrugged. Her hands were warm, her eyes saw only him. "I shall look in the southwest corner of the temple. The chest is not over large, but it is as heavy as two strong men can lift. And I shall not let my foot slip between any rocks." He sighed. "And I know full well that if I do find it, I may pay for it with my life. But that information came from Killian, not Janie."

Srolan nodded. "I thought I felt the tingle of wind magic in the air this morning. It's a good sign, Vandien. They fear you, and try to scare you off, but only because they fear you may succeed where others have failed. That is because you have the will to succeed."

Srolan rose suddenly, dropping his hands. She paced a turn around the room, her blue cloak billowing about her with the energy of her movements. When she stopped, it was sudden, and her eyes pierced him for secrets. "There is much more afoot with the Windsingers than our hunt, Vandien. I have been far afield this day. The winds will tell secrets, to any who know how to listen. I have been listening hard. The Windsingers' minds are turned from us, are focused on things closer to their home. Killian fears, because she knows she stands alone against you. No help can be spared to her. Your stubbornness scares her. Believe me when I tell you this: her little demonstration for you this morning cost her. Summoning a wind is no trifling task. She will have to rest now, and reassemble her strength for this evening. My suggestion is this. Do not wait for her to be ready."

Vandien found himself nodding. Through the unshuttered window was coming the early noise of a village that rises to festival instead of work. Idle talk and laughter rose. Beneath, the inn floor shook to the tramp of early traffic. Voices called for spiced wine, for a hot bowl of chowder. But in Vandien's room they planned, no merrymaking, but battle.

"Janie suggested that I follow an old custom. She told me to follow the tide out, not wait for it to ebb and then go out. The difference seems small."

"An ebbing tide reveals things, Vandien. She gave you sage advice. As the water drains out of the temple, you may catch a glimpse of something revealed for a moment by moving sands. If you spot it then, and get a rope on it, you have all of the tide to haul it in. I've rope for you, by the way."

"I assumed a fishing village would have plenty."

"Not like this. This will not slip out of a knot, nor stretch when it gets wet." Srolan produced a coil from within the voluminous cloak. Vandien looked at it in dismay. The line was no thicker around than his finger. She tossed the coil to him. It landed heavily in his lap. He fingered the smooth grey surface. He twisted it against its lay, but could get no strand to buckle.

"Kerugi made," Srolan replied to his questioning glance. "A friend sent it to me. Fine stuff. Those tiny fingers can weave the smallest strands into a tight whole. You can trust it, Vandien. As you can trust me."

She strode to the window and glanced out at the alley and street below. "The jugglers did come. That's fine. I must go now. You will be wise to get what rest you can, for your tide will be late tonight. But for me, holiday goes on below. There will be festival cakes and rare good drink. There will be stories, too, and song. Old as I am, I am a child for those things. No matter how they weary me, I cannot deny them to myself. Rest well."

"What of Janie?" Vandien's voice halted her by the door.

"Janie? I've no doubt that she's out and about, below. She works a bit for Helti, you know, for he watches over her little sister by day."

"I mean, when this is over, what of Janie?"

Srolan's shoulders fell. Her steps were slow as she came to lean on the foot of his bed. "Janie. A pity we cannot save it all, make it all end as happily as an old tale. Well. If you succeed, her story will be vindicated. She is the granddaughter of a hero. For a day or so, that is. Then Janie will find that the doings of our ancestors carry little weight today. She will find she is still Janie, the daughter of a drunken wreck. She will be treated no differently. In fact, it may make things worse. If you are the granddaughter of a hero, folk expect more of you than if you are the granddaughter of a liar."

"And if I fail?"

"You won't."

"But if I did?" he persisted stubbornly.

"Then it would be just one more year. She would be teased for a few days past Temple Ebb, and then she would be forgotten. In a few more years, her sister will be old enough to help her with the dory, and they will earn a better living. She will have coin of her own, and more young men will look at her and consider that they might do worse. Not that I think Janie will ever take one of them. She remembers too well, that girl. She could list for you every taunt she has received since she could toddle. That's one problem of a village this size. All the children grow up as playmates. I doubt there is one man in this village who has never made a jest of her."

"Except Collie."

"Collie." Srolan pursed her lips thoughtfully. "That's so. He was too busy defending himself to have time to tease others. She might take Collie."

"Might she leave False Harbor?"

"I doubt it. Few born here do, you know. Look at me. I was born here." She came closer, her shadow falling over him. Her voice was soothing suddenly. Vandien did not start when her fingertips touched his face. She trailed the backs of her nails lightly over his forehead. His thoughts went wooly. "Rest now. You can do nothing about Janie. She was here before you came to False Harbor, and will be after you've gone. Let her weave her own life strings. Go to sleep, Vandien. We shall need your full strength. I'll see that you are called in plenty of time to eat, before you go to follow the tide."

She smoothed the pillow beside his face. He felt her deft tuggings as she pulled blankets up to cover him. It was odd, but he could not recall lying back on the bed. "Sleep," she told him again, and her touch was gone. He thought he heard the closing of the door, and then sleep took him.

SEVENTEEN

THE points of light shimmered. That did not disturb Ki. Whether she stared at still lights or shimmering ones, it was all one to her. They could have all blinked out and left her just as calm. Some large translucent body was coming between her and the lights. It did not concern her. The closer it came to Ki, the more lights it smothered. After an eternity of observing it, it filled her eyes completely. The shimmering lights were all blotted away. The thing had swelled larger, or come nearer. It was all one to Ki, until it engulfed her.

With reawakening came terror. Ki screamed, sliding back to life on the sounds of her own fear. She had no sense of location or time; only that she was alive and wished to remain so. Sensation after sensation struck her. She was cold. She was spattered with a foul-smelling liquid. Bells clanged close to her ears. She was blasted with sand that scoured the skin from her flesh. Brilliant lights pulled her eyes from their sockets, seared them to blindness. She was plunged into a darkness so intense that pastel sparks of light danced upon her brain.

Was it for seconds or days that she endured this? Ki did not know. But she knew that pain was life, and clung to it

even as she fought it. The head on her arm chattered inter-
minably to itself, but she paid it no heed.

The universe split open like a rotten canvas sack and Ki
spilled out of it, tumbling through light and cool air. She landed
badly, thumping the air out of her lungs. Her head bounced
against the hard-packed earth. The wizard's body landed heavily atop hers. His head was crushed between them.

With a grunt and a shudder, Ki shoved them off. She could
stand that contact no more. She scrabbled blindly away from
them, to collapse on her belly. Sweet, sweet grasses poked
against her face, precious earth pressed her grasping hands. A
stream of muffled curses rose behind her. She rolled farther
away from them, onto her back. Her eyes watered as she stared
gratefully up at a pale morning sun beginning to blaze in a
pink and blue sky. She breathed deep of the smells of earth
and grass and river water. Somewhere a horse snorted noisily.
Ki gave a glad wordless cry at the sound of it. She heard her
name called. She lolled her head in the direction of the call,
grinning foolishly.

Dresh's body had struggled to a sitting position. His handless arms groped awkwardly about seeking for his head. The
head was face down in dry grass where it had tumbled when
Ki pushed it off her chest. The grass was muffling his shouts.
More by chance than guidance, one of the block hands clunked
against the head. With judicious pushes, the body was able to
right the head on its mounting block. Ki watched in fascination.

Dresh's grey eyes blazed as he spat soil from his mouth.
Like blind puppies seeking warmth, the hands were crawling
up the body's trunk, dragging their shared block of stone behind
them. Ki could summon up no amazement at the sight; it only
seemed mildly comical, a clown's charade in early morning
light, after the darker magic just survived.

When she could compose herself, she took a deeper breath
of the fresh morning air. "Are you alive?" she asked inanely,
ignoring the stream of invective she interrupted.

"Small thanks to you, but I am!" Dresh retorted acidly.

"So am I. That's good, I suppose." She could not call her
mind to order. A thousand questions bubbled through her
thoughts. None seemed pressing now. She asked at random,
"What brought us here? How did you call it?"

Dresh stared at her, his eyes bright with tears. He coughed

and spat out more dirt. His voice was hoarse. "The summoning of that one is beyond my skills, teamster. There are those who say that only a Windmistress of the Windsingers has a voice that can call up one of those. And it is too draining of power for them to consider it worth their time. No doubt it was only our good fortune that one was in our path."

"No doubt," mumbled Ki as she rose to dust the leaves and dirt from her clothes. She had hardly heard his words, too many other things claimed her attention. She stretched, enjoying the freedom of possessing her own body and senses. It seemed a luxury beyond belief. And this world of hers! Had there ever been a more lovely place? The perfection of autumn leaves pressed against the blue sky, the subtle blending of scents in the crisp air! There was a wagon drawn up in the shelter of the trees. It was her own. Dust streaks marred the brightly painted panels of the cuddy. The open freight bed was splintered and worn from a thousand loadings. Never before had she seen it so clearly, or so gratefully. Beside it a large grey horse cropped grass. Harness marks scored his hide. Would she ever tug at the reins again without remembering Dresh's pre-emption of her body and will? A newly hatched guilt uncurled in her soul. Before it could nibble, Dresh's voice broke her thoughts.

"Ki." His voice was weary, almost saddened. "My powers are ebbing lower with every breath I take in this form. It has drained me more than I expected. I can no longer reassemble myself unaided. I must have Karn Hall at Bitters, with its congenial convergences, and my servants to assist me. And we must hurry. Rebeke may have given me up, but there are other Windsingers. Take my hands, if you will."

As if to mock his words, a sudden breeze gusted up from the river. A prickle of fear stirred Ki's hair. She scrabbled to her feet, snatched up the hands on their block of stone, and tucked the head on her arm. The body lumbered after her as she ran to her wagon.

The hands she set within the cuddy on her bed, the head on the plank driver's seat. The body had to be tugged and hoisted awkwardly onto the box. It all but tumbled into her cuddy. She shuddered as she watched it push the hands over and casually usurp her bed.

"Now get that team hitched! Forget the rest of it; there isn't time! Cut the picket ropes, don't bother to untie them! Ki!"

She ignored Dresh's useless directions and commands as she jostled her horses into place. Buckles and straps resisted her weary hands.

"Ki, the wind magic will be upon us in moments! I have no strength to stave them off! Leave those trinkets and let us be off!" If the head had possessed a set of lungs to power it, it would have been roaring. But Ki turned a deaf ear as she scooped up her kettle and mugs, to tumble them pell-mell into the dish chest strapped to the side of the wagon.

"Trinkets to you," she explained breathlessly as she vaulted up onto the seat. "But for me the trappings of my life. I will not abandon them. Get up, you two!"

The last she called to her team. The greys lunged against the traces as another gust of wind buffeted the side of the wagon. Clouds swirled up from nowhere to obscure the blue skies. The wagon bounced and rocked as Ki forced the team back to the main trail. From the roots and potholes, she tried to pretend, but she knew it was the gusting wind hitting the square side panels of the top-heavy Romni wagon.

"Put me within!" Dresh's voice finally broke through the rush of the wind and reached Ki's ears. She glanced over, to see that the head on its stone had slid dangerously close to the edge of the seat. One more jolt would have sent him over the side. With one hand on the reins, Ki reached out to slide the head back to her side.

"Have you no fondness for the open road on a fine day like this, Dresh?" she asked innocently. "After all, the show is in your honor." The gusting wind seemed to switch directions every minute. Ki's hair streamed across her face, whipping her eyes. The horses plunged against their harnesses, fighting the sudden windstorm. The sky had greyed; morning was twilight.

"If we meet someone on the road, the show will be in your honor!" Dresh shouted breathlessly above the roar. "I suppose you prefer to be stoned to death as a witch rather than feel the wrath of the Windsinger?"

"Neither has much appeal," Ki admitted. She pulled in her team long enough to slide open her cuddy door and place Dresh within, none too gently. As she shut the door on his complaint and took up the reins, a bitter smile touched her mouth. This was what too much association with wizardry did to one. She had not even considered how peculiar it would be to meet a lone teamster with the head of a wizard on the seat beside her.

A spattering of yellow-green leaves ripped early from the trees recalled her to her danger. She called to the team and they picked up their pace.

She forded the river recklessly, not trying to pick the best path but the quickest. The team plunged into the grey rush of water. The tall wheels jounced over rounded river stones. The great hooves slipped and nearly floundered. The wind whipped water white against the wagon, and flung it up into her face. It drenched her, and suddenly the wind was icy against her, reddening her hands and making her body tight with chill.

On the far side of the river, the trail became wider and straightened itself. The team heaved and strained to haul the heavy wagon up the slippery bank. It seemed to take an age, and once they were up on the trail again, Ki dared not halt to let them breathe. She longed to whip them up into a full gallop, to carom down the trail, away from this accursed forest and river and the magic it seemed to invite. The wind battered and threatened her. She forced herself to calmness. Her ponderous beasts could not maintain a gallop long; it made no sense to burn their strength that way.

A peculiar high-pitched note mixed with the wind. It was not at all similar to air moving through trees. Suddenly her team showed no inclination to settle into their usual plodding pace. Ki watched the four ears flicking about nervously. The incessant wind continued to rattle the wagon as they jolted over the little-used trail.

The stench hit them with the next gust of wind. Sigurd screamed and plunged forward in his harness, dragging Sigmund along. Ki couldn't hold them in. She tried to keep the reins firm, to let them feel some measure of control from her, but she knew they had taken their heads. The wagon jounced and rumbled alarmingly. From within the cuddy she heard muffled curses and cries. Dresh was not enjoying this rattling. But Ki could not take her eyes from the trail or spare him a thought. It took all her skills to influence the team as they careened down the trail. She kept them, as best she could, to the middle of the path. The great hooves threw up chunks and clods of earth. Foam laced the grey backs. She prayed that they would meet no one coming from the other direction. She tried not to imagine her team colliding with another team and wagon.

But it was not a team and wagon that suddenly confronted

them. It was no creature Ki could put a name to, and the source
of the terrible stench. It dropped from the sky to hang before
them on the unnatural wind. Its wings were like tattered sea
canvas, at once in this world and some other. Its body was all
claws and eyes. The plunging team reared and tried to halt,
but the impetus of the wagon pushed them on. Ki heard the
screech of the protesting wood as the balking team racked the
wagon, and then jerked on in terror as the wagon rode up on
them. The creature kited over them, giving a cry between a
screech and laughter. Ki saw it fold in its gruesome wings. It
dropped. It would land squarely on the backs of the panicked
greys. It was twice Ki's size, with wings added on. The wind
boiled about her, whipping her hair across her face, stifling
her with the stink of the beast, and adding its roar to the
distressed screams of the horses.

But even as the noisome creature extended its claws to land,
a sudden gust of a new wind buffeted it from the side.

The perfume of the warm wind cut through the stench of
the creature. It swirled against the chill wind that rattled Ki's
wagon, to put her and her team in the calm eye of a storm of
warmth and fragrance. The hapless sky creature was sucked
up in it, thrown aloft and spun about. Its tattered wings flapped
like the stained rags on a street beggar as it was flung about
in the suddenly hostile wind. Ki strained to master her team
and keep them on the trail. They needed no encouragement to
run now, and she no longer wished to hold them in. She sent
tremors of encouragement down the reins to the greys as their
huge legs stretched and reached, snatching up lengths of the
trail and flinging it behind them. The trees on either side of
the trail were flogged clean of leaves by the battling winds,
but they traveled in a tunnel of silence, moving in the eye of
a storm that moved with them, sheltered by a buffer of warmth
and scent.

She heard wild cries and the snapping of branches as the
sky creature was mastered by the warm wind and flung to its
fate in the reaching branches of the trees. Ki sensed that she
moved through the midst of a great battle of wills. She felt,
not protected, but possessed. These winds battled over her and
her wagon, and more so over its contents. No matter who won,
she could not expect mercy. Yet, hoping against hope to be
claimed by neither, she urged on the team that was racing to
exhaustion.

She did not feel the rain. The warm wind did not let it through to pelt her with its icy blows, but it could not prevent the rain from soaking the trail ahead, changing its hard-packed surface to slick mud. The wide hooves of the team slid and scrambled, the wagon fishtailed madly behind them. Ki wished vainly for her freightload of earth and stones in crates. The empty wagon was too light to travel at this pace over wet earth; a heavier wagon would have made it possible to control the frenzied horses. The greys raced on, the wide backs rising and falling before her frantic eyes. If one did not slip and break a leg, they would run themselves to death.

The forest began to thin. They passed two small farms in clearings on one side of the trail and the trail grew wider and showed signs of more use. Ki and her storm of destruction had invaded the periphery of a farming area. She watched the fields crumpling under the onslaught of the storm she brought. Wind harvested the grain; cattle fell under the hail. No Humans or Dene moved outside their farmhouses. All had doubtless fled to shelter from this unnatural weather. Ki doubted that they even heard the rumbling passage of her wagon through the rumbling of the thunder that rose to confront her.

The team was slowing. Lather scraped against the leather traces and dripped down their sides. Ki heard their blowing even in the midst of the swirling winds. Her heart went out to them. They were running to their deaths and it was not even their quarrel. She could not save them.

Suddenly she felt Dresh join her vision. She could not explain how she knew that he, too, peered from her eyes, but she felt his weariness drag at her, and guessed that he sucked at her stamina as well as his own. Ki felt her anger rise, and then quail inside her as she realized the uselessness of it. She was used by him as she used her team. She did not know why he wanted her eyes, until she felt the sudden strength flood her arms. She found herself fighting her team, standing up to drag harshly at the reins. The foam at the bits went pink, and she turned them down a rutted abandoned road. Karn Hall, she immediately knew, was at the end of it. The destination of her freight was closer than she had known.

The winds clashed more furiously than ever. Twice the desperate icy onslaught broke through to Ki, once hard enough to fling her back against the cuddy door. The circumference of the storm eye shrank. The greys felt the icy blast on their muzzles. Ki heard the rattle of hailstones in the empty back of her wagon. The protective circle around them could not last much longer. Ki guessed that by now Dresh was exhausted. Now what? Ki did not want to wonder.

A bend in the rutted path, and Karn Hall loomed before her like a broken tooth in a mossy skull. Its white stone was stained greenish with neglect; the stone window sills in the upper tower were crumbling away. Its courtyard was overgrown with grasses and low brush, and trees clustered close to its walls. Their limbs did not stir. No gale buffeted them. Like a sudden plunge into quiet water, the team gained the magic circle that surrounded those walls. The wind and storm died behind them. Suddenly Ki was given the strength to rein in the team. They were too weary to fight her will. They slowed, trotted brokenly, then halted, their great heads drooping to trembling knees. Ki let the wet reins fall from her welted hands. She shook as badly as her team. Folding her body, she let her tousled head rest on her drawn-up knees. Blessed, blessed silence embraced her. Not even the sound of the storm that still raged outside the circle would reach her here.

When she finally lifted her head and looked about, she saw the waning storm moving off in defeat. The trees of Karn Hall still stood tall, but outside Dresh's sphere of influence, the trees were wretched battered things, weeping leaves in the wake of the holocaust. Ki thought she scented a trace of fragrance in the air. Before she could identify it, it was gone.

Ki dismounted shakily. Her stiff fingers could scarcely work the buckles on the heavy harness. The leather was warm and wet, the metal slick with lather. She let it drop away from the exhausted team. The greys did not move.

A muffled thudding reached her ears. She stumbled back to her wagon, struggled up onto the seat and slid the cuddy door open. It was the body, thudding one of its stony arm ends against the door. The head lay on the floor where it had fallen during their mad flight. A leak of blood snaked from one aristocratic nostril. Dresh's eyes were dull in his grey face.

"Tell the folk in the house to fetch me in," he whispered. The tip of his tongue ventured over his dry lips. She noted a chip off the corner of his mounting block had crumbled on her cuddy floor.

"No need, Master!" Ki was too weary to jump at Bird-eyes' voice coming from behind her. She moved out of the old wom-

an's way as she shouldered herself into the cuddy. Ki dropped
gracelessly from the wagon to the ground. She opened her
mouth to warn off the stable hand that was approaching her
team with rubbing rags, but the normally fractious Sigurd was
standing quiet under his ministering touch.

"And that is the strangest wizardry I have seen yet!" Ki
murmured to herself. The door of the hall had been left ajar.
She wandered over to it, glancing back to her wagon, where
several serving men had materialized and were lifting Dresh's
various parts down, under the sharp-tongued supervision of old
Bird-eyes. Normally the sight of strangers swarming over her
wagon would have enraged her. Now she felt only relief.

Through the open door of the hall, a bright fire burning in
a huge hearth beckoned. She stepped into the cool dark of the
entry hall, and through the second lofty door into the welcoming
chamber. A low table laden with food and drink was surrounded
by soft pillows and finely tanned skins. It drew her like a candle
draws a moth. Ki sank down onto the soft cushions and poured
wine for herself into a glass of cut crystal. She sipped at it and
felt warmth flood her weary body. How long since she had last
slept? For just a moment, she closed her eyes and let her head
sag onto the cushions.

"And there she has slept, like a dirty stray dog, in the middle
of the best room, since yesterday afternoon! Master, she acted
as if . . ."

Ki did not hear the *sotto voce* reply. She opened her eyes
and lifted her heavy head to see voluminous black skirts whipping out of sight around a corner. Dresh stood alone in the
doorway. He looked peculiarly tall to her, with his head atop
his body. He smiled mockingly at her as he raised his hands,
rubbed his wrists lightly, and then waggled his fingers at her.
"All in working order!"

"So I see." Ki struggled to a sitting position and tried to
gather her scattered thoughts. "Is my team all right?"

Dresh frowned lightly, as if he found her concern for mere
beasts inappropriate at this moment. But he replied, "They are
resting as comfortably as you have been, and no great harm to
them. I regret I had to force such speed out of them, but they
have taken no permanent damage from it."

"I suspected you had a hand in their new-found stamina.
As to damage . . ." Ki remembered her manners and calmed

her voice. "Thank you for the hospitality you have shown my
team and me."

"You are more than welcome. And was I right?"

"About what?"

"That I am a well-made man, when I am in one piece."

His voice was confident. He smiled his contagious smile,
which was more attractive with his head atop his body. She
was suddenly aware that he *was* a well-made man. The sleeve-
less brown jerkin trimmed in gold set off his olive skin and his
smooth arms. His belly was flat, without apparent effort or
binding; his hips were of a flattering narrowness.

She kept her voice casual. "As well-made as many I have
seen."

"Thank you!" he responded imperturbably. He crossed the
room with an easy stride, to drop down on the cushions beside
her. He leaned his elbow on the low table beside hers and
brought his grey eyes close to her green ones.

"There is a lovely chamber upstairs, with a tub of steaming
water in it. There are perfumed oils to choose from, and two
trunks full of soft gowns of many colors, trimmed in Kerugi
lace. You could bathe and change, and return to dine with me
here. Time enough after dinner to settle our, ah, accounts."
Fascinated, she watched his small even teeth nibble at the
wedge of cheese he plucked from the table. The bath was
tempting. Despite her sleep, her body was still weary. Hot
water would soothe her bruised and aching muscles. She owed
herself a little time to relax after the trials of the last few
days . . . was it only days?

"I'd like to, Dresh, but I've an appointment to keep," she
remembered belatedly. "I'm to meet someone in False Harbor
tomorrow or the next day."

"Let him wait," Dresh suggested. "You're already late, you
know. Or do you? Do you realize just how much time our little
detour took? By late tonight, I imagine Vandien will be up to
his nose in cold water, trying to fish up that chest. Not that I
have the faintest hope of his doing so. Still, it seemed an
amusing idea at the time, and who knows?"

Ki straightened up from the cushions. Her stomach roiled
with dread. "What had you to do with Vandien's errand in
False Harbor?"

"Me?" Dresh smiled smugly. "Why, who do you think steered
Srolan to him? Who but Dresh could have told her what bait

to hook him on? One glance at Vandien, and I knew what he
would risk all for: the lifting of that scar from his face. It was
so obvious to me, and yet she would never have thought of
it." Ki was silent, staring at him with wide eyes. Dresh grinned,
delighted at amazing her so. "You'd never guessed it? How
could you not see it? Have you not seen him sitting thus, his
hand held before his face?" Dresh fell into a posture Ki knew
well. Thus *did* Vandien sit, thumb at the side of his jaw, his
index finger stretched beside his nose to touch the center of
his forehead, his other fingers curled before his mouth. It was
a pose he adopted when deep in thought. or exceptionally tired,
the way another man might rest his chin on his fists. It had
never before occurred to her that the gesture also covered most
of the scar down his face. But now it did. It was more than
she could bear to see Dresh's sly grin around his hand as he
struck the pose.

"Stop that!" she growled.

Dresh flung himself back against the cushions with a laugh.
"I knew it the first time I saw him. I spotted him as soon as
he came to Dyal, and I knew you would not be far behind. I
had, ah, shall we say, arranged for an errand to bring you there.
Why Ki, you may ask? A friend pronounced you the soul of
discretion and recommended you; something to do with a sealed
book that you transported for him some years back, under rather
tricky circumstances. So, favors being owed, Ki was given a
cargo of beans that would bring her to Dyal. But there was the
matter of this Vandien. He was an unknown in my equation.
I could not tolerate that. He could be a thief or worse. So, I
arranged for him to be busy elsewhere, and made certain that
you would be receptive to a generous offer for a simple task.
More than half my skill as a wizard, Ki, comes from my being
able to have people do as I wish them to, all the while believing
that they are following their own best judgment. So, whilst we
were about our little detour, Vandien aimed his steps to False
Harbor, in the hopes of being rid of that scar. I doubt not that
he'll do his damnedest tomorrow to drag up that mythical chest.
But that need not concern us. For now, let us . . . Ki!"

Ki had risen. Her heart was pounding and tears stung her
eyes. The desolation in her heart was an actual physical pain
in her chest. *That* was what he had not told her; that was what
had been proffered him over any coin. That was what had
prompted him to volunteer her team, to overstep the carefully

set bounds of their friendship. She suddenly despised herself for ever letting those bounds come into being, for being so careful of the *mines* and *thines*. Vandien wore that scar in her stead, had taken in his face the Harpy claws intended for her. He had not paused to consider if he would interfere with her life, had not weighed the merits of his face over her death. But when she should have been the giving one . . . it choked her. That he had not even told her was salt on the wound. Damn him a thousand times for the words he held back behind that crooked smile! And damn herself ten thousand times for not seeing what this twisted little wizard was throwing in her face. She whirled on Dresh.

"Wizard, I've an appointment to keep. I must be on my way." She cursed her shaking voice.

"Let him wait," Dresh repeated. "We've our accounts to settle."

"They'll keep!" she growled. The wagon was still fully supplied; time enough to worry about cash later.

"No. They won't." Dresh was smiling insistently. "The gowns will keep, the dinner will keep; even the bath can wait. But I wish to settle our accounts now." The door before Ki swung soundlessly closed. Even before she put her hand against it, she knew it would not yield.

Whirling, she advanced on Dresh angrily. "I've had enough of your wizardly shows. Open that door!"

Dresh smiled at her. "Certainly." The door swung open.

She turned to the door. As she stepped toward it, it closed again.

"Damn you, Dresh! This isn't a game!"

"Isn't it?" He laughed.

Ki longed to smash that smile from his face, to rend his grinning lips from his face. She swallowed her fury. "What do you want of me?" she grated.

"To settle our accounts," he explained calmly. "As I said. If you'd only sit down and listen . . ."

"I listen fine standing."

Dresh sighed. "The reknowned Romni stubbornness. Listen then, Ki. Listen well. *Come here, Ki.*"

Never before had her name sounded like that. She stepped toward him, then stopped, frowning. But she could not stop. She circled her steps away from him. He watched her in amusement. Like iron drawn to a magnet, she moved ever closer to him, no matter how she diverted her steps. Her heart hammered in her throat. No words came to her. Why had she never noticed the soulless look of his eyes? She slowed her steps, she bridled and shied, but at last she stood before him. She stared down into a face that smiled joylessly at her.

"That's better. Sit down with me, Ki." His soft voice lapped over her.

Her legs trembled beneath her. Her knees bent to his command, not hers. She balanced herself stiffly as she sank down onto the cushions before him. She found herself leaning into Dresh, relaxing into the arms that awaited her. As her mind fought like an unbroken filly on a lead, she found herself tasting those narrow lips, running the tip of her tongue over his even white teeth. She tasted the smell of funeral herbs. His mouth was wet and cold. Disgust and fury blazed up in her as her traitorous hands slipped behind his shoulders. Anger freed her tongue.

"You have no right!" she growled through clenched teeth. Dresh pulled his head far enough back to smile into her face.

"No? I said we have accounts to settle. How else do you propose to repay the agreed-upon portion of the advance? I know you have not a coin to your name. As I told you, due to our little detour, you are a full day late delivering your freight. In scarcely perfect condition, I might add. How else shall I reclaim what you owe me?"

He smiled down at her. Ki felt her arm muscles tighten as they drew him closer to her. He pillowed his head upon her breast.

"I shall find a way to kill you!" Ki promised heartily.

"Was ever a conquest so sweetly spiced with resistance?" Dresh wondered laughingly.

Dresh's body pressed hers down. Her hands played over his back, slipped under cloth to feel warm flesh. Ki shuddered internally. Her mind raced and veered, seeking escape, seeking any kind of weapon. Desperation blazed up in her as she flung words at him.

"Did you play this game with Rebeke, Dresh? Is this what drove her to the Windsingers? You used her as a toy, made her less than a beast! Shamed her, broke her! It is no wonder she fled your arms! The wonder is that she sent her wind, wrapped us in her protection until we reached Karn Hall. A breeze scented like wind-flowers, like anemones!"

Ki landed on the cushions on the opposite side of the table like a flung doll, repelled from Dresh's body as easily as he had attracted her. Anger and pain burned in his face. She knew she had gone too far.

"She only did it to shame me! To humiliate me with her mercy! Because she knew . . ." His mouth worked with unsayable words, and then his lips went white.

"Are you certain of that, Dresh?" Ki gambled words as she picked herself up. "What do you suppose the Windsingers are doing to her now, while you indulge yourself? Tell me of it, Dresh. Why not further entertain yourself by recounting what her torments are while you pass the time with me?"

Dresh was silent, choking. His eyes were a thousand years older, but they were the eyes of a stricken child. Then a chill mask of amusement took sudden control of his face. He rose, tugging his jerkin straight and gave a shrug and a sarcastic little sigh.

"You are a disappointment. I had hoped you would yield to my persuasions gracefully. I had also hoped you would bathe first. We might have passed a diverting hour or so. You miss the chance to learn many things. Ah, well. There are prettier puppets than you, Romni teamster."

The door was ajar. He had forgotten it. "Undoubtedly," Ki spoke recklessly. "But puppets will never content you, Dresh." She began backing toward the door as she spoke.

"My last little weakness," he admitted disdainfully. She hated the way he smiled at her retreat. "When I weed it out of myself, then shall I come to the fullness of my power. This foolish regard I have for the Human spirit, this sentimental sympathy . . ."

"Is your last shred of Humanity, Dresh. As it is Rebeke's. Cling to it, Dresh. I salute your weakness!"

She felt the jamb of the door behind her. With a sudden tug and spring, she was through it and dashing down the entryway. She pulled and jerked wildly at the slowly opening door of Karn Hall. Morning light blinded her as she squeezed out into the courtyard and dashed across the the dust strewn paving stones.

A door crashed behind her. She whirled, lost her footing, and sat down flat in the dust. She froze, her heart shaking her. Then her tightened shoulders loosened and dropped in puzzlement.

There was no pursuit. The tall door had been slammed shut behind her.

Her wagon was standing ready in the yard, the greys already hitched to it. They looked tired, but not broken. Ki frowned. Dresh had been ready for her to leave, had prepared her wagon for her, expecting it. She rose and dusted herself off, shaking her head at his final charade. There was no sense in trying to understand wizards. She spat the taste of him from her mouth. She wasted no time in crossing to her home and mounting the tall wheel to her seat.

She picked up the reins. Sigurd twisted about to send her a reproving look. The team was weary, had been drained yesterday. They had rested no longer than she, and she knew how she still ached. It was not right to ask this of them. She was no better than Dresh. But there was Vandien. There were no right answers to her dilemna, but the one most wrong was to let him face his task alone. She stirred her team to action, glad to put Karn Hall behind her. "I'll send you the damn coin I owe you for late delivery," she promised the stone walls in a venomous whisper. "Yes, and with a snake in the sack for an extra payment!"

Two days to False Harbor, was it? They would be there by this night . . . or by tomorrow's dawn. If she was not there to help him, at least let him see that her heart had been with him. Vandien. Shaking her head, she stepped the team up, while keeping a watch on the sky.

Dresh drew back from the tower window, smiling his narrow smile. "She'll go now, like an arrow shot to the mark."

Bird-eyes chuckled.

Eighteen

VANDIEN picked at the knot on the railing. The woven rein came loose in his hands and he moved to stand behind his slumbering team. His belly was cold with dread; discouragement made him weary before he'd even started. He longed for nothing so much as to go back up the stairs and fall into his bed. Perhaps he could sleep the hours away until tomorrow, and then wake up to a different life as a different person. How he wished!

He had slept, and risen to eat. Helti himself had served him. Though he had peered about for a glimpse of Janie, he had not seen her. The common room had been a lively place, with competing groups singing snatches of different songs. Sticky little cakes poked full of slivered spiced fruit were presented to him. Folk stopped by his table to offer him chunks of a poisonously sour fish pickle. Vandien watched in awe as they wolfed mouthfuls of this dubious treat, following it with hunks of white cheese cut into bells and moons and stars. They had laughed uproariously at his inability to choke down the fish, and tried to soothe his feelings with mugs of potent drink. He had been affable. It was festival, and the fisherfolk were determined that all should enjoy it. When Vandien took a sign from Srolan and rose from his table, few asked him where he was going. And when he told them, none of them followed. "Too early," they said. Festival was still strong and noisy in the common room of the tavern. When their bellies were full and their heads were reeling, then they would come to watch the teamster flounder about in the water. They pressed him to stay and drink with them. He would miss the best parts of festival. Didn't he want to hear Collie's harp again? Before long, there would be dancing, and contests of strength. Had he seen the jugglers yet? Wouldn't he stay? No? Then they wished him good luck, and would come to watch him in a bit. Vandien left.

He shook the reins and his team uncoiled. He realized then that he had been hoping they would refuse to budge. He would have preferred to struggle with them in the late afternoon sun here in the alley, but they were limbering up their sinuous bodies, arching their short ugly necks, their tails coiling and recoiling like springs. They made chopping sounds with their snouty muzzles. Without warning, they scuttled down the street with Vandien in their wake.

He scarcely had time to respond to the greetings of folk in the street. "Early to the task, make a fine catch!" shouted someone. "Let's follow!" suggested a woman, but the man at her side pointed to the tavern and said something Vandien did not hear. He found a hard smile on his face and a perverse merriment took over his soul. To the task, then. Be drowned if you must, but do it with style. He gave one glance to the trail that wound down the cliff face. He longed for the sight of a tall panelled wagon on yellow spoked wheels, but he knew better than to hope for it. It wasn't there. He was alone, and the moon alone knew where Ki was. He might be running her head into the noose as well as his own. He doubted it. It sounded to him as if she had already drawn her own battle lines with the Windsingers. Well, this was his chance to settle a point he and Ki had long argued about. Did he make a greater fool of himself when he was alone, or when in her company?

His team scuttled from side to side in the roadway, flanked by the wooden sidewalks that fronted much of the road, and urged on by the sounds of Vandien's steps behind them. On one shoulder he had looped the coil of line from Srolan. The prod was tucked securely into his belt. The air off the sea was

cool, but not too frisky. A fine day for a festival. Helti had
pointed out to him the bluff where the festival Windsinger
traditionally stood. Vandien could see no sign of blue robes.
Perhaps he and Srolan had outmaneuvered her. She would not
expect him to be hastening early to his encounter, not after
flattening him this morning.

The wooden sidewalks and tidy cottages gave way to gear
huts cobbled together from whatever the sea tossed up. The
rocks in the road became larger, the puddles deeper, as the
way made the transition from road to footpath. The path itself
then spread out and dispersed over the pebbly shores. Vandien
had a clear view of the bay now. The only structures now were
boathouses and boatways, and then the docks standing stork-
legged and tall above the retreating tide. The pilings were black,
crusted with barnacles and festooned with sea plants.

Vandien's team whiffled suddenly as they went, and pulled
him on eagerly. He put himself between them and the sea and
paced them as they scuttled on, past a pier that trailed out into
the water like the rocky spine of some long dead beast. They
seemed to become more anxious with every step. Their splayed
feet slapped the pebbly beach, the rounded stones damp and
bare from the sea's retreat. Vandien stepped on a stray rag of
seaweed, he slipped, and was jerked to his feet again by the
pull of the leather rein in his fist. The skeel were making for
the sea. Over their swaying heads, Vandien could see the
emerging walls and truncated chimneys of the old village. Beyond them he could sight a darker huddle beneath the waves.
The Windsingers' temple was still covered.

Sixteen splayed feet flapped and splashed into the water.
As soon as it felt the damp, the left rear skeel sank to its belly
and tried to lie motionless. The team seesawed around it, the
others eager to go but unable to pry their teammate loose.
Vandien could see it attempting to work its flat feet in deeper
among the pebbles and sand. The other three squealed and
struggled to go on. Just as Vandien bent to give its tail a tweak,
one of its brethren gave it a stinging slash with its whiplike
tail. A bubbly welt rose instantly on the mottled grey hide, and
the recalcitrant skeel squeaked and surged to its feet. The team
plowed into the retreating waves. Vandien followed.

The water was cold but not numbing as it rose over his low
fisherman's boots. The loose trousers flapped around his calves
and then grew heavy with water, but the wool held its warmth.

Vandien soon found himself grateful for that. The skeel were more eager to advance than the tide to retreat. Vandien held them in with a firm hand, but he soon found the waves licking about his hips. He braced his feet and prodded his team to a temporary halt. They stopped, but there was no lessening of the tension on the rein. As soon as he yielded, they would surge on.

Vandien stood wondering about the team's usefulness, and catching his breath. They were not swimming. They had scuttled out belly deep and, with no hesitation, pressed on, ignoring the waters that rose to cover their squat bodies and then their ugly heads. Vandien looked for rising bubbles, but either there were none or the action of the waves obscured them. His team squatted completely underwater, straining at the leash. Well, at least they seemed willing to pull.

Slowly the sunken village ebbed into view around them. Walls rose from the falling waters. There was not much left. Sturdy stone walls had worn down until they stood no higher than Vandien's knees. The small artifacts of a fishing village were long gone, either salvaged by the survivors or buried and eaten by the ocean. Rooms had been silted in with fine sand. Barnacles crusted chimneys. Crabs scuttled behind the angle of a crumbled doorway. Little had survived except for walls and hearths. Anything wood had long since been nibbled away by the sea. Metal items such as chimney spits had been eroded to skeletal remains. Vandien wondered how long it would be before even the walls were gone, how long until not one stone remained atop another. When that time came, would False Harbor still hold Temple Ebb, and would it still remember why?

He loosened his hold on the team and they promptly surged forward. It was hard to guide them now, for all he saw was the rein following them like a diviner's rod. The sun was sliding down the sky. Its light glanced off the waters, all but blinding Vandien. The breeze that rose was only the ordinary evening breeze off the sea. He stumbled over stones of walls long fallen as his team dragged him into deeper waters; the reins caught on the corner of a sunken building and the pull of the team whipped Vandien around it. He barked his shins on hidden obstacles, stumbled and caught himself. The water was nearly to his chest now. He had to fight both the pull of his team and his own buoyancy. If ever they dragged him completely off his feet, there would be little he could do about it.

He squinted his eyes against an orange and rose sunset. The light made sea and sky one before him. As the skeel dragged him inexorably deeper, the cold of the water began to close tight around his body. The heavy wool shielded him, hugging his body warmth to him, but the weight of it was becoming frightening. Although it helped him to keep his feet as the skeel pulled on, it would make it harder to rise if he were dragged under. "So I won't be." He smiled inanely at the sound of his own voice. The shushing waves and the tragic cries of the sea birds were a special kind of silence, not to be broken by the voice of a mere Human.

Ahead of him, a wave suddenly tipped white in the middle of its green-capped family. Again, and again, there was that flash of white amidst creamy green. Then a black tooth began to rise slowly from the water. The uppermost of the surviving walls of the temple were beginning to emerge, tracing the outlines of their old foundations. The temple was as jagged as a decayed molar of black bone. The sea water trapped inside it swirled angrily, seeking escape. Vandien heard the rattle of stone against stone. The pull of the tide was thwarted by the stubborn walls. The frustrated water seethed within the temple.

The ocean had not wrought its will upon the temple. It had been built in old times and by old ways. What powers had lifted and arranged those huge blocks of black stone? No mortar showed, but there were fine seams showing blacker between the stones. No seaweed dared to cling to them; even the barnacles were only scattered white dots over the surface. The few crustaceans that clung to it were small ones. There were no generations of barnacles clinging to the backs of their parents like on the walls of the submerged village. The black stones stood immune to their encroachment.

The closer Vandien got to the temple, the more monstrous it loomed. Only a sunken building, he reminded himself as its ominous shadow fell upon him, shielding his eyes from the glaring sunset. It stood open to the sky, its vaulted ceiling long gone. If ever it had boasted a lofty bell tower, that, too, had fallen. Vandien wondered briefly about the legends of the bell ringing. How likely was a bell in a cellar? Perhaps there had been a bell tower that had stood after the temple sank. Perhaps

it had rung beneath the water, dampening the spirits of the
villagers long after the fall of the temple. Such a sound would
not have been forgotten in a generation, or even three. It did
not matter that it no longer rang; if it had rung but once before
it fell, it would have been enough to spark a legend.

The skeel stopped. The black stone wall blocked them. They
could not surge over this wall, and drag Vandien after them.
He stood chest deep in cold water, looking up. The black stones
rose higher than he could reach. His team pulled left, and then
right seeking a route around this obstacle. With a sinking heart,
Vandien realized that he did not know where the entrance was.
He had assumed the walls had been worn and crumbled away
like the village huts. How was he to get into the place to search
it? If the entrance wasn't on this side, it was on the other, still
underwater. The temple was huge. Even one circuit of it would
take up precious time. The light was ebbing as fast as the water.
Vandien's courage sank with it.

A stab of light and a slosh of white turned his head. The
light and the slosh returned for an instant. Sound poured forth
from the temple with the ebbing water. The descending water
bared the arched portal of the temple. Now a handsbreadth of
light showed above the water. The waves swirled in and out
of the draining temple, creating a current, and eddies. Waves
rushed in and then gushed out almost immediately. Vandien
bided his time, staring up at the chiseled lintel. A row of
Windsingers was depicted. Their outstretched arms were linked,
their robes fluttered in a petrous breeze. Their lips were wide
with song. A common enough scene to be carved in such a
place, but Vandien found it unsettling. A subtle wrongness
teased his eyes. He saw the lintel only as it was illuminated
by the same flashes of sunset that blinded him. But were not
the mouths stretched too wide in song, the eyes inhumanly
puckered? Humans were not the only species to become Windsingers, he reminded himself. Perhaps these changelings were
some other race. Their arms were sinuously long from shoulder
to elbow, but stout and stumpy from elbow to wrist. The robes
sheltered his eyes from the rest of their bodies. Vandien continued to stare at them. "Probably just a poor sculptor," he
remarked reassuringly to his sunken team.

The light of the sunset that broke through the portal was
dimmer now. Soon the sun would sink completely, and he
would have to work by touch. He did not want to waste what

little light he would have. He could pass safely through the
door now, if there were no steps down into the temple.

His groping feet edged behind his team. They scuttled away
from him, following the wall of the temple. As soon as they
reached the portal, they surged through it. Vandien saw no
sign of his beasts except for a skirling in the waters. The stout
rein followed them. The water became deeper, rising shoulder
high. Before he could check them, the team dragged him on.
Salt water licked his stubbled chin as the Windsingers danced
over his head. He stumbled, but could not catch himself though
his free hand flailed the water. The strap twined around his
wrist dragged him ruthlessly on. Vandien went down and under.
His sodden clothes sank him as his team towed him on.

The water cushioned his impact as his chest met the stone
steps that rose just inside the temple's entrance. Vandien scrabbled to his feet spitting water. A toss of his head flung wet
curls from his eyes. Water from his hair streamed over his face.
He gasped in air gratefully. His team had stopped. He stood
within the temple of the Windsingers.

Jagged black walls cupped the orange sky of the dying sun.
As much of the temple had fallen within the walls as outside
them; huge stones nosed up from the swirling waters. The voice
of the water was amplified here as the sea breathed in and out
through the temple door. Vandien felt it tug at him with each
passage. The temple stretched before him, immense and sullen,
glory fallen on hard times. Bas relief figures had paced those
walls once, but most of their heads had crumpled away with
the upper walls. Their gilt adornment had peeled and fled,
remaining only as traces in the corner of a mouth, or an unshed
tear at the angle of an eye. No barnacle or sea plant had ventured
within the temple. The retreating waves left the black walls
bare. The tumbled stones could have hidden a thousand chests
from a hundred searchers. A fool's errand.

Feeling with his toes, Vandien edged up four steps. Pushing
his foot forward, he found a flat floor beneath him. The water
reached only to the bottom of his ribs. Either he was at the top
of the steps or on a small landing. His motionless team was
invisible under the water. He had ceased to wonder if they
needed air. Those big feet would paddle them up to the surface
if they wanted a breath. For now, the less bother they were to
him, the better.

He slipped the coil of rope from his shoulder and stooped

to knot one end of it to the center ring of the harness. The skeel had settled. He intended to explore the temple, and he did not wish to have the reins fouled on hidden stones. The skeel remained still as he stepped away from them. Slowly he paid out the grey line as he clambered and sloshed to the southwest corner of the temple. It had nothing to recommend it except Janie's story; one stone-jumbled corner of the temple looked much like the other to Vandien. The water eased in and out of the temple, but the level continued to gradually fall. The submerged floor of the temple was littered with pieces of stone ranging in size from the ones that barked his shins to the ones he had to clamber over. He went slowly, testing his footing. If there were steps up into the temple, then Janie's tale of a chamber below was probably true and he had no wish to suddenly plunge down into it. But the stone underfoot was as sound as the stubborn walls.

The light on the water was wrong. He could see nothing through it. Everything within the walls of the temple shone with the same wet blackness. Time leaked away as he moved slowly through the temple, prodding the floor with his toes, and occasionally stooping beneath the cold water to try his fingers against objects he encountered. He found many rocks, some more or less rectangular in shape and feeling, to his shod feet and chilled hands, much like metal chests. Three times he raised such objects, only to find a square rock as his reward. How many times had this temple been searched since the days of Janie's grandfather? How many times had stones been raised and dropped? Whatever the old man had found here could have been buried even deeper by the searchers that followed. In the corners of the temple, sand and smoothed pebbles had been heaped by the endless dance of the waves. The chest could be buried there, the metal gnawed away by the salt water, and whatever treasure it held, scattered. It was a hopeless task. And the light was failing.

The water was only waist deep now. Vandien climbed out of it for a moment, and sat on a pile of leaning stones jutting up from the water. Their hard cold surface was no comfort to his chilled body. The skin of his hands and fingers stood up in tender ridges. Calluses made harder yellowed patches on his hands. Within the sodden boots, his feet were tender and sore. The constant immersion had softened his skin until the least abrasion felt like a blow. He could not count how many times his toes had rapped against immovable stones beneath the surface. The weight of his woolen clothes sagged on him. Vandien's spirit, shored up all day by black humor, sank into the depths of the cold water.

A voice rose in a paean of loneliness. Higher than bird song, purer than the wind's whistling, it soared into the greying sky and hung there. The note stretched, breathlessly, impossible, filling all the sky with sound. It called forth the stars that suddenly shone there. Night cupped the world beneath its hand. The temple walls were a starless blackness against the speckled sky. Then the voice fell suddenly, sliding down the scale, swirling music through the night sky. The wind began to rise. Higher, the voice now went, higher, and the winds followed it, rushing up to match its pristine flight. Then Killian let her voice fall again and the winds dashed down with the weight of dropped stones.

The water around Vandien boiled, tipped with white in the darkness. The line to his team grew taut in his hand. It slid through his water wrinkled fingers. He tightened his grip but the rope burned through his palms. He rose, feet braced, both hands gripping the line that was, despite all his efforts, ripping through his fingers. Then, like a breaking axle jolt, the knot at the end of the line caught behind his fists. He was jerked from his pile of rocks, dragged floundering through the water. His body caught between two upthrusting rocks. Vandien dragged himself to his feet, fighting the line and braced himself against the two stones. The line tightened in his grip, seeming to stretch with the tension. His hands burned, his shoulder gave a creak of protest. Vandien's teeth were bared and he would not loosen his hold. Let the rope break, or his hands be jerked loose from his body, but no one would say he had let go.

As suddenly as the line had pulled, it went slack. He fell backwards in the water, catching himself before he went under again. Black and silver shone the watery temple in the starlight. The voice sang on.

Wind blew his soaked hair from his face. Vandien struggled through the choppy waters within the temple. Spume flew up whenever the water dashed against a rock. The salt stung his eyes, leaked into his tightly closed mouth. His scar shrank and pulled at his face. The old pain of it began to eat into his flesh and send spasms of agony into the bones of his skull. And still the Windsinger sang, never pausing even for a breath, rising impossibly high and raining down in streamers of pure sound. It whipped the wind to frenzy, and the wind battered the waves to froth. The cold came.

This was no chill of autumn, but the full slash of winter's claws, brought down from the moon's cold heart. Vandien shuddered before that attack. He was blinded by the salt spray flung into his face. The wind buffeted him, filling his ears with a roaring that could not drown out the silver notes of that distant singer. Vandien leaned on a rock, sucking in air between clenched teeth.

"Vandien!"

A woman's voice called his name through the howl of wind and hymn of Windsinger. More than that he could not tell. Hope surged up in him as rapidly as it had fallen. He squinted his eyes through the dark and storm.

"Ki! Over here! Ki!" He stood up on his rock, waving his hands, reckless of his balance. "My damn team's bolted, but I've got a line on them. They're somewhere in this mess." He leaped down from the rock without waiting for her reply, and began winding up the line. It was a struggle to follow its twining course between the rocks in the darkness, but he'd be damned if he'd let her see just how out of control the situation was.

Wood scraped against stone. A dark lantern was partially unshielded; its yellow light guttered brightly in the darkness. Janie sat on a crude driftwood raft, the lantern firmly fastened to its center. Her drenched clothes showed that she had pushed the raft out to the temple through the ebbing tides. She rested on it now, one hand hooked on an outcropping of rock. Her eyes were stony as the walls of the temple, and as cold. Her fair hair was a colorless flame blowing about her face. The lantern illuminated little besides her. She shouted to be heard.

"I thought you deserved at least an audience of one, for your sincerity." She paused. "The others are too well into their drinking and singing, you know. Killian has stirred up too much of a storm to make it entertaining to watch you. Only a handful turned out last year to watch the teamster. Perhaps in a few more years 'teamster' will be an honorary title given to whatever minstrel or clown they can find to entertain on festival night." She stared down at his face. His curls had given up their spring and lay dank against his skull and neck. Chill reddened his face except for the scar like a white brand. His clothes hung sopping from his narrow frame. His eyes were dark pits, his mouth a flat line.

"In truth, I had forgotten to expect an audience," he said.

"Yet you sounded glad when first you answered my call. I thought for a moment that you had found the chest."

"I thought you were someone else. A friend of mine who had said she would try to come and help me with this task."

"Well, I don't suppose you would name me as your friend, but I have come to help you."

"Janie. That isn't what I meant."

"Explain later." She cut him off roughly. "The singer's in full voice now, and we haven't much time until the tide turns. Hard to believe that's little Killian up there, isn't it? Who would have suspected lungs like that in her dainty form?"

"There are many shades to the word 'friend,' Janie."

"And none of the colors suit me. Stow it, teamster. We've work to do here. Have you found any sign of the chest?"

"None!" The wind snatched his reply away, but she read his face. "Let me get my team in hand again," he roared to her, and she nodded.

She sat cross-legged on the bobbing raft, watching him wind up his rope as he followed its zigzag course through the temple. Twice he had to duck under dark and heaving water to unhook the line from jagged projections. He finally reached the knot that attached it to the ring. He nearly stepped on the team huddled in a corner of the temple, not far from where he had entered.

"Now what?" he demanded of Janie. It was a comfort to roar out words at someone. She would hear him over the wind and slam of waves. It was a small vent for his frustration.

She shrugged. "Pull some rocks over!" she yelled back. "Start in my grandfather's corner!"

"Why not? Giddap, team." Vandien stooped under the water and gave a coiling tail a tweak. The team sidled off and he herded them to the southwest corner. "Pick a rock!" he invited jovially.

Janie used both hands to push the hair from her face. The salt water borne on the wind had soaked it already. Tendrils clung to her forehead and cheeks. "That one!" She pointed to the tallest, a narrow jagged thing like a crooked finger pointing at the sky.

"Fine!" He kept a grip on the rope near the ring. The free
end of the line he tossed to Janie. "I'm the teamster," he
reminded her. "You're the fisherwoman, and the world looks
to the seafolk for sturdy knots. Make it fast to the rock you
picked, and let's see what we can turn up."

His twisted grin was not to be refused. A wry smile lit her
usually sullen face and she slipped willingly from the crude
raft into the chill waters. Vandien watched her settle the line
in loops around the stone, throwing the line into a knot as easily
as he told stories on his story-string. She threw up her hands
to show she was finished and waded clear of the rock.

Vandien stepped toward the team and stooped and felt for
tails. But before he found one, the rope snapped taut, stinging
his hip as it burned past him. His movement had been enough
to spook the team. He dodged back from the thrumming line
and threw up a forearm to shield his face. The silver grey line
shimmered with the intensity of the pull. But the stone did not
budge. The wind whistled past them as Killian's voice rose
and fell. The cold water boiled around them as the skeel maintained a steady pull. But the stone was adamant.

"Let's try a different one!" Vandien suggested loudly.

Janie nodded with a grimace. She was plainly unimpressed
with his efforts. But Vandien would not fault his beasts. The
humming line attested to the steadiness of their pull. He doubted
that mules or horses could do better, given these circumstances.
He could not even picture Ki's great grey horses standing among
these rocks; they would have no room to maneuver the bulk
that made up their pull. He stepped toward his skeel, intending
to prod them to stillness so Janie could unfasten her knots.
Churning water told of the skeel's agitation at his approach.
Before he could tap them down, he heard Janie's scream of
warning.

The stone was coming. Silently it fell like a bludgeoned
giant. Vandien gave a hoarse cry and tried to scramble out of
its path. His frantic efforts were swallowed by the clinging sea.
The water cradled him as he fell backwards. The line never
went slack. The scrabbling team kept it taut as they surged
away from the falling stone. Vandien saw the line pass between
two standing stones before the black water closed over his head.
A wall of water washed over him and pressed him down.

A hundred years later he came up out of the darkness. A
searing cold wind was a blessing on his aching face as he spat

and coughed and snorted. He could hear Janie screaming his name, but he had no breath to answer her. Water poured down his face from his sodden cap and hair, flooding his nose and mouth with water when he tried to suck in air. It was pitch black now, night, all trace of evening gone in the moment he had spent under the water.

His eyes found Janie's lantern first, a tossing bit of yellow light in the blackness. She crouched over it, unharmed. His team had vanished. The tall stone they had pulled down lay where he had last seen them, partially jutting from the water. He could see one loop of the rope still knotted about it.

"Janie!" he roared, and she heard him at last. The lantern light caught the wildness of her eyes as she turned to him. She jumped from her raft into the water and waded toward him. One hand, hooked into a log of the raft, towed it along behind her.

"I thought you were dead!" she screeched. "I thought it had landed on top of you." Her face had gone white, fear dragging at her mouth. She reached him and let go of her raft to seize him in a convulsive hug. Vandien was amazed at the strength of her arms as she clung to him. "You were under so long!" she said into his ear. Her body trembled against him.

"Just long enough to learn how stupid I was to jerk at the stone that way." He patted her shoulder lightly. "It's all right. No one was hurt."

Janie stiffened and was instantly apart from him, the frightened child swallowed by the outraged woman. "And small credit to you, you stupid landsman!"

Vandien let the wind blow her words away. "Did you see my team?" he asked. She shook her head, still torn by conflicting emotions. She turned away from him, and hurried over to where the stone had stood, to begin poking diligently about in the water. Vandien trudged forward through the water to where the line was still wrapped around the fallen stone. He managed to latch his hand under it and followed it forward along the length of the fallen giant. The rope was tight against his hand, but not singing with pull as it had been. He grimaced in the darkness, making his scar wrinkle painfully. Despite their ugliness, he had grown more than tolerant of the skeel. He hoped they had come to no harm.

He clambered over the fallen stone to follow the line as it snaked between two standing pillars. He took another step and found himself in water to his chin. The line still led down. Vandien slid his booted foot forward and found emptiness. His toe slid across a straight edge of stone. The answer came to him. He was standing on the first downward step of a stairwell. He backed up, staring down at the black water before him. The beasts had scuttled down those submerged stairs and taken the line with them. He pulled at the rope and felt an answering tug. At least they were alive. He could imagine them huddling their bodies down flat, digging those splay feet in for purchase. Four beasts that could pull down that standing stone weren't going to be budged by his pulling on a line. He'd lost them.

Janie sloshed up to him. The waves alternately cloaked and revealed her breasts beneath her sodden smock. Vandien became suddenly aware that the water was higher than it had been. The tide had turned and was advancing on them. It would be easy to be trapped here. The Windsinger's voice stirred the tide to new energies. Every wave that came in the temple's door surged higher than the previous one. Once the door was covered, they would grow exhausted long before the waters rose above the black walls. They'd drown like rats in a pit. The urgency in the story Janie had told came home to him. Leave or die. That had been their choice then.

He looked at Janie's lantern raft. If he abandoned his team, they could cling to it. It was no more than a few driftwood logs hastily lashed together, but they could hold onto it and survive. He pictured the rising water carrying them up slowly, until they could float free over the temple's walls. And probably be driven out to the sea, still clinging to it, to drown there. Scarcely an improvement over drowning in the temple.

"There was nothing under it!" Janie was shouting in his ear. "We'll have to try another one. Back up the team. My knot's trapped under the stone, but with some slack I may be able to work it loose. Otherwise, we'll have to cut the line."

He stared at her silently. Laughter welled up in him, but found no voice. The wind drove salt water between his lips and into his mouth. All things were lost to him; his chance for his face, for the gold, to earn Srolan's respect, to ease Janie's woes, even the ugly team he had borrowed. He had lost it all, and this child did not even comprehend that. Janie took his silence for assent. She turned from him, still towing her raft, and struggled along the falling stone. She stooped by the rope, and then shook her head. "Back them up. I need some slack."

"They went down stairs." Vandien spoke low, but somehow the words carried to her.

"They couldn't. We covered it up years ago!" Janie was incredulous. "I was a little girl, then, but I heard about it. They covered it up because someone fell in it and nearly drowned, during a Temple Ebb. Everyone was so busy watching the teamster, no one saw the danger until it was almost too late."

"Well, it's not covered now. And my team's down there."

Janie sloshed over to stare down at the water in front of him. "I guess this gives you an easy out," she said with sudden bitterness. "There's never been a teamster yet that put his heart into this. Why should you be different? Keep your scar, damn you! Go back to the inn, laugh and drink! Damn you, damn you, damn you!" Her voice rose in shrillness and vehemence, cutting through the wind to beat against him.

Gripping the rope loosely in his hand, he took a deep breath and a step down. Water lapped his chin. He steeled himself, and stepped down again. His eyes were useless now. His body wanted to float back up to the surface, but he kept his grip on the rope. He'd see how far down these steps went, if nothing else. He reached his other hand down and gripped the rope to pull himself deeper. His feet lost their contact on the stairs. He trod water and felt his feet scrape and glance off the stairs. His lungs were beginning to swell within his chest. He resolved to try one more step. He reached his free hand, got a good grip, and hauled himself deeper.

The surge of the team jerked Vandien deeper before it snapped the rope free of his grip. Salt water stung the abraded skin of his water softened hand. It took a moment before he realized the rope was gone. His tuggings had spooked the team. He'd have to find the rope and start again, but first some air. His bursting lungs prompted him to kick strongly, reaching up for the air. With two strokes his outstretched hands met smooth stone. He scrabbled along it in the dark, hoping his sense of direction was good. The opening of the stair well had to be nearly overhead, unless the team had jerked him farther than he thought. Unless. A bubble escaped his mouth.

NINETEEN

AT the bottom of the hill, Ki took off the wheel brake. She was amazed it had held. She let the team stand for a short time; their sides worked in and out with their breathing. Sigmund dropped his head down nearly to his knees; Sigurd's heavy mane was streaming out in a grey sheaf. Ki's own hair was twisted into a braid and trapped inside her hood. She leaned off the seat to look back up the cliff road they had come down in the roaring wind. The wind still felt as if it might blow her wagon over, but at least now it would not bounce down a cliff face if it fell. The Windsinger's voice was a pure thread of sound in the wind's rough weaving.

She squinted her eyes against the wind's lash and picked up the reins. Two heavy slaps were required before the horses grudgingly began to move. The team was finished, and Ki nearly so. But she must get to the lights of False Harbor and find them a shelter for the night. The team needed a dry stable out of the wind, and she needed a warm bath and a hot meal. Much as she disliked inns, she'd be glad to find one tonight.

She pushed on. The wind was a living thing with a rapacious appetite, a beast out to destroy anything that moved against its

will. It snatched at her clothing, and snapped and fluttered the
horses' manes and tails. Ki clenched her jaw against it. She
had known there would be a sung wind here this night. After
her recent dealings with Windsingers, she feared them more
and respected them less. The winds were only extensions of
their own fickle moods, subject to all the vagaries of pride and
the distractions of personal power struggles. They would rip
this little village off its foundations and fling it into the sea
with no more thought than she gave to driving her team over
an anthill. Somewhere tonight, Vandien was opposing the will
of the Windsingers, daring the full brunt of their power. She
cursed herself again. She should have talked him out of this.
She should have offered to let him use the team, and then come
to False Harbor too late. But she had told him it was all a joke,
a charade. This wind was no charade.

Ki could not forget the bait that had drawn him here. To
lift the scar from his face! An impossible thing, an offer only
a fool would believe. But Vandien wasn't a fool; he was only
a man trapped into a fool's act by a hidden hunger: to have his
own face back.

She tried to remember what he had looked like before he
was scarred. The image was vague. She had a blurred memory
of the night he had appeared in her camp, attempting to steal
her horses; he had been so starved and weak that she had easily
wrestled him to the ground. She remembered thinking he was
handsome in a ragged way, but she had felt little attraction to
him. She hadn't wanted any man then, hadn't had any love
left to give after the Harpies had taken the lives of her beloved
husband and children and then come after her own. She had
agreed with reluctance to let Vandien ride with her team out
of the mountain wilderness near the Pass of the Sisters. When
the Harpies finally caught up to her, it was Vandien, not Ki,
who fell before those gruesome claws; Vandien who carried
the physical scars of that battle. She had never really seen what
it had done to him; not until now. It had taken Dresh to throw
it into her face.

She had been more than insensitive. She had been callous.
She had felt guilty about the pain it gave him on cold days.
She had regretted it being there, so visible a reminder of that
battle. But it had not mattered to her. It had not affected her
feelings for him, had never made her see him as anything less
than Vandien. The scar that divided his face was no more to

her than a splash of mud upon his cloak, or a rent in his leggings. It was a minor detail, subtracting nothing from the man. But how had it seemed to him? Ki saw it now, in her mind's eyes; a jagged rent down his face, always paler or redder than the rest of his face. She thought of the innkeepers and hostlers who casually called him Scar, in the same way they called her Teamster. More than once she had noticed children peering up at him wide-eyed, curious, but too shy to ask about the strange mark down his face. He was still as quick spirited as he had been when she first met him, but had his humor always had such dark edges? She had no way of knowing. That Vandien had scarred his face for her was bad enough. That his life should be scarred as well was unbearable.

Ki found the inn more by the sounds and lights than by the sign swinging in the wind. Snatches of song and rags of laughter carried through the wind's roar. She turned her team into the alley. The inn broke the worst of the wind from them. The sudden cessation of its constant roar was like awakening from sleep. Ki's cheeks stung from the wind's caresses. She found her lantern and managed to kindle it.

The stiff leather and heavy buckles resisted her chilled fingers, but the harness finally dropped away from the team. Behind the inn was a building, more shed than stable. A lone cow turned rebuking brown eyes on her as she opened the door to admit her team and the windstorm. She hung her lantern from the hook and turned her team loose in the shed. It was not intended for such massive beasts. There were no stalls, but there was plenty of hay heaped in a loft. She shook some down for them, left them loose in the shed and made her way back to the inn.

The sounds ebbed as she stepped within. Ki thought at first it was the result of the blast of wind that came in with her, but as eyes scanned her and turned away, conversation resumed. "Not the teamster yet," she heard a woman remark. "You'll have to give him credit for making an honest try, Berni, even if he isn't much to look at." The chance words squeezed Ki's heart. Not much to look at. A slow anger nibbled at her as she pushed her way through to the fire. The worst of this, she thought, was that it made her think too much.

Her relationship with Vandien had been a thing that had happened, a pleasure accepted as casually as clean water and fair weather. The give and take of it had been natural, the cares and restrictions of it balanced by the camaraderie and the sharing. That was all gone now. She asked herself now what that relationship had cost Vandien, and she looked at the debts of it. Even the finest jewelry will have a flaw, if one looks at it closely enough. Once she had found every nick and scratch in their partnership, would she ever easily enjoy it again?

This had to be the innmaster, pushing up to her through the crowd. He looked down on Ki from his height, and she stared up at him. The black hair on his arms matched that raked scantily over his head. Grey-blue eyes were frankly puzzled by her.

"We didn't expect strangers this night. Few come to our town during Temple Ebb Wind. What can I bring you?"

Ki found a smile and plastered it on her face. "Anything hot to drink you may have, innmaster. I've already taken the liberty of putting my team in your cow shed, to get them out of this storm. Hope you don't mind that. I actually came seeking a friend of mine, with whom I was to meet here. Vandien?"

The Innmaster raised his eyebrows. "Vandien. That'd be our teamster—about so tall, with a scar down the middle of his face, right?"

Helti saw the woman's face spasm as if with sudden pain. "Yes. Is he about?"

Helti smiled. "He should soon be. No one lasts long in a storm like this. Killian surprised us all. To think that a little slip of a Windsinger like her could bring up a storm like this. We haven't seen an Ebb Wind like this, for, oh, must be close to five Temple Ebbs. Such a merry, friendly little thing, so close to Human you might forget what she was. And then she sings up a storm like this. Surprised us all, but the teamster most of all, I'll wager."

"I'll wager," Ki agreed grimly. "Where will I find him, then?"

"In the Windsingers' sunken temple, but you've no need to go out in this wind. Nor wish to, either, I suppose. The tide has turned. Water will be rising, and they'll be headed in by now. You needn't worry about him forgetting the dangers of the tide. He'll be more than ready to come in by now, and Janie is with him. Whatever else Janie is, she's fisherfolk, and she won't forget a tide. She knows how it rips in over the flats when it comes. I'd be surprised if they weren't already wading back by now. It'll take them a while, in this wind. Sit a bit, and have a hot mug of spiced wine, and wait them out. There's rare fine food from the kitchen this night, hearty as well as the sweets. If you're the teamster's friend, I'll put your bill with his, and you'll both owe naught tomorrow. Damme if he hasn't surprised us all with his spunk. It's little enough he's asked from us. We'll be kind to his friend, if he won't let us be generous with him. Sit down, now." The innmaster smelled of his own spiced wine. His generosity to himself was making him generous with his words and his goods.

Ki rubbed her face wearily. The warmth from the fire was finally beginning to reach her. Her clothes felt steamy against her skin. She could just stay here and wait for him. She did not need to go back out in that windstorm. To do so would be a meaningless gesture. But she felt like making gestures tonight. Vandien might not find it so meaningless.

"I'll take the spiced wine, Innmaster. But then I think I'll go out to meet Vandien."

"Well, if you're so insistent, I suppose you'll have your way."

"I suppose I will," Ki agreed.

The heated wine warmed her hands, and then her whole body. Helti's directions were simple. The others were too caught up in their own holiday to pay much attention to the stranger. Ki pushed the door open against the wind, and stumbled down the narrow streets, buffeted by the storm. Her boots discovered every rut and pothole. She wished in vain for a lantern that would stay lit in this storm.

The unfamiliar road stretched into the darkness. She could hear the boom and crash of waves eager to reclaim the beach. The wind whistled past her and the Windsinger sang on. The beach came into view, white frilled waves dashing up the dark sands and falling back in a lace of foam. Rising fast. Ki walked out to the incoming edge and stood.

"Vandien!" she called loudly. The wind blew her voice landward. She strained her eyes until she saw the dark hulk of the Windsingers' temple. "Vandien!" she shouted again.

She put one boot in the water. A wave grabbed her foot threateningly, and slid a cold hand up her calf. Sand slid away from under her. So damn cold and so damn wet. "And so damn stubborn!" she yelled at Vandien, wherever in hell he was. Angrily she sloshed out toward the temple, struggling through rising water. Past her knees it rose, coldly familiar, up to her hips, and then waist high, and still she was wading. The shape of the temple resolved itself into jagged walls against the sky. The water crept up her ribs. Every wave she met threatened to lift her off her feet. The wind dashed sea water into her face. Her hood streamed water in a trickle down her cheek and down the back of her neck. "Vandien!" she screamed, expecting no answer.

"Vandien!"

It was either an echo or someone mocking her from within the temple. Ki was not positive she had heard it; perhaps it was only a trick of the wind through the ruins. She pushed on, half swimming through each incoming wave. The crumpled wall of the temple loomed above her, and she caught a sudden promise of light from within; only a glimpse, but it showed her the portal of the temple. Unfortunately, the bottom seemed to drop deeper between her and that portal. She set her teeth and plunged through the water. Her clothes dragged at her; she should have left her boots on shore. But she was within the temple at least. She tried to tread water and get her bearings, but her boots suddenly rasped against a floor. Thank the moon the temple was higher within than without. She could stand again, though the suck and push of water through the portal sought to sweep her balance from her. The light she had glimpsed was gone.

Again she heard a voice. "Vandien!"

A dim flash of light broke from beyond two standing pillars. "Vandien!" Ki echoed, plunging toward the light.

A sodden child hunched shivering on a makeshift raft. A lantern was burning out beside her. Her colorless hair was slicked to her skull, and her clothes ran water. She turned a startled face on Ki at her call. A look almost of anger, or jealousy, crossed her face. She squared her shoulders at Ki, revealing the thrust of young breasts against her smock. Ki wondered at her presence here, but had no time to worry about it.

"Where is he?" she demanded, advancing through the whirling water.

"Who are you?" countered the woman on the raft.

"Ki. Where is Vandien?"

Janie glared at her. "He went down there." She managed to make her shout sullen.

Ki's eyes followed where she pointed. Dark water met her

gaze. Fear squeezed her, colder than the sea around her. Anger surged up in her for this woman who pointed so coldly at the water and said Vandien was down there. She wanted to throttle her and make her scream out when, why, and what in hell he was doing down there, but she had no time. The cold water mocked her, sucking at her limbs as she tried to hurry over to where the girl had pointed. When one of her boots suddenly met only water, Ki rocked back, shivering. Janie quailed before her look.

"He followed the rope down! His team went down there!" Janie suddenly volunteered. Her eyes denied any guilt.

"His team?" It made no sense, but sense didn't matter. He had been down there too long. Ki groped along the fallen stone, following the rope. It was tight to her touch. He must still be at the end of it. With a shudder of horror and fear, she drew in a shaking breath and stepped down into black water.

Coldness pressed inside her ears, tried to sneak up her nose. She stared blankly into the watery darkness. She forced herself down another step. It changed nothing. Gripping the rope with both hands, she took a third step down.

A glancing blow swept the side of her head. She staggered from the impact and nearly lost her breath, but not her grip on the rope. She tried not to wonder what was in this blackness with her. Flesh-eating fish, perhaps? She couldn't change that. She pulled hard at the line, hoping to feel an answering tug, but it remained taut. It could be snagged on something below. She did not believe Vandien could be holding it so tight; not after being under so long. She could not see him, she could not call him. If Vandien had chosen to come down this way, it was the last choice he had ever made. Ki's eyes stung with salt water. She backed up a step.

Again she felt a turbulence, and something brushed her shoulder. But there was less energy to the movement now. As it passed, she felt the rasp of cloth on her cheek. Ki grabbed.

She lost the steps, but not the rope. She would not loose her grip from that. The leg she seized gave a feeble kick and was still. A hand brushed her hood and caught in the cloth there. In the darkness she trapped the leg between her chest and arm and again gripped the rope with both hands. The leg was limp against her, but the hand held on. Stay with me, she thought desperately as air tried to press out of her lips. Hang on. She fumbled her way back up the rope.

She felt his weight on her back, and then a hand caught at her burden as she emerged from the water. Janie had an awkward grasp on his shoulder and was heaving ineffectually at his limp weight. Ki caught him at the hips and tumbled him up onto the raft, nearly upsetting the lantern and putting the top of the raft awash. Water streamed from him. Breath burst out of him with a spray of water. He snorted and choked feebly, without even enough energy to drive the water from his mouth. Janie was paralyzed. Ki glared at her, but Janie was unaware of it. She stared at Vandien as if at an unfamiliar fish. Ki reached up and grabbed one of Vandien's shoulders, to roll him to face her. She could find no words to speak, nor breath to say them. She drew gasp after gasp deep into her own lungs. Vandien sputtered again, and coughed, this time with more energy. One eyelid slid open. He regarded Ki miserably.

"I nearly drowned down there." His calm voice barely reached Ki. He would have used the same tone to complain about a badly rutted road.

"I noticed that," she heard herself reply conversationally.

Vandien's lips sneered up and she thought he would choke again. But after a couple of gasps, he began to laugh. He tried to sit up, but could not. His laughter was broken by coughing. Ki found herself grinning as she gripped his shoulders by the baggy smock. Janie stared at both of them, not comprehending that survival was the most basic joke of all. When he could no longer laugh, he lay motionless on the raft, still smiling and coughing intermittently. Ki glanced up at the solemn faced young woman. "Let's get out of here," she suggested. She put her weight against the raft, pushing it toward the portal.

"We can't!" Janie's voice went raw and high.

Ki's glance shot to the portal, but there was still enough space to push through it. The raft might scrape on the tapering sides of the arch, and Janie would have to duck low. But they'd make it.

"We haven't finished!" Janie's cry was outraged. "We can't go yet. We haven't found the chest of the Windsingers." Ki received these words with a cold look. She continued to lean against the raft, moving it along. Janie turned on Vandien. "If we leave now, teamster, you haven't succeeded. You haven't earned your fee and you've lost your team. Think on that, Vandien! No team! No money! And you'll wear that scar to the end of your days. Forever!"

"He would in any case." Ki kept her voice low, but it carried through the wind. "Why not offer an impossible reward for an impossible task? Maybe next Temple Ebb it will be a mountain of gold."

"It's not impossible! It's not!" Janie grabbed at Vandien, shaking him. He was powerless to resist her. Her shaking flopped him about like a rag doll. "Srolan would never offer the impossible. And the chest is here! It is! My grandfather saw it. He held it in his own hands."

"Leave him alone!" Ki roared. Her green eyes flashed as with a back-handed blow she struck Janie's hands away from her friend. "Isn't half-drowning him enough to please you? Do you have to keep on tormenting him with offers of what can't be? Not finished here? You came damn near to finishing him anywhere!"

Even in the dim lantern light, Ki could see the rush of blood to Janie's face. Her eyes distended, her hands became claws. Ki did not flinch, but she tightened her muscles in preparation for the attack she was sure would come. But only hard words pelted against her, screamed out in a voice shriller than the wind. "You know what it is, Vandien? She doesn't want that scar lifted from your face. It marks you as hers. She knows that while you wear it, she need fear no rival, for no other woman would look at you. She came out here to stop you!"

Sickness swept Ki. Vandien reared his body up between them, dragging himself to a crouch. His black hair hung dripping on his forehead. The yellow lamplight made his skin sallow. His scar was a brand and his mouth a puckered slash. He turned accusing eyes on Ki. For one rending instant, Ki supposed that he believed Janie's accusation. "Can't leave my team!" he gasped out. He shook his head, scattering drops of salt water into the wind. "Got to get those skeel out, Ki! Four of them, and that's four more than I can afford."

"Skeel?" Ki was incredulous. "You brought a team of skeel out in salt water?"

"Why not?" Vandien was visibly recovering. He held himself between Janie and Ki, using his body to block the tensions that hummed between them. "They seemed to like fresh water well enough."

Ki laughed. She roared with laughter, and began again to push the raft toward the temple portal. Vandien coughed and stared at her. Janie was silent and sullen. A slow puzzled smile

began to dawn over his face. "Tell!" he demanded. "What in
hell is so damn funny?"

"Skeel!" Ki choked out the word. "In fresh water they soak
up moisture reserves. Makes them frisky, and gives them a lot
of stamina. But in salt water..." Ki dissolved in helpless
laughter. Vandien leaned forward, his dark face on a level with
her own. He kept trying to smooth out his face and be solemn,
but a smile kept tugging at the corners of his mouth. "In salt
water," Ki gasped out at last, "they go into rut. They go as
deep as they can, twine together in a knot and mate. For hours!
Days, sometimes! They don't stop until they're all mutually
fertilized. Then they'll come up and head for the open sea."
Another bubble of laughter from her. "Don't worry about them,
Vandien. We'll come back for them at the next low tide. They'll
be fine until then. In fact, they'll enjoy themselves immensely.
Most teams seldom get a chance to mate."

Vandien grinned feebly and swung his legs off the raft. "I
don't need help," Ki protested, but he only nodded toward the
portal. An incoming wave lifted Ki off her feet and for an
instant filled the portal. As the waves gushed out again, the
water sucked at the raft. Vandien and Ki braced to keep from
being dragged into the swirling water.

"Jump off, Janie!" Vandien called. "We're all going to get
wet going through that portal."

Janie didn't move. Her head came up, eyes narrowed. "I'm
not leaving. And you aren't taking my raft, nor my lantern.
You may not have the courage to see this through, but I do. I
won't leave until I have the Windsingers' chest."

"Or until you die?" Vandien asked.

"Or that." Janie spoke in a lull of wind, and her voice was
flat.

"Leave her," Ki suggested. Her stubbornness seemed the
whim of a spoiled child, and Ki had no intention of indulging
it.

"Wait," Vandien interceded, but Ki pointed at the portal.
The lintel disappeared at the height of each wave. As the water
receded, only a sliver of door showed.

"Time and tide wait on no one, Vandien. It's a long cold
swim back to shore. I don't think you'd make it. Our only
hope is to get out of here before the water gets deeper."

Vandien nodded at Ki, and made a gesture that hushed her.
He turned to Janie. "We're going now, Janie. There's no hope

of finding the chest now. The water's too deep and it's too dark. So you'll stay and die, and your legend will die with you. The village will remember your family as drunks and liars, and you as a fool. There's your little sister, of course, but she can grow up sweeping out the ashes of Helti's fires. She'll survive. Many children grow up on less. And each Temple Ebb to come will mean a little less. Teamster *will* become a meaningless title. Ebb will be when the jugglers come to entertain, and a Windsinger graciously performs for your village. That might be a good thing. Maybe it's time to end this ridiculous custom. The village would be wiser to forget the past and go on to other things. Your dying might be a very good thing."

Halfway through this speech, her face had crumpled, but Vandien pressed inexorably on. The veneer of womanhood cracked; the child's eyes welled angry tears that mingled with the salt spray on her face. Without a sound she swung off the raft and clung to the edge beside them. Ki took breath for a sarcastic remark, but Vandien's look stopped her.

"Let's go," he said, his deep voice cutting under the wind to reach them. They braced for a moment against the incoming wave. As the wave retreated and swirling water sucked at the raft, they pushed off. The raft was caught up like a bobbing cork. Their treading feet found no purchase. The raft sought the portal of the temple and wedged in it. The arched top of the portal was not wide enough for the raft to fit through it. "Put some weight on it!" Vandien yelled, hoping to sink it down to where it could pass. But it was too late. A fresh wave surged into the temple and they clung to the raft as it was pushed away from the door. They whirled, their feet no longer finding bottom. The wind shrieked with laughter.

"It's too late." Janie's voice was soft and hopeless. The portal was no longer visible. The water sloshed and rose within the temple, but the hole it entered by was covered. As if in sympathy with their hopes, the lantern flared once and went dark. Ki felt sick. "Too far to swim. Too cold," she whispered. The others couldn't hear her. But they already knew.

Vandien dragged himself back onto the raft. Ki did not blame him. She had not been out here as long as he had, nor had she been half-drowned. But her strength was draining, and Vandien must be at the dregs of his.

The black sky flecked with stars taunted them. Frills of froth were white within the temple, but little else showed. Ki clung to the water-slick logs of the raft. She could feel Janie beside her. Neither kicked anymore. They would save their strength until they had cause to struggle.

"What are you doing?" Ki asked as Vandien hunched in the center of the raft. Vibrations traveled through the logs, but before he answered, the raft went suddenly to pieces.

"Grab the log!" she heard Vandien scream, and then she went under. She came up sputtering in cold darkness. Luck bumped the log against her shoulder and panic helped her clutch it. "Vandien! Janie!" she yelled. The dark pressed down on her. "Here!" came a voice from the end of the log. The log jarred as Janie came up beside her. A flung rope slapped Ki in the face. She mananged to catch it before it trailed off into the water.

"We should be able to force a single log down and through the portal!" Vandien yelled. "If we keep roped together, we should make it back to shore."

"If we can find the portal!" Janie yelled back. Ki silently agreed. Her ducking had confused her, and the whirling water had finished the job. She was not even sure which wall the door was in. "Just follow!" Vandien shouted. He said no more, but began to push against the log. Ki tried to kick in the same direction. For a moment Janie just trailed in the water beside her; then Ki felt her begin to kick.

The water eddied and swirled. Ki couldn't see where they were. The wind held them back, howling with laughter. She could no longer separate the sound of the wind from the voice of the Windsinger. Both were full of cold mockery and power. Abruptly the log jarred against a wall.

"I can feel the door with my foot!" Vandien shouted. Ki could feel his movement but could not tell what he was doing. "I've got the rope knotted to the log," he shouted. "I'm going to dive down and through the door, and take an end of the rope with me. When you feel me pull, force the end of the log down, and I'll try to pull it through. But keep an end of the rope with you. When the log is through, dive and follow. Keep a grip on the rope."

Ki nodded idiotically, then stopped when she realized no one could see her. "Be careful!" she called.

"He's gone," Janie said. The two women clung to the log in the swirling water. Ki strained every sense, trying to feel

some tug that would be Vandien's, and not just the push of
the sea. Long moments burned away, and she felt nothing. "He
must be through by now," she yelled to Janie. The jerk came
like the tug of a fish on a line. The end of the log bobbed.
Together Janie and Ki moved to put weight on it, to push it
down below the surface until they felt it jogged away from
their grip.

Vandien fought the shivering that tried to convulse his body.
One could not shiver and swim. He tried to forget the pangs
from his face that numbed his nose and burned between his
eyes. He braced his feet against the outer wall of the temple
and heaved on the line. He felt first the buoyancy of the log,
and then the scraping as it edged through the portal. He went
under again as it came bobbing suddenly free, bursting up from
the water nearly under him. He swam up and clung to it, waiting
for the women to swim through.

Janie came up quickly and Ki followed. They clung gasping
to the log, feeling the unimpeded strength of the wind outside
the temple walls. At least the waves favored them now. The
tide was racing in over the flats. It helped them push their log
toward shore. Vandien forced his head up and began to kick
feebly. No one had the strength to speak, but he felt the efforts
of the others as they joined in. Far away the few lights of the
village shone like yellow stars. He wondered if any of them
thought of Janie and him, out in the water and wind. What did
they hope for? That both would drown, and put an end to the
troublesome girl? Did any besides Srolan hope he'd return with
the chest? Just as well that they didn't. Fewer would be disappointed.

There was a muffled cry from Ki, and then Vandien's feet
also scraped bottom. A few more kicks and they were able to
plant their feet securely. Janie alone made no glad sound. "Your
sister will be glad to see you alive!" Vandien tried to cheer
her.

"Helti will have sent her off to bed hours ago," she replied
dully.

They staggered up on shore. Vandien sank down, gathering
strength. But the wind continued to howl mercilessly; it could
not forgive them for having escaped the sea. The chill of their
garments soaked into their bones. Vandien felt the weight of
the water and hanging wool as he arose. Ki came up beside
him, fitting comfortably under his arm. He laughed softly at

the solid touch of her against him. They had come through alive again. He reached for Janie in a hug, but she shrugged him away. Dark emotions radiated from her. She would have nothing from them, not even the human comfort of companionship. She staggered to her feet and limped away from them. He and Ki were able to keep her in sight until she turned into the door of a dark cottage, smaller than most in the village. The wooden door thumped behind her.

"Vandien?" Ki began softly, but "It would take more than an evening to explain," he said. Ki let it drop.

The wind was less in the town among the houses. The darkness still pressed upon them and the slinking cold peeled the warmth of their bodies away. Another cold welled up inside Vandien, rising to fill him. Janie was gone now; he and Ki were two, as they had been so often before. But there was a difference. Janie's wild words in the ruined temple came and fluttered darkly between them. Ki knew why he had risked all for this ridiculous quest. He was not sure how he felt about his own actions, but he could think of a dozen reactions Ki could have to them. None of them were appealing.

"How's your face?" she asked, suddenly but softly.

"Ugly," he replied, telling her in that word things he had never said before. They did not speak the rest of the way to the inn, but her arm slipped about his waist and held him firmly.

Ki dragged the inn door open against the push of the wind. It slammed it shut again behind them. Sudden warmth and silence greeted them. Fisherfolk sprawled on benches and stools. Half-drained mugs rested on tables before them. Platters held scraps and crusts and crumbs in untidy heaps. Helti was warming his broad backside at his own hearth. He found his tongue. "So you made it back alive!" His words were friendly if drunken.

"Aye. And Janie, too." Vandien dropped his words into the silence, speaking more to Collie with his muted harp than to anyone else. Perhaps Collie nodded slightly, or maybe he was only resisting drowsiness.

"Well, Janie would. It would take more than a Windsinger and a storm to dampen that one. She'd be a fine woman, if her deeds matched her tongue."

Vandien bit his lips to keep back a sour reply. It would do no good. The mumble of conversation was rising again. Most of the drinkers were too far gone in their cups to be much interested in his return. But Berni called loudly for a drink, "For the teamster and his friend." "And tell us the tale of your night!" called another from a far table. A young fisherman by the fire seconded the request. Fisherfolk cleared a bench for them. Vandien sat gratefully. He reached and caught Ki's wrist, pulled her down with a tug to sit beside him. He felt her uneasiness. Left to herself, she would go to her wagon, or straight to his room above. Inns and strangers never appealed to her. Tonight that was truer than ever.

When they sat, their wet clothes streamed water onto the benches and floor. The fisherfolk paid it no heed. Ki shivered and drew closer to Vandien, as much for the comfort of his presence as for warmth. He pushed his curls back from his face and summoned up a grin. It sent ripples of pain through his scar, but he nailed it in place. Helti placed hot mugs of brew before them.

"Well, you've paid me well with your hospitality and your songs. I haven't brought the chest of the Windsingers back to you. The least I can do is give you the tale of how I failed. Right, Ki?" He jogged her elbow.

"Right!" she echoed, with a venomous smile for him. He'd best keep it short, he knew. Ki was full of words for him. The longer she honed them, the sharper they'd be. She reached for her mug and drank deep. Vandien reached up to his throat. Long habit made him lift his story-string from around his neck and loop it over his fingers. It did not matter that these folk could not understand the symbols he would weave as he spoke; he could no more tell a story without weaving it on his string than Ki could look at a horse and not guess its price. He looked down at his hands, at the twisting his fingers had put in the string, and frowned. It hung there, the crooked web that stood for scar, maim, disfigure, ruin. A snap of his fingers made the string back to a loop again. He reached and took a long swallow from his mug. It stung his nostrils and warmed the length of his gullet.

"Come on, teamster!" someone called, and Vandien sent a smile around the room. So they thought he kept silent to tease them to attention. Let them.

"How shall I start?" he asked them rhetorically. He glanced at Ki, who held her mug aloft for a refill. "Let me ask you this. Did you folk know what an amorous beast a skeel is? Did you know of the hidden stairwell in the temple of the Wind-singers? Have you ever marked how the kneeling Windsinger over the fallen altar watches one with a tear at the corner of her eye? How her hands seem to rise and fall with the waves that kiss them?"

He had them. With a few questions, Vandien had them in silence, hanging on his tale, as if the temple he spoke of was not at their doorsteps, but a mystic place a legend away. Ki listened to him, and watched his flying fingers as he wove for them a tale full of omens and misfortune, spiced here and there with knowing laughter. Vandien made himself the fool, the teamster who came not knowing of the trickiness of the task. To Janie he gave the role of courageous village girl who saves the foolish teamster at the last possible moment. Ki listened silently as he gave every fact the twist it needed to tickle the villagers' vanity most. He painted them in their best colors, a doughty folk who braved the treacherous seas that bewildered and awed a simple teamster like himself. Even Ki found her self smiling at his words as he described how his own team had nearly dragged him to his death. And if he gave Janie the credit for pulling him back from the water's grip, Ki did not begrudge it. She knew what he was trying to do, and knew that he could not succeed at it. The village would not see Janie as a plucky young woman, no matter how Vandien turned the story. He might temporarily soften their feelings for her, but he could not change how they thought of her.

"And so here I am, alive but wet!" he was winding it up. "And if I haven't a stack of gold coins to show for it, at least I've the experience. I'll never hear a man tell me what an easy life fishingfolk have without knowing he's never braved the sea. And that's a good bit of knowledge to have, worth as much to a man as a purse full of coin." With a grin, Vandien snapped his string back into a loop. He settled it over his head again, and drained his cooling mug.

"Another drink!" called Berni, but Vandien shook his head.

"We're for bed," he replied, rising slowly from the table.

"Let the woman stay!" A guttural voice called from a back table. "She shouldn't have to climb in beside you until the light's out, teamster!"

That got a general laugh. Ki narrowed her green eyes, and parted her lips to speak, but Vandien caught hold of her shoulder and gave it a squeeze that silenced her. With a knowing smile, he turned the taunt, saying, "Not Ki. She's a wise one, and knows that handsome is as handsome does."

"I'll wager the fisherwomen know the same," Ki added tartly. "For I see that you drink alone, fisherman!"

The laughter was turned upon the man at the back table now. The sound of it followed them to the base of the stairs that loomed before them. It took an inordinate amount of time to climb them. Vandien's pace and steadiness were no better than that of the revelers in the room below. Ki slipped a hand under his arm. She found him trembling with weariness and cold, but he pulled away from her support. They reached the landing at the head of the stairs. Vandien turned and gave her a smile that rippled his scar but did not reach his eyes.

They stood like strangers in the semi-darkness on the landing. All the words that Ki had prepared since Dresh had told her how Vandien had been baited here were suddenly ashes on her tongue. She thought of the days and miles they had traveled together, the times when it seemed that Vandien knew the thoughts of her head before she voiced them. She had found comfort in their long silences. She had thought that Vandien shared that comfort. In those long evenings when they had ridden in silence but for the sounds of the horses' hooves meeting the road, when Ki had been watching the fir trees turn from green to purple against a darkening sky, what had been in his mind? When they swayed together on the hard seat, their shoulders jogging companionably against one another to the rhythm of the greys' pace, had his thoughts turned to his marred face and wondered why it had to be? A cold winter memory came to her. She had wakened in the darkness of the cuddy, jarred from sleep by a dream whose ending she could not abide. When she opened her eyes, the moon was shining in the small window. Her pale light touched the objects in the cuddy without giving detail to any of them. Vandien had rolled away from her and was sleeping on his back. The moon silvered the skin of his face making him look like a very old carving of yellowed ivory. The proud jut of his jaw and the straight line of his nose were sharply delineated, but his eye hollows were filled with blackness. His still features were an empty-eyed mask, a mocking cold thing put into her bed to remind her of her loneliness. Her half of the bed seemed chilled and empty, but she could not bring herself to move closer to his warmth. For if that

warmth were not there, if his profile were only an icy sham,
a monstrous cheat of some sourceless magic . . . she had shivered then as she shivered now, with more than cold, with the
child's sudden fear that the things she knew best she knew not
at all. As she had shuddered in her bed that night, he had
stirred, turning his face to her, and silently pulling her into his
warmth and man-smell, holding her close and making the world
real again. She had never wondered, then, at his wakefulness.
But now she did. What dark thoughts had he followed as he
lay on his back in the cold moonlight staring at the cuddy
ceiling?

She watched him walk away from her. His shoulders sagged.
The short darkened hallway closed in on him, folding him away
from her in its depths. Ki felt the sudden sting of tears, so long
foreign to her eyes. She straightened her body and took a deep
breath. *I am just tired,* she told herself, *and I am letting my
emotions run like unbroken yearlings.* Vandien kicked open a
door. Yellow lamplight flooded out in a folded rectangle on
the floor and opposite wall. Ki hastened to follow him, but he
was standing in the doorway, not entering the room.

"I've failed you, Srolan." His words were slow and deep,
sounding drunken. Ki moved up to peer past his shoulder.

A woman was sitting on the bed. The imprint of her body
was on the blankets and pillows. Emotions swirled up in Ki,
anger, surprise, jealousy, and then subsided as she realized the
age of the woman. Her night black hair was smoothed back
from her face to hang in waves down her back, her jet eyes
shone, but her mouth was framed in lines. Crow's feet brack-
eted her eyes. The papery skin of her cheeks had fallen, abandoning the proud bones of her face. Ki could see the beauty
she had been, but youth had fled that face, leaving only the
shadow of its memory and its proud lines.

Ki glanced at Vandien. He stood in the doorway, brow
furrowed, staring as if he did not trust his eyes. The woman's
gaze fell before his. "So you see me. Just an old woman now.
It's a hard glamor to maintain. And it grows harder with each
passing year, especially before eyes as discerning as yours.
You tempted me as I have not been tempted in years, Vandien.
You love and hate and hope with such abandon, with such a
plenitude of emotion. I could feel you burning to achieve my
goals for me. You were like a hawk on my fist; I could have
flown you at the sun, and you would have gone. You should

be grateful to me, woman." Srolan was addressing Ki now. "I could have had him, you know, body and soul. I could have made him burn for me in any way I pleased. But didn't. I've that much honor left to me. As you say, you've failed me, and there is no reason to deceive you any longer. Is Janie all right?"

"She's alive, if that's what you mean. She is scarcely 'all right,' nor do I think she ever will be. Tonight she spilled every last bit of courage she held. I do not know what she will use to face the village folk after this. Bitterness may have to suffice."

"Well. She has plenty and to spare of that. As do you, teamster. Do not think too hardly of me, for I am not as cold as I seem. Only old and disappointed and weary. You made an effort, teamster. That's more than has been done for many years."

"But not enough. You will keep your gold, and I'll keep my scar."

"Yes. But take my good will with you when you go. That's not a bad thing to carry off with you."

"And all it cost me was four skeel and a near drowning."

"I've heard of worse bargains. It isn't as if this were done solely for amusement, Vandien. Do you think you are the only one disappointed this night? It is beyond your imagination to guess what I have lost this night. I believed you could do it, Vandien. I looked into you. You are a man whose feelings drive him to do the impossible. So I hired you. So I opened the door on my caged dreams . . . and now I see them, feet up in the straw. I am too old to try again. And I have so many regrets. If only I had found you years ago; if only they had left young Killian to sing the wind, instead of bringing in that Windmistress; if only I were young enough to have one more chance."

Srolan rose slowly to go, an old woman lifting her tired bones. Her body moved with the rasp of her breathing. Vandien stepped aside from the door. But Ki didn't move. *Windmistress.* Her lips formed the word, but she could not utter it. Rebeke? Who else? Her antagonizing of the Windsingers had led to Vandien's defeat. She had drawn their attention to herself and her friend.

"How much?" Ki demanded suddenly. Vandien and Srolan were startled back to awareness of her. Ki didn't step out of the door. Her sopping hood hung down her back. Lank brown hair framed her narrow face. "How much?" she repeated, more insistently. A note of anger crept into her question.

"How much . . . what?" Srolan stood puzzled, seeking to leave, but blocked by Ki.

"How much to lift his scar . . . if you can do it."

"That's not a thing bought with coin."

"Damn you, that's not an answer! You can't do it, even if he brought you the whole damn temple! Admit it!"

Srolan stared at Ki. Ki knew her measure was being taken by those dark eyes. A chill power flowed behind them, but Ki was too angry to be wary.

"She's right, Vandien. I couldn't lift the scar. But if I had the chest, there is one who would be persuaded to lift your scar for a single peek inside the box. I would have carried out my side of the bargain, if you had yours. But you didn't."

"That wasn't the only possible bargain in the world. Who is this one who can lift the scar from a man's face?" Ki was not screaming. Screaming would have been pleasanter than the cold hoarseness of her voice.

Srolan looked at her with knowing eyes, and the corners of her withered mouth turned up in mockery of a smile. "Do you really need to ask that of me, Ki?"

Ki could find no words to answer. She felt shamed by Srolan's appraising eyes, but could not imagine what Srolan knew, or thought she knew, about Ki. No deed in Ki's past could be as loathesome as her tone implied. But Ki found herself drawing aside to let Srolan pass. A chill wind seemed to follow her, that set Ki to shivering until her teeth chattered in her head. She clenched her jaws against it. She looked down the hall, but Srolan was already gone. She turned back to Vandien.

He stood in the middle of the room stripping efficiently and dropping his sodden clothes into the bathtub. Ki came into the room, drawing the door shut behind her. She watched him undress. His feet were wrinkled and red with their long immersion. As he drew his wet smock off over his head, his neck bent in a graceful curve, the arch bared to show the small dark shape of a hawk printed on his nape. The woolen smock slapped into the tub on top of the rest of his clothes. He stood rubbing his face. Putting one hand on each side of his face, he pushed firmly. His scar went narrower, no longer dragging at his eye. But when his hands dropped away, his face fell again into its marred configuration. He was surprised to find Ki watching him.

"It hurts all the time, doesn't it?" she asked gently.

"No." He denied it flatly. "Only when it's cold. The rest of the time it's just a stiffness, a place of no feeling. It doesn't really trouble me all that much, Ki. It was just a chance to be rid of it, and have a pouch full of coin into the bargain. Anyone would have jumped at it."

"Certainly. Even I, if anyone had bothered to tell me what the stakes were."

He looked acutely uncomfortable. Vandien turned away from her and went to the bed, to climb in under the covers.

"Vandien." Ki groped for words. "I never stopped to think what a burden that scar must be to you. But now that I know . . ." Ki floundered. "Let's go to Srolan in the morning. Let's find out who can lift your scar, and go see . . ."

"Just like taking a kettle to the tinker. 'Here, fellow, patch this up, and I'll give you a coin for your time.' Ki, dammit, it's *my* face. I'll not have you paying to have it repaired. Must we dredge all this up and talk about it now? I'm tired and cold."

"So am I." Ki sank down onto the stool and began to work her boots off her feet. For a time, the silence held. The boots dropped to the floor and she rose to pull her hood and tunic off. Her voice came muffled and bleak through the fold of damp cloth. "As I put the scar there, why should I not help to remove it?"

"Must this damn thing come between me and every other person in my life?" Vandien demanded petulantly. "I'd prefer you continue to ignore it, Ki. You didn't put the scar on my face. A Harpy did that. You had no say in it. You never called to me for help. Up to that moment, you didn't even welcome my company."

"You offered me a bargain, once," Ki recalled. She had freed her hair from the braid and was combing her fingers through it. "You offered no debts between us, nothing given, unless it was given freely. As I offer this now. What harm can it do to spend a few days upon this, to see exactly what can be done?"

"The same kind of harm that is being done right now!"

"Harm." Ki gave a choked laugh. "That's what I am best at. You might have succeeded, if they had not brought in a Windmistress to sing. Did not Srolan say that?"

"I have no idea what she meant." Vandien shouldered himself deeper into the bed.

"I'm afraid that I do. You have not asked what errand kept me away from False Harbor."

"You don't need to give me excuses."

"Not usually," Ki said gravely. "But I suspect I brought the Windsingers down on you. Did I tell you in Dyal not to risk their enmity? I should have advised myself. I did more than earn their anger. I owe my life to one Rebeke, Windmistress. She kept me alive; but I doubt if she has any fondness for me. Or for my friend."

Vandien propped himself up on an elbow. His dark eyes bored into hers. With an effort, he lightened the mood. "It sounds like a tale worth the telling, but one that deserves a night fire under high stars. Let it wait awhile, Ki. And remember, there is no changing what is done. Even if there had been no Windsinger, I doubt if I could have found that chest. The night was too dark and the water too deep. Besides," he tried for a smile, "I can't let you steal the only morsel Srolan threw to my vanity. Let me believe the Windsinger Killian knew herself no match for me, and called in reinforcements."

Vandien flopped back to stare at the ceiling, Ki bent to blow out the lamp. In the chill darkness she found the bed and crawled into it. She rested beside him, their bodies not quite touching. She could not see in the blackness of the shuttered room. Uncertainly she reached out to put her hand on his chest. She felt the hair bend softly beneath her fingers, felt the chill of the sea on his body still. He made no sound, and she grew bold enough to huddle closer, fitting her body to his. She eased her head onto his shoulder, until she felt the softly bristling stubble on his chin tickle against her forehead. "Did you believe Janie . . ." she began cautiously, but could not go on.

Vandien shifted. His hand moved to tousle her hair. It rested on her head, lightly pressing her to his chest. When he spoke, his weary voice hummed by her ear, with a shade of his old humor in it.

"What Janie said out there in the temple? That you would like to see me stay scarred? As soon as she said it, I knew it would gnaw on you. It's just the type of insidious suggestion you can't abide." He fell silent.

Ki waited. Vandien sighed out a deep breath. He bent his

head and she felt the brush of his moustache as he kissed her lightly on the forehead. His body relaxed as sleep took him.

"I asked if you believed her!" she reminded him in an exasperated voice. She punctuated her reminder with a light jab in his ribs.

He jumped and chuckled infuriatingly. Ki knew he had baited her into repeating her question. A little of the day's tension went out of her. If he could still laugh and tease, then their companionship could survive this day's folly.

"It bothers you that much, does it? It's like this. Every person hides inside her some small bit of ugliness. Perhaps it makes Janie feel she is not so wicked and selfish if she can imagine you are no better than she. Did you notice Collie, the mute harper?"

Ki nodded against his chest. Their bodies were beginning to warm the bed. She liked the way his chest thrummed against her ear when he spoke.

"Janie likes him better mute. Had he a voice, other than his harp, he might mock her as the other men in the village do. Then she would have to sneer at him and reject him as she does the others. But while he is voiceless, she can care for him, in the depths of her blighted little soul, and rest assured that other women will not find him too attractive. I doubt if she has put her feeling into words, even to herself. But some part of her knows, and her guilt stings a little less if she imagines you share a like sentiment for me."

"Oh." Ki rolled over and arranged herself so that she could lean on her elbows and look down into Vandien's face. She could see little but her eyes weren't needed. She lightly trailed her fingertips over his face. The lines in his forehead smoothed away under her touch. She fluffed the damp curls away from his face and cautiously ran a finger down the stiffness of his scar. A light touch told her that his eyes were closed. She stroked his face. "Does it ease the pain when I touch you like this?"

Vandien sighed and gently pushed her hands away. "It eases the physical pain of the scar. But every time you touch it, it is a reminder to me that it is here. Ki. We have asked very little of one another. But now I ask. Let this thing go. Between us, let us not speak of it, or touch it, or let it matter. I've made a fine fool of myself these past few days. I've not a coin to show for it, and I've a team sunken in that temple. Help me get the team out and return them to their owner, and then let's find a haul for your wagon that will pay us a few coin and work me hard. As for the rest of my folly here . . . will you let me forget it? To only you my scar has made no difference. Yet it is you who I wish could look at me and not see it."

His body had gone tense against her. As close as she was to him, she felt she could not warm him. She moved to cradle his body against hers. She wondered if he even felt her touch. She whispered, "Between us, there is never a need beyond asking. Go to sleep, Van, for there's a cold wet task before us tomorrow."

"Vandien. My name is Vandien."

"Vandien," she amended softly.

He was silent after that, and Ki lay still against him. She wished for sleep, but it was a long time coming.

TWENTY

Ki sat in the open freight bed of her wagon and wondered if things could get worse. Her clothing was plastered wet against her; that had become routine. Sigurd and Sigmund, dried and blanketed, nosed disgustedly at the coarse salty grasses sprouting up at the margin of the beach. Ki would have to lead them to better grazing and picket them after she built the fire and changed her wet clothes, if she could get up that much energy.

Last night she had told him her tale of Dresh and Rebeke. He had listened quietly. The events she related seemed unreal, even to Ki. The sheer physical effort of the past few days had drained her, making all yesterdays vague. Medie's death loomed more monstrous and she regretted her part in it. Hardest of all was to speak of the debt she owed. Rebeke had saved her, maybe with no more thought given to Ki than to her horses, but saved her nonetheless. Ki had finished her tale with, "I hate a debt that can't be settled."

"Don't we all," Vandien had replied, staring into the flames, and she knew he was thinking of how Dresh had sent him to False Harbor. She had come to hate this place. The chill water over the sunken temple with its secrets baffled them both. And

Vandien went about strangely abashed, ashamed to admit the hopes that had been dashed. It was a bad place that gnawed at old pains without devouring them.

Another tide had ebbed and risen. They were no closer to recovering Vandien's skeel. Ki was privately wondering if they were still at the end of the line. Perhaps they had tangled it in the sunken crypt of the temple, and then scuttled off. Maybe she and Vandien had spent the last two days trying to pull the bottom of the temple up through its own stairwell. She was discouraged, her team was sulky and tired, and Vandien had found new depths to black humor.

She looked down the beach. Vandien stood staring out at the waves over the temple. The grey waves curled at his feet and slunk back to the sea. He'd have to move soon, or the sea would be creeping up his legs. In his hands he held a coil of rope whose end disappeared into the surf.

On the first low tide following Temple Ebb, they had been able to recover the end of the line Vandien had left looped around the fallen stone. Janie had provided sulky dory service to the temple and Vandien, against Ki's advice, had himself dove down to cut the line free and fasten a fresh length of line to the cut end. There had been a second dive to go down and thread the fresh line through the temple door, for Vandien maintained that Ki's team might be able to break the skeel free of their grip on the bottom, but could scarcely haul them over the jagged temple walls as well. Ki had traded dried fruit and sausages for three more lengths of rope. These sufficed to reach the shore and be fastened to her team.

The team had pulled from shore at high and low tides, and at the turn of the tide. She had taken the team out into the surf, approaching the temple at the low tide, and pulled from there. All to no avail. *If* the skeel were still at the end of that silvery piece of line, they were dug in firmly and likely to remain so for as long as their rutting instincts held.

"Vandien!"

He turned at her call and plodded toward her, his shoulders bunched against the chill sea wind. He still wore the bulky wool garments of the fisherfolk. They hung on his narrow frame. His dark eyes were shadowed. He doled out loops of rope as he came, finishing by knotting the end firmly to the wagon tongue. "I'll build the fire while you take your nags to

grass and change your clothes," he offered as he came to lean
against the wagon box.

But Ki did not rise to his use of the word "nags." "Vandien,
let's do one of two things. Let's quit dragging at that rope and
sit back and relax until the damn things finish copulating and
come up for air. Or, and this I prefer, let's cut the rope, hitch
up, and leave. We're low on coin, but we could trade hides
or blankets or something to the T'cherian against the value of
the lost team. We could even trade whatever we can for salt
fish here, settle with the T'cherian on the way, and haul the
fish inland until it becomes a rarity, and trade it then. I've
some good contacts back in Greenwood. That's only five days
past Bitters."

"No." Vandien replied when she paused for breath. "I'll
haul those skeel out of there, one way or another, and get them
back to Web Shell. Having made a tangle of everything else,
let me at least splice the ends in smooth. He loaned me the
team in good faith; I want to return them to him. Why don't
you go change into dry clothes while I take your nags to grass
and build the fire?"

"Maybe if I argue a bit longer, you'll change my clothes
for me, as well as give grass to my nags and build my fire."

"Maybe I will. To hell with the grass and the fire!" Vandien
suggested.

"Braggart. You're as tired as I am."

"More so. Is that Janie coming down the sands?"

Ki turned to follow Vandien's nod. She saw a cloaked figure
with a smaller one in tow. The little girl's hair blew free of
her cap, and she skipped merrily to match her sister's longer
stride. The wind blew snatches of her birdlike chatter to them.

"Couldn't be anyone else," Ki remarked. "The rest of the
village has been too busy fishing since Ebb to bother with us."
They watched silently as the two approached, Janie striding
determinedly over the shifting pebbles and sand, her eyes steadily fixed on the wagon, while her little sister hopped along
beside her, taking an interest in every shell and pebble they
passed. Janie's hair was trapped under her woolen cap. Her
loose smock was belted tightly at her hips and her trousers
were tucked securely into her boots. The child's smock was
longer and unbelted as was village custom. The hem of it was
edged with a narrow band of blue. Her trousers had come out

of her boot tops and flapped jauntily with each step. Just before they reached earshot, they stopped, and Janie stooped to say something to the child, who listened gravely.

"Have good manners, don't speak unless you're spoken to, and don't be a pest," Vandien guessed solemnly.

"And wipe your nose!" Ki added with a low laugh.

Janie trudged up to them. As soon as she let go of the child's hand, the girl ran to the side of Ki's wagon. She began tracing the brightly colored pictures on the high panelled cuddy. Janie sent her an exasperated look, and turned back to Ki and Vandien.

"There's an easy way to raise your team," she began without preamble. "I was in a foul temper when I took you out to the temple to get a line on them. I felt I owed you nothing, and that the sooner you gave up and left, the sooner the village would go back to normal. But I was wrong. I've heard how you told your tale of Temple Ebb. I don't say thank you for that, but I appreciate what you tried to do. It's also become obvious that you won't give up and go away. I may as well help you raise the team."

Janie ran out of words. Just as the silence became awkward, the child spoke. "I had some Romni tea once," she announced loudly, but to no one in particular. When she drew no response, she added, "I liked it very, very much."

"Sasha!" Janie exclaimed in rebuke, but Vandien laughed aloud. Then he drew his brows down in a frown and turned to the child.

"Have you never heard how the Romni give sleeping tea to little girls, and then steal them away in the night?"

"Idiot!" hissed Ki. "She'll believe you." Turning to the child she explained, "The only little child I ever stole grew up to be that nasty-tongued man. So I gave up the practice. But if you'll help me to gather sticks and twigs, and a bit or two of driftwood, I'll show you how the Romni brew their tea on an open fire beside their wagons."

As Ki stood up, the girl dashed down the beach to ferret out bits of twisted white driftwood. Ki threw Vandien a shrug and followed her. Vandien raised an inquiring eyebrow at Janie. He quickly lowered it when he realized she was staring in horrified fascination at what this made his scar do to his face.

"Well. You know how to raise my team?"

"The whole village knows. There's even been a round of

bets at the inn as to when you'd figure it out for yourselves."

"And for giving me the solution, no doubt the village will be pleased with you?"

"Who cares? It matters little what I do, the village is always ill pleased with me."

"I see."

"I doubt if you do, nor does that matter. The point is this. To lift anything off the bottom, one does not battle the tides. One makes the tides do the work." Janie paused to give a small smile to Vandien's incredulous look. "Can your team match muscles with the Moon herself? Make yourself a bundle of sturdy logs bound together with rope. You have plenty of rope. At the next low tide, take the raft out to the temple. At the lowest point of the tide, reef the line up straight, so there is no slack between your team and the logs."

"And then?" Vandien prodded, for Janie thought she had finished explaining. She gave him an exasperated look.

"Then wait for the high tide, of course. The waves lift the log raft, and either your team will rise, or the rope will break. But I know the line Srolan gave you. I think the team will rise. And once you've lifted them off the bottom, any child could tow the raft back to shore. They may hang up a bit on the temple walls, but you should be able to handle that."

"I should." Vandien squinted down the beach. Ki and Sasha were returning, each with a small load of wood. They were laughing, and Ki's brown hair blew about her face.

"Why don't you both come with us, Janie?"

"Just like that? You don't even ask Ki, but just ask us along? And do you expect me to say, certainly, I'll leave my dory and my cottage and come? How would we live?"

"As the Romni do. Believing that the road will take care of you, as long as you don't worry about it. The luck of the wheels. Ki is something of a heretic, you know, with her freighting and trading. The other Romni I've met trust to the luck of the wheels. It's not a bad way to live, Janie. I think Sasha would like it. . . ."

"She probably would." Janie spoke quickly. "But that doesn't mean it would be good for her. She'd lose all sense of who she is and where she comes from. She'd forget. . . ."

"I know she would. Maybe you could, too. Be Janie, instead of Duce's granddaughter."

Janie stiffened perceptibly. "I came out here to tell you how to lift your team and to offer my help. But if you're . . ."

"I'm not. How do we get logs?"

"There's always some snagged on Rocky Point. We'll have to use my dory."

"Then let's go get it. After I move these nags to better grasses."

The moon had claimed the sky when they returned. Janie brought her dory up on the beach. As the keel of the double-ender scraped, Vandien sprang out into knee-deep water to pull it up on the beach. Janie followed to help him.

The silhouetted wagon had yellow edges. Ki had built her fire on the far side so the bulk of it blocked the breeze off the water. As Vandien and Janie rounded the end of the wagon, Vandien saw that Ki had gone to all efforts for Sasha. A traditional Romni camp had sprung up by the wagon. Sasha was enthroned on a fat pillow and snuggled in a quilt. A red head-scarf with gaudy purple tassels confined her hair. Cushions had been placed about the fire as if Sasha hosted a dozen guests. In both her small hands she cupped a steaming mug. Vandien peeked into it as he passed and saw an extravagantly large piece of dried spiced fruit floating on top of the fragrant tea. Ki had changed clothes. She wore a traditional skirt and loose blouse, topped with an embroidered vest, and a belt interwoven with silver wire and tiny bells. Only Vandien could appreciate how deeply she had dug in the cuddy to come up with those clothes. She had let her hair go wild and long, and was even wearing the gaudy enamelled earrings he had bought for her on a long ago market day. Sasha would remember this night, not as the night they lifted the team, but as a night when she drank tea and broke bread in a real Romni camp. Ki was fully into the spirit of it. Many bracelets clattered on her wrist and interfered with her cooking.

"Romni stew, I see." Vandien leaned over the cooking pot.

"And Romni bread with Romni cheese," Ki rejoined, letting her green eyes glow with a mysticism that made Sasha's eyes go wide.

"And a not-Romni raft, tied with not-Romni knots, to four skeel at low tide," Janie added in a voice that broke the fragile spell. Ki looked at them askance.

"After we built the raft, it seemed foolish to let another low tide go by. Before the night is out, the rising tide should lift the skeel clear of the temple floor, and then we drag them in."

"Up the staircase, and through the jumble of stones in the temple and then..."

"Over the temple walls. It was hell's own errand to rethread that rope in the dark. They will be dragged over the walls, not through the portal, raft and all."

"Well, that should make it simple," Ki rejoined skeptically.

"I didn't say it would be easy," Janie broke in. "Only that it would be possible. Your methods weren't."

"I didn't mean to belittle your help. Sasha and I saved food for you two, even if we did not wait for you before eating. The bowls are in that chest."

"No. Thank you. Feeding Sasha and entertaining her are more than I expected. I thank you for that, also. But we must be back home now, for morning comes early for fisherfolk, and for small girls who must help out at the inn."

Sasha's bright face fell, but she did not protest as she stood up and shed her bright scarf. "No, keep that," Ki told her quickly. Janie bid them thanks and good evening in a formal voice and made to lead Sasha off, but the child broke free of her grip, to tackle Ki with a hug, and then dart off after her older sister before Ki had even recovered her balance. They were gone in the surrounding darkness. Ki slowly began to fold up the quilt as Vandien served himself stew and a hard round of bread.

"I could get used to having that one around," Ki said to no one in a very soft voice.

"I already asked. Not a chance. Janie feels she will shirk a family responsibility if Sasha grows up free and happy and unshackled to the past."

"Um." Ki sank down on a cushion, the quilt pillowed in her lap. Vandien sat across the fire from her, eating. One hand held his bowl and one his spoon, while he balanced his bread expertly on one knee. Her brow creased as she tried to remember how he had looked the first time she had fed him at her fire. Skinnier, certainly. And more ragged than she had ever seen him since. His hair had been shaggily unkempt, brushing his shoulders. His face had bristled with whiskers. She knew those details, but could not bring that image to mind. For all she had seen then were his eyes, unsettlingly dark, and hungry. "Tea?" she asked him now, and his dark eyes rose briefly to meet hers as he nodded. His eyes were still bottomless, she thought, but now she understood their hunger. Vandien devoured life, and was ever filled with it but never satiated. The tea streamed into the mug from the earthenware pot, as golden as the firelight and spiced to sweetness. The mug warmed the chill away and the fragrance filled her with memories of spring. She handed the mug to Vandien and refilled her own. "How long until high tide?" she asked to fill the silence.

"Not until dawn. But it will be high enough for us before that. Damn, Ki, I've learned more about tides and moon pull since I came here than I ever cared to know. I'll be glad to leave the coast and forget it. Tides never flow when you need them. It will be high enough for us soon. Too soon for me to lie down and sleep, but too long for me to just sit here idly, for then I'd fall asleep and miss it."

"There's the team to bring back," Ki suggested. "And harness to put on them. Pots and dishes to wash and pack. And the cuddy to be straightened up for the road. Because as soon as we have that team up, we're going. I'm sick of the water and salt. Every bit of metal on the wagon is going green."

"As to leaving right away, fine. As for the rest of it, some day I shall learn not to tell you when I have idle time."

"If I ever have idle time, I'll tell you about it," Ki offered. She fetched her harness from the wagon. With a rag and some oil she began to supple the leather and polish the sea tarnish from the metal. Vandien watched her, a wry smile twisting his lips. Then he rose to gather the dishes and spoons.

When Ki could see the flames of the fire moving in the harness buckle, she gave a nod of satisfaction and returned it to its peg. Vandien had resumed his seat by the fire. He stared into the flames, rubbing a slow finger up and down his scar. Ki watched him unsmiling until he became aware of her gaze and looked up. His hand dropped to his knees. When he smiled, it was his old grin. A cloud had lifted and Vandien had returned. Ki felt a flood of relief she could not help from showing.

"It was silly, wasn't it?" Vandien concluded. "Now that I have finally thought it through and let go of the notion, I feel at peace. Strange, isn't it? Until Srolan offered to lift my scar, I had never thought of it. As soon as she offered it, I wanted so badly for it to be possible that I willed it to be true. I was willing to make a fool of myself, and drag you into it, for the sake of a smooth face. Now when I come back to my senses and see what a fool I have been, I cannot believe the things I did. It's like waking up sober and remembering all the witty words of the night before. They don't even make sense." Vandien shook his head deprecatingly at the fire. "Accepting the scar as part of my face may be the only gain from this."

"Accept and grow, my father used to say," Ki agreed.

"Accept and die, say the fishermen." Janie stepped into the circle of firelight. Ki and Vandien both startled. The shushing waves had covered her footsteps on the soft sand and pebble of the beach. "Where's Sasha?" Ki asked, and the militant set of Janie's face relaxed as she warmed her hands.

"Asleep." Her face was soft with affection. "Nothing would do, except that she must heap up her bed with every blanket and cushion in the house. With her doll and a cup and two wooden spoons, she has gone to sleep in her Romni wagon. No doubt she'll have a pleasanter night than we will."

"We?" Vandien ventured.

"I've brought my dory back. *Rainlady* is pulled up on the beach. I gave some thoughts to the stones standing in the temple and the snaggled walls. That rope will hang up somewhere. But if Ki can manage the team on shore, I can manage the dory while Vandien tries to unsnag the line. I've brought him a hook-pole."

"We're grateful for your help."

"I'm grateful for the afternoon that was given to Sasha. She chattered of nothing else. She has never been treated so, as an honored guest and indulged as a child. Because of who she is, she doesn't receive the toleration usually given to children. Her curiosity is deemed nosiness, and any lapse in manners is malicious, not naughty. So, for her to speak so brightly of her afternoon with Ki. . . ." Janie faltered for words. "I could wish I were a child again, and could have the old aches smoothed away with such an afternoon." She finished awkwardly. Her voice flinched as if she expected laughter. But Vandien was slicing a chunk of fruit into the steaming mug of tea that Ki had poured. Janie sank onto the fat cushion Vandien indicated and took the warm mug.

They spoke little after that, of unimportant things only. Janie sipped at her tea. Her eyes lost some of their wariness. She took off her wool cap and shook out her pale hair, bringing Vandien to remark, "With your hair loose on your shoulders and your eyes full of flames, you look like you belong by a Romni fire."

"An evening like this makes me think well of it," Janie

replied with no trace of her usual sharpness. All was silence but for fire sounds, and the waves creeping up the beach. The sea breathed hoarsely as the waves rushed in, giving a pebble-rattling snore as the water retreated. Janie suddenly cleared her throat.

"The tide is high enough," she announced in a businesslike voice, and began tucking her hair back under her cap. The moment was gone. Ki went for the team while Vandien meekly followed Janie to where her dory floated nearly free on the rising tide.

TWENTY-ONE

"WHOA! Hold steady!" Vandien's voice was a thin echo breaking over the incoming waves. Ki relayed the command to her team, backing it up with a steady pull on the reins. The greys halted. They shifted their big hooves miserably. They had no desire to pull at a rope in the dark of night. Sigurd stamped, and then tested his weight gently against his collar. "Hold!" Ki reminded him, and took a better grip on her reins.

She turned to stare at the dark heaving blanket of sea. Her eyes could not pierce the night. The voices of Vandien and Janie reached her like the thin anxious cries of seabirds. At least there was no Windsinger singing this night. For that she was grateful.

"Pull!" Vandien's call whispered across the water.

"Get up!" Ki told the team. The trailing rope slowly went tight as the greys moved up the sands. Ki glanced back and saw the taut line rising up out of the waves, to hang dripping. She listened anxiously for Vandien's call for her to halt. It didn't come. The greys plodded on, the rope singing higher with every step they took. Ki felt a hitch in their pulling, and suddenly the rope was just tight, not strained as it had been. At the same instant, a wave of dizziness swept over Ki.

She stumbled over nothing. The sand shifted slightly under her feet. Her team swayed suddenly before her with snorts of disquiet. A vibration rattled the sand and pebbles; a rising of sound from the sea itself speckled the dark surface of the water with its throbbing. Again she lost her footing and staggered to regain it.

The silence was like a giant drawing breath. Then again there came the subsonic thrumming that mottled the surface of the water as if the waves were being pelted with hail. The greys snorted and tossed their heads, snatching more rein through Ki's startled hands. They stepped up their pace in spite of her efforts to hold them in. "Vandien? Janie?" she called. She heard a murmur of voices from the village, welling up questioningly. The vibration stilled for an instant; Ki felt steadier upon her legs. She drew a breath to call to Vandien again, but his yell came first.

"The Bell!" His Human voice was blasphemy after that inhuman knelling. As if in confirmation, the deep throbbing voice spoke again, simmering through the sand and waves to pulse in the night air. The sound chilled Ki. But the silence that followed it was even more daunting.

Ki's eyes flickered from the team to the rope to the sea and back to her team. They would load those skeel tonight and be on their way, even if she had to drive up that cliff in the darkness. Her mind traced again the convoluted path that had brought Vandien here. She winced as she thought of her own involuntary part in it. Damn Dresh and all of his wizardly ilk! He had tossed Vandien into this foul mess with no more thought than if he were discarding the outer leaves of a cabbage. But time and distance would heal all things; had not they done so before?

"Whoa! Hold up!" Vandien's voice came stronger to her. Ki pulled in her team and waited. Her flesh was warm but she shivered. The Windsingers' bell, no legend, but a rare event. Ki wondered what trick of the tide had made it ring. She could hear Vandien and Janie discussing something in muffled voices. She heard faint splashing and felt the rope vibrate with small tuggings. "Pull!" came Vandien's command. Ki started her team. She felt the difference instantly. They no longer towed something through the water. What they dragged now was scraping bottom, for the rope throbbed and hopped beside her as the team pulled.

The team left the peak of the beach behind them and began to trudge through the sedgy grasses of a salt marsh flat. The mud smelled foul and the big hooves made plopping noises in the wet ground. Ki considered moving the team back to take a fresh bite on the rope, but decided instead to pull on, keeping the line tight. Skeel had a reputation for making the most of a slack line.

"Hold! We've got them!"

Ki gave a sigh of relief, but the tension in her didn't ease. The tolling of that sunken bell had chilled her soul. The Windsingers had reached down and tapped her, reminding her they knew her name. She turned her team and headed them back to the beach. Time enough to coil up the rope later. Just what in hell would she do with so much rope? Sell it in the next town?

From ahead, Ki heard wild yells. She halted the team and stood in the darkness, straining all her senses. Had it been Vandien's voice? And now, that voice, it must be Janie! Her fear changed to puzzlement as she heard a wave of mingled laughter. She started the team again, scowling as she followed their plodding steps. What in hell was so funny? She could understand Vandien's relief at recovering his team, but this sounded like hilarity.

"Ki!" Vandien bounded up right under the noses of the horses. Sigurd stamped, and then snapped at Vandien while Sigmund looked disapprovingly down on him. His clothes streamed water. Drops were flung from his outstretched arms. He seized her in a soggy hug, jouncing her about excitedly; it was all she could do to hold the team steady. "The skeel have got the chest, the Windsingers' chest! Janie saw it! When we hauled them up on the beach, they were all tangled up in one big knot, big as a foundered cow. Tails wrapped here, snouts buried there, legs tangled about until it might be three animals or six! We stared at them wondering how to pry them apart. Then Janie saw it. There's a corner, just a corner, poking out from the middle of them. It must have been beside them when they decided to mate. It's trapped among their bodies, held by legs and tails and snouts! But it's the box and no mistake. Just as Janie said it would be. We can see the edge of the belt that binds it shut. It shines like gold, with no trace of tarnish, and each strand of it looks as fine as baby's hair, but to the touch is cold hard metal. Come on! Come!"

He pranced and danced about her, finally seizing her arm and dragging at her. "I can't leave my team here," she protested, but Vandien boldly grabbed Sigmund's reins below the bit and dragged the big horse into a trot. Ki hurried along beside them, sharing her team's baffled amazement.

"We'll hitch up the team and load the skeel on the wagon," he decided as they ran. "We'll take that tangle of skeel into the village and by the Moon! We'll roll it right into the inn! Let Janie have her triumph, and for me there will be coins and a new face!" He laughed wildly, breathlessly. His dark eyes caught and flashed the starlight at Ki as he let his thoughts race. "These fine beasts of yours shall have all the grain they can stuff down! When we return the skeel to Bitters, there's a stall in the marketplace that had a cloak just the color of your eyes that we must have! Yes, and a rapier and scabbard for I am determined that you shall have your own, if only to keep my own skills sharp! And we shall eat . . . oh, everything, except fish! And presents for Sasha! We must find things for Sasha, bright and foolish robes, and a dozen tinkling bracelets and . . ."

Ki listened as Vandien spent his coins a dozen times over, in ways ever more extravagant. She smiled to hear him, but could not find belief in herself. It was too good a thing to have happened. She did not trust it yet.

But there was the corner of the chest, protruding from the tangle of skeel. Ki stared at it, not daring to touch the cold black metal. The skeel themselves were a sight. The long whip-like tails twined about the outside of them, binding them together like a climbing vine. Their eyes were lidded in ecstasy. Legs wrapped over legs, and snouts tucked neatly in. The wad of animals was as close to an orb as their squat bodies would allow. Most surprising of all was the rosy glow that suffused their formerly dull and mottled skin.

The greys grudgingly submitted to being harnessed to the wagon. Ki coiled up the ridiculous lengths of rope while Vandien and Janie, with much laughter, rolled the ball of skeel to the back of Ki's wagon. Loading them demanded a group effort. More than once the wad of skeel slipped from their grasp to thump again on the ground. It disturbed them not at all. By the time the bundle of beasts bumped over the edge and into the wagon, Ki was as weak with laughter and silliness as the other two.

They broke camp quickly, loading gear anywhere. Vandien kicked the fire apart and scooped sand over it. The night was broken only by the lantern on the wagon seat. There was a moment when all voices were stilled and the waves spoke. To Ki they whispered secrets and warnings. She felt her light mood slipping away, but "To the inn!" roared Vandien and the greys moved to his command. Ki peered ahead, trying to guide them around large chunks of driftwood and stone.

"Finally. Finally." Janie whispered softly on the seat beside her. "They will have to see that I am right. The chest will say it all, prove it all. Things will change."

"I've an idea," Ki ventured, not knowing what inspired her. "Let's not go to the inn. Let's pick up Sasha and keep on going. We'll return the skeel, and sell the chest for whatever it brings in Bitters. Then let's look ahead, not back, and go."

"Are you mad?" Vandien asked incredulously. "Why under the Moon do that? There is gold coin to be had for this, even if you have no thought for my face."

"Shall I slip away in the night, let them after make mock of my name? Shall I let them think I have slunk away in shame?"

"It was only an idea," Ki mollified them. She fell silent, wishing they'd agreed. With every step the team took them closer to the tavern, to the confrontation Janie lusted for and the payment Vandien believed in. But peering ahead, Ki saw only the blackness that outlined the yellow windows of the village. Just as darkness swallowed the town, melancholy swallowed Ki.

The inn sign swung in the sea breeze like a hangman's noose. The hubbub inside the tavern leaked out. Ki decided that the tolling of the bell had roused the village and driven the folk from their beds to the inn for companionship and drink.

"Announce us, Ki!" Vandien laughed as he jumped lightly from the wagon. "Janie and I will roll it in."

Ki set her wheel brake. Janie and Vandien giggled insanely as Ki heard their thumping efforts to roll out the skeel. Envy twinged as she knotted her team's reins to a hitching post. The euphoria eluded her. With a grunt and a thump, the wad of skeel hit the ground. Vandien and Janie wrestled them along, bundling them up the boardwalk. Ki pulled the heavy door open.

Light and sound spilled into the street.

"Stand clear!" Ki called out in a commanding voice. All within the tavern fell silent. Eyes turned toward the door.

"You're letting in the night wind!" Helti protested, and then gaped in amazement as the ball of skeel wedged in his doorway. Vandien put his shoulder to it, and with a shout they were through, the skeel rolling a half turn before they halted. Fish-erfolk were rising, to gape at the tangle.

"What in hell is that?" demanded a voice, and others echoed him.

"Are they doing what I think they're doing?" Berni asked in mild amusement.

"Not on my clean tavern floor!" Helti roared in outrage. "Get them out of here! Damn inlander's trick; nothing but barnyard humor! I don't want my place stunk up with musk and rut! Get them out of here, teamster. Now!"

"Be silent!" Srolan's voice carried and ruled. Her dark eyes went from Vandien's grinning face to Janie's shining one. Slowly her back straightened. When she threw back her head and shook her hair loose, her laughter rang out like bells. "Don't you see?" she asked her folk. "You heard the bell and ran here for courage. Can't you see why it rang? Look!" She circled the ball of skeel. Her hand trembled over the protruding corner of the chest. "The Windsingers' chest! They've brought it up to us!"

"It is just as my grandfather said it would be!" Srolan fell back as Janie advanced to place a proud hand on the chest. Her eyes were not shy as they swept over them all to linger on Collie by the fire.

Ki braced herself. The silence in the tavern brooded like the hills before a thunderstorm. Some cast their eyes down to their mugs. Helti stood drying his hands over and over on the sack tied below his belly. The man that had traded rude remarks with Ki on Temple Ebb night stared stonily at the skeel. The hood he wore threw his features into shadow, but Ki bristled under his scrutiny. "Temple Ebb has come and gone," he said in a guttural voice. He raised his mug and drank, dismissing them.

"That's so," said Helti stoutly.

"You bet that's so!" One old fisherman rose slowly. He moved to warm himself at the fire, awarding the skeel less than a glance. "Janie, what do you want to be stirring up this kind of trouble for?"

Janie's mouth sagged open. Her eyes went round, not comprehending. Her brows knit as she struggled to find words. But Ki understood. The village didn't want to change, didn't want to lose its festival in success, to pay gold to a stranger, least of all to admit the truth to Janie's story. They wouldn't. It was that simple. It did not matter what evidence they gave the village. They wouldn't accept it.

The greybeard by the fire looked up from warming his hands. "Teamster, you knew the agreement. Gold was to be paid for that chest, *if* 'twas brought up during Temple Ebb. To have done it on that night, in that storm, well, that would have made it a mighty feat, worthy of gold and honors. What you've given us here is no hero's task, but only a good bit of salvage work, such as any of us might do. A hard job, and no belittling it, but not a wonder. You can't expect us to part with gold for that."

Ki swallowed as she saw Vandien's eyes go cold. Only a small portion of her noticed the outrage on Srolan's face.

"Cowardly misers!" Srolan lashed out at them. "Beasts and fools, all of you! It's the chest he has! The chest! And you will turn him away, as if he were selling rags in the street! Have you no memories, no pride? Would it choke you to admit that Janie's grandfather spoke truth? Was a one of you even there? All the village council can think of is the coin they must part with to be honorable men! You shame me! I wish there were other folk I could call my own! I will not be judged with you. Vandien! Know this! My part of the bargain shall be kept!"

"And what part of the bargain was that, Srolan?" It was the gravel-voiced man at the corner table. "The village council has told you, they will not pay gold for a deed done late."

Ki's eyes flickered from face to face. Vandien stared at Srolan in an agonized suspense. Longing blotted out doubt, letting the child peer out of the man's eyes. Ki's heart leapt out to him in compassion, for in her own heart was a knowing. That which he ached for was not to be.

Janie no longer stroked the chest, nor stood straight and proud. Her arms clutched one another. Her face was pinched and her body was shrinking in on itself. A different sort of child peered from her eyes.

Srolan snatched her gaze from Vandien's face, to stare in consternation at the cloaked man in the corner. For the first time, Ki marked that no other fisherfolk shared his table.

"Well you know that I don't speak of gold!" Srolan rasped out. "What is this treachery, Dresh?"

"Ah, well." Slowly Dresh pushed the hood back, letting the lamplight finger his foxy features. He gave a little sigh and a mocking shrug cf resignation. "I have never yet been able to trust to the discretion of a woman's tongue. But must we be so public, Srolan? Surely our little arrangements were between you and me."

"It appears I have a stake in it as well," Vandien growled.

"You would have. *If* the chest were brought up on Temple Ebb, and *if* I had first access to the contents, then I was to perform two minor favors for Srolan. Do you think she frets over your scar, teamster? The vigor of youth is not enough to content her. She hungers for a youthful body as well. But I do not honor agreements tardily carried out. If you don't believe me, ask Ki."

Srolan's eyes flashed to Ki in confusion. Ki glared at them both. Memories burst in her mind like fresh wounds. She suddenly perceived the whole tapestry Dresh had woven. Wizards and Windsingers were creatures cut of the same fabric, stuffed with the same vile weeds! "It is true, Srolan," Ki said. "I have never yet been able to trust the honor of a wizard's word. Yet my mind cannot stoop to the depths of their deceit, cannot roll in the same gutter to follow their devious plans. Was this your little amusement, Dresh, to arrange this play for us? How well you wrote the parts, and how finely you assigned them! It has been better than any Temple Ebb pageant these folk have ever seen. It matters little to you that the tragedy doesn't end with the falling of a curtain. Nor do you see fit to pay your actors. From the first, we have all danced to your tune, but Vandien and I have trod it best of all."

"Does it end with a soliloquy?" Dresh asked drily.

"It does," Ki snarled. Her glance swept the room. Fisherfolk gaped like stranded carp. Ki saw no empathy, no regrets. She and Dresh were a spectacle to them, a last treat of Temple Ebb, the unexpected entertainment. Srolan alone had sustained a loss among them. She had aged in these last few moments. When she croaked out, "Dresh, please!" even the music was gone from her voice.

"My friends," Ki said slowly. "My first idea was the best. Let's roll our skeel out of here. Janie, run to fetch Sasha. The Romni know the truth of it: There's always another buyer, down the road apiece."

Ki stepped up and put her shoulder to the skeel. Dresh stood up so suddenly he nearly overturned the table.

"Hold!" he cried as he strode toward her. He shouldered Berni out of the way like a transfixed sheep. Boldly he put a hand on the opposite side of the skeel. Ki felt the resistance. "Hold up, teamster. Take your skeel, please. But not the Windsingers' chest, for it does not belong to you."

"And you would claim it as yours, wizard?" Vandien's words were politely questioning. But in his eyes there was a threat, and in his stance and face a promise. Dresh's eyes met his. Dresh didn't flinch, but Ki saw a sudden revising of opinion. For the first time she realized how much of a size the two men were. Dresh would have been the handsomer of the two, even if Vandien had not been scarred. But there was a slinkiness to his beauty that put people on their guards, and a coldness to his eyes that ruined his face more than any scar. If Vandien were the hawk, Dresh was the intricately patterned poisonous snake. He was coiled to strike.

"Vandien!" Ki whispered, cautioning. But Vandien was beyond caution. Dresh had twisted the man's hopes until they had broken off short. He smiled, and Ki's belly curled up at the sight. "There are customs, wizard. Salvaged goods belong to the one who brings them up. Me."

"You are mistaken, teamster," Dresh said smoothly. He glanced about at the village folk, warming them with his smile, including them in this debate. "It was the village that knew of the chest. It was the village that set you after it." Dresh paused to fit a wedge. "Srolan does deserve their thanks for hiring you. Perhaps I could help the village make her a reward." Fanatic hope kindled again in Srolan's eyes. Dresh smiled at his success. "The chest belongs to the village, I think. If I hired a teamster to bring my goods from here to there, and the teamster is late, does that mean the teamster may keep the goods? I think not." Again his smile swept the room, but he let it rest over long on Ki.

"That is so," Helti agreed cautiously, and here and there

heads nodded hesitantly. Even Srolan looked at Vandien with her heart in her eyes and begged, "Leave it here for me. It is my final chance."

"The chest cannot be taken from the village!" Dresh decreed. "It belongs to the village! If they had not told you of it, you would never have recovered it. Who told you where to look, and what to look for? The village folk alone knew that. On that basis, it must belong to them."

"To me, then!" Janie's voice began as a shriek and ended in a whisper. Dresh's eyes snapped to her face in shock. "By your own reasoning, wizard! It is mine! I alone knew where it was, I alone knew what to look for! And I helped bring it up! Mine, wizard, and you will kill me before you touch it!"

There was no rationality in Janie's eyes. She advanced fearlessly on Dresh, and he retreated. In madness there is power and Janie wielded it. Her hands settled on the chest's corner, a priestess blessing relics.

"Janie. Now, Janie, calm yourself. Listen to me . . ."

"Shut up!" Janie screamed savagely, and Srolan fell silent before her wrath.

Srolan turned anxious eyes on Vandien. "Do something," she pleaded. "Make her see reason."

"Do what?" Vandien demanded. "It seems to me that Janie is correct. I've no wish to take the chest from her."

"It's mine!" Janie asserted again. She glared at Dresh who had ventured forward a step.

"I've no wish to kill you," Dresh said reasonably.

"Then don't," Vandien growled.

"She leaves me no other course!" the wizard flared. His fingers waggled in agitation until he clenched them into fists.

Vandien grinned. "Be ready with the team, Ki. Janie, shall we load it?"

But the eyes she turned on him didn't know him. "It's mine!" she warned him.

"She's broken," Ki said in a hushed voice. "They've finally broken her."

"It is *mine!*" she screamed in an inhuman voice.

She was echoed by an inhuman roaring. Cold swept through the inn borne on a wind that snatched their breaths and snuffed not only candles but the fire on the hearth. The fear-stricken cries of the fisherfolk were drowned in its immense vibration. It was a blinding, numbing wind that paralyzed all Ki's senses.

A heavy wooden table skidding across the floor struck her on the hip. She found herself on hands and knees in cold darkness. Other people blundered blindly around her. A foot trod heavily on her hand and a knee struck her in the ribs. She scrambled away in the confusion, but could find no safety. The roaring wind ceased, but the darkness remained. Confused cries filled the room.

"Vandien!" Ki cried out. An answering shout came from across the room. In darkness she blundered toward him, only to trip on an overturned bench.

"It is mine!" shrieked a voice scarcely recognizable as Janie's.

"It is mine," responded another voice. The resonance of that voice nullified all other sounds. There were a few more scufflings, then silence. Ki brushed the hair from her eyes and rose silently. In the darkness, yellow flame blossomed. Two slender well-formed hands cupped it. They transplanted the fire to a candle on one of the few tables that remained standing. The tall figure straightened. The flame on the candle struggled and tugged at the wick, trying to illuminate the darkness. A hushed expectancy grew. Then another yellow flame bloomed within those tapered fingers. The inn gasped as the fingers snapped it away. The ball of fire arched through the air, to land on the hearth and burst into a roaring blaze. "Make light from that," the voice commanded, and those few who had found candles crept forward to kindle them.

The inn was a shambles. Tables and benches were overturned. Broken crockery grated underfoot, while the sour smell of spilled ale mingled with the fishy odor of slopped chowder. As Ki's eyes adjusted to the semi-darkness, she saw folk huddled like frightened sheep. Their eyes darted about furtively, seeking someone to blame. A hand squeezed Ki's shoulder and Vandien stood beside her. "Look at Janie!" he whispered.

The other villagers had retreated from the skeel. Of Dresh there was no sign. Janie alone stood protectively by the wad of animals. One hand rested possessively on the chest as she glared at the one who sought to take her treasure. Defiance and despair had driven out caution. Her shoulders were squared as she defied the blue-robed Windsinger.

"Rebeke," Ki breathed in dread, and Vandien replied, "I thought so."

Rebeke ignored them. The dancing firelight struck a sheen from her finely scaled face. Her hands were innocent of weap-

ons as they hung peacefully at her sides. She needed no threats;
her face radiated her power. She scanned the room once, eyes
lingering a moment on Ki. But she found no opposition. Folk
turned their eyes away, or crouched with bowed heads. Even
Srolan winced away like a kicked cur. Slowly Rebeke turned
her gaze back to Janie. She did not break the silence, and no
one else dared. Long she stared at the woman-child with eyes
that reached and touched and probed. A little of the tension
went out of Janie's stance, but still she repeated, "It is mine."

Rebeke smiled as a mother might smile on her curious child.
"Yes. I can see that. But it is also mine."

"No!" The defiant shout shook the room and trembled on
the air. Villagers cowered, expecting retribution. Rebeke waited
until the echoes had ceased. No trace of anger marred the
serenity of her browless face.

"Killian spoke of you. For you must be Janie."

Janie hesitated, then tossed a grudging nod.

"Do you believe I will take the chest from you?" Rebeke
asked her.

Janie's eyes flickered over the assembled villagers. She
found no support. Her eyes locked with Vandien's, but she
looked hastily away. He had offered her the only taste of friendship she'd had. She wouldn't draw him into this.

"She . . ." Vandien began.

"Silence!" Rebeke said calmly. Rebeke made no gesture,
but Ki felt the impact as Vandien reeled against her from the
unseen blow. No other saw it.

"You say the chest is yours," Janie said as Rebeke continued
to gaze at her questioningly.

"And yours. I said it was yours as well. Having said that,
do you think I will take it from you? I have come for the chest,"
Rebeke spoke to the villagers now. "But I have also come for
Janie and Sasha. Run and fetch your sister, Janie."

"By the Hawk!" Vandien swore, but his voice rose no louder
than a croaked whisper. Janie stared at Rebeke and did not
move.

"Didn't you hear me, Janie?" Rebeke repeated, smiling more
gently. "I've come to take you and Sasha away. You don't
belong here. Any fool can see that, and I am far from being a
fool. Your own spirit knows it. The chest called to you because
of it. And only one of your spirit and determination could have
dragged it up. Because you are a Windsinger, Janie. You were

never born to drag up smelly fish from cold water, to bend your back to the wind as you sliced the wet meat from their bones. You were born to find power and wield it. You were never meant to be part of this village. It is beneath you. You knew it from the time you were a small child. And the village knew it as well. Am I right?"

Janie's eyes were riveted to Rebeke's smiling face. She teetered on the edge, for Rebeke called to her hungry heart. The only one who might have wished to call her back was voiceless.

"Why hesitate? What holds you here, sister?"

The simple kinship offered overbalanced the scales. "I must fetch Sasha," Janie began hesitantly.

"Didn't I just say so?" Rebeke's laughter was warm as a summer wind. "Hurry, for we have far to go this night. Take no time to pack, just bring the child. All else we have prepared for you."

"Prepared..." Janie's voice trailed off in awe. The implied welcome warmed her cheeks. Life flowed in her eyes, bringing animation into her face. "You will wait for me?" she asked fearfully.

"Hurry!" Rebeke chided her with a smile. Ki looked at Janie's glowing face. She was the peasant child in the tale, who finds herself the true daughter of a queen. A smile bowed her mouth as she looked down on them crouching in the dark before her mentor. Her eyes paused on Collie, but the silence that had prevented him from mocking her now prevented him from asking her to stay. "Hurry!" Rebeke warned her again, and Janie broke free of Collie's eyes with a laugh.

"Janie! Go with us, and be Human!" Vandien croaked. The slamming door answered him.

Rebeke turned rebuking eyes on him. She considered him, and how he and Ki stood together, apart from the villagers. "I did not think to find you here, Ki," she remarked. "But the Romni are renowned as a thick-headed folk. Perhaps that means that when you learn to respect Windsingers, you will learn it in such a way that you will never forget it." Her cold eyes appraised Vandien. Ki shuddered. Then Rebeke smiled. "You stand as friends stand. That man would defy me, would take from me not only the chest, but Janie as well. Does he know that you owe me, Ki? Didn't Killian hint to him that you traveled under my shadow, and only by my tolerance? But as

he runs with Romni, perhaps he is as stubborn as one. I chose
to let her live, Vandien. Murder is distasteful to me, but I had
other options. Still, I chose to let her return to you. By that
choosing, some would say I betrayed my own interests. I don't
think so. But I angered some that could be mollified by this
chest. I could use the chest as justification for letting Ki live.
However . . . some other Windmistresses might see it as neg-
ligence on my part if Ki went on living and we had nothing to
show for it. They might even try to remedy that."

"Vandien does not share my debts!" Ki cried out in anger.
"Ask of me what you will for my life, but don't . . ."

"You have nothing I want." Rebeke stated it flatly. "And
he is not really in a position to bargain. As I have said, murder
is distasteful to me. Vandien may either say, 'We made a trade,
the Windsinger and I,' or he may resist me when I take the
chest, and die."

Vandien gave a harsh laugh that drew all eyes to him. "Take
it!" he croaked. "Take it and be welcome to it. As the village
will not pay me for it, why shouldn't you have it? But not as
barter for Ki's life; neither of us would want to live under that
burden. Consider it this way; I return the chest to the original
owners, as would any honest man."

"Asking no reward?" Rebeke marveled drily.

Vandien afforded her a courteous nod.

"Then I shall remove your team from my property."

Rebeke circled the tangle of skeel slowly, frowning as she
examined them. To the villagers she paid no more attention
than she would to a flock of curious birds. After her third
circuit of the skeel, she stepped back from them, massaging
her narrow hands. She stared for a moment, then flicked her
fingers at the chest. A cracking sparked momentarily from her
fingertips. Instantly the chest glowed, moving through a dull
red to blinding white in the space of two heartbeats, and as
quickly fading back to its dull black. The skeel didn't even
twitch.

"I don't like to be harsh," Rebeke muttered in consternation.
She folded her hands together and extended them in front of
her. Her thumbs were stiffened, pointing straight at the chest.
The crackling lasted longer, and three times the chest pulsed
white. Rebeke lowered her hands and stared wordlessly at the
motionless skeel still entwined around the chest. She gave
Vandien an apologetic glance and began to raise her hands

again. But the skeel began to loosen. Like melted wax they slid bonelessly down, to puddle around the chest. The blinking of a wide eye showed they were still alive, but they lay in postures skeel had never assumed before. One whiplike tongue flicked lazily out and leisurely slid back in. Yet they looked not stunned, but satiated.

Ki's eyes moved up to the black chest. With heart squeezing shock, she saw the widening cracks in it. Even Rebeke's hands were clutched tightly in front of her breast. Her finely scaled lips were pinched shut. One villager cried aloud and many turned aside their faces. But Ki could not resist the awful temptation of knowing what so much had been risked for. Slowly the black pieces fell away from one another, like a flower shedding its petals.

The thing within was white, a dead white without shine or shading. It stood no taller than Sasha, but it creaked of age. *And Evil,* Ki thought to herself, *but no, not evil, but a wisdom so far beyond Human reach that it could not seem good.* Its high knobbed forehead domed above a scaled face that was noseless and lipless. Its mouth stretched as far as the hinge of its jaw. The thin sexless body crouched with its knees drawn up to its ribby chest. Folded arms rested atop the knees, almost Human, but owning too many joints, and most of them bending the wrong way. Its eyes were open, round and white. An indescribable flowing, neither bone nor hair, cascaded whitely down its back.

"What is it?" Helti demanded sickly.

Ki knew, with a jolt of recognition.

"It's a Windsinger!" shrieked Dresh. He leaped up from his crouch by a table near the door. Pushing back his hood, he let a cube of brown chalk drop from his hand. "And the thrice-damned thing is mine!"

"Dresh!" Rebeke mouthed the words, but no sound came. She did not move. A brownish glow came from the earthrune carefully chalked on the floor. Dread rose in Ki as she knew that Rebeke could not move, had fallen to Dresh's power. Ki remembered how he had bent her will. Sickness rose in her as she imagined how he would twist Rebeke. Ki had been but a casual entertainment for him. The spurs of retaliation would goad him on with Rebeke. Always Ki had dreaded and despised Windsingers. Those feelings weren't gone. She feared Rebeke and shuddered at how Janie had been seduced away from her own Humanity. But sympathy squirmed within her, overturning old loyalties. Vandien shot her a questioning look as she eased away from him. Her sideways movement was lost in the stir of folk edging forward in fascination to stare at the revealed image.

"Look at it!" Dresh gloated. He stepped past Rebeke to put greedy hands on it. Rebeke cringed as if his questing fingers violated her personally. "You see what hasn't been seen on this world for so many generations that it is now a legend; a true Windsinger. This is not some transformed Human or T'cheria or Dene, but a Windsinger hatched and grown. Not a statue of one! This is what they did with their dead, folding them neatly and tucking them away in chests. No temple that building, but a mausoleum unbelievably old."

The village folk dangled on his words, mesmerized by what he said. Ki slipped slowly through the crowd.

Dresh smiled at his audience. "See how she flinches at my words! This is what the Windsingers wouldn't have you know; that they are shams, chameleons who have taken the shapes and powers of an older race. Control of the winds was never given to them; they seized it! And how? By a process as gruesome and twisted as themselves. This body can be ground to a powder, and ingested through nostril and mouth. Then the changes begin. Imagine the small girls, stolen from their homes, who are fed a secret measure of this filth with their food. Once the transmutation has begun, there is no stopping it. The children never have a choice!"

No tears flowed on Rebeke's face, but it was twisted in agony. Her eyes denied what Dresh was saying, but her lips were silent. Dresh smiled at her pain.

"Do you know why they want this so badly? It is this. They have no lack of this powder of Windsinger, for the race was multitudinous, and their burial places, though hidden in inaccessible places, are said to be many. But few of the bodies are intact, and none of them are as perfect as this one. That they need. For, while the powder starts the transmutation, the brain must guide it. The would-be Windsinger must focus her mind on the shape her body is to become, to guide it through the change. The closer she can approach the true shape of a Windsinger, the more power she will wield. But when their temple sank, the last true body sank with it. That quake was not the act of the Windsingers, as you believe, but the very vengeance of the Moon herself, angered that the Windsingers would take to themselves the powers she had trusted to that ancient race only. For many generations of Windsingers now, there has been no guiding image for the younger singers to grow by. They've had to pattern themselves on the older Windsingers, straying even farther from the true form. Their power is slowly dwindling because of it. This corpse would have let them re-capture it. But it has fallen to me." Dresh put his full attention on Rebeke. He leaned close to her without touching her. "To me, Rebeke. Did you hope to match me? You were close, when you snatched my body. But you let me go! And when I dangled my puppets before you, you had eyes only for them. You watched a scarred fool and a Romni teamster dance, while their master walked up behind you. It's funny, isn't it? You see the humor, I'm sure. Smile for me, sweet one."

Dresh's brows knit lightly in concentration. A smile crawled onto Rebeke's face and squirmed there, mocking the revulsion in her eyes. A gasp of awe rippled through the fisherfolk and then a sprinkling of cruel laughter.

Heads turned to the opening door. Janie was framed in it, the blackness of night her backdrop. The thin light of the candles touched her confused visage, outlined the sleepy face of little Sasha who stood bundled before her. "No!" she moaned at the helplessness in Rebeke's eyes.

"Traitors!" someone cried. The crowd surged forward.

"Run!" roared Vandien, pushing a bench into the crowd nearest him.

The glowing brown runes seared Ki's smearing foot. She jerked in its grip, her body twisting and snapping out of control. Blurred images scalded her brain: Vandien going down under a wave of villagers, Sasha's mouth red in a scream, Dresh's eyes wide as he spun on her, Rebeke's hands finally moving, her fingers weaving in the air before her.

"Ki."

She opened her eyes, wondering when she had closed them. Her face itched where her cheek pressed against woven wool. Vandien looked down on her. A dark shining stream rilled from a split at the edge of his scar. When he spoke her name, she saw blood on his teeth.

Realizing her head was pillowed in his lap brought her to her senses. She sat up slowly with his help and stared around the inn.

The fisherfolk were herded to one end of the room. Those on the fringes of the group were trying to squirm into the middle. They pressed back against the wall. Helti lay in the center of the room groaning softly. Someone's feet thrust out from under a table. "Sasha?" asked Ki, and Vandien pointed.

The child was looking up wonderingly into Rebeke's face, watching the lipless mouth that smiled down on her. The blue windrune hung glowing in the air, singeing Ki's eyes when she looked too close to it. Dresh looked smaller as he stood by the door with his hands folded between his shoulder blades. Rebeke had left him the movement of his eyes, and they darted frantically about the room, seeking an ally. No one met his eyes.

"Is she all right?" Rebeke asked.

"Are you?" Vandien passed on the question. Ki realized they spoke of her, and managed a nod.

"Good," said Rebeke. "We must be on our way now. There will be a storm after I leave. All would do well to stay within these walls. I'm sure you will have much to chat about. If boats are damaged, you must remember you brought it upon yourselves. It will be a wind such as has not been seen before. When it passes, not a block of our temple will be left standing for you to sniff and pillage. It should have been done long ago, but always we cherished the hope that *this* could be recovered. Now that we have it, there is no longer a reason to leave any sign of the temple."

Ki stared at Rebeke as she spoke. Her features had melted and merged. Her patrician nose was now no more than a smooth swelling in the center of her face. Her fine-lipped mouth had spread across her cheeks. And there was a fluidity about her hand movements that reminded Ki of the sinuous flexings of a skeel's tail.

"It's true then!" Ki cried out. "Janie, you must not. Think of Sasha!"

"She does think of Sasha. Sasha will be loved and cherished as never before. They will go with me." Rebeke answered for them. "True? As true as a rumor and a scrap of gossip when they are woven together by guesses and filtered through the mouth of a fool. To make you understand the truth would take longer than I have. Such secrets are not for Humans anyway. We will be going." Rebeke stepped toward the door and paused.

She looked again at Ki and Vandien over the white image in her arms. "It occurs to me that I do you no favor in leaving you here. Leave now, if you wish, and the storm will not begin until your wagon reaches the top of the cliff road."

Vandien glanced at the huddle of villagers. "Let's go," he suggested, hauling Ki to her feet.

"Wait!" Ki begged, hanging to his shoulder as she got her balance again. "Rebeke! What will be done with Dresh?"

"You make me think less of you, Ki, that you even ask. But I will answer, for the courtesies that are owed between us. I will put him in a place where he will be stopped. Not killed, for I refuse his blood. I think you know where he will be. His life will pause, and the pause will stretch forever."

Vertigo swept Ki as she remembered the airless emptiness of the void. "Leave him!" she begged, surprising even herself. At the outrage in Rebeke's eyes, she groped for her reasons. "He is, at least, still Human."

Rebeke ran her eyes over the folk in the tavern. "And this is something to be proud of?" she asked contemptuously. "Ki, you don't know what you ask. He has started down a path that will twist him. He may keep the shape of his body, but he will be no more Human than I am. Little folk like you will feel the pressure of his heel more often than those whose skills equal his own. Will you inflict this on your own folk?"

Ki looked at Vandien and forced out the words. "I have a selfish reason. It is said that he could lift the scar from my friend's face."

"A lie," Rebeke stated flatly. "He claims more power than he has." A curious smile crossed her immense mouth. "I must deny you what you ask, Ki. But I shall remember the voiding of the earthrune."

"So shall I," Ki said stubbornly. "Twice I have gifted you with revenge that left your hands unbloodied."

"I remember that, also," Rebeke replied coldly. "I still refuse what you ask. Go now, Romni teamster, without another word, before I forget that I have said I will hold the winds back until your wagon is clear of them. Trust a Romni to try to barter with a Windsinger. Was there ever such a mulish folk? Take with you, not my favor, but not my ill will either. Go now, knowing that I remember what is between us. But do not speak."

"We're going!" Vandien injected, giving Ki a warning glance and a shake of her arm. He could not resist adding, "Farewell, good fisherfolk. I trust this Temple Ebb you have been entertained, even if I cannot juggle."

He stooped and seized the hind legs of one of the blissful skeel. With an exasperated sigh, Ki grabbed the front legs and they lugged it out the door to her wagon. Already the winds outside were beginning to toss, and they loaded skeel hurriedly. As they carried out the last skeel, Sasha spoke.

"Good-bye, Ki!" she called boldly. She looked up into the foreign visage of Rebeke and then back to Ki. "Even when I am a Windsinger, and strange to your eyes, you will know me by my Romni scarf! I will remember you!"

"By the Moon!" gasped Ki as the child happily flapped the scarf at her in farewell.

"Try not to think of the implications," Vandien suggested as they loaded the skeel into the wagon.

"Go!" commanded Rebeke from the doorway, and the team started before Ki and Vandien were even seated.

"I am sorry he must keep the scar," Janie said dreamily as the wagon was obscured by the night. "He was kind to us."

Rebeke lifted her hand and the wind rose another notch. Her blue robes swirled around her. The lipless smile she gave Janie rippled her cheeks into folds. "Perhaps it is a shame." She looked up the cliff road. Her eyes were indulgent as she turned back to Janie. "Let him be patient for a year or so," she suggested. "Let him be surprised at how well his body heals itself."

"Thank you," Janie whispered.

"Come, Dresh," Rebeke commanded. She seemed not to have heard Janie's thanks. The wizard came on stiff-kneed legs, an unmouthed scream bulging his cheeks. The wind slammed the inn door behind them.

TWENTY-TWO

THE gusting wind pushed against the high panels of the wagon. It rocked gently. Ki lay awake, listening to the small creakings of the cuddy. A grey wash of dawn light filtered in the cracked shutter. She struggled to sit up in the welter of blankets and sleeping furs and, leaning precariously over the edge of the sleeping platform, peered out the little window. The big grey horses stood with their rumps to the wind that streamed their heavy tails and manes. They grazed peacefully in the wind-storm, cropping the sweet grass of the rolling hillside.

"It's morning," Ki said, nestling back into the blankets.

"So what?" grumbled Vandien.

"We've not a coin between us, and a wagonload of pregnant skeel."

"Will any of that change by noon?" Vandien asked.

"No." Ki surrendered to the comfort of the bed and her own aching muscles. Vandien's body was warm against hers. An idea slowly grew in her mind.

"Your scar," she began lazily. "You really wish I couldn't see it?"

"Ki," Vandien groaned in protest. "Let it be. I was a fool.

267

Let us pretend to forget it. Can we go on as if we had never been to Temple Ebb?"

"No." Ki trailed a slow finger down his chest. "For I know a way to make you forget it. A way I can't see it."

Vandien sank into a sulky silence at the levity in her tone. A moment later he *oofed* the air out of his lungs as Ki's body landed squarely atop his. He found himself nose to nose with her. He blinked, but couldn't focus his eyes at such close range. A single green eye appeared to peer down into his.

"When we are like this," Ki said conversationally, "I cannot see your scar."

Wind whispered under her wagon, filling the long silence.

"Scar?" Vandien wondered aloud.

The wind rocked the wagon.